MW00909642

Chance Encounter

A Post-Holocaust Story

Sanford R. Simon

AuthorHouse™
1663 Liberty Drive, Suite 200
Bloomington, IN 47403
www.authorhouse.com
Phone: 1-800-839-8640

©2008 Sanford R. Simon. All rights reserved.

No part of this book may be reproduced, stored in a retrieval system, or transmitted by any means without the written permission of the author.

First published by AuthorHouse 11/13/2008

ISBN: 978-1-4343-9316-6 (sc)
ISBN: 978-1-4343-9317-3 (hc)

Library of Congress Control Number: 2008909207

Printed in the United States of America
Bloomington, Indiana

This book is printed on acid-free paper.

To Arlene:

You have been my friend, wife, and companion.

Foreword

In the American Jewish community there are thousands, perhaps millions, of assimilated secular Jews who grew to their maturity in the period of World War II and the postwar era. They learned of the Holocaust but emotionally buried the tragedy as a historical occurrence that impacted others, not them. They supported Israel, gave money to Jewish causes, but buried any strong emotion concerning the deaths of the six million.

On the other hand, there were Germans who grew up during this period. The Holocaust was something not to be mentioned or discussed, and the popular notion was that the German populace were victims of the war. The view was that they were victims of Hitler, the Nazi party, and the Allies who bombed the cities, killed their men, and forced twenty years of reconstruction. The rebuilding of the country was more important than the acceptance of either guilt or responsibility for the tragedy of the European war or its dirty secrets. Some things were not to be spoken about.

This novel is about two men: an assimilated American Jew and a successful postwar German executive. This is their story.

Chapter 1

Newark, New Jersey: Prewar and the War—George's Story

It was over 65 years ago, but I still remember the letters. Each Monday, my grandmother would hand me three envelopes, two addressed to her brothers and one to her sister. The address was to town with a strange name, "Ozarow" in the Kielce region of Poland, which didn't mean much to a skinny eight-year-old kid who looked for every possible distraction on the way to school. My thoughts were on dodge-ball and tag played in the schoolyard and on the marbles in my pocket. Getting to the yard early assured me of being on the better teams playing before the first school bell.

Grandma was Bella Wall, just past her fifty-second birthday and in the United States nineteen years. She was "Big Grandma" behind her back and Mama to her face. Since my mother worked in the candy store with my father, I was often left in her care. I felt I had the privilege of two mothers, both of whom loved and cared for me. "Big Grandma" was five feet two inches of iron will, and dominated her household of my father, mother, me, an aunt who was born two years after she'd come to the US, and, of course, Grandpa.

Her instructions, in excellent and practiced but slightly accented English, were precise: "Go to the mailbox first, then to school." Mail was first collected by the postman at 11 a.m., Grandma wanted me to mail the letters on my way to school at 8:45, so the round trip of family news could be on the way. A green box on top of a cement pole base, this mailbox had a little square instruction plate about my eye level. I'd put my schoolbooks down on the dirt between the sidewalk and the street, always protecting the geography book, since it was my favorite subject, reach up and drop the letters into the pivoted slot, and swing the entry port twice to be sure the letters dropped. The cast metal entry port had a distinctive squeak and off-key clank as it rotated and slammed closed.

In return, each week there were one, two, or three letters written on very light, almost translucent paper with strange postmarks and unusual stamps that I always asked to be saved for my collection. The postman dropped the letters through the mail slot at the front door, where they formed a small pile at the foot of the stairwell. Grandma would first gather those letters with scraggly inked addresses and separate them from the other mail. She would hurry to the north corner of the living room, which had the best light, and sit in her favorite overstuffed wing chair and read the letters. In the summer, this was the cool corner of the house, with the porch just outside shaded by two oak trees. In the winter, when the light was faint and gray, Grandma turned on the tall multi-bulb floor lamp and a lighted upper portion that was surrounded by a huge, tasseled, cream-colored shade. The lamp had three levels of intensity that lit the room with a pleasant glow. She would select the light level that was comfortable, and with the fixture towering over her seat, huddled into the corner, she would read quietly until she had devoured the family news from the Old Country.

We loved our Newark, New Jersey, home. The house was a frame "2½"—that is, the building was a two-story home on top of a separate ground floor apartment (with one bedroom of that apartment on the second floor; for a maid?), allowing the owner to live comfortably above a tenant renting the lower floor. The front of the house had four tall columns that rose from the street-level porch and ran up the full front two stories of the building, framing the façade, and made this home just a little more distinguished than those on either side that were built with flat front facades and stone stoops rather than full porches. The house faced north, ensuring that the screened porches on the first and second floors were cool and protected from the heat of long summer days and evenings.

With the added income from the "flat" on the ground floor, the owner's family could live well on the second and third floors. For many families in Newark, owning this type of property was the first step in building capital. Buying the house was a step to some financial security for families who survived the hard days of the Depression. This was so for Grandma, but she had purchased the house with something more in mind. With great care and planning, alterations were made. The interior was modified so each floor would house part of her brood. My mother and father and I were on the top floor, Grandma and Grandpa had the middle floor, and the first floor was reserved for my aunt Sophie for when she married. It was Grandma's family plan: The entire family would be living under one roof and there would be a place for the cousins when they eventually came from Poland.

My grandfather's name was Jacob, "Jake" to his friends but always Jacob in his home. A house painter by trade, he painted the house in off-white and the columns that supported the porches slate gray.

Grandma was a strong woman. She said, "Grandpa left me in Europe before the First World War broke out, because he didn't want to be taken back into the Russian army." He had been conscripted during the war between Russia and Japan and was fortunate to be released from an onerous long-term conscription. She would explain that "Jake didn't want to leave again, so he left me in Ozarow with the children and said he'd send for me after he became established in America."

She and five children were stranded in Poland during the First World War. Three of her children died from diphtheria and the flu that ravaged the area. A fourth, my mother's twin brother, died of rheumatic fever just as the war ended. By 1919, with money saved from running a dry goods store and some savings and a steamship ticket that Jake had sent from the US, she and my mother left Ozarow. In addition to traveling with full trunks of clothes and belongings, Grandma purchased fur coats and jewelry—not only to show their means, but to possibly use as barter for services or needs along the way. She and my mother, Bella, who was eight years old at the time, managed to negotiate their way across newly independent Poland and postwar Europe to the German port of Bremen, where they boarded a ship to the United States.

Grandma joined Grandpa in Harrison, New Jersey. She had survived the war, the separation, and the deaths of four of her five children. She had another child, Sophie, and became a believer in her American dream of becoming a financially independent woman.

With her drive and acumen, she and Jake opened a dry goods store in Harrison.

Bella quickly Americanized, went to school, and, with a unique knack for language, lost any trace of a foreign accent. By 1929, she had grown into a confident nineteen year old who had worked in the store, had made it through high school, and met Michael. He was a tall accountant in training who played and taught the piano, had a small dance band, could dance well, and had a charm that disarmed Grandma and swept Bella off her feet. Bella married Michael in December 1930, after knowing him six months. I came along eleven months later and was named George. I was named after a poet my mother had admired during her Polish/Russian youth. Everyone called me Georgie.

Bella and Michael and their new baby, Grandma, Jake, and the young Sophie became a family unit. They worked and lived together. At first they prospered, but the Depression and the closing of the major factory in town caused the dry goods store to fail. Jake became a house painter. Michael worked as a bookkeeper and they survived the Depression. Little by little they improved their situation, and by 1937 Grandma had scraped enough money together to buy the Newark house. It was just around the corner from a rundown candy store that Michael purchased in an area that was becoming predominantly Jewish, known as the Weequahic section.

Grandma was a happy woman, comfortable and proud of her large home. Just as a captain would command a ship, she commanded the three apartments from her kitchen in the back of the middle floor. In her backyard garden she grew her roses and "snowball" flowers and each year planted table vegetables such as tomatoes, corn, lettuce, cabbages, and, of course, radishes, which I delighted in pulling up for additions to lunch or the dinner salad. Her pleasure was having her family gather in the evenings for dinner. The meals were of "old country food" such as borscht, stuffed cabbage, and the fish courses of herring, whitefish, and variations of carp. Hot evening meals at least once a week would feature "boiled beef" (Flanken) with horseradish and heaping mashed potatoes laced with garlic and chicken fat. I often found a carp swimming in the upstairs bathroom tub on Thursday afternoons when I came home from school before she would perform a swift execution to make her gefilte fish for the Friday night ritual dinner welcoming the Sabbath.

The summer of '39 was a happy time for me. Although my mother and father had wanted at least two or three children, I was an only child. My mother had "women's problems" and my father told me, "Mom can't have more children." Just coming up to my ninth birthday, I discovered sports, loved baseball, the Yankees, and Lou Gehrig, my hero. There were no night games back then. On free afternoons I would lounge in the living room, turn on the freestanding radio in its ornate mahogany veneer and simulated gold trim box, and listen to the ballgame, imagining each pitch and hit. I was bored only when the team was on the road and the broadcasts were simulated, punctuated by the sound of the ticker relaying the play by play to the announcer who improvised the crowd reaction and described what he thought was happening.

By then my father had converted the candy store to a luncheonette. The store was on a main shopping area, Bergen Street. There were eight stores along the street with apartments called "railroad flats" on the second floor above the stores and large backyards the neighborhood kids used as their playfields. I had plenty of friends to play with.

"The Shaker twins," Carol and Barbara, lived across the street. Boys and girls played together and they were part of "the gang." Naturally blond and slightly plump, they loved to climb and run with the boys. My best friend, Sammy, lived on the next block and was the neighborhood's best athlete. He was a year older than I, taller and much better coordinated. We liked each other's company and shared our local adventures. We were outdoors playing on our own all day, but we were never far from the house or the store. This little neighborhood was our safe territory.

Of course, being the child of the luncheonette/candy store owner was a great advantage. I could parade my friends into "my store," go behind the counter, and mix sodas. I was particularly adept at reaching up and getting the right amount of seltzer into the chocolate mix, reverse-charging the gas, and then adding a splash of milk to produce a marvelous "egg cream." The sodas were "on the house" when my guys came in with me, and they came often. The store had a large newspaper counter along the left wall as you entered, and my father normally was at the cash register opposite this magazine and newspaper display. He would stand behind the old NCR mechanical cash register which went "kerchang" every time he had a sale, pressing hard on the big numerical keys. The register had a mechanical keyboard at a 45-degree angle over the cash drawer and a glass display window with little flags that popped up to indicate the amount of the sale. I used to love hitting the keys for a "no sale" just to hear that ring: "kerchang! kerchang!" Most times my dad would stand with the latest novel propped up on the register keys, reading as he awaited the next customer. Often people would rush in, late for an approaching bus at the corner, and ask for a "loosie," one cigarette out of a pack of twenty and sold for a penny. It was near the end of the Depression, and a penny a cigarette was a good sale when cigarettes sold for between twelve cents and fifteen cents a pack. People often got their single cigarette "fix" before jumping onto the coming bus.

The soda fountain and luncheonette counter were on one side of the store, with the cash register and the cigarette display behind the register. The cigarettes were stacked pack by pack, by brand, out of their cartons, each brand in its own cubby. Along the far back wall, next to the pay phone booth with the interior corrugated green wall surface and the split hinged door that creaked each time it was opened or closed, there were several show cases holding candy assortments and penny candy, loose delights that had to be weighed and scooped into little white bags. At this counter the store sold candy "chances," chocolate-covered marshmallows with white centers, except for three or four in the box of forty that had pink centers. These were the "winners," the winning being a free second candy from the box. As the son of the owner, I knew how many of the pink centers had been taken. This was knowledge that made me very popular.

Even with all the activity around the neighborhood, my mother and father sent me to four weeks of day camp. I was a happy kid. Each morning I would go to my father's store and take a newspaper or magazine, walk to the back of the soda fountain, sit at the counter on the last round chrome and red mock-leather seat resting on a fixed single pillar, and have a diluted cup of coffee and a buttered kaiser roll (a baked roll with a hard crust and poppy seeds) until I was picked up by a taxi at about 8 a.m. from Monday to Friday to be taken to Crystal Lake Camp in the Orange Mountains about 10 miles from the house and store. The camp had a great swimming pool, and we were able play, swim, and be home at night. I learned to play baseball on a real kids-sized diamond, to hit a hardball and play the infield. I didn't want the summer to end.

When September came I didn't notice the news of the beginning of the war. Sure, the headlines on the rows of newspapers—the *New York Times,* the *Newark News,* the *Star Ledger,* the *Herald Tribune,* the *Daily News*, the *Mirror, PM*—in the newspaper rack shouted that Hitler had invaded Poland. Being young, I just didn't relate to the news. I sensed that Grandma was worried by the way she would stop her work and listen to the radio and how she would measure her words when someone mentioned either the war or the family. She was silent to all of us. After all, she and my mother had survived the First World War in Poland in that same area where battles were now being fought.

Her routine didn't vary. Each week Grandma would write the letters sitting in the kitchen surrounded by the marvelous smells of her cooking. The rich odor of cooked cabbage and warm aroma of chicken soup that was being distilled into the plasma of strength for her family always wafted through her kitchen. She sat at the square kitchen table covered in the rose patterned oilcloth that served as our table for meals, family gatherings, and Grandma's workplace. She was always dressed in her patterned housedress protected by a white halter-top apron. Her stockings would be rolled down to just above her black dress shoes, purchased years before, now comfortable with a broken back and relegated to being worn around the house. Even though the news told us that Hitler was moving rapidly through Poland that September, the letters were still written, and I was faithfully dropping them in the mailbox on the way to school. This continued through the autumn and beginning of winter—until one morning in January 1940, when the postman put three of the

September letters through the mail slot. They were returned stamped "UNDELIVERABLE." If Grandma was worried about the receipt of the returned letters, she didn't share her concerns with the family. Every letter mailed after September came back the same way, until in April they stopped coming back.

Grandma stopped writing.

Chapter 2

Stuttgart, Germany: 1934 to 1939—Willie's Story

Willie Kirchenmann's first memories were of the wonderful aroma of bread baking as he awakened each morning. He would stir from his sleep and then, lying awake, he would smell the aroma from the coal-fired ovens in the basement of the store below the apartment. He would slip out of bed onto the cold floor, still in his pajamas, tiptoe past the large bedroom where Mama was still sleeping, and carefully descend the rear wooden stairs, holding the bare rail for balance, making his early morning journey from the comfort of his huge feather bed to the warm, fragrance-filled bakery. Starting just past his fourth birthday, he would make his early morning journey to Papa's world of hot ovens and freshly baked bread. Then, hiding behind one of the huge racks where new bread was cooling, he would watch Papa place a dozen kneaded loaves into the fire-hearth using a long-handled wooden pallet filled with either the popular brown rye breads or the pumpernickel that made the bakery so well known in the neighborhood.

After about five minutes, Papa would feign surprise, come over to his Willie, pick him up, and hug him as he spun him back and forth with joy, pressing the boy against his flour-saturated apron, kissing his son on each cheek. Then he would reach for one of the fresh, warm black breads, break it in half, and give it to his son to sample the morning's work. With a grunt of satisfaction and a nod, the day's bread production for the bakery had passed Willie's inspection.

Hans Kirchenmann was a baker in Stuttgart, Germany. In 1938, at twenty-eight, he felt that he had satisfied and accomplished many of the goals he had set for himself in his early life. He married his first sweetheart, the one he dreamed of since they met in primary school, and three years ago had purchased the bakery from his uncle. The store was on a busy street two city squares from the central rail station. The bakery's window, filled with the day's fresh goods, faced a thoroughfare lined with small shops that fed, clothed, and bejeweled the Stuttgart middle class. Herr Strasser owned the greengrocer's across the street, and Cohen the jewelry store. Rosenfeld was the proprietor of the men's shop, and his brother-in-law Groswasser had the ladies ready-to-wear across the way. The fish store, with the tank of live carp and pails of iced herrings from the North Sea, was on the corner. It was a small retail community near the city center. The street, Stephanstrasse, was close to the railroad station. Shoppers coming from the station and the town square would pass by on their way home and stop for their bread and delicacies in the nearby stores.

Hans grew up during the turmoil of the post–First World War years. His father had served on the western front while Hans was an infant. He remembered his father's struggles to feed the family during the hard years after the war, and when the chance came, when he was fifteen years old, he welcomed the opportunity to apprentice to his uncle as a baker. Now, at twenty-eight he felt secure. Life was good for the six-foot-tall, powerfully built, blond-haired baker. He wasn't a political person and didn't vote for the Nazi party when they had their last election, but he was satisfied that this government had the answers that would make Germany great once more. He had his beloved wife, his son, and a good shop. For five years now, the country was prospering under the Nazi Hitler government. What more could he expect?

Since he was a toddler Willie had been welcome in all of the local shops. He was the baker's boy. When he visited Strasser's store, the affable, tubby vegetable seller would break a carrot in half, take the knife from his belt, clean it with five or six quick scrapes, and give the snack to Willie. At the jewelers, Cohen would fit a loupe to his eye and let him inspect the diamonds received from Amsterdam. When a new shipment arrived at the haberdashery, Herr Rosenfeld let Willie try on the hats and caps that filled one of the two windows. At the delicatessen there were samples of the cheeses and the wursts and liver, blood, and ham sausages. In turn, Willie would experience the rich aromas of the full shopping bags that came into the bakery. From the mere scent that followed each shopper he could tell the path they had taken in their stroll along the street.

The merchants were friends and neighbors. They looked after each other's children and shared their problems, worries, and joys. They had lived through the postwar inflation and endured the turmoil of the past ten years of economic change and political uncertainty. These merchants had survived the economic depression of the 1920s and remembered the Brown Shirt street gangs marching just a few years before. There was a new government, and business was improved and stable. Shoppers had money once more and there were goods to be purchased. The politics of the Nazi party didn't appeal to most of these storekeepers, but business was business. Behind each storefront there was a family. Children were conceived, born, and matured. Mothers tended the store while rocking the cradle, and fathers worked hard to see that their stores were stocked and attractive. They were proud to be Germans; pride had returned to the country.

It was so at the Kirchenmann bakery. Papa would be out of bed at 4 a.m. and start the ovens. Mama would open the store at 8 a.m. and give Papa a rest from his early morning task of baking the day's supply of breads, rolls, and specialty buns. Mama worked, and as Willie grew, Papa also put Willie's hands to work. Willie's first job was to take the formed, still cold, raw doughy loaves of black bread and roll them in caraway seeds. He would then organize them on Papa's pallet, a dozen at a time, ready to slide into the hot glowing oven for baking. The heat of the oven would radiate, and to young Willie the warmth was an extension of the love his father generated. Papa would reward Willie for his assistance with a pat on the head and a hug at the end of the day's baking and send him off to school with a fresh loaf to share with his classmates. If Papa had baked *stolen,* the doughy, sugar-coated buns would be in the bag as a bonus treat for Willie and his friends. At Easter and Christmas times there would be *hutzelbrot,* holiday cakes, to please the classmates.

When Willie was old enough to reach over the counter, he would assist in the store, waiting on customers. He did the math and calculations for each sale. "It's better than school," Mama would say. Willie loved the experience. He was part of the family team.

Mama was the first to notice when the jeweler Cohen was visited by several Brown Shirts from the local SA organization in late 1934 and a sign was posted in his store window that said "JUDE."

"Hans, did you see the sign in Cohen's window?"

"Yes."

"Should we say something?"

"There is nothing to say, but go over to them and speak to his wife and ask if they want anything." He shrugged his shoulders and heaved a sigh, "I think the Jews are in for a bad time. I don't like what Hitler is doing, but we are not in much of a position to resist these laws he is imposing."

"But Hans, they are our neighbors. We have known the Cohens for a long time."

"The government must know what they are doing. Just stay out of this."

"But . . ."

"No buts. We have our own lives to think about."

By the time Willie was five years old, the sign in the jewelers window was an accepted part of the neighborhood. Brown-shirted men with black trousers tucked into jackboots, carrying truncheons and pistols, became a common sight around the train station, just a few blocks away. Sometimes one or more would come into the bakery; their hobnailed boots would resound on the tile floor and announce their presence. They looked frightening to little Willie. Papa, when he was in the store, would always be the one to wait on them. Mama would retreat into the back of the store and find some tidying up to do.

"They are lower-class bullies. I'm afraid when they come into the store. They come here, buy bread or a few rolls, and then always seem to bang on Cohen's window when they leave. Poor man."

"Mama, it's not our business!" was Papa's comment.

Then one day, right outside the bakery, Willie saw an elderly man pushed into the street in front of an oncoming horse and wagon by a brown-shirted trooper. The man wasn't hurt, but the trooper stood over him, and Willie heard: "The walkway is for me, the gutter is for you, Jew."

"Papa, why did the man push the old Jew?"

"I don't know Willie. But that is the way it is today."

Willie was too young to be recruited into the local Hitler Jugend Bann that was organized at his grade school.

He was five years old, in the last year of his kindergarten in 1936 when it became the law that all parents had to register their children for the Hitler Youth.

"I don't want Willie to be part of those tough guys," Mama was heard telling Papa.

"The government says we must, they must know what is right."

"I don't want my son marching in the streets and acting like a soldier."

"But he is only five years old. It doesn't matter at this stage."

"A five year old should not train to be a stormtrooper."

Papa was silent and shook his head with bewilderment at his wife's seemingly anti-government attitude. However, Hans, respecting Mama's comments, resisted the idea of the Youth registration. But after several days' delay, reluctantly Willie was taken to Town Hall and registered. The registration placed young Willie in Deutsches Jungvolk, the preteen organization for indoctrination before young men were admitted into the more militarily oriented Hitler Youth. When they arrived home from the registration, Mama would not speak to Papa until well after dinner. Her silence was a protest over the day's activity.

Willie looked forward to Sundays. The store was closed, and when the weather was good, the family would take the street car to the end of the line. Mama would pack a picnic basket, Papa would find a cool place in the woods, and they would have a picnic. Papa in his lederhosen and Mama in her dirndl skirt, white blouse, and green vest would sit and sing to Willie after the lunch. Later Mama would nap on the blanket they had brought along and Willie and Papa would walk in the woods. Sometimes Mama would change into shorts and join the "two boys" for a hike.

Willie was just seven years old and attending the *gymnasium,* the more select school for young children with academic potential, when in the middle of March he came from school and excitedly ran into the store. Mama was behind the counter, but he looked for his father. "Where is papa?"

"He is upstairs finishing his nap."

Willie ran up the stairs and jumped onto the edge of the bed with his street clothes and outdoor coat still on.

"Hey, you are cold!" Papa exclaimed.

Willie was flushed, with a red face, and, gasping for air, started to talk rapidly. "Papa, the boys beat Hershel Cohen on the way home from school. We were walking together, just as we always do, when five of the brown-shirted guys jumped on Hershel and started to hit him. They pushed me away. They called him a 'dirty Jew' and I was called a 'Jew lover.' Why did they do this? Can you come to school and get them to stop?"

Papa hugged Willie and stroked his hair. There were tears in Willie's eyes, and Papa reached over for a handkerchief, wiped the tears away, and had Willie blow his nose. "I don't know what to do about this," Papa said. "I am against what these people are doing; I think it is wrong. But these are strange times, and our Jewish friends are being blamed for things they have nothing to do with. They are being hounded. Many are leaving Germany. Our government has reasons, and we can't question them. I don't know what Herr Cohen is going to do. I hope he can leave and go somewhere where he is welcome. I'd like to help him. I don't know what to advise him, I feel quite helpless. He is a good man."

"But, Papa, what am I to say?"

"Say nothing, obey your teachers and don't tell anyone what we think about this."

Willie shrugged his shoulders as Papa got out of bed, took his coat, and affectionally patted him on the backside. "Go play, or help Mama in the store."

It was early in Willie's course at school that he came home with his books and Mama saw a thin picture book, *Introduction to Mein Kampf.* It had a photo of Hitler on the cover. "What is this?"

Willie replied, "That is the new book the teacher gave us to read. I'm supposed to read it and we are all going to be quizzed on what we have learned. It tells us of the ideas the Führer has for making us all great as a nation."

Both Mama and Papa let the incident pass until about a week later, when Willie brought home another book. This was *Der Giftpliz* [The Poisonous Mushroom]. Mama picked up the book and said, "Who gave you this book? It was written by that man Streicher. This is trash!"

"But Mama, everyone in school received one, it's a gift."

"Willie, don't believe what is in this. It is full of lies. You see the Cohens across the street. You have played with their son, he is one of your best friends. Jews are nice people. This book is propaganda, lies that someone is telling for politics. Don't believe it."

Papa came into the room as Mama pushed the book aside.

Mama asked Willie to come upstairs, and the two rested in the sitting room corner.

"Willie, some of he messages in this book, and in *Mein Kampf,* are not good," she instructed. "That's what propaganda is all about. You have to learn them because that is the law and the government's curriculum. But understand that I don't approve of this book. Telling lies about people doesn't make it true just because the government printed the message."

"I understand."

"It's confusing, but these books teach hate and that the good of the state is more important than the good of individual people. Papa and I don't hate anyone. We believe that all people are basically good, no matter where or how they pray. Jews didn't do the things the Nazis say. The Cohens across the street are nice people and so are most of the people who pray with them." Mama took a deep breath and paused, trying very hard to make a point, but not feeling that she was up to the job. "When you are older, we hope you will understand."

In early 1938 an official-looking letter arrived at the bakery. It was a notice for Papa to report for review for the military conscription that had been introduced three years before. It was a summons to show up at the town hall for a review of his status. Mama was silent after the letter arrived. She would go over and hug Papa from time to time. Often there were tears in her eyes.

"I don't want you to go into the army. This is all wrong!"

"Don't worry, Mama, I'm a married man with a child. They really don't want me," Papa said as he left the store several days later to face the review board. About three hours later, he returned with a smile on his face. "See, I'm back."

"What did they say?"

"Well, I'm safe here at home until a call-up, which they don't think will come."

Mama didn't like the answer. A scowl of worry would pass across her face anytime someone mentioned the conscription or the army's preparations. Her periods of silence became longer and her face showed the first lines of a worried scowl. She was concerned, and when Papa was near she seemed to hold him just a little closer than she had done in the past.

The call-up came just five months later. It came the day after the night the Brown Shirts broke Cohen's windows and pulled him out onto the street. With Cohen's wife watching, they beat him. From behind the curtains of the upstairs apartment, Papa looked out.

"Mama, I don't want you involved, but when they go away, go down and help Mrs. Cohen. See if she needs anything."

"Yes, Hans."

"And these are the people who are calling me into the army?"

"I don't want you to go, but I understand your orders from the government," Mama said. "You must go."

"It's the law, and we must listen and follow. But to leave my family, to possibly associate with people who do things like we just saw, is not my idea of a proper life."

"We are told it's just for a year."

"I hope so."

Just three days later Papa, with a small overnight bag in hand, kissed Mama and left seven-year-old Willie, the bakery, and Stuttgart to serve his one year of conscription. Mama was crying and held on to Hans until he pulled away, leaned back, and gave her a final kiss as he walked out the door.

Before he left, he had turned to Willie and said: "You are the man in the house now. You must help take care of your mother. I trust you to do the right thing."

Two weeks later Mama wrote to Hans that the Cohens' store was boarded up and the Cohens had left. She didn't know where they went.

They had left their furniture and many of their belongings. Within a week the store was reopened with a proprietor who was a relative of a Nazi politician. The apartment was occupied by a German family. The husband, Bruno Schmidt, was one of the local Brown Shirts.

Chapter 3

Newark, New Jersey: The War Years—George's Story

My grandfather had been a butcher in the old country. After his arrival in the United States he settled in Harrison, New Jersey, and started a dry goods business, first selling remnants and then full bolts of fabric. Grandmother and my mother came in 1920 and the family prospered for several years, only to have the Depression wipe out the business when the largest manufacturing plant in town closed. He became a house painter. With a barrel chest and arms made rock hard by work on a stout body, he was a powerful man. His workingman hands were callused and chapped from the hours of stroking a paintbrush, and dried by the turpentine used to remove the paint stains. He had thinning gray hair combed straight back. Although he always bathed as soon as he came home, the faint fragrance of leaded paint and turpentine were infused onto his body, and the scent of the drink of schnapps that fortified him for the evening after a day's work was on his breath. After dinner, he would sit in his grand wing chair and listen to Gabriel Heatter, then New York's leading newscaster, present the news for fifteen minutes on WOR.

Heatter would start each broadcast with his signature baritone voice intoning: "Ah, there's good news tonight." Of course, on a few nights there would be a solemnly intoned: "There's bad news tonight," followed by a deep sigh. With Grandpa comfortably leaning back in his chair and listening, I would spread a map on the living room floor, tracing the movement of the Germans as they first swept across Poland, and then divided Poland with the Russians. The peace that lasted for eighteen months on this eastern front suspended our evening map exercise until June 1941 when Hitler attacked Russia.

Grandpa would comment on the cities and towns mentioned in the news. Villages that were part of Ukraine were battlegrounds, and on many of these evenings I would get a geography lesson describing the land and customs of Russia. We traced the German advance to the gates of Moscow in the north and watched the blue pins, representing the German army on our map, move east past Kiev and all the way to the Volga River and beyond. The red pins, marking the Russian positions, were constantly being reset back toward Moscow.

On December 7, 1941, our focus on the war became more personal. We had been attacked by the Japanese at Pearl Harbor and now it became "our war." Our sessions of following the news became more intense.

We were caught up in "the war effort." Grandpa worked painting the new barracks that were quickly built in our local park. My father took a job in a defense industry, first as an apprentice machinist and then as an accountant in one of the formerly German owned factories where the government had expropriated the business for the duration of the war. My mother and Grandma kept the store open and I collected scrap aluminum pots and pans, steel junk, and, of course, bacon grease from the local restaurants; all for the war effort. We attended bond rallies and purchased "saving stamps" at school which we proudly redeemed at the bank for war bonds when we reached the magic goal of $18.50, the cost of buying a $25 war bond, the lowest denomination sold.

In September of 1942, the high-water mark of the German advance into Russia came with the battle of Stalingrad. Then the tide turned and Grandpa instructed me in the geography of his native Poland and Russia as we moved the battle lines back, marking the Russian offensives pushing the Germans west. By late 1944 the battleground was the area around the Vistula River. My grandfather and grandmother both told me that we all came from there: "That was home of the relatives; that was where they would be."

On the Monday after Victory in Europe Day, Grandma once again sat down at the kitchen table, took out her box of paper and envelopes and wrote letters. She sat for three evenings. They were longer than usual, judging by the weight of the envelopes. There was a lot of news: My dad had sold the store. My aunt Sophie had married and moved into the first floor of the house; her husband was in the Air Force stationed in the Pacific and I was just about to finish grammar school. For the six years of the war, Grandma hadn't written, and there was a lot of news to share and many questions to be asked. If Grandma was worried, she didn't say anything.

Grandma had received no letters during the war years. I was older now, but with this group of new letters, I still made the trip to the mailbox for her. Within weeks the letters came back and were dropped into the mail slot at the bottom of the stairs. The identical stamp was imprinted on each in bold red ink: "No Addressee Known." Grandma read the newspapers and listened to the radio. She read about the death camps and the slaughter of millions. She heard nothing from the family. Other letters she wrote were never returned. Often I would see her sitting in the corner in the north light, white handkerchief in hand, crying.

That year, on Yom Kippur, the Jewish Day of Atonement, the holiest day of the year, she lit Yahrtzeit (memorial) candles for her entire family. As she prayed over the glow of more than a dozen of them, tears glistened as they streamed down her cheeks.

Chapter 4

Stuttgart, Germany, 1945: The End of the War—Uncertainty

It was Willie's task to walk to the post office each morning and see if there was a letter from Papa. There hadn't been a single message since January, and the realization that Papa had either been killed or captured had demoralized Mama. In the absence of word from the army, she still hoped that her husband was alive.

It was early spring 1945, and the Allied armies were across the Rhine just north of the city. Just a few months before, Willie and Mama were relieved when the bombing stopped, the previous July. The air raids had been a continuous threat for nearly three years—the British bombing at night and the Americans bombing in daylight. Mail was no longer delivered to their house. Herr Brenner, the postman, had been killed in the February attack, and his wife took over the post job and would not deliver mail in clear weather, as these were the daylight bombing days.

The fear and apprehension of the nearly daily sounding of the air raid sirens and the rush to the basement shelter had worn away the effervescent joy of his youth. The smells of burning buildings and the dust and odors of death were slowly receding. The city rubble was all around. Lanes were cleared in the streets to allow minimal passage of carts and trucks. The Allies had come ashore in France in June the year before, and a few remaining fanatics were claiming that the Americans and British would be thrown back into the Channel. As the news of German defeats became known, Willie noticed that the morale of those who came to buy the limited supplies of bread was mixed. There were those who realized that the war was lost and drawing to a close, and then there were those who still believed there could be a miracle, a victory, or at least an armistice. There had been hope of a "great German offensive" in December 1944 that would have driven the Americans and British back and forced an armistice. When the offensive failed, the people's spirits plunged into deeper despair. The word of the Allies' advance across France and the news that the Americans were approaching the Fatherland created fear and apprehension about the uncertain future.

Willie and his mother were living in the cellar since the last big raid in July. That raid destroyed most of the rail yards and leveled the area near the city center. Incendiary bombs had set fire to and destroyed the upper floors of their old house. Their cellar "home" was two basement rooms in the bakery area, all that survived when the house burned. The "store" was open a few hours a day, more of an open stall within the shell of the ground floor. The former green painted front was now blistered from the incendiary fires' heat, and the large windows were gone, shattered in one of the first raids and replaced by boards from nearby rubble piles. The multi-hued colors of their makeshift shelter kept out the cold and the rain. Inside, the store was dark, and candles served as light. The loaves of bread that used to be spread on clean white pine shelves were now displayed on a counter made from a salvaged door. Mama would post a little sign that bread had been baked and was for sale, and the housewives would queue with their ration cards and little baskets, sometimes waiting hours for the sales to start.

Willie and Mama lived around the bakery ovens with furniture that had been reclaimed from the floors above and from neighbors who had either been killed or were not returning from their flights from the city to the safer countryside. Mama and Willie had become experts in finding old rugs and carpeting to cover the walls, provide decoration, and keep the sounds of the city from their little space.

Willie knew that over 100,000 people had been badly injured in the last raid and that there were many dead. Luckily he and Mama had been in their basement shelter during the raid. Willie hated the scream of the falling bombs and the thump, thump of the impact. There were often six or eight explosions with each falling bomb series, and Willie and his mother would count as the impacts got closer or receded. When the raiders switched from high explosive bombs to fire bombs, the incendiaries had set massive fires. Much of the last months were spent by the women working with their older children clearing the rubble in the streets, trying to salvage the valuables that weren't destroyed, gathering and sorting building materials, and getting cover over their heads.

Willie was just under fourteen years old and in the last year of the pre-university stages of study at the *gymnasium.* If he had been six months older, he would have been enrolled in the Hitler Youth and drafted into one of the home guard units. Several of his friends, just a year or so older, were now manning anti-aircraft positions in the city defense ring. Admission to the university was being postponed because of the war.

Willie and his mother were alone. He hadn't seen his father since Papa was home over two years earlier in late 1943. During home leave, his father spent a lot of time with Mama and, when he could, would hold Willie close to himself for long quiet hugs, without saying anything. The soldier was embracing his son. Willie would feel his father's warmth and listen to him breathing. It was comforting just to be held. Willie loved these moments. He sensed Papa's reluctance to leave to rejoin his army unit in the east. Mama cried for days after he left. His posting to "the East" was bad news.

The Kirchenmann bakery was located on a main street, a shopping area just to the east of the center of the city. By 1945, his mother could no longer bake the quality pumpernickel and rye breads, heavy with the rich taste of grain and filled with caraway seeds, that she had sold with great pride before and during those first victorious years of German conquests. The good flour that came to her from France, Poland, and Russia in the early years had been replaced by dry ersatz powder that the government distributed. When baked, it didn't fill the kitchen with the full wondrous black bread aroma that Willie had remembered. It was bread to satisfy hunger, not the bread of a pleasurable meal; bread to sell to the housewives who arrived early each morning waiting for the bread to be placed onto the store's wooden counter.

Every other day in the early months of the war, Mama would get a letter from Papa telling her that everything was "all right" and how much he loved her and wanted to be back home. Mama would take the letter from Herr Brenner, walk to the rear of the store, and sit and read, reading some of the passages out loud so Willie could hear his father's story. Most often, Mama would immediately take out her writing pad and the box of envelopes and answer the letter. Of course, there were entire sections of the letters Mama wouldn't read to Willie. These she would read silently, often with a smile and a little flush in her face as she treasured each loving word. Late at night, she would take the letter received during the day and read it again. Tears would often accompany her second reading. Papa had taken his F2 Leica along with him into the army, and as the war progressed, there were pictures of Papa in cities with strange names like Tarnowo Podgorne, Krakow, Radom, Lvov, Aleksandrov, and Rostov, often with Papa and his buddies smiling and sitting in a town square or on destroyed enemy equipment. These were assurances that all was well. The names of the cities in the letters moved east with the news of the army's advances.

Willie would follow the army's conquests on his school's geography maps. After the army entered Russia, Willie went to the local stationery store, purchased a map, and used colored pins to show where the army had driven to deep within Russia. He would mark those boundaries with red pins and little blue pins to signify where he believed Papa was garrisoned.

As the war moved on, the pictures that accompanied the letters were fewer and noticeably different. Pictures of beautiful or quaint town squares no longer fell from the envelopes. Now there were scenes of destruction, and the happy cooks and bakers were replaced by combat troops and riflemen. These were pictures of *Landsers,* infantrymen. Papa's role had changed. Then, the letters continued, but there were no pictures. The later letters were mere quick scribbles on scraps of paper. The words were comforting, but the condition of the letters was an ominous sign that all was not well.

Mama's mood had changed about two years earlier. The letters came less frequently; and the visits home from the war zone ceased. During Papa's last home leave just before Christmas in 1943, he seemed to feel dejected, and although he and Mama were happy to be together, Willie sensed that his mother cried a lot while Papa was home. Papa had told her the truth: The war was being lost and the situation was so bad that men who were bakers and cooks in 1939 were now fighting in the front line. He had lost many friends. Many of the men who'd trained with him just a few years before had been either killed or wounded. Papa told Mama that the morale at the front was very poor and he was afraid.

Whole armies had been lost. The horrible defeat at Stalingrad had shocked the people at home. Other news from Russia told of huge German losses in places Willie and Mama had never heard of. It wasn't like the victorious advances in 1939 and 1941. The optimism of the early days had eroded into a fear of the future. The air raids destroyed large areas of the cities. Every family knew of soldiers lost in the battles and civilians killed or maimed in the raids.

When Papa left to return to his duties on the Eastern Front after that last leave, he promised to keep writing. The letters came regularly, not at the former every-other-day rate, but more like once a week. In January 1945 those letters stopped.

The first of the Allied troops into Stuttgart were the French, who arrived just before the final surrender in May. Willie stayed close to his mother during the days when the French were securing the city. No one knew what to expect. The French army and administrators were very thorough and strict. Curfews were strictly enforced, and the population was screened for Nazi party members. There were arrests of some of the local officials. Everyone was interrogated and issued new identification papers; Mama and Willie worked to keep the store open. The French army made some supplies available, and Mama could bake once again. The women returned to their shopping. The damaged store was repaired and busy. Mother and young son lived in their protected underground home and worried. They had survived the war, but they didn't know where Papa was and presumed that he had been killed during the January Russian offensive.

The rumor was that Stuttgart was to be in the American zone of occupation. Willie and Mama came out of the cellar when Willie heard the movement of the heavy equipment—the tanks and many, many trucks foretold that the Americans had arrived. The American GIs were different from the French; they were men with smiles, candy, and huge amounts of supplies and food. They were well fed and well dressed. For every battle-hardened man, there seemed to be dozens of trucks, quartermasters, support soldiers, and medical personnel. They all seemed to come from a place called Kansas or another called Brooklyn. Willie was given his first chewing gum by one of the GIs, and one of the soldiers gave Mama chocolate just for answering a question about directions to the train station.

After a while, the men from the defeated German army slowly returned to the city. Of course, the first to come home were the men released after duty in the west and those captured by the Americans and British in the campaigns in France and the recent battles along the Rhine and the Low Countries. Then, weeks and months later, the men who were captured in battles in Africa and interred in England, Canada, and America arrived. These were well fed, healthy, and energetic returnees. There was just a trickle, very few, returning from the east. The first were men who had escaped before the Russians moved forward, men who had eluded Russian capture. Many of these had walked all the way across Germany to get home. There were the very few who were captured and released by the Russians. Those that came from the east were defeated, hollow-cheeked, gaunt men. Their uniforms were in tatters, some had boots that were worn tissue thin, with threadbare socks protecting their swollen feet as they hobbled home.

Papa did not come home. Mama made inquiries. She would go to the railroad station and the area where the veterans gathered seeking work. She asked for men who served with or near Papa. She found no one who had survived from the battle segment from which Papa had written his last letter. She went to the local American military governor and asked how to find a missing German soldier. She tried the few official channels of government set up to trace the missing. She didn't get answers. The military archives were in disarray. She met with other wives who also were looking for their husbands. There was hope that the Russians had captured Papa, but that hope died when the Russians released the names of the soldiers they held. There were "channels" set up to account for those missing. Mama registered with every agency that possibly could help her. It was a full year before Mama heard that the best they could say was that Papa was unaccounted for after an "action" in January 1945. The action was somewhere near the Vistula River.

Mama gave up all hope.

Chapter 5

Leaving Newark, 2005: The Trip to Memory Land—George's Story

As an investment banker with European clients, I traveled regularly and extensively to the major cities of Europe. Four months earlier I retired and started to wonder what to do with my newfound leisure time. Moving to Florida was not an option; that was "God's waiting room." Years earlier my wife Nancy and I agreed that we would not change our lifestyle in retirement. Our goal was to stay active and enjoy the "golden years." Cruises, resorts, and stops in cities around the world where museum visits filled the day became our life. Our son and daughter had children of their own and lived independent lives. Being grandparents was wonderful, and we enjoyed our visits, but we were still very independent. However, I felt there had to be more to do, something meaningful.

Many projects had been delayed during my working years. I started to sort areas of the apartment and storage closets as a major activity. Nooks and crannies that hadn't been examined in years were invaded. Junk that should have been thrown away long ago went into the trash. A little label maker was among the items discovered. It became the instant "newfound friend" tool of the day, and the remaining boxes that were kept all received proper tags in coded colors. I felt proud of each task completed.

Culling and cleaning our library, a room with floor-to-ceiling bookcases containing volumes representing fifty years of our collective reading became my next major project. The books ranged from college texts we couldn't part with to the latest novels by favorite authors. Nancy helped, and we organized the collection by topic and separated the novels from the nonfiction. Facing reality, we regrettably gave away many books. The room was now neat and it was time to look for another project.

Turning my attention to the large mahogany desk, with its deep drawers, I found a treasure of memorabilia and many years' accumulation of useless trinkets and documents. There were old greeting cards from birthdays remembered and friends forgotten. Buried in the drawers were used ticket stubs from shows, both good and bad, and reminders of hotels in exotic locations. There were lost pictures of the children taken twenty and thirty years before. At the back of a file drawer was a folder with my grandmother's will, immigration papers, and a large pack of correspondence she had received from Poland before the war. The postmarks ranged from the early 1930s to those that had been returned marked "undeliverable." I looked at the yellowed envelopes and felt where the paper had grown crisp to the touch and was starting to crumble at the corners. At random, I opened a few of the envelopes. The letters were in Yiddish and I couldn't read the language.

Curious about the contents, I called a translation agency and arranged to take twenty-five of the letters into New York. Within a week, the translations were done and were returned in a FedEx package to my condominium. Now it was my turn to read, just as Grandma had done years ago. At the dining room table I sorted the letters by date and years and, choosing a few, went into the living room and started to read them, eager for the information I might gather. The first letter, selected from the middle of the pack, was dated August 1938:

Dear Feggie,

All is well here. Leizer is away in the forest seeing that the wood is cut for the coming year's sales. He leaves on Mondays and comes back midday on Friday in time for Shabbas. The challah [bread] is in the oven and the noodle kugel is baking. The cholent [stew] is made, and after I finish this letter I will hurry over to the baker to have him put it in his oven to be warm until tomorrow sundown. Since Leizer is away, I have time to sit and answer your last letter. Everyone is well and the weather has been nice, not too hot and not too cool, a good summer. Business has been good and we are looking forward to Rosh Hashanah next month. I have bought some new dresses for myself and Miriam for *younthf* (the holidays). As you know, Miriam will be getting married to the young man I wrote you about last month. He is a student at the Chadar [religious school] in Cracow. His family is from a nearby shtetl [town] and they are in the dry goods business. His father is a leader at their shul. They are fine people and we are all pleased at the match. His family is prosperous and wants him to continue his studies. He may want to be a rabbi. On the other hand, Leizer told me there is a place for him in our timber business. He always wanted a son in the business. No matter, Miriam will have a good marriage.

We would love you to come with Jake and see us all. I know that will not happen, but it's a wish. Of course, you realize that we are so tied to our world here that I can't imagine us coming to live with you in America, no matter how attractive you make it for us. Maybe the children will come to you, *Baruch Ha-Shem* [God willing]. Sadie's little boy, Eli, is now five years old and can recite poems in Polish and in Yiddish. He is very tall for his age and we think he is very smart. Of course, as grandparents we would! The community has set up a new school that young people attend before they start the real school. Do they have this in America? We all would like to know more about your life. There are so many stories. Is it really easier there? Although life is good here, the young people all want to leave and go to Palestine or to America. But it is hard. It isn't only the money, it's all the restrictions. Maybe you can investigate how some of the boys can come over to you. That would be nice.

I will close now. I must continue preparing my cooking for Shabbas, going to the baker and cleaning the house.

My regards to Jake and your family.

Love,

Your loving sister Selma

The other letters described a loving family. I was absorbed and read on and on. Brothers and sisters who were once very close were now separated by land and ocean. The letters were their bond. They told of the "old country" customs, the superstitions and rituals, the cycles of the seasons, the holidays, and the events of life. They were chronicles of peaceful people, some tied to the land where they lived and others with the ambition to move on. There were cousins who left and went to *eretz Israel* [land of Israel] and others who wanted to go to America. This was the story of my family—Grandma's family, the Eisensteins; and Grandpa's family, the Walls.

Reading the letters, I wondered who these people were. Yes, they were my relatives, but I really didn't know or relate to them. To me they could have been any family. Who was Leizer? Who was Selma? The names of their children and other names were all a mystery to me. My new knowledge left me hungry for information. In reading I realized that I had never identified with this family. They were Grandma's family—but her family was my family. It was a startling realization that came upon me. I was lost in my own family. Having never identified with the writers of the letters, I found myself thinking about them, their lives, and wanting to know what happened to them. I was becoming curious. How could I find out about them?

The translations told of life in a small Polish town, a *shtetl,* with about 3,000 Jews and perhaps 7,500 gentiles. I looked up the town and found that Ozarow was a village located near the Vistula River on a slight rise above the river plain. I used Google Earth and observed that the ground between the settled area and the river was excellent fertile farmland, and the land to the west for several miles was a pasture and wheat fields. Beyond, there was a forest supplying timber to the area. That must have been the forest mentioned in that first letter, where Leizar had his business. This was a farming community and crossroads for local commerce. The general store was owned by one of Grandpa's brothers, and the kosher (of course) butcher was a cousin. Selma's husband, Grandma's brother-in-law, was a timber merchant owning what Grandpa called a lumberyard now that he was "Americanized." All had a dream of a peaceful life.

This was described in the letters. There were items of gossip and news. There were stories of births and deaths.

The letters brought back the memory that Grandma had told me about the Jews having built a magnificent synagogue over two hundred years before, which was the center of their life. The synagogue had a history of housing distinguished rabbis. The Jews had a good relationship with the local Polish people and the congregation of the small Catholic church at the heart of the town. The church was located on top of the hill that crowned the approach to the main square and the market that was the center of the social life of the non-Jewish town folk. In modern history, the Jews of Ozarow never had a problem with their gentile neighbors. The letters told of the peaceful life, an almost religious utopia, as the community prayed and lived without interference.

Those few who emigrated followed older brothers or husbands who'd left to avoid army duty during the time the town was part of Russia before the First World War. I was told that this was why my grandfather left. He didn't want to serve in the Russian army for a second time, as he had served for a short time during the Russo-Japanese War. Under the new decrees, conscription was for a term of twenty-five years, and for Jews it meant service in labor battalions without weapons. Of those relatives who stayed in Ozarow, there seemed to be a peaceful and rather idyllic life in the independent Poland that emerged after the 1920 revolution, in the new Polish republic broken away from Russia. During the 1930s, the letters frequently mentioned that there were cousins trying to emigrate to Palestine, in the hope of becoming part of a new Jewish homeland. Several of the letters talked about the hardship of getting "proper papers" to gain entry into "the Holy Land." I thought about it and remembered my grandmother's *pischkah,* a blue and white metal collection box with a slot in the top for collecting money, with a picture of Jerusalem on the side and the initials "JNF," standing for Jewish National Fund. The cash collected went to support the costs of bringing Jews into Palestine. Even when we were poor, in the depths of the Depression, Grandma always saw to it that loose change in the house found its way into the JNF box. She would even send me to stand in the cold outside the door of local restaurants shaking the box and approaching the diners as they each left the restaurant, still holding change in their hands after paying their checks. Many of those pennies, nickels, dimes, and hopefully quarters would be dropped into my shaking box. When I would came home, Grandma would set the box in a corner to await the visit from the rabbi who would collect the money for delivery overseas.

Each letter gave me a morsel of information. Each letter left me wanting to ask my grandmother questions. Of course, I couldn't. She had passed away thirty years before. Oh, what wonderful conversations we could have had if I'd only had the interest then!

I read other letters, filling my mind with images of the life and culture of people who were both so close to me and yet so distant. Then I read the last letter. It was dated September 3, 1939:

Feggie,

I am writing this in a hurry and will run to the post office in the town square to mail it. As you know, we have been attacked and we are at war again. The Germans are about fifty kilometers (30 miles) away and we are told that they will be here within days. The Polish army isn't able to hold the Nazis back.

We don't know what the future will bring. In the last war the Germans weren't bad occupiers, they left us alone. Now we have heard rumors that they have laws that are very bad for the Jews. This all worries us. Hitler has said things that do not make us comfortable.

Leizer's nephew has left and is trying to go overland to Palestine. We were all sad to see him leave, but he was very determined that he wanted to settle away from Europe. We kissed him and sent him on. Pray for him. Miriam's new husband has tried to enlist in the Polish army. He left yesterday and we have no news from him. Miriam is pregnant, and for this we are happy. With a husband away, Leizer and I will have to be watchful over her.

I don't know when I'll be able to write again. I hope the Germans will allow post. Please write and give us some good news.

Your loving sister,
Selma

Looking at the addresses brought a nostalgic feeling, and the more I touched them, the more they seemed to say, "Go see." My mind had said that the war had happened to "someone else." That was the sense I always lived with. Now with these letters, I had a sensation, a stirring, within and a curiosity that needed satisfaction.

There was a part of me that denied a connection to the people to whom Grandma wrote and who wrote back. What had been missed in the transfer of knowledge from generation to generation? These letters were a connection to the past. Now I wanted to know these people. I knew it was too late, but my reaction was that I must go and see this town in Poland to understand my family origins. I had to see what was there, if anything.

Transatlantic trips had been routine for most of my career. I was comfortable with the process of arriving in a foreign city and making my way. However, never having been to Poland, there was a slight sense of adventure in planning this trip. This wasn't business; this was all personal. What would I find? My curiosity was driving me.

I told my wife of the possible trip and immediately had second thoughts. After all, I was a comfortable retired businessman and had few needs. Why was I going? It was difficult to leave home for an unknown journey to satisfy an interest in what had happened sixty years ago. To spend time away from my comfortable apartment high above the Hudson River commanding a spectacular view of New York City for an uncharted adventure seemed foolhardy. Yet there seemed to be a force within me that drove me to want to go to Ozarow, the town where the letters were addressed, and determine what had happened. Had anyone survived the war? Where might they be? Also, what was there before the war? What was left? The correspondence only told the detailed life of the family, some gossip, and little else. Information was limited. How did my relatives die? Did any survive? How were they killed? Were they sent to concentration camps? Were they massacred?

Strangely, I never had an impression growing up that there was a link between our family and the Holocaust. Grandma had a connection, but the family never talked about losses or missing relatives. Yes, I was Jewish and those slaughtered were other Jews. They were "over there," not here. Insulated as an American Jew, it didn't happen in our world. It didn't happen to me. Reading these letters brought me a sense of loss I hadn't experienced. I had been protected by my family during the period after the war when Grandma was in mourning over her lost relatives.

In reading the letters, I started to question my reactions over the years. Yes, there were contributions to Israel fund-raising and to my local Jewish causes and charities, but it wasn't with much thought other than the community expectation that giving money was the "right thing to do." Had something been missing? I was active in the Jewish community—wasn't giving money being "active"? Making your expected contribution put you on the dais at the local fund-raising dinner. Now I was thinking about the disappearance of the people who were in the letters.

I remembered the grief my grandmother felt for her lost family those many years ago. Did it just happen to "them"? Who were "they"? Were they really my family? I was an American secular Jew. For most Jewish Americans, the family history begins with a grandmother or grandfather landing in New York and going through Ellis Island. Grandparents seemed to want to leave all history behind. There was a "wall of knowledge" between America and the Old Country. The Holocaust involved some other unfortunate men, women, and children. Or did it? I was starting to question my actions and thoughts of the last sixty years. Should there have been more interest? Involvement?

I spoke to my wife about these feelings. We had just celebrated our fiftieth anniversary. Nancy's first comment was: "Isn't it a bit late for you to find religion?"

"This isn't a matter of religion. I feel I've avoided something."

"Darling, you've missed very little in life. But, if you have this feeling, you should go and see what happened to the town where the letters were addressed. Go see what happened to your relatives. After all, they were really your family."

Her words were a shock. I had never put the letters and the people to whom they were written into my mental framework as being "my family." They were Grandma's and Grandpa's, not mine. Now, I really wanted to know what happened. Would there be any trace of their fate?

Nancy said, "Go! This is something you have to do to resolve your relationship with your past. It's a trip of closure for a chapter in your family history. It's a story you want to be able to tell to our children."

My preparations for the trip began. The next day a TravelSmith catalog arrived, offering comfortable and lightweight travel clothes to make packing easy and limit the weight and bulk of a suitcase. The clothes worn on my business trips would not do—they were mostly pinstripe suits and tailored monogrammed shirts, the uniform of the business world. My wardrobe did not contain clothing that ranged from a suitable blue blazer to underwear and socks sold just for light-packing travelers. What was needed were casual and indestructible clothes; clothes that could be washed in bathtubs and sinks, hung to dry, and be available in the morning. The best of the hotels existing in the small towns were of two-star variety. There would be no laundry ready in a day, no dry cleaning. I wanted clothes that were comfortable, relaxed, and still looked good. After all I still had my standards.

During the next several days the items needed for this trip were assembled, including a black carry-on rolling suitcase like an airline employee would use. I was excited and ready to go. This was unlike previous business travels. It was a strange exhilaration. Traveling with the small, rolling carry-on instead of a briefcase felt liberating from my usual heavy suitcase. The carry-on held some of the travel brochures and a small tape recorder so I could capture my thoughts and perhaps record one or more interviews. Also, carrying a small digital camera with an extra chip would give me the capacity to take over 800 pictures and share some of the experience with grandchildren and friends. It was just a final thought that made me go into my den and find a small Reform Jewish prayer book I had purchased many years before. I placed the book into the luggage and heaved a sigh.

As I packed, I thought of Grandma's and Grandpa's stories of the Old Country, trying to visualize what might remain of their old town, the area they lived in, and the world they left. What was the life they'd left behind? What would be found? How would I feel? What was there? Again and again, I asked myself, why am I going? There were still doubts about the trip, but the planning and preparations went forward.

Warsaw would be the obvious starting point. I could go there, find a guide, rent a car, and make my way to the town of Ozarow. It seemed quite logical and easy. United Airlines had a code-share flight with LOT, the Polish airline running Newark to Warsaw, and was the best deal. I thought of Grandma, who saved money by buying day-old lettuce at the vegetable store. She would have been proud of me getting frequent-flyer mileage on United and points on my American Express card. The contrast between modern luxury air travel and Grandma's journey many years before by horse-drawn wagon on poor roads, train, and ship astonished me. Thoughts came to mind of the problems she'd had of crossing borders, dealing with corrupt customs agents, exchanging monies, and caring for her nine-year-old daughter while traveling. She never told me how she'd done these things; she'd just said that she'd "made her way to Bremen, Germany" where she'd waited for a ship and had come to America. Thinking about this, I was awed by the enormity of her accomplishment. She was a determined woman to manage that passage from Poland to New Jersey. For her it was a voyage between two worlds that took two months. For me it would be only a plane ride for nine hours and a week of exploration. The world had certainly changed.

Since retirement, my lack of a secretary made booking travel and hotels a challenge. For the first time, I made reservations online. It wasn't as hard as I'd first thought, and frankly the process was enjoyable: searching for the flight and then selecting and booking a hotel, at least for my arrival in Warsaw.

When the day of the flight came, I was packed and ready to go to the airport several hours early. Nancy said, "You look anxious." I denied any anxiety but admitted to being a little excited at starting my adventure. When it was time to leave the apartment, Nancy got a big hug and I told her to enjoy her visit with the grandchildren. I quickly waved and got into the elevator with my baggage. In the limousine to the airport, the driver wasn't chatty, and pleased to be left to my own thoughts, I relaxed, trying to imagine what I would experience during this trip. I was filled with questions.

With a first-class ticket and the privilege of a rapid check-in, there was time to sit in the lounge, have a drink, and avoid the frenetic scurrying of the pre-boarding routine. Passengers were buying duty free as I sat in the deep black leather armchair with a drink of Johnnie Walker Black and twirled its lemon peel.

I ignored the several guidebooks on Poland in my bag, choosing instead the latest *Time* and *Newsweek* for pre-boarding diversion. The time went quickly. When the flight was called, I abandoned the newsmagazines in the lounge and began the long walk to the departure gate. The crowd at the gate seemed eager to board and get to their seats. I boarded and reached my first-class seat early, stowed my luggage, and gave my jacket to the flight attendant. Then, comfortable in the ample-sized luxury seat, I accepted the offer of the courtesy preflight scotch from the flight attendant, a lovely tall blond girl dressed in a starched United blue shirt and attractive blue skirt that displayed an athletic figure to her advantage. At 6:45 p.m. the airplane taxied away from the gate and we were off. We were due to arrive in Warsaw at noon the next day. As the plane became airborne and climbed away from the runway, I reclined in the plush seat and sleep came within a few minutes.

Chapter Six

Stuttgart, 2005: The Retirement—Willie's Story

Willie Kirchenmann sat at his huge slate-gray executive desk and gazed through the floor-to-ceiling double-wide office windows. It was his last day at the bank. All that was left was to await the senior managing director to shake his hand and say goodbye. His glass-enclosed office, on the top floor with the coveted panorama of the southwest of the city, was in the management suite of LandesBank Baden-Wurttemberg, or LBBW, as insiders in the banking world knew it. The building occupied the whole area of the southeastern corner of Arnulf-Klett-Platz, directly across from the Stuttgart main railroad station. It was a distinguished modern four-story building with not only floor-to-ceiling exterior office windows, but long and elegant corridors. Postwar Impressionist paintings hung along the solid interior walls, adding color to the otherwise stark glass and steel construction. For Willie, the building and the bank were monuments to his carreer.

The Landesbanks were the savings institutions of postwar Germany. Until recently state owned, they also acted as commercial lending banks. Their small-business lending speeded the "postwar miracle" of German development.

Willie had come a long way from sweeping rubble in the destroyed center of Stuttgart. In those months just after the war, it was the only work available. His position as a bank senior officer was a great achievement for someone of his generation born to the middle classes and educated in the public schools. Sitting at his desk, he reflected that he was less than a kilometer away, across the square below, from the bakery location that once was the center of his family's life.

He remembered when he was a skinny, half-starved, and eager teenager, confused by the events of the German defeat and fearful of the future for himself and his mother. It was a time when dust from the bombings, the odor of burnt wood, and the acrid smell of decay covered the whole area. He thought of his lucky moment when he had been singled out by an American officer for a job because he'd had a slight command of the English language from his *gymnasium* curriculum. Willie had worked in the Americans' camp doing odd menial tasks; then, because of his quick mind and winning personality, other, more challenging duties had been given to him. He'd become the protégé of an American finance corps brigadier general supervising the funding of postwar projects in the American occupied zone. It had been the start of his banking career.

Now he was seventy-four years old, and unlike many of his fellow executives, he was still very slim. A full six feet two inches, he was taller than his father had been. He had never taken to the diet of beer and wurst and had always watched his appearance and weight. Hanna, his wife, had always admired his appearance and discipline toward food and exercise. She loved his flowing head of hair, now slate gray. He didn't smoke, and when he took a drink, it was only for social occasions. In all the years of their marriage, Willie had never raised his voice in anger. He was known as a quiet man who attended his Lutheran church on select days, when Hanna insisted he show some reverence. She led the children to church on a more regular basis. If asked, he would say that he believed in God, but wasn't religious. He respected his wife's wishes concerning observance and at each meal sat quietly as Hanna said the blessing. Now, as a widower, when the children and grandchildren would visit, he led the prayer. Willie was a politically conservative man who loved and cherished his family and enjoyed the quiet, respected life of a prominent banker.

He appreciated that the bank had kept him on long after the normal retirement age because of his established and essential relationships with the old guard of clients. These men had built their businesses after the war, often starting with nothing but willpower and a loan from Willie. His clients trusted his knowledge and integrity. Now he was well past the mandatory retirement age, and the bank couldn't change its policy. Although this was his life's work, he knew he must step down and retire.

Willie had been instrumental in designing the bank's modern glass and steel building as an architectural statement for its prominent position in central Stuttgart. The offices had glass walls so that all could see the occupants and observe their activity. It was as if visual openness raised confidence in the bank and displayed honesty.

Willie had cleared his desk. He looked across the plaza below his window at the Hotel Graf Zeppelin, a five-star hotel built within the walls of the original bombed-out building. He liked to reflect upon the dissimilarity between the old hotel facade of red stone taken from nearby quarries and his bank's modern glass and stainless steel walls.

To him the contrast of the classic hotel representing the glory of the past and the futuristic glass facade of the Bank were two sides of Germany's twentieth century. He'd enjoyed his time in this modern building where he'd spent his working hours. From this executive floor he could see the Stadtgarten, the large city park; and the huge dominant hill, the Birkenkopf. This was the "hill of the dead." It was an artificial small hill containing the rubble of the old city. The destruction from the fifty-three Allied bombings was bulldozed into a mass of destroyed brick and dirt. The past was buried there. Now it was a beautiful park, a great hill to climb on weekends. It was an awesome silent monument. The grass and tree-covered slopes were a far cry from the rubble and dirt of 1945. The locals called it "Mount Sherbelmo," the mountain of shards.

Willie had been a senior officer of the bank for the last twenty years. He was on the supervisory board and managed the relationships with other Landesbanks. His office was spartanly appointed, as were the offices of all the senior managers. The plush carpet covered the slate floor, and the chrome trim of the ample modern desk contrasted with the black leather desk blotter and chrome Cross double pen set. The entire floor had a sterile aura of respectability and power. Each office had a small plaque at the door with the occupant's name and position at the bank. Willie's door had his name and title, Willie Kirchenmann, Verantwortlicher Direktor.

Willie could see his group of friends and executives walking along the corridor toward his office. The throng of well-wishers filed in through the open door. As the men entered, Willie stood, greeted them by name, and extended his hand. Some grasped both his hands and warmly held them for an extra precious moment. He pulled several of the older men toward him and hugged them, a gesture far removed from his normal formal behavior. He had been instrumental in hiring many of these men, training them, and bringing their careers along within the bank. He was a respected mentor and friend. The large office immediately filled, several well-wishers were standing at the door and in the hall. The head of the bank, Jasowarsky, cleared his throat and removed a plush box from the black briefcase with the bank's monogram emblazoned on the side. Willie knew what the contents would be. He had attended many of these farewells over the years. It was "the watch and the medal." This was the reward for forty years of loyal bank service. The watch was traditional gold, a valuable token, with Swiss movement and a black leather band with a gold clasp, a classic design. The engraving was: "Willie Kirchenmann, Verantwortlicher Direktor LandesBank Baden-Wurttemberg, 40 years service." On the medal, also gold, would be another inscription: "For forty years service," and the dreaded phrase "upon his retirement."

Willie listened to Jasowarsky's speech. To him the words were meaningless. This was happening to someone else. The sounds echoed in Willie's mind as if he were in a bubble and seeing through a mist. He smiled at the right places. The scene around him and the speeches seemed to be in slow motion and rang hollow in his ears. The managing director said, "We want to congratulate you on this, your retirement day."

Willie felt the pain of leaving and going to his empty home. He still felt young. He knew that this was the end of his business life, but it was hard to take. Where was he to go? What would he do with his days?

After forty-five years of marriage, his beloved Hanna had passed away three years ago. He was alone. Their four children were scattered all over the world. One of the boys, Thomas, was working in New York for the bank and lived with his wife and family in Connecticut, an American state that Willie had trouble pronouncing. Thomas had the first two of his grandchildren, a boy now eighteen years old and a very lovely blonde granddaughter who was sixteen and the darling of Willie's eye. He could deny her nothing that she requested, and during the weekly Sunday afternoon telephone call, she often did ask. His other children lived in Europe. His second child, a daughter, was living in Paris and had not married. She had gone into the fashion business and was designing, living joyously, and loving men and life too much to spend much time with her dear father. His other two children, a boy and girl, were living with their spouses in Germany and between them had five children. They were within a hundred miles of Stuttgart, but as Willie mused, they were living their own lives. Willie thought how strange that he, a child of the Hitler era was a parent of a boy with grandchildren who considered themselves American. The grandchildren, all of them, were fun to visit, but not a life's pursuit.

He would miss the everyday challenge of business, a task that had occupied him since the war. He reminisced about those first years after the war when, at only fourteen, without a father, he had faced the fear of hunger each day. He had become the man of the family and worried about Mama, watching as she'd sunk into mental depression over the struggle and her memories of the husband who never came home from the war. The burden had fallen upon Willie to pull her through and to keep them together. Then there had been the early years of supporting a wife and children as he'd worked, completing his education, and sustaining the family. Of course, later had come years of comfort, recognition, and security as his banking career had blossomed and he'd risen in the bank's hierarchy.

He recalled the day when General Zion, a Jew from Paterson, New Jersey, had found him clearing war rubble, taken him off the street, and asked him to come to his office to help process the huge number of business and reconstruction loan applications that had accumulated in the American Aid Agency as part of the Marshall Plan. Although Willie had been one of the youngest in the office, it had been apparent that he had an aptitude for cutting through the red tape and getting aid money into willing and needy hands. There had been piles and piles of applications for reconstruction loans and grants, and it had become his job to review each one, speak to the applicant, determine need, check out the use of the money, and recommend whether the loan or grant should be made. Willie had become the friend of many of these postwar entrepreneurs, met their families, helped them organize their businesses, and, despite his youth, become their adviser.

The bakery was long a thing of the past. Postwar shortages and the ravaged, half-destroyed building had forced its closing. Willie had helped Mama get a job, getting her secure and settled. He had been the man of the family and had fully accepted his responsibility. While working with the American administrators and the occupation staff under General Zion, he had completed his education at the general's insistence. After getting his degrees, he had been hired at the bank. It had been a natural progression for Willie. Many of the customers were the men he had helped in those earlier days when he was working with General Zion. Then, as time had gone on, the processing, sorting, due diligence, and decision making hadn't been on behalf of the occupation administration, but for the private banking sector. He had been happy and successful in the job.

He often thought about his first meeting with Hanna—homeless, without a family, a life destroyed by the war, her mother killed in an air raid, her father dead in Normandy during the 1944 American invasion. He had first seen her clearing rubble, working with threadbare gloves and wearing cast-off army boots. How beautiful and dignified she'd looked doing such manual labor. Though they had all been destitute, clearing rubble had been a good job that had paid enough to get some bread and keep one's pride. Many years later, she said it was the dust from the rubble that infected her lungs and gave her the cancer that killed her. After forty-five years of marriage, she was gone. Willie was alone.

When he arrived home from the bank, he put the awards on a shelf in the study. Then with a beer from the refrigerator, Willie sat looking at the orderly, book-lined room where he and Hanna used to have their evening meals. They would sit side by side in two lounge chairs reading and watching television those years after the children had grown and left. His eyes drifted around the room, remembering how each book was purchased and the reason it remained in their collection. His gaze stopped at the box in the corner top shelf. It was Mama's red leather box, containing the letters Papa wrote, along with the pictures he sent. For the first time since Mama had died, he took the box off the shelf, untied the ribbon, and started reading the letters. He had never gone through them. While Mama was alive, he'd felt they were too personal for him to invade her memories. After she died, he'd never had time. Now was his time.

The first letter was dated October 1938, just after his father had been conscripted. The start of the letter was simple:

My dearest wife, my dear Willie,

I miss you more than I can write. This has been a difficult time for me, as we have never been apart a single night since we married. I am trying to adjust to being away, but I awake during the night and reach out for you. My army cot is narrow, and of course you are not there. I miss your smooth skin next to me and how excited I become when I touch you in the middle of the night. I miss your scents, the taste of your skin, and the comfort you bring me when I am tense and worried. My first reaction to the barracks and being with all these strange men was to be depressed. Yesterday I sat next to my locker and cried. Oh how I miss you. I know this will pass, but all I can do is think of you being alone with Willie and the store. I hope Willie is all right. Please write and tell me how he reacted to my going away.

The letter went on describing the camp and telling of some of the other men in the group conscripted with Papa. Toward the end of the letter, Willie felt the flush of embarrassment as his father once again detailed how much and how he missed his mother. The words were very explicit about the great physical hunger their separation created.

He examined other letters, skipping through the orderly pile that was in the sequence in which they'd been received. In several envelopes, there were pictures. Willie took these out, looked them over, and replaced them in their envelopes. Several times he rubbed his hands to remove the dust. Once he sneezed as the fine mist of the past invaded his nose. He was diligent in maintaining the order and condition of the letters.

Other letters told a love story and memories of the painful separation of over six years. They chronicled one man's journey through the war. They were a diary telling how Papa had been conscripted, trained, and assigned to a unit, then telling his war history on the Eastern Front. The written words told that although he was a Christian Socialist and had little sympathy for the Nazi party or its actions, he was imbued with a German sense of duty, order, and country and had to serve and do as he was instructed. He felt he was a man called to do a job for his country. His country was at war, and he was a German. Papa used the term "a loyal German" to describe his mission:

> Being in the Army isn't the choice I want in life. I am here and must make the most of it. There are times I just sit and think, What will become of me? I have been issued a "soldbuch," a book that is my pay record and will hold all of my transfers and vital information. I must carry this with me at all times. The soldbuch has the names of our entire family and your addresses. It is a very complete history of who I am. It amazes me that my life is summed up in this little book. We are told that we will be here for only a short time, and probably be released into the Home Army. I hope this is true, although I am learning that army and bunkhouse rumors are seldom true. There are some men who believe all that we are told; I cannot be of this mind. We have had several indoctrination classes. Officers from the SS and the Party come to talk to us. We are told that if we want advancement, we should volunteer for the Party. I will not do this. I am a baker, not a fighter. There is a great difference between those men who are members of the Party for years and are now in the army and those

of us who consider ourselves civilians in uniform. I am frightened when some of these Party members talk of "our German destiny" and the power our leader brings to us. These men seem ready to fight. Some men have been in the Hitler Youth before joining the army. For them the military life has been a natural step. They are hard men. I am pleased we tried to avoid the Hitler Youth for Willie. The men who are enthusiastic for a war frighten me, they use words like "master race." I do not feel this way. I want to be home with you and Willie.

Other letters were opened and read one by one. Willie was absorbed by his reading for several hours, and it was late in the evening before he finished. The correspondence was an individual's chronicle of going to war, the adjustment to military life and training, the early battles, and the victories and defeats. The early letters told how the German army was expanding. There was a letter written as the army marched into Poland, and Papa's unit had gone along. The tone in the early letters was happiness to be a baker, working in his civilian trade. He took great satisfaction in his work and prayed every day to come home to his loving wife and little Willie. There was joy expressed for the early victories of 1939 to 1942.

At first the letters were uncensored. Halfway through the stack, Willie started to read those that were written after the first defeats. The tone changed from optimism and joy to despair and even grief. He sensed that many unsaid things were being expressed, talked around, but not spelled out. There was an underlying fear in the letters that was never spelled out. Some letters from the last two years of the war, from mid-1942 after the defeat at Stalingrad, were covered with black censor's marks as they traced the retreat from

Russia. There were changes of units, letters from "rest areas," and at least one from a field hospital. Were there letters that never arrived? Postmarks showed that as the war went on, the time between the letter being written and the time it arrived in Stuttgart increased. Near the end, it was taking four to six weeks for letters to get from Papa to Mama.

Willie imagined he heard his father's voice as the descriptions changed from those of a conscripted civilian to a hardened, combat-experienced soldier, a Landser. The many letters contained innocent, enjoyable comments that evolved to hardened texts alluding to the facts of war with desperate actions and bloody events. The letters described what Papa was doing and seeing. Long correspondence became short notes on soiled and often tattered paper. Willie was reading a chronicle from the day Papa entered the army to a location somewhere in Poland. The last letter was dated January 15, 1945, and described an area near the Vistula River. This was where it all must have ended. Willie had never thought of the specific location where his father was reported missing. He just knew he had disappeared and knew of his and Mama's loss.

The letters stirred his emotions. Willie was normally a staid man. As he was reading, he started to cry. Although in tears, he continued reading until he finished the last letter. He breathed deeply and tried to maintain composure. He felt the pain his mother must have experienced: her husband taken away, the long absence, the uncertainty and the final bereavement.

Willie held the letters and felt he was touching his father. He wanted to know more. To him Papa was a hero, a man who had served his country, a loyal German and a good man. Willie knew the Nazi cause was unjust. These postwar years had instilled in him and Mama a sense of justice and love of others. He knew how evil the Nazis were and recognized that horrible acts had been committed by that government. Willie believed that the German people were victims, first of Hitler, then of the war. His father was his idol. But weren't they all brave, good men, those who were conscripted to serve? The more Willie thought about the letters, the more he had a desire to determine what had happened to his father all those years ago.

The idea of following his father's travels started to form in Willie's mind. He had never been to Poland or Ukraine. What was there? Could he find some trace of his father? He had the time and now could satisfy his need to find out what happened. He had a mission: to follow the path the letters described, to go see the land and the towns Papa traveled. He wanted to see the battlefields, trace the travels, experience his father's footsteps, and find where it all ended. With a heavy heart, he folded the letters, placed them in chronological order, and arranged them in the box. He knew so little of his father because he had left to go to war when Willie had been so young. Now Willie wanted to know.

The box was placed on a table near Willie's desk in the den. The next morning he found an atlas and marked the travel route as best as he could. On notepaper he meticulously outlined the maps he would have to purchase, the guidebooks, the clothes he would take, and the other items he would need. He called his children and told each one that he wanted to take this trip and that he would be gone for two or three weeks.

A sense of adventure replaced the pain of separation from the bank.

Chapter Seven

Arrival in Warsaw: The First Lessons—George's Story

The flight from Newark to Warsaw was uneventful. After a light nap on takeoff, I ate lightly and slept most of the way across the Atlantic and Europe. My dreams had nothing to do with the Holocaust or my future plans. When I awakened, on the nearly flat, comfortable seat, my reminiscences were of pleasant past journeys. Then I started to contemplate what I would see when we landed. Warsaw had been devastated by the war. Had it been rebuilt? I started to think about how this postwar, post–Russian controlled country would appear. Would there still be ruins? What cultural difference would I see? Would I experience any latent or overt anti-Semitism? It would be an exciting adventure. About an hour from touchdown, breakfast was served and I calculated that I had had about seven hours of sleep.

The flight approached Warsaw from the northwest, dropping out of the sky beneath fluffy white clouds to reveal farmers' well-organized fields, beautifully planted for the spring season. Clusters of villages dotted the countryside. They consisted of twenty to thirty detached homes with red tile roofs, country lanes, and a town square. The midmorning sun reflected from the farms' hothouse roofs, and I could see the neat, well-trimmed, fertile landscape. The fields had a precise herringbone pattern, as the rows of brown and dark and light bluish green delineated the different crops—the wheat, potatoes, barley, rye, and, of course, beets and cabbage that were staples in the Polish diet. The roads between the villages were tree lined with tall thin poplars that cast their early morning shadows against the spring growth. The landing was smooth, and some of the passengers applauded as the plane touched down. At Frederic Chopin Airport in Warsaw, a modern, multi-terminal facility, the plane was assigned a central gate, an easy walk to the immigration kiosks.

Passing through immigration was trouble free; no visa was necessary, and my American passport was stamped by the officer behind the glass cage. He didn't even glance up as I stood before him. Without checked baggage, I walked straight through the baggage hall, passing customs agents standing at the Green Lane Door, and entered the main airport hall, where there was a *bureau de change.* There were only two customers in line, and when my turn came, I asked to change three hundred dollars, which came to nearly 1,000 zlotys at the exchange rate. Stopping at the Hertz rental car desk, a pleasant young lady confirmed that a car would be delivered to my hotel in the morning.

Stepping out of the Arrivals Hall to a taxi stand, I hailed a cab and I settled into the back seat while the driver put my luggage into the trunk of the slightly old but well-kept light green Mercedes with a plastic yellow Taxi sign on its roof. Soon we were on Zwirki I Wigury Avenue, a very wide tree-lined boulevard, heading directly into the central area of Warsaw. On the way, the driver asked where I was from. His English was surprisingly good. He said:

"I have a brother in Pittsburgh; he works in steel mill. I was in your country visiting last summer."

As we rode, he waved his arms pointing out sights he thought would be of interest. We passed a huge monument, to the left of the boulevard, backed by a large well-kept grass field, and he said: "This was a military cemetery for the Russian troops that died during the Second World War." I was impressed by the massive memorial. With some irony, he said in his accented English, "That is a gift the Russians left when they departed in 1991."

The ride was pleasant and I appreciated the little travelogue. His arms kept waving as he spoke, punctuating his sentences with jabs into the air or pointing in one direction and then the other. The traffic around us was heavy, and I was a little concerned about his keeping both hands on the wheel.

"All of this was destroyed in the battle for the city," he said, again waving his hands to illustrate both sides of the road, as we approached the center of the town and passed several very modern buildings. They were obviously office complexes. Pointing across a large grassed public area, he turned his head and yelled into the back seat: "That monstrosity was built by the Russians as their central administration building. Another leftover from their stay, it's the 'Palace of Culture.' It was built during the 1950s. Once it was called 'Stalin's Palace.' We call the building 'The Gift.' "

Indeed, I looked out the car window and saw a towering, massive ugly brick building about forty stories high crowned by a clock tower and what appeared to be a television spire. There were four smaller buildings in the same style, one at each corner of the mammoth structure. The style of the building reminded me of old New York structures built in the early part of the twentieth century. It seemed out of place among the more modern, sleekly designed postwar buildings such as the obviously new Supreme Court or the classically designed architecture that made up the rest of the city.

Greeted by the ornately uniformed doorman at the hotel Le Royal Meridien Bristol, I was ushered across the marble-floored lobby to a chest-high registration desk. Check-in at the hotel was quick. My Platinum American Express card had been used to guarantee the reservation, and as a member of the hotel chain's "Loyalty Club," I was pleased to be upgraded to a junior suite. The desk clerk asked how long the stay would be, and I answered, "Probably two nights, but returning in about a week."

A bellman who appeared to be in his late sixties grabbed my roll-along bag from my hand and escorted me to the room. I seemed to be in better shape than he was. At only about five feet tall, he was so thin that he looked as if he needed a good meal; I felt that I should be managing the one piece of rolling luggage, not him. His formal uniform was both colorful and amusing, more like a Prussian general's than a bellman lifting suitcases. In almost unaccented English, he was very polite. Opening the door to the room, he checked the temperature and gave a quick instruction on how to regulate the thermostat. He walked me into the sitting room and gave me a tour of the large marble-floored bathroom, which was dominated by a massive white porcelain bathtub and a bidet. With pride he pointed to the ample supply of towels. He turned, leaving me standing in the bathroom, and left the suite saying, "I'll be right back." Within a minute he reappeared with a full ice bucket from the bar downstairs. "All Americans want extra ice." I started to tip him and he asked if I knew the history of the hotel.

"I hadn't thought of it. What's the story?"

"This hotel was the seat of the first parliament of a free Poland in 1920. Paderewski, the famous pianist, was our first prime minister and was the owner of the hotel. So, they held the new country's first parliament meeting on the first floor of this building. In the lobby, you'll see a large bust of Paderewski."

I thanked him for the information. He didn't turn to leave; instead he asked, "Are you in Warsaw on business?"

Being candid I told him: "I'm tracing some family roots."

"You must be Jewish."

"How do you know?"

"We get two or three families a week looking for the places their relatives lived either here in Warsaw or out in the countryside. Also there are many 'Jewish tours' that come here to see the Uprising monuments and cemeteries and are shown the camps. Some come just to see the cemeteries, others to see the camps, and then they leave. We get about one of these groups a month."

"How do you feel about that?"

"It's all behind us. We all suffered and have stories. It was a long time ago, so much has happened since then. It's a new world."

He shrugged his shoulders as he spoke. "There's nothing I can do about the past." I tipped and thanked him, and he left.

Looking around, I found there was a very comfortable sitting room with a separate bedroom and huge king-size bed. It was a very well appointed suite, and the rich fabrics covered comfortable, if slightly overstuffed, furniture. The sitting area had a flat screen television and a small couch. It also had a balcony facing King's Walk, one of Warsaw's most fashionable streets, which overlooked the presidential palace next door. The floor-to-ceiling windows served as the balcony portals. On either side were heavy earth-toned damask drapes held back by matching gold braid cords. Parting the drapes, I stepped onto the balcony. Breathing deeply to absorb the fresh air, I looked at the street below bustling with shoppers scurrying by. From my vantage point, I saw the changing of the two-man palace guard. Six uniformed men goose-stepped through the changing routine with an officer counting cadence and issuing crisp commands.

Seeing the city seemed to give me a second wind, and I abandoned the idea of taking a nap. I unpacked a few items and showered to freshen up and lose the jet fuel odor that seemed to cling to my skin. Then, I had one task before leaving.

In my old business address book I looked up the phone number of a former associate, Morris Diskowski. Morris was now about forty-five years old, a first-generation Polish American brought up in Chicago. His parents were academics who had immigrated to the United States after the war and become American citizens. Morris was an only son, and with adoring parents, had lived a privileged youth. He was bright. His parents were professional teachers, and he had been born when they'd both been well over forty. They'd doted on their child and devoted their attention to his education. Morris had a distinguished academic record, starting at the University of Chicago and then earning a master's degree in business from Yale. After working with my firm, he had come to Poland in 1991 as part of the United States economic assistance program when the Solidarity political party had taken control of the country and had broken from the Soviet bloc. By 1995 he'd had enough experience to leave the US government agency and start to do independent investment banking as Poland emerged into the capitalistic world. He had done very well during the last several years. After three rings, Morris answered the telephone.

"Hello Morris."

"George, is that you? Where are you? Are you in Warsaw? What are you doing here?"

"Yes, I just arrived and wanted to speak and perhaps meet with you."

"That would be great, how long will you be here?"

"Don't know. It all depends on how quickly I can get some things done." I invited Morris for dinner at the hotel, and he agreed and would bring his wife, a much younger Polish woman he had married three years previously. After the call, I experienced the satisfaction of having made my first contact on this trip. I now wanted to get out of the room and see some of Warsaw. Stopping at the concierge, I asked for directions and a map of the area.

"What do you want to see?"

"Having just arrived, I would like to take a walk to get some air and see a few sights. I want to see the remains of the Warsaw Ghetto."

"That's a lot to see for a short walk. The old city and the area of the Ghetto are to the left when you leave the hotel. It's about a ten-minute walk."

I thanked him and walked out into the fresh air, heading in the direction of the old town. Indeed, Warsaw in the late spring afternoon was a delight. The fresh air worked its magic, and jet lag seemed to fall away as my mind cleared. It was a modern city, mostly rebuilt since the war. I strolled observing the name brands in the windows of the fashionable stores that lined the boulevard. The scene changed from fashionable to historical as I walked into the old town area and passed some unique Polish themed restaurants.

The old Royal Castle was on the right, and I detoured to just have a quick look. It had been destroyed during the war by the Nazis—just as about 90 percent of the city had been destroyed as well. The castle had been reconstructed between 1971 and 1984. Looking at the building and the open square around, I could not believe that it had been damaged and that this was a reconstruction. As I strolled, I started to see and realize that there were numerous memorials and monuments everywhere. The people of Warsaw had been dedicated to creating memorials for those martyrs of the Second World War and the German occupation. The reminders ranged from little plaques to large dramatic pieces. These commemoratives were side by side with statues and memorials that marked events and persons prominent in their historical past.

Growing impatient with myself at "sightseeing," I had a feeling that I had to see something more substantial than old buildings and the rebuilt castle. Hailing a taxi, I asked to see Mila 18. The taxi driver didn't know what I was talking about and took me to a nondescript postwar housing block. Shaking my head, I said: "This isn't what I want." His English was near nonexistent. Taking a pen from my pocket, I wrote the word "Jews" on the map. He nodded, drove about a quarter of a mile farther, and left me in a parklike setting with a huge monument in the center of the area.

I approached the impressive stone and marble memorial honoring the Heroes of the Warsaw Ghetto, commemorating the uprising that lasted from April 17 to May 16, 1943. The parklike setting was about the size of two city blocks and was crisscrossed by paths that seemed to be favorites of mothers strolling with their young children. There were several oak trees scattered between the paths and just enough shade to allow for the blankets of a few couples lazing about in the afternoon. I was amused that between the curb where I'd left the taxi and my approach to the impressive monument was a pushcart stand that had a placard saying that souvenirs were for sale, and the guide books were in English, French, and German. A large placard read "Ghetto," and sample pictures were for sale.

The man selling souvenirs was about thirty-five years old, with a salt-and-pepper crew cut and cropped beard, wearing a gray cut-off T-shirt. He could have been selling bric-a-brac at a flea market almost anywhere. Litter, old beer bottles, and dog feces were on the ground. I purchased a guidebook in English and approached an impressive stone wall with a huge bas-relief fascia and read that this was the "Heroes of the Ghetto" monument. The Jewish uprising had occurred here as the Germans began the process of evacuating the Ghetto, shipping the occupants to Treblinka for elimination. Standing before the monument and reading from the guide book, it was ironic that the stone used for the memorial had been ordered by Hitler in 1942 from Sweden, to be used as part of a Third Reich victory monument. The bas-relief by the Israeli sculptor Natan Rapoport showed the figures of men standing boldly facing the world. The sculpture was an awesome display portraying defiance.

There were many Polish inscriptions around the monument, and a few in Hebrew. I could find none in English. I looked around and found a young lady. "Do you speak English?" I asked. "Can you translate the inscriptions for me?"

"Gladly," she replied. "The first one says, 'The Jewish Nation—to its fighters and martyrs.' " The young lady was a perky brunette about five feet two inches tall, with an engaging smile that showed brilliant white teeth. She was well dressed, wearing a pleated skirt, a pale green blouse, and saddle shoes with white socks. She didn't carry a purse but had a backpack that I surmised had books and her personal items.

I asked her name. With a smile she answered, “Anna.” She walked around the monument with me, translating each plaque. Taking my arm, she ushered me to a large circular embedded disc on the ground in the park to one side of the monument. There was an engraved palm leaf and a raised plaque with the Hebrew letter *beth.* The young lady directed me to the part of the guidebook that explained that this was commemorating the very few survivors among the heroes of the ghetto who escaped. She explained, “The letter *beth* is symbolic because it is the first letter in the Torah. The word *Bereshit,* ‘in the beginning,’ symbolizes hope and survival and the opportunity to start life anew.”

On the side of this huge imbedded disc was a raised sandstone set of four steps. I sat on the side of the monument visualizing what had taken place sixty years ago in this area. I was awed that in this relatively small area hundreds of thousands of Jews had been confined and then herded to the trains and their deaths. Sitting there, part of the sophisticated veneer that shielded my denial that I was related to all of this was stripped away by thoughts of what had happened in this area sixty years before. This was my first realization that this trip was more than I had planned or bargained for.

I felt ignorant of this entire chapter of Jewish history. This was going to be more than a visit to Ozarow and some gravesites. This was going to be more than learning how the Jews of Ozarow died.

As I read from the guidebook, the young lady came and sat next to me.

“Where is Mila 18?” I asked. “Is it nearby?”

She smiled politely: "This memorial is for the people who fought in the uprising. The Mila 18 site, the location of one of the Jewish fighter's main bunkers, is just about two blocks away."

"Anna, tell me about yourself."

"My father's entire family was rounded up and killed at Treblinka. They were marched away along this street to the railroad. My dad was a 'survivor.' He slipped away from the deportation train and spent the war in the forests. Later he came back to teach mathematics at the university. He tells me that the entire Jewish population was liquidated by the Germans. There were over 300,000 Jews deported to Treblinka from this neighborhood. Between here, where we are sitting, and the railhead is about ten blocks. This was the path of the deportations. Let's walk that way."

She accompanied me to the Mila 18 Bunker memorial, about two blocks away. Anna pointed and went on: "This is a mound, a high grave mound. The height of the mound is the height of the level of rubble from the destroyed Jewish district. I think you know the story. Your American Jewish author, Leon Uris, wrote it very well. This site was the HQ of the ZOB, the Jewish Fighting Organization. Mordechaj Anielewicz was the Jewish commander. They were very brave. With only nine rifles, fifty-nine pistols, and a few hand grenades they fought against massive German forces from April nineteenth until the end of May. At the end, Anielewicz committed suicide along with his staff rather than let the Germans take them alive. The Nazi command issued orders that not only were the fighters to be killed, but the site was to be destroyed and leveled without a trace. We know the story because the Gwardia Ludowa, the GL, a Communist fighting organization, led just a few of the fighters out of the bunker through the sewers. There also is a monument to the GL."

"What about the destruction of the Ghetto?" I asked.

"The Germans used flame throwers and burned out home after home, bunker after bunker, block by block. The pistols and Molotov cocktails the Jews used to fight with were no match for the machine guns, flame throwers, and artillery pieces the Germans used to blast through the Ghetto house by house."

"How did it end?"

"On May sixteenth, the German Army blew up the Tlomackie Synagogue, thinking that this would end the uprising. It was a dramatic signal, and the German general declared that the fight was over. It wasn't! As late as May thirty-first, Jewish fighters tried to break out of the Ghetto and failed. There actually was sporadic fighting into the autumn.

"Down the street about a half mile from here, from a ramp known as the Umschlagplatz, on Stawki Street, they loaded the remaining Jews. They were herded out of the Ghetto just like cattle onto the railroad cars and shipped to Treblinka for extermination. The trains were loaded with anywhere from eighty to one hundred twenty Jews in each railroad car. There were fifteen to twenty cars in each train. About two thousand people in each shipment. Each family was allowed one little suitcase of personal belongings. The people and their luggage were packed in so tight that they were standing, compressed into the cars. There was no water or food and no sanitary facilities, and many died in transit. The Jews were told they were being relocated to work camps, but they were heading to their death."

We walked together for a short while as she showed me more plaques with the etched names of the heroes and engravings depicting the events in 1943. "This is called the Path of Remembrance."

My throat went dry, and I felt my heart pounding as she recited the numbers of the deported Jews. She told of stragglers and purely innocent people shot on the spot on the way to the death trains. I was overwhelmed by her recital of the statistics.

I stopped her, holding her sleeve while I took a breath and looked around. The peaceful scene about us was a pleasant cityscape with mothers pushing strollers and happy children playing. It was hard to fathom this modern pleasant world full of sunshine and happiness contrasted to the horrors of Jews being treated as cattle herded toward their destruction.

She went on, continuing as my tour guide. "There were actually two Warsaw uprisings. The first was the Jewish uprising. The Polish underground helped the Jews during their fight, and some of the few Jewish fighters who escaped the final destruction of the Ghetto joined the Polish underground. They fought again in August and September 1944, in the second uprising, which was by the Polish resistance. In that battle the Polish underground took a large part of the city under their control as the Russians approached and were only about thirty kilometers away. In that battle, the Poles started to fight the Germans just as the Russians approached the city as liberators. The Russians backed off and allowed the German army to crush the Polish civilian and paramilitary effort. The calls for help from the Poles went unanswered. As the Russians stood by, the Poles were crushed. The resistance was betrayed by the Russians and destroyed by the Germans."

Anna took me to the second monument, the memorial to the heroes of the second battle. The monument cited that over 200,000 Poles died in that battle. Its bas-relief depiction of noble people fighting in a desperate cause with bare hands, stolen guns, homemade Molotov cocktails, and captured grenades struck a chord of futility. Sadly, I had the feeling that this memorial was kept in much better condition than the Ghetto memorial. The area of the Jewish monument was unkempt and seedy. The Warsaw Uprising monument was spotlessly clean and well groomed. Being in the presence of the memorial I felt exhausted. I had had enough touring!

I said goodbye to Anna and thanked her for her time. The jet lag and the impact of seeing the memorial monuments and hearing the story of the clearing of the Ghetto filled me with a tremendous sorrow and weariness.

I remembered that Morris and his wife were coming for dinner. I took a taxi back to the hotel to have time to nap until dinnertime. While in the taxi, I realized that I had come to find what happened to my grandparents' family, but I was going to be exposed to the far greater tragedy of the Holocaust. My grandmother's grief was just a small slice of this near total destruction of my people. For the first time in my life I started to think of these Jewish victims as "my people." I remembered a quote from something I'd read by Simon Wiesenthal: "The death of one person is a tragedy. The death of millions was a statistic." The "statistics" were becoming personal to me.

I tried to imagining what six million Jews would look like if they were assembled in one place. I thought of an afternoon at Yankee Stadium, where a sold-out game was just over 50,000. Then I thought of the six million Catholics, Gypsies, and political prisoners. What a huge mass of humanity. With each death, there were individual stories. Whole families—mothers, fathers, and children, along with uncles, aunts, etc.—all people with names, lives, and futures, were in those groups herded into the trains. All were huddled together and driven to their deaths in the gas chambers or beaten and shot while in transit. What did six million look like? How could I grasp the enormity of this Holocaust?

Arriving at the hotel, I went to my suite and fell onto the bed for a well-needed nap.

Chapter Eight

The Long Road, Spring 2005: Stuttgart to Poland—Willie's Story

It was just before dawn as Willie left his home in the fashionable suburb of Weisstannenwald, just northeast of central Stuttgart, traveling through the nearby town of Muchingen and east toward Heilbronn. The scene was awe inspiring as the sun broke over the horizon and appeared to be sandwiched between the earth and the puffy morning clouds. His tinted aviator sunglasses and the Audi's lowered visor shielded his eyes. With stylized glasses and a khaki windbreaker, he felt quite dashing in the morning chill, quite different from the buttoned-down banker of a few short days ago. He took deep breaths, enjoying the clear fresh air of the late spring morning of his first travel day. These were familiar local roads as he worked his way to the Autobahn A6 so he could head northeast toward his first goal, the Polish border.

The sedan was packed sparingly. He was driving alone, didn't expect to attend "state dinners," and only needed casual clothes and toiletries. Willie couldn't relax his personal dress code, even though he was retired. Pressed khaki slacks color-matched his light tan shirt and cashmere sweater. He wouldn't wear jeans, as he was critical of the current generation wearing jeans all the time, even with a sport coat. Willie was still of the generation that believed that the cut of a man's clothing made the man, and "good appearance" created the first impression. The shoes he wore were brown lace-ups, and even in casual attire his socks were calf length. In the trunk of the car were two relatively small suitcases arranged so he could take one out on any overnight stop and be quickly and comfortably unpacked and repacked again in the morning. He was on his way.

Willie kept the letters from Papa in their chronological order on the seat next to him, along with his camera, the maps, guides, and some army history fact sheets he had purchased or downloaded and printed from his computer. He also had a printout of several unit histories of army detachments and divisions that had been identified in his father's letters. These histories described the German army's deployment during the war. The hardest ones to get were good maps of Russia and Ukraine. Many place names had been changed after the war. Some towns and villages that Papa had mentioned were renamed, and the new names were unrelated to the past. Spellings had been significantly altered. The Cold War had been over for more than fifteen years, and maps depicted the current roads. These highways and side roads did not coincide with the roads of sixty years ago. Local guidance would be needed if he was to trace the routes where Papa had traveled. Language in Poland, Ukraine, and Russia would be a problem. He had little knowledge of Slavic languages. His skills were in German, of course, and English. Most businessmen in Europe spoke more than one language, but Willie wasn't going to be speaking to businessmen; he was traveling well away from large cities and would have to understand the local people. He hoped there would be someone to interpret at each stop along the way.

At one of the first rest stops, Willie opened one of the early letters his father had written from training camp:

> I don't know what they want a poor baker to do. I'm in the first course that they call "Prussian Basic Training" and "Infantry Training." Often we are in a meadow and they teach us how to "hit the dirt." I think I have been able to recognize each blade of grass in that field. I've also learned to crawl on my hands and knees for several hundred yards with a Mauser 98k rifle cradled in my arms so it doesn't get dirt in it. Also I can take the rifle apart and put it together with my eyes closed. I have learned to march and salute and know how to keep my uniform pressed and ready for inspection. When I get up in the morning, I have been trained to have everything in its right place. I now have also learned to drive a truck. What good this would do for a baker I don't know, but apparently the Führer thinks this is all for the best. Since I now know how to drive, we will have to purchase a car when I come home.

The letter was actually quite cheerful, and Willie thought about his father crawling in a field and learning to drive. Before he'd left for the army, Papa had been only a passenger. They hadn't owned a car, and there'd been no need to learn. These thoughts passed through Willie's mind as the Audi seemed to eat kilometers speeding east. Willie set a goal of traveling about 800 kilometers on this first day. He was aiming for the entry point into Poland mentioned in one of the letters Papa had written when the war had started on September 1, 1939. He wanted to find a town named Tarnowo Podgorne.

My first training is complete and I will now be going to "cooking school." I don't know what they expect to teach me, but they know best. After the last six weeks of training, they consider me a soldier. I will have to disappoint them, I'm still a baker. There are many here who are loving army life. I don't. The emphasis on discipline, making beds, and absolute obedience does not make me happy. The punishment I've seen when a soldier doesn't comply is harsh, so I have learned to go along. The conversion from civilian life is easier for those younger men who have been through Hitler Youth. They are well disciplined and don't get into trouble. I miss being home. They will give me a leave after I finish the school. I look forward to being with you and Willie once again.

Papa had finished the school and been assigned to a company of cooks, bakers, and quartermasters. He'd spent two weeks at home and left to rejoin his new unit. A month later, the Wehrmacht in all its might marched into Poland.

Willie was heading toward the first wartime bivouac area that Papa mentioned for that Army support group. After driving seven hours, at the fast speeds allowed on the Autobahn, he crossed the German/Polish border at a quiet and peaceful checkpoint. He hardly had to slow down. Willie imagined what the border crossing might have been like sixty-five years ago at the start of the war.

At a rest stop, he opened the leather box and read a letter that had been written on September 3, 1939, three days after Hitler had ordered the army into Poland:

. . . Well, we are at war! Some of the men are thrilled and keep saying 'what a glorious mission we are on.' We are riding in a long supply column into Poland. There are about one hundred trucks and behind us many horses and wagons. Our trucks are painted battle gray and we are trained to stop and set up our kitchens in less than an hour after arrival in a bivouac area. In front of us and to either side, several miles away, our Army is moving quickly and efficiently across the countryside. The Army has protected its supply column with outriders on either side. We feel safe when we see these units as we ride along. When we come to a town, the local people seem to be in shock and stand by the roadway as we pass by. They don't wave, and many stand in tears. Many of the buildings are draped with white sheets indicating surrender. Here and there we see Polish flags lying in the street, torn from buildings or flagpoles. Our men seem very efficient and well trained. I saw my first dead soldier. It was a Pole and I was shocked. Apparently he was part of a rear guard action and our troopers just blasted their way through. I wonder who will bury that poor soul. The population seems to distance themselves from the flags and move aside as our column moves through. The silence of the people was awesome.

For the next two hours, Willie slowed the car to absorb the landscape and reconstruct the scenes described in the letters. His father wrote of the almost effortless German army advance, and from Papa's viewpoint there had been almost no resistance as the supply groups followed the invasion. These were the "blitzkrieg" days; the "lightning war" that placed armored troops at the front racing forward with direct Stuka air support. The bakery and supply companies followed behind.

Now, years later, Willie saw the fields planted with late spring crops, row upon row of the Polish diet laid out neatly in the fields. There were wheat, rye, and oats in the larger fields and cabbage, potato, and corn in the narrow fields of the smaller holdings. The road gently curved, following the contour of the land, and the furrows formed a multi-hued green herringbone on either side of the highway. In his imagination, Willie placed himself in the supply truck with Papa. He visualized the side of the roads lined with silent Polish citizens, defeated but proud; worried, not knowing what was to come. He imagined the white bedsheets draped from the buildings signaling the surrender of the local towns and garrisons, the older women with tears flowing down their cheeks, and middle-aged men hanging their heads in the somber posture of defeat. From a letter dated two days later:

This afternoon as we were moving the supply column, I saw how destructive war can be. Destroyed buildings were all about as we passed through a town where some of the Polish Army resisted our soldiers. There were many burned out buildings with just the chimneys standing as monuments to what was once a home. Our bombing and fighters had done a job clearing out the Polish fighters. We are amazed by the efficiency of our army. I saw more war casualties. It wasn't pleasant. I think most of the dead were Poles. There were also some civilians who got in the way. My commander said this was unfortunate and we had to ignore what we had seen. It is difficult.

Willie spent that first night in a bed-and-breakfast between Tarnowo Podgorne and Poznan. The innkeeper and his wife were pleasant and tried to make him feel welcome in excellent German. They offered a light dinner, which Willie declined, but when they offered a coffee and tray of Polish pastry with poppyseed rolls and sweet apricot kolaczki triangle cookies, Willie could not resist. As he sat with his hosts, they politely talked about the weather and spoke of their dedication to the bed-and-breakfast life. The hosts said they loved to meet guests.

Their names were Stanislaw and Apolina. After some pleasantries, Willie asked how they came to own this bed-and-breakfast. Apolina was the least shy of the two and led the conversation with her explanation: "We came from East Germany, where we worked for over twenty years to save money to own this bed-and-breakfast. We purchased it after the Wall came down in 1989."

Stanislaw, emboldened by his wife's explanation, said: "Owning our own place has given us the hope of a good life. We feel independent and worthy. It's very satisfying."

Willie asked, "How did you choose this place?"

"This town was the ancestral home of Apolina's family," Stanislaw replied. "Her father and mother tried to move west in the final days of the war to escape Russian occupation, only to be trapped in what became East Germany. The Russians weren't very kind to volksdeutsch [persons of German background who had settled in the East]. Her mother and father struggled and survived those difficult days after the war."

Willie was interested in their story. It was similar to so many survival stories he had heard from bank customers. He listened politely but wasn't forthcoming about his background or the reason for his trip. Indeed, he was weary from the drive. After about an hour carrying on a light conversation, Willie excused himself and went to his room. The yellow walls bedecked with the flower-design wallpaper weren't to his taste, but the very comfortable feather bed was welcome. As he undressed, he placed his clothes in a neat pile organized for the morning, then took the shaving kit and toothbrush out of the single suitcase he'd brought to the room. It was a minimal effort to get to bed. He was weary from his first day on the road.

After a good night's sleep, Willie was up early. He spread the two or three letters Papa had written about this area and the army's movements on the bed and read them again. He refreshed his memory:

> . . . The fields are full of grain and crops. We have moved so fast that the Polish government hasn't had time to destroy the crops or burn the countryside as they retreated. Why should they? They will need the food to feed their people. It's September, and the harvest is nearly ready. The people seem afraid. They don't talk to us, but also they do not want to fight us. Our group of kitchens and the bakery are miles behind the fighting. At night we stop and prepare the meals for the troops for the next day. Our last stop was at a town named Tarnowo Podgorne. Have Willie look it up on the map and show it to you. I think we will be staying here for a few days. . . .
>
> I have been promoted. I am no longer the lowest of the low *schutz* (a private). I am now an *oberschutz* (private first class). This means I am going to receive more money and you will receive a larger allowance. My duties are the same, I still work in the

bakery, but I'm on the way to becoming a master baker, with men reporting to me.

Apolina and Stanislaw served breakfast in the country-style kitchen on their massive butcher-block wooden table. It was clean but stained by many years of hospitality, family meals, food preparation, and being a meeting place to sit and talk, just as they had last night. Breakfast was simple: pickled herring, black bread, and strong coffee. Willie ate well, and as he was leaving, Apolina gave him several of the sweet babka coffee cakes and two of the gooey doughnuts like paczki pastries to take with him. "This is just in case you become hungry during the ride." Shaking Stanislaw's hand, Willie thanked his hosts and was on his way.

Papa had described that his unit was north of the stiff fighting which occurred near Lodz, where the Polish army had stood and defended the Warsaw approaches. The landscape Papa described had dramatically changed. Then it was war torn. Now it was a peaceful countryside with small towns. The straw-thatched huts of 1939 weren't there anymore. The Russian sweep through the area later in the war had destroyed most of them. In their place were postwar Communist-designed buildings—uninspiring, identical white cement four-story apartment blocks that didn't vary from town to town. It was as if the design came from a central planner who had no imagination. The fields with their crops and the rolling countryside were still there. Papa the baker, who loved food and its preparation, was evident in his description of the scene:

We traveled past many farms where the crops were ready for harvest. We saw wheat that had been cut by hand and stacked in

> stooks ready to be gathered and brought to the miller. There were fields of black kasza ready to be harvested for gruel, and fields of hops for beer, and many fields of cabbages, cucumbers, and rhubarb. I can't wait to have some of the fresh vegetables brought to cook for the men. It will make the Army rations palatable.

Willie observed that the wheat fields and the smell of the farms were just as Papa described. He was driving in the late spring; Papa had traveled in the early autumn. On the other hand, this rolling countryside had been suitable for German tanks and so deadly for the Polish mounted cavalry. Willie just had to look, open his mind and imagine the past:

> The roads are clogged with troops moving forward. Refugees leaving the towns obstruct the highways. There are often battles between the advancing army and the hordes of people running from the war. The Wehrmacht just pushes these poor people aside as they move on. The front-line troops are motorized, and there are many tanks leading the advance. We are traveling with teams of horses pulling our supply wagons and kitchens. Sometimes we have a hard time keeping up with the front-line troops. Our horses aren't that fast, and the civilian refugee traffic gets in the way.

In Papa's units, just as in much of the army rear, they'd had horse-drawn wagons, and the support troops had followed behind the rapidly moving mechanized forces. Willie contrasted the German army rolling forward across Poland with his nearly effortless ride on today's modern east-west roads. Papa's letters told nothing of conquest, only of movement, encampment and missing home.

> Life in the Army is one of making camp and then breaking camp. We arrive at a destination and are told to set up the kitchens and prepare for feeding troops. Some of the men work with me in the kitchen and others tend the horses. Our supplies are brought to us by the quartermasters, who always seem to know where we will be and how much we will need for the troops and the horses. We seem to stay a night or two and then fold the tents, pack our kitchens, and move on. We then repeat all this again.
>
> I miss being with you and Willy. There is no time to think about what is happening around us. It is far different than being with you, loving our home, and sleeping with you. I miss your reaching out to me in the middle of the night and feeling your breath tickling my skin as you breathe deeply as you sleep. I miss your tenderness. I miss you telling me that it will all be all right. When will we have these pleasures again?
>
> I love you.
>
> I hunger for you.
>
> Hans

The highway toward Warsaw was just south of the Vistula River, where the waterway runs east to west before turning toward the north and eventually emptying into its delta and then the Baltic Sea. As Willie drove, he thought of the area's history he'd learned as a schoolboy many years ago. This river had been a major trade route for hundreds of years, acting as a water highway for the transport of goods from as far away as central Russia. The lessons of the old classroom echoed in his head: the Baltic Sea–Vistula-Dnieper–Black Sea water route. This was a trade route that carried amber from the north and silk from the south. It had been as vital to trade two hundred years ago as the highway he was traveling on was to commerce today.

In the previous centuries many armies had come through: the Swedes, the Czars, and the Polish princes had all conquered and in turn given up control of these fertile lands. Willie thought of the First World War battle of the Vistula River, or as some called it, the Battle of Warsaw. This was the battle where von Hindenburg, commanding the German army, pushed to the gates of Warsaw, only to be defeated by the Russians. This countryside had been a battleground long before Papa and the Wehrmacht had approached in 1939.

In five hours of meandering past Poznan, Konin, and Bemovow, Willie arrived at the outskirts of Warsaw, searching for a village named Prosta. According to Papa's letters, his unit had spent the better part of a year garrisoned near this town. It was near the Vistula River as it turned and entered Warsaw. Willie found a small, almost Tudor-style white stone guesthouse. He asked if they had a room for the night and accepted the innkeeper's terms and price for a delightful light-filled room with a high ceiling and another huge feather bed. There was an adequate bathroom "en suite." Willie then took his toilet kit and the few things he needed for the morning and items he wanted to review and read:

> The campaign here in Poland is over, and my group has been garrisoned in this wonderful little town of Prosta. It is very quaint and in some ways reminds me of towns in the Stuttgart countryside. All of the talk is about those assigned to leave for

the Western Front. Many of the men want action. I'm very happy to stay where we are. I hope to get some home leave to be with you and Willie. Also there will be some sightseeing and buying of some local items. What would you want? I will write you just before I get the leave. I must end this letter as I must go to a "political indoctrination." This is a new thing. Once a week we are visited by an officer from the Party and told the objectives of our being in the army and how the world respects us for our protecting Europe from the incursions of the Jews and other Eastern types like the Gypsies. We are told that we are supermen and the Reich is our vehicle to greatness. We are not allowed to doze off during these lectures.

After these indoctrinations I think I should end my letter with a salute to Hitler and the fatherland.

Love, Hans

In two days, Willie had driven just over 1,200 kilometers. Now he wanted to slow the travel pace and absorb more sights, sounds, and tastes of the countryside. He needed to understand the experiences of the army life of his father, the man he never really knew. He wanted to walk in his father's footsteps. He hoped to capture some of his father's missing essence.

There was no moral judgment in Willie's thoughts. He wasn't condemnatory as he read Papa's letters of garrison life and troop support and compared these thoughts to the combat stories he had heard from his war veteran friends. Willie sat on the bed before sleeping and reread these early letters. He realized that Papa had kept them vague for the most part, clear of description of any action, and always reassuring Mama not to worry.

The German army had essentially completed its conquest of Poland by the end of September 1939. In an act of betrayal of the Polish government, the Russians had joined the war and attacked Poland from the east on September 17, and the Germans had captured Warsaw eleven days later. It had been a quick campaign for the Wehrmacht, with the last of the Polish army laying down their arms on October 5. Some of the troops of the victorious German army had then been shifted to the West, where the Germans faced the combined British and French armies. This had been a "quiet period," from late 1939 until the spring of 1940, when the campaign in the West had begun with rapid attacks through Belgium, the collapse of the British army, and the capture of Paris.

For the Polish invasion, Papa had been assigned to support units of Bock's Army of the Center and Guderian's Second Group of divisions. This group had been the phalanx of the German advance, and with the Polish campaign completed, they'd spent the autumn of 1939 in the Warsaw area resting, being reequipped, and serving garrison duty as an occupation force. For Papa it had been a time of peace, with an occasional quick leave to see his family. The letters home were filled with descriptions of the countryside and often contained pictures of Papa and his buddies—two, three, and four men, with a monument in the background or a landmark like a town signpost forming an anchor in the picture:

> I have come to enjoy the work of the Army. We have a set routine, getting up very early at four a.m., starting the ovens for the breads, and preparing the dining area. In addition to the baking, I supervise the morning meal, feeding about 2,500 men. They start marching in for breakfast at 7 a.m. and we feed them

in waves for about an hour and a half. Afterwards we clean up, with the help of some Polish prisoners and laborers the SS has brought to work for us. We are told that the civilian "helpers" were volunteers from the local population. Some of us spoke to these workers and they said they were arrested by the SS and brought to our camp to work. After breakfast we turn the responsibility of the meals and kitchens over to the shift of cooks responsible for the midday and late-day meals. Since I had supervised the baking early in the morning, I have the rest of the day to visit the towns and see some of the sights. I miss being home with you and Willie, but Army life isn't that bad right now. I am happy not to be in the West. I don't want to be in the fighting. All is quiet here, I hope to be on leave and be with you soon.

Chapter Nine

Warsaw First Evening: The Enlightening Dinner—George's Story

Dinner in the hotel was a convenience to avoid my going out this first evening in Warsaw. My reservation was to be at the Malinowa Restaurant, which the concierge said was "an award-winning dining experience, not to be missed." At seven I was in the lobby and easily spotted Morris as he walked through the revolving door. Over six feet two inches tall and absolutely bald, he wore no hat; the lobby lights reflected off his head. A lightweight well-tailored camel-hair coat was casually thrown over his shoulder; the quality of the coat advertised his prosperity. Just behind him was a stunning woman who I presumed to be his wife, also fashionably dressed. His dark blue custom-tailored suit showed well on his tall, trim body, and she was wearing what appeared to be a designer dress that clung to her attractive slim torso, showing her curves with a modest amount of décolletage. Her perfume was a pleasant rose fragrance that didn't precede her but was noticeable as I came close, and her jewelry was expensive but modest enough to be in good taste for the evening.

I greeted them near the center of the vast two-colored marble lobby floor. I hugged Morris and took his wife's extended hand in a warm handshake.

"Elsa, this is George from the States. George, this is Elsa, my wife."

"I was told this bar was the best place to start an evening."

"Whoever said that was right. We've been here before. The atmosphere is perfect for conversation."

With a nod as a reply, we stepped off to the side into the "Column Bar." They gave their coats to the shapely young lady in a black uniform and white apron and we were escorted to a cozy corner table with brown kid leather banquet seats and one green leather chair in the corner. Each seat had a brown square pillow as a back support. Elsa and Morris sat on the banquet seats and I sat facing them. A round mahogany table was centered knee high between us.

"Isn't this a delightful room," Elsa said. "The Grecian Key columns appear to soar into the sky because of the lighting."

I turned my head and observed that the ceiling was about thirty feet above us, and each column was ringed by sets of light fixtures that filled the room with a soft glowing ambience contrasting the light against the dark wood surfaces. The bar was quiet, and we could easily converse without raising our voices.

Elsa was as tall as Morris and had blond hair, which advertisements proclaim as the "typical" Polish woman. Very attractive, she had the confident air of a woman who knew her effect on men. Morris seemed to enjoy letting her take the lead in the conversation. After we ordered drinks (Lilet for Elsa, a Gray Goose martini for Morris, and my Johnnie Walker Black), she opened the conversation. "Morris told me a great deal about you. It's so good to meet 'the man' in person."

"I hope some of the things he told you were nice," I retorted.

"Only pleasant things," she said with a coy smile and a very slight but pleasing accent. "As a matter of fact, he thinks working with you years ago was a highlight of his early career."

"I'm flattered."

The drinks were set in front of us, and Morris quickly lifted his glass and toasted, "To old times, a good friend, and a happy evening together."

The three of us started nibbling at the small dish of olives and nuts in the center of the table. We reminisced over the drinks, catching up on what we had done since Morris and I had last met. Morris wanted to know the news regarding my family, and asked about some of his former associates. He told me he was heading a group investing in companies that had been privatized from the government since the 1991 breakaway from the Soviets and the establishment of a free and independent Poland.

Time passed quickly as we bantered back and forth, and it seemed like only a moment later when the maitre d' said our table was ready. A uniformed waiter appeared and placed our remaining drinks on a silver tray to be delivered to us at our table in the dining room.

The dining room was luxurious. We were escorted to plush enameled white wood armchairs with red damask cushions. The red of the chair cushions matched the plush carpet, and the six large wall panels had padded red quilting that muffled sounds within the room. The decor created an atmosphere that allowed us to continue our conversation in comfort.

The sound level was subdued, and I could hear Elsa's delightful, soft voice: "This is lavish. Morris has taken me here only once." And with a sly smile directed at her spouse, she said, "And he was courting me then."

Morris ignored her comment and raised his hand, beckoning for the wine list. We made ourselves comfortable and ordered our dinners. I chose a filet mignon with a sauce that was a specialty of the chef. Both Morris and Elsa ordered the salmon and shrimp featured by the chef, who came to our table to describe the preparation. Thumbing through the wine list, Morris selected a good Polish wine produced by a new vineyard, the Golesz domain in Jaslo.

He explained, "This was from a vineyard competing with the Slovakian and Ukrainian wines that have dominated the Polish market." He said that his group had invested in the vineyard, and he was proud of the product. He had chosen a Seyval Blanc as the white wine and a rich Rondo for our meat course.

The red wine was opened at the table and decanted into a carafe. The chilled white wine was poured for our first salad course. Morris raised his glass and looked straight at me: "To my friend George, who has come a long way on his personal journey. May he find what he is seeking and may we all live in peace and harmony."

After my first sip of the white wine, I raised my glass and returned the toast. "To Morris and Elsa. It is my pleasure to share my first night in Poland with you."

As an afterthought I said, "You should be proud, this is very drinkable."

As we started our first course, Elsa said, "Morris said that you would tell us why you have come to Poland. Do you have business here?"

"No, this is not a business trip. I want to trace what happened to my grandmother's family. I understand they all died in the Holocaust, and I want to visit the town, the family cemetery, and the surrounding countryside and find the circumstances of their deaths."

"Oh my, I can't imagine why you would come to trace your family, visiting the cemetery and all that. Isn't that dredging up ancient history?"

"I think it is more than that. They were Jews and we don't know how they died. We know about the Holocaust, but that's the large picture. I want to know specifically what had happened. I feel compelled to see the town my relatives came from and see for myself what became of their graves. I want to be a witness to their lives and find out how they died. My American family deserves to know what happened. It's an open wound. The Holocaust was part of our parents' and grandparents' generation. My generation distanced ourselves from the events and even the specific knowledge. We heard about the horrors, but then we couldn't identify with the crimes and extermination. What happened, happened to 'them.' Perhaps we marginalized the tragedy. I'm really trying to see where this all fits in my life, and perhaps the lives of my children."

Morris interjected, "George always had a sense of right and wrong."

"What do you expect to find?" Elsa inquired.

"I really don't know. I've read a great deal of how some Holocaust sites have been memorialized and how others, particularly the graveyards, have been neglected or even desecrated. I don't have any specific expectations. I just want to discover what happened to the community that lived there."

Morris asked, "How many days will you take to explore?"

"Again, I really don't know. I plan to stay in Warsaw a day or so, and then see the countryside and small towns between here and Ozarow."

Elsa looked around, spread her hands, and said, "You will not find this type of luxury as you travel around. Poland is not as luxurious or modern a country as would be indicated by this hotel. Are you prepared to rough it?"

"I only brought casual clothes and this blazer."

"I'll bet this is the last time you will wear the jacket to dinner."

Our dinner was served and the conversation continued in a light vein. It was after the main course was cleared that Morris then turned to me. "How do you feel about the Germans?"

I didn't expect Morris's question. I was slightly taken aback. I thought a moment before answering: "Of course, I feel angry about the horrible things the Germans did to the Jews. I guess part of my trip is to gain perspective on what we accept as the crimes of the Hitler era. They were mass murderers, and as time passes it appears that we have allowed the horror of that era to fade into a recognition that some evil is part of the human condition. In the case of Germany, I really can't say how I feel. It has been sixty years. Being an American and having some sense of fairness, I can't say I believe in collective guilt. However, I wonder how a people enabled a regime like the Nazis to get away with the massive killings that occurred. Ask me more after I've made my trip. I want to see and feel what they did to my family. This is putting a personal face on the terror of the Holocaust."

Elsa was determined to make a point. Her blue eyes seemed to light up in a blaze of anger and she flushed slightly. "The Germans were barbarians. They destroyed the Polish nation, dismembered it, and slaughtered not only Jews, but also millions of Poles. They killed six million Poles, half of whom were Jews. The three million Jews were ten percent of our population before the war. The three million Poles who went with those Jews to the camps and the gas chambers were our army officers, our intelligentsia, and our leading politicians. The Germans killed them first to subdue the population and ensure there were no postwar leaders left."

She paused to take a sip of the red wine and then, still animated and punching the air with her finger, said: "We Poles lost twenty percent of our people to the Germans. We find that most Jewish visitors only think of the six million Jews. They don't focus on the others who were murdered. Please look at more than the Jewish Holocaust. We too were bloodied for much of the twentieth century.

What the Germans didn't do they inadvertently left to the Soviets, who blasted their way through the country and then made Poland a subservient client state to them for over forty years."

Morris calmly added to Elsa's commentary: "Poland was the meat in the grinder between Germany and Russia. Poland today is the remnant of that country that existed before the war and contains many people displaced by the war. We are a proud nation, victimized but proud that we survived the war, and then the Soviet domination after the war. Today we are now more Western than middle European."

Her passion and Morris's calm voice resounded in my ears. I was stung by her blunt talk. Having always looked at this from afar, I felt confronted by someone who was personally involved. Her national pride was a surprise. Surely, I wasn't offended by her animation and ardor. "I find myself an outsider when it comes to Polish history," I confessed. "I only know the story of the last seventy years."

"George, a famous scholar, Professor Piotr Wrobel, recently said, 'To most Americans and West Europeans, World War II constitutes the proverbial ancient history: vague, remote, and irrelevant. To most East Europeans and to the Poles among them, the war is a recent memory, the emotional wounds are still fresh, and new important events, rooted in the World War II tragedy, continue to develop.' I might add that I believe those words also apply to the world's Jews."

It was almost an afterthought by Morris when he turned toward Elsa and said, "George is interested in this area's Jewish history. Jews lived in Poland since the early 1400s and had a rich history here. We had a Jewish cultural base that was part of the fabric of this country. Jewish and Polish culture were interrelated. Most of that was destroyed." Then he turned to me, almost apologizing, "You will need luck to find anything to see of consequence. Most of those small towns have changed. There is precious little of the old Poland left."

Morris made a point of telling me of some of the areas of Poland I should see on the way to Ozarow and the southwest. "Before you leave Warsaw, you should visit the Jewish Historical Institute. There is an exhibit that will give you a good background in what you want to see. They show a film that not only depicts the horror of the Ghetto but also shows what the deportations were like. Of course, you then really should see Auschwitz. If you have come this far just to find your family's story, you should see the larger picture and understand fully what inhumanity was. Murder and shooting and beating were atrocious enough, but when you understand the building of a killing industry, you will see that there was more than deportation, prison, work camps, and murder. The magnitude of the crimes of the Holocaust is beyond what was done to the Jews, or indeed to the Poles and other innocents. The crimes reached a stage that most of our minds cannot process. The killings, the scale of the process, the institutionalization of the hate, and the sheer cold bloodedness of murders made the Holocaust unimaginable. Ordinary men did these killings. How could these men live with, or have lived with, these crimes that were committed is the unexplained human factor of the times."

Morris gave me a travelogue on what I would be seeing and named a few towns I should find. We then spoke about our former business associates, and I updated him on the careers of friends. He added to his earlier comments on his work. Then his conversation turned back to my journey and he advised that I find and talk to as many of the "older" people as possible. "Sadly" he said, "they will remember. The young ones don't want to know."

All in all, the evening was pleasant. It was good to see an old friend and realize that he had married a goodlooking and intelligent woman. At the end of the meal, I walked them through the ornate hotel lobby and bid them goodbye.

As he was leaving, Morris turned back to me, stepped one pace away from Elsa, and said, "You'll find that we haven't marginalized all this. But we are still trying to fit the experience of the last sixty years into a perspective we can understand and live with. We still hear of discrimination in some of the small Polish towns and we are horrified that any hate still exists. During the war we had Poles who helped the Germans. We are not proud of those few. We had people who turned Jews over to the Nazis to be taken away, as well as those who protected their neighbors. There are many stories of those who sheltered children for the entire occupation. Most of us prefer to remember the good stories, and many suppress the thoughts of the bastards who betrayed Poland and the Catholics and Jews. George, I hope you don't judge Poland by the horror stories you will hear. We have been through too much. We pray for peace and understanding."

Morris hugged me. "Enjoy your trip. If you need anything, call me. Be sure to call before you leave for home." He pressed a business card with all his contact information into my hands.

We embraced one more time. I was drained from the day's events and the conversation over dinner. There was a lot to think about, and I was too tired to process my thoughts. I went back to my room and was asleep by eleven. It had been a long day and night.

Chapter Ten

Peace and War: Time in Warsaw—Willie's Story

It was six in the morning and Willie had fallen asleep with his father's letters spread across the bed. He had not moved under the covers and was surprised at how undisturbed he had slept. He showered and read a few more of the letters, particularly those written from this area. As he read, he was jarred for the first time by an account in an uncensored letter. There was a disturbing note. Papa wrote, just several lines in the midst of a more pleasant letter:

> We heard shots the other night. It was strange because the fighting seems to be over. The shots came from an area not under our Wehrmacht control, but from an area under the command of the SS. We didn't see anything, but the next day some of our prisoner workers told us that the local mayor and some Jews were executed for not complying with orders to bring all the Jews into the town where they were assigned to live in a confined district. The Jewish population isn't trusted and the SS is relocating them where they can be watched. The prisoners were made to clean the site after the executions. I was disturbed by all this.

Papa had been able to come home on leave for as long as a month at a time during this period. He had been happy, the army had been victorious. The Führer had made the nation prosperous; people had been at work, flour brought from Poland for bread had been inexpensive, vegetables from Poland and occupied France had streamed into the homeland, and Mama had been able to expand the little bakery by taking the adjoining store and deepening the cellar for storage.

Willie remembered these days of Papa's furloughs. He remembered his father coming into their home wearing his uniform and quickly embracing Mama and changing into his civilian clothes. Willie remembered the almost antiseptic smell of his father's coarse woolen uniform and how quickly Mama made him hang the clothes in the entranceway cupboard where they kept their rainwear. The uniform stayed there all during the time Papa was home. He remembered the fresh clean smell of his father after he'd bathed within minutes of arriving home. He remembered being asked to go and play at Cousin Elena's for the afternoon and wondering why he couldn't have stayed around the house and be with Mama and Papa. Now he understood. He remembered how sad Mama was when the furlough was over and his father put his uniform on and went out of the door carrying his rucksack. He remembered. He remembered. He remembered.

Papa had remained stationed in Poland; he hadn't been transferred to fight in the west in 1940, as the Western army had quickly swept back the French. Paris fell to the Germans, and the British were pushed into the sea. Papa had been happy to remain comfortably assigned outside Warsaw. To him the war had seemed to be over; he had been safe in Poland and wrote of coming home for good:

I don't know what is next. Perhaps we will be discharged. Many of us thought that after we finished with Poland we would be coming home. From the preparations, it is apparent that the Fuehrer may have other plans. We have been reequipped. Motorized trucks have replaced much of the horse-drawn equipment. I now know why they taught me to drive. Our camp is on one side of the Vistula River, and about 20 kilometers on the other side of the river is a Russian camp. This is the new border between Poland and Russia. Control of this area has shifted many times over the years between these countries. None of the peasants are very happy about this, as they also have seen fighting twenty years ago on these same grounds. The people just seem to shrug their shoulders over the changes. The families all seem to have relatives on the other side of the border. We go out and talk to them and we are able to buy fresh eggs and other produce for very cheap prices. The Army gives us as much food as we want, but there is nothing like fresh produce. Some of the locals are very nice. One of the men in my group met one of the young girls and seems to have taken up with her. Our commander does not like this and the man is being given the worse possible duty, cleaning out the kitchen grease traps. When he wasn't assigned to this we had local laborers doing this work. My friends and I are a little uneasy; there isn't much to do. We'd like to come home.

Willie was in great spirits as he left Prosta and drove the short distance into Warsaw. The weather cooperated; it was a pleasant spring day. As he entered the city, he observed the wide boulevards and buildings that had been built during the post–Soviet occupation.

He quickly navigated toward the city center and found the Europjski Hotel. This hotel was centrally located and was advertised as being in the tradition of serving "old Polish royalty." It would also serve as a good base for exploring the town and nearby countryside.

The next morning, Willie, acting as a tourist, wandered around Warsaw. He saw a rebuilt city and made the inevitable comparison with Stuttgart. Much of both cities had been destroyed in the war. Now Stuttgart was a modern city with varied contemporary architecture. The contrast of the modern glass-and-aluminum structures back home and the five- and six-story postwar Communist flats struck Willie as a huge difference between the architecture of the West and the East, and the cultures that sponsored the rebuilding. Willie observed that it was only after 1991 that imagination seemed to come back to the Polish builders with several modern, well-designed contemporary public buildings to contrast with the blight of Soviet-style central planning. He noted the socialistic influence in the postwar architecture; the uniformity of many oblong cement five-story apartment buildings, which didn't have the variety and good taste prevalent in rebuilt Stuttgart, with its amazing blend of contemporary modern buildings and traditional structures salvaged from the wartime destruction. He was proud of his work at the bank, where he'd been part of those reconstruction years, financing projects that had been architecturally challenging and had brought pride to the German people. "What a great job we did rebuilding after the war."

The scent of the early spring blossoms was in the air, and as he walked by the rebuilt Royal Castle, Willie saw the castle gardens being replanted. The smell of earth being prepared for the new flower beds pleased him, and he savored the peace and beauty of the surroundings.

He enjoyed seeing the formal garden arrangement and imagined how pleasant they would look when work was completed.

His reached the Chopin Monument, where the annual Chopin festival was held. Papa had mentioned this in his letters, describing how the grounds were prepared for a concert he'd attended and how the music had made him feel homesick. Willie wandered to the Wilanow Palace, the summer residence of King Jan III, which dated back to 1677. In the stack of letters there was a picture of Papa and several buddies in front of the palace entrance. Willie compared the picture and smiled because here was a place that didn't seem changed. He felt a bonding with Papa just by standing there.

Papa also had visited the National Museum. Willie walked there, enjoyed the art collection, and stopped by the reconstructed St John's Cathedral. At this point he purchased a guidebook. In the book, beside the usual lists of attractions, there were two sections describing the uprisings of the Poles during the Nazi occupation. Over a coffee in the museum cafeteria, Willie read about the revolts, one about the Jewish Ghetto uprising and liquidation, and the other on the fight in 1944 that ended in the destruction of much of the city. This was a "must see" in the guidebook.

Hoping to see both sites before dinner, he hailed a taxi and asked to be driven to the Jewish monument. Within minutes he realized the driver was lost. From the passenger seat Willie handed the driver the tourist map, and after some difficulty, the driver let Willie off in the two-city-block park area dedicated to the Warsaw Ghetto Uprising. He walked around the massive Jewish martyrs monument and, following the map, found the old bunker of Mila 18 about two hundred yards away. He remembered that there had been a book written with that title. He hadn't read it. He observed the tributes with respect but couldn't identify with what he was observing. There were plaques written in Polish and English all around, and he stopped to read many of them. He paused at the monuments in the plaza, but he didn't relate to the message inscribed on the base and walls of the monument or the cause the statues and inscriptions represented. To Willie the messages were academic; they didn't tell him of his father's travels. He thought, "Papa wasn't involved in this." Willie looked for signs of the old city—there were few. He was more interested in how the city had been rebuilt. This was all a rebuilt postwar area.

Willie walked on into the district known as Zolibirz, tracing the streets of the old city from Wola to the Saski Gardens and near the Kierbedzia Bridge, the area of the 1944 uprising. He knew that this had been the Polish-underground revolt. From his guidebook, the plaques and inscriptions told of the siege and the liquidation of the Polish patriots during August 1944. He was able to grasp the extent of the total destruction sixty years before. According to the letters, Papa hadn't been involved; he had been far to the south in Ukraine at the time. Willie saw the area as a historic battlefield and was merely a tourist, an observer. He noticed the crumbling corners of the Jewish memorials as contrasted to the well-maintained facade of the uprising monument. The litter around some of the monuments, including dog detritus, annoyed Willie. He thought, "Memorials should be maintained with respect."

As Papa had spent nearly two years garrisoned near here, Willie stayed in Warsaw an extra day. He wandered about trying to identify sites that were in the pictures enclosed with the letters home. Tired of walking and taking taxis, he got into his car and visited the surrounding countryside. He found town squares that were mentioned in the letters and shown in the pictures. Late in the day, he wandered about sixty miles northeast of the city and came upon the area of Treblinka. Driving down a secondary road, he saw a large granite marker pointing down a dirt road into a pine forest. The marker had a Polish inscription that was quite clear even to Willie, "Hitler Era Death Camp." He was intrigued and curious.

Knowing the name, Willie stopped the car and found the reference in one of his tour books. He scanned the description and decided to investigate the site. He turned into the forested area and drove about two hundred meters. He parked near the sparse, pine-house souvenir stand at the edge of the parking lot. The shack was no more than twelve by twelve meters square and was made of gray board with a small clerk's inquiry window. There were very few people around, and he walked slowly to the stand and requested a guidebook. The charge was nominal, eight zlotys.

Willie walked about thirty steps into the forest along a gravel path. The tall pine trees obscured any vision of the site beyond about twenty meters, and he felt the isolation of being in the vast woods. In front of him he saw what appeared to be an unplanned memorial. It was different from the granite or brass monuments and plaques that he had seen. It wasn't mentioned in the guidebook or the pamphlet he'd received at the parking area. There was a Hebrew inscription on a small painted sign resting on the ground with an English translation, "We remember those of our people who died here." Beneath the plaque was a pile of at least a thousand multicolored stones, none larger that his fist, many smaller. They were painted and inscribed with what appeared to be names and dates, mostly in Hebrew, a few in English. He looked carefully at them and walked back to the souvenir stand to ask about the stones. The lady behind the counter replied, "We get many Israeli schoolchildren here. It is a Jewish tradition to leave a small stone at a gravesite when making a visitation. That isn't an official camp memorial, but it has become the place that visitors, particularly the children, leave their small visitation stone. The names are the names of both the visitors and relatives who were murdered here."

Willie turned, walked back to the pile, and looked closely. Some of the stones had multiple names painted on them, and others just a single name. There were inscriptions in different languages. They were in all colors, and several had intricate designs. He was impressed by the efforts and care that had been crafted into preparing each marker. There were so many.

Willie slowly walked away from the improvised memorial and turned down the wide path that led to Treblinka. After about fifty meters he faced two signs at a junction in the path. One said "Labor Camp" and the other "Extermination Camp." A bit farther along, there was a large map with the layout of the surroundings. Willie studied the board with its detailed "Selected Features" list and then walked toward the area marked "Reception Platform, Ramp and Square."

During the next hour, Willie wandered about the two camps. He was most affected by the massive monument that was centered in the "Extermination Camp" area, a vast field with irregular boulders strewn about. He stood before the fifty-foot-tall granite cenotaph built of massive rough-cut square stones that had a Jewish candelabra at the top and what appeared to be a fracture running up one side. "How simple and yet eloquent." It appeared to be a large broken heart. He then walked around and through the irregularly shaped boulders that surrounded the massive memorial as if they were standing guard. Some were marble, others granite, and others were nondescript-shaped alabaster that covered the huge field. Each boulder had the name of a town, some of which were recognizable to Willie. The guidebook indicated that each represented a town or village whose people had been exterminated here at Treblinka. Willie shuddered at the thought. There must have been hundreds of thousands of people represented by these unsculpted monuments. To one side between the large memorial and the field of boulders was a large inscribed granite marker with an inscription in seven languages, "Never Again."

He stood before the large pit with the remains of burnt coals that the guidebook said represented the funeral pyre. It was a huge trench. He read that the fires burned for thirteen months, being fed by the bodies of the murdered. Train after train of ten to twenty cars arrived with anywhere from 150 to 200 men, women, and children in each sealed car, ten and twelve cars per train. Four and five "cargos" of stinking, emaciated, weary, and defeated people arrived each day; many not having survived the brutal conditions of the trip. Half-alive people staggered out of the boxcars begging for water or food. Bodies remained in the transport to be dragged to the pyre before the trains were sent back for their next cargo. The journey's survivors were beaten, stripped of their clothes and possessions, and murdered within hours of arrival. They were forced into gas chambers fed with the carbon monoxide from old tank engines. Then, soul by soul, they were thrown into the fires of this pit, now a memorial. He was revolted reading that women's bodies with slightly more fat had been used as the base of the cremation fires, giving the flames more substance. Most had been Jews from Poland, indeed from the Warsaw Ghetto, where he had been just yesterday. Willie paused and said a quiet prayer. It was an involuntary reaction to seeing the charred stones that were symbolic of the thousands that had been immolated at this spot. The plaques he'd seen yesterday now had a deeper meaning.

Willie turned and slowly started to walk the several hundred meters back to the parking lot. The ground was covered with thousands of little pine cones. He changed his stride to avoid stepping on them. "Let them live and germinate," he mused. At the entrance to the path to his car, there were another six monuments all in a row, each in a different language. He stopped at the memorial inscribed in German and read that 800,000 Jews had been murdered here in Treblinka and that 10,000 Poles had been murdered in the nearby labor camp. His shoulders slouched from the effect of reading the text. Willie reached his car and sat silently in despondent thought. He tried to catch his breath. Did Papa know of this? As he headed back to Warsaw, he drove in silence, alone with his thoughts, the car radio off. "How could the Nazis have been so inhuman?" A slow rage stirred within Willie's stomach, and bile rose to his throat. He wanted to stop and cry for these people, but his emotions were confused. He mourned the deaths of these innocent victims, but the sheer numbers were difficult to absorb. How could he have sympathy?—he was a German. But what he had come upon was inhuman. The day disturbed him. It was uncivilized; he could not absorb the reasoning of these killings, but he could not deny what he had seen.

When he arrived at the hotel, he went to the bar and ordered a beer. Everything was so normal. The barman with his starched white shirt and apron and the orderliness of the room made Willie ask himself, "Does this generation know what I saw today? Do these people mourn for those murdered just a few miles from here?" It had been sixty years ago, but were these people even aware of what had happened, or were they just caught up in listening to the light pleasant music playing in the background? Was the world just listening to the music? Was it all buried in the past and forgotten? Anguish filled his heart. What kind of men could do this? In all of his years, he had avoided visiting any of the labor or death camps. He hadn't talked about them to his children. This was a subject he had ignored. Had he not wanted to face the shame of these acts? Did his avoidance of the past make him part of the Nazi scheme? Was there guilt in silence? He wanted to talk to someone, but there was no one near, only the preoccupied barman and a few couples. They wouldn't be interested. Any appetite for food had left him. Willie ordered a second beer, skipped dinner, and went to his room.

> We often leave our encampment and travel to see the Polish cities. Our money is very strong and we can buy just about anything we want. I'm sending you some dresses I purchased in Poznan, a city we often visit. Several of the men and I visited Warsaw. We went on a tour conducted by Kraft durch Freude [Strength Through Joy] an organization that takes care of soldiers with leisure time. We had a bus tour through the area where the the Jews live. Later I went to the market just outside this Jewish town and made some purchases. I have a new leather handbag for you and I bought a Persian lamb coat from one of the Jews. I will bring the coat home with me when I come on my two-week leave next month. I'm told it is a very fashionable coat. The Jews are everywhere selling goods at very low prices. There are many

luxury items for sale in the local markets, and many of the men go shopping there. The tailoring is so reasonable that I had several uniform shirts made so I will look extra good when I come home. There are no shortages here, and the area is very peaceful. I visited a town near our encampment, Zelazowa Wola, the birthplace of Chopin. The house was partially damaged in the fighting, but it has been partially repaired and I understand some of the art was taken away to Berlin. There was a concert for the troops and it was a very nice evening.

Willie visited Zelazowa Wola the next day, and indeed it was a beautiful place. The Chopin house had been restored and sat in a large peaceful park. Willie walked across a small wooden bridge to get to the house and imagined Chopin crossing this bridge as a young boy. The house was a white stucco bungalow with a gray slate roof, the interior spacious, with high ceilings. Willie saw the restored furniture and copies of family portraits that adorned the walls and read the little statement in the guidebook: "All of the furniture and the portraits are reconstructions, as the originals were lost to the Germans in 1939." Then, in his mind's eye he envisioned Papa and his army friends visiting to hear the concert. Willie thought, "Papa was a cook, a baker. What a shame that there were others who weren't as civilized."

Then Papa's world had started to change. The German army had begun sharpening its sword and upgrading its armaments and transport. Many of the horse-drawn supply vehicles had been replaced by trucks, and the cooks, bakers, and supply personnel had been given extra training in handling weapons:

I have become an expert shot. The Army has taught me to shoot a rifle and I have become proficient with a new type pistol called a machine pistol. Willie, it shoots very fast and sounds like paper tearing when I shoot. I must say that this was fun to learn, but I hope I never have to shoot in combat.

Chapter Eleven

The Road to Ozarow: Peter's Tour—George's Story

The super-soft mattress and down comforter were sheltering and protecting me from the world as I slowly awakened. It was the beginning of my second day in Warsaw, and I was excited about what I would see and the people I would meet. Based upon what Morris had told me and the meeting yesterday with Anna at the Holocaust memorial, I realized the need for a translator and a guide.

After a shower and leisurely full breakfast, during which I read the *International Herald Tribune* in the ornate breakfast room, I went to the lobby to speak to the concierge. He was eager to assist. "Where do you want to go? What do you want to see, and what is the purpose of the trip?"

He made several suggestions about sights and routes, and was generous with maps and guidebooks. He said he knew of a young man, a licensed guide, fluent in English, who had led several Jewish tours. He assured me that this guide knew the Holocaust history and was familiar with the countryside southwest of the city all the way to Ozarow and beyond.

Within an hour I was interviewing the suggested guide. I estimated that he was about twenty-five years old, and he met all the qualifications and seemed eager for the job. His name was Peter. He was tall, slim, and blond, with a flashing smile.

He said, "I'm a graduate history student at the university—just finished with all of the course work and I'm writing my dissertation paper." I asked him what was its topic, and he replied, "I'm writing about the politics of the first Polish republic, established in 1920. Indeed, right here in this hotel they held the first Parliament. That's how the concierge knows me; I've been in and out of here doing research."

He displayed excellent command of English, even using some colloquial expressions.

"How come your English is so good?" I asked.

"I have an uncle in Toledo, Ohio, who had worked in the steel mills. He now owns a small restaurant, and I spent two summers working there, sharpening my English. Then during the last two years I was able to work as a guide for one of the tour companies that brought American and Israeli tourists to the Jewish cemeteries."

I thought he was perfect; I liked him and agreed to his rates. At 7:30 the next morning, the rental car was outside the hotel, my bag was in the trunk, and the guidebooks were on the floor in the front of the car. I saw Peter loping along the street with long strides carrying his backpack. His greeting was a cheery, "Good morning."

I took the very light bag from him. "Is this all you'll need?"

"What more? Several changes of underwear, an extra shirt, and another rolled-up pair of khaki pants along with my toothbrush. I travel light."

We stowed his gear in the trunk alongside my bags and he said, "I'll drive" as he jumped behind the wheel. We reviewed the maps, and Peter said that we would be heading south out of Warsaw. We were under way.

As we navigated away from the hotel, I was pleased that he started our conversation by saying that he was fascinated by my motivation for this trip. "It is unusual for someone to come and try to visit on their own. Usually people come in tour groups and they choose to see the cemeteries or visit the death camps like Auschwitz and tour the old cities like Krakow. These are standard tours—you know: forty people and a guide in a bus for seven days with a good going-away dinner on the last night."

"I'm not the tour type of person. I'm not comfortable riding in a bus and being programmed like everyone else."

"It is just unusual for someone to do this on their own."

"As I said yesterday, I'm tracing my family history and I want to see how our Polish relatives died. I want to see where and try to understand their end. If possible, I want to see some of the towns between here and Ozarow and see what happened during the Holocaust, but that is more curiosity than interest. I'm obviously aware of the stories of the Holocaust and the death camps. I'm not naive, but I'm here to understand more."

Peter nodded his head: "George, we can probably find out what you want to know, where it happened, and some of the details. Much of what was here is lost. Time is cruel, and until the breakaway from the Soviets there was little interest in preserving the past. For the most part we will find no visible signs of the Jewish existence other than the cemeteries, a few faded signs, and perhaps a shadow or indentation on a doorpost where a mezuzah once marked a Jewish home. One thing I can't do is explain why any of this happened. Few of the younger people understand the hate of that time and the motives. Most don't care. We know the story and the events, but my generation just doesn't comprehend what motivated the Germans to do their killing, or indeed, why some Poles were complacent."

"You don't understand anti-Semitism?"

"I understand that kind of hate. It has been prevalent for hundreds of years and should be deplored and purged from the minds of Catholics and non-Jews. What I don't understand is the killing, the murder, the death camp mentality. Indeed, what kind of a man does this to a fellow man? Why did the Germans act the way they did and why did certain of my people support that hatred and also act badly?"

We were riding along and Peter was pointing out sights along the road when he mused, "It's strange; we had the death camps, postwar pogroms, and years of Soviet rule. Now throughout the country there are 'Jewish style' restaurants serving ethnic food and young people dancing to Jewish songs and dances. There is even a Jewish festival. The dancers and the diners all are Poles. There are no Jews. There are only 10,000 Jews among the 39 million now living in Poland."

"What does this mean to you?"

"I'm young, so are the others. We are of a generation that realizes that more than the Jews disappeared. The food, music, literature, and the other arts all are missing. A culture vanished. Part of the Polish soul of six hundred years was destroyed."

I told him about the mailing of Grandmother's letters all those years ago, and how they came back.

"You are here to solve a mystery."

"Yes."

"Do you want to see the camps?"

"I wasn't planning on it."

He said, "We will see a great deal. I am going to recommend that you see Auschwitz. So, if you change your mind, we could travel a little to the west to be there."

He seemed to want to take control of the trip, and I felt this was a good sign. He was young but aware of the history and enthusiastic to impart the knowledge he had. He also had brought along some guidebooks and maps, all of which supplemented the items I had. "George, our first goal will be to visit Radom, a city about sixty miles to the south of Warsaw and on the way to Ozarow. Along the way we'll visit several cemeteries I think are interesting, based upon my prior visits."

"I'm in your hands. As long as you think these are places I should see, I'm game."

"A lot of restoration work has started in some of these cemeteries."

"Restoration work?"

"Yes, the war destroyed many of these sites. The Germans and indeed some of the local Poles desecrated these cemeteries and in some cases used the gravestones for building materials."

"Who is doing the restoration?"

"In several cases there is an American group funding the work. In a few instances the local population is helping, and there are families scattered around the world who come back and want to fund the cleaning and maintenance."

As we drove along, I expected to see rural scenes. My eyes looked for small villages with thatched-roof homes, villages where there would be a church, general store, and maybe a dozen homes at a crossroads. My mind had this picture, nurtured by my grandmother's descriptions many years before. But Poland had changed.

When I asked Peter about the countryside, he replied, "The war created much destruction. The Germans tore through in the '39 invasion and then there was the steamroller effect of the Russian advance in early '45, along with the ruthless defense of the German rear-guard units that leveled many of the 'old towns.' The Soviet influence in the postwar years and the emerging New Poland resulted in planned towns, located at the crossroads of the highways."

What I was seeing wasn't what I had envisioned. The towns were quite modern, and the landscape wasn't filled with poor peasants. In many towns I saw the rebuilt Catholic church in the center, with graveyards alongside. The postwar buildings often had a "cookie cutter" appearance that must have come from a central planning desk manned by a designer whose only pride was to create quickly constructed affordable housing. My eye was able to pick up charming little pieces of the old world. In one town I saw a one-story schoolhouse, a street market full of produce, and a small clothing store that must have been founded after the opening of the economy following the Soviet years. There were also some of the smaller produce farms that surrounded the villages, with people working the fields without modern farm machinery.

Peter stayed off the main roads to let me see the local economy. We slowly passed through several of these rural towns. I told him that I wanted to see how my grandmother's family had lived. How the uncles, friends, families, and the great host of Jews who hadn't migrated in the years from 1890 to the mid-1930s had lived as they'd farmed and practiced their religion. These were those who had stayed behind, for whatever reason, perhaps not believing the stories that came back that America was a land of golden opportunity, or because inertia held them in place. They may have felt secure in pre-war Poland. For some there must have been the fear of change. Roots held them fast to a way of life. Perhaps some were unable to raise the meager money to break away, abandon this corner of Europe, and find their way into a new world. And there were many, many who just did not want to move on and saw no need.

At several of the rural crossroads Peter would show me a marker indicating that there used to be a village here. Some were now completely abandoned, designated in some cases by the little plaque placed by relatives from the US. These were the visitors, mainly from tour groups who had made my journey before me and found their site, their cemetery, and their past.

I said, "Tell me about Radom."

As we drove, Peter briefed me. He would hold the wheel with his left hand and punctuate his words with his right, holding his forefinger in the air as if he was lecturing at a university. "The area we are traveling in was part of the 'General Government' set up by the Germans as the governing territory of eastern Poland right after they took control in 1939. The notorious Hans Frank was assigned by Hitler as the administrator of the area. He set himself up in Krakow and ruled like a king."

"In March 1941 Hitler ordered Frank to turn this region into a purely German area within 15 to 20 years. In the cynical terms of the Nazi regime it was a direct order to eliminate the Jewish population. Throughout their corrupt rule, the Germans used polite catch-phrases to avoid putting in writing words like 'eliminate' or 'kill.' Living within the General Government were both the indigenous Jews and many who had been transported into the area from Germany,

Austria, and the surrounding countries. Frank was diligent in accepting those orders. The Jews were forced into ghettos, and the 'elimination' was started by the process of starvation, outright killing, and exploitation by demands of hard labor. Then, of course came the death camps. The goal was to convert an area where there were 12 million Poles, including the Jews, into a place to be populated by 4 to 5 million Germans. His objective was to make this as German as the Rhineland."

I was impressed by Peter's command of history. He was a good lecturer. He went on to tell how Jews expelled from Germany were initially "resettled" in this area, forced into the Polish ghettos that were set up. In turn some Poles, not Jews, were deported to work as forced labor in Germany.

"Peter, I didn't know about the deportation of Poles," I said.

"Yes, about a million Poles were taken for slave labor. One of my uncles was a slave laborer in a factory near Hamburg. Many died in Germany. My uncle was lucky, and he survived. Another uncle wasn't as lucky. He was an officer in the Polish army. He was imprisoned and executed in Auschwitz. We also lost much of our intelligentsia, and many whom the Nazis identified as persons who would resist."

As we were approaching Radom, Peter continued his commentary. "In 1939 there were about 90,000 people living in Radom, and about one-third of them were Jews. The town was taken by the Germans within eight days of the invasion and became the site of one of the German administrative districts. In December 1939, many of the Jews were rounded up and sent to forced labor camps. The remaining Jewish population was confined to two ghettos, one in the center of the city and the other, a smaller one, in a nearby suburb. During the first days of 1942, the German garrison initiated several so-called *aktionen* events, which was another name for murder, the murder of local Jews. By using machine guns and rifles, these atrocities were committed. But this wasn't efficient enough for the Germans, and several thousand of the confined Jews were deported to Auschwitz. Radom became one of the railhead towns, with regular trains departing to Auschwitz and Treblinka. Jews from nearby towns were rounded up, confined in Radom, and then herded to the railhead. This was the collection point. The trains were scheduled, one a day, with as many as fifty or more boxcars in a train, two thousand or more people in a single railroad shipment. People were jammed into a boxcar with their luggage. They were told they were being relocated. Again, the German cynicism, 'To the promised land.' In the rail cars, the people were jammed in inhuman conditions without water or sanitary facilities, for journeys as long as a week. They were shipped like cattle, many died in the crowded cars. Within six months the two ghettos of Radom were totally destroyed. The Jews had been shot or sent to forced labor or to the extermination camps."

As Peter spoke, I felt blood rushing to my face and my pulse seemed to race. I experienced a feeling of futility and sorrow hearing of the horror and injustice. I was speechless; voicing anger was useless. I felt frustrated. We reached the outskirts of Radom, and Peter slowed the car as we entered the town from the north. He showed me the location of the large and small ghetto areas. We parked the car and Peter continued his tour.

I was silent, hung my head, and followed slowly as he carefully walked through what had been the Jewish neighborhood, the site of the old ghetto. He pointed to many plaques citing the whereabouts of synagogues, homes, families, and buildings that were landmarks to the Jewish life that formerly existed. He was familiar with the story of the Jews of Radom. "The Germans cordoned off one area of the town and designated it to be the new home of the local Jews. First they filled the section with displaced Jewish families, bringing Jews from nearby neighborhoods and towns and dumping them into the ghetto section. It became unbearable. The conditions became deplorable, and deaths from starvation and random executions became a daily occurrence."

Peter paused. He guided me into the shaded area of a small park and we sat down. I welcomed the opportunity to catch my breath.

He continued. "Life in these ghettos was beyond horrible. Several families were crammed into a single room. One toilet served fifty to a hundred people. Disease broke out, and there was no medicine. The old or the infirm died first. The dead were lying in the streets, to be picked up just the same as trash. Food rations were inadequate, in most cases less than two hundred calories per day per person—that's about the calories in one potato. Starvation was rampant. There were no jobs, as there were few industries. The Germans did not permit leaving the ghetto area to work unless you had specific permission. It was a massive bureaucracy designed to psychologically destroy the Jews and deplete them physically. The Germans did take a few out of the ghettos to work as slave labor, but for the most part the ghetto was a place to die or sit and wait for the Germans' next move."

"I understand that the Germans forced them to form a quasi-government."

"Yes, it was called the Judenrat, and was established to have the Jews govern themselves. Those who were appointed served between the proverbial rock and a hard place. On one hand, they tried to serve their co-religionists and deliver some government, including services; and on the other hand, they were subservient to the impossibly hard and unfair orders of the Germans. Those German demands included giving the names of those who would be in the 'transports,' the people selected to be next in line for the extermination camps."

"How did they select the victims for the camps?"

"Systematically, each day, often late at night because it raised the level of terror by arousing people from their beds, the Germans would seal off a ghetto section and search for Jewish families. Sometimes there would be a list of those to go; other times it was just a wholesale roundup. The Jews were forced out of their homes and lined up in the streets as the Germans took inventory of their nightly catch. The Germans would send men into the buildings to roust out any stragglers. Those who were found hiding or old or ill were shot in their beds. Like I have seen in the movies, you would have an American cattle drive, they herded the Jews and marched them to the railhead with nothing more than one suitcase for each family, holding their most precious possessions. There was no resistance. Indeed, it was hard to resist. Those who resisted would be beaten or shot on the spot. The streets to the station would be lined with the bodies of those who stepped out of line or were too weak to continue."

"Why did they have the one suitcase?"

"I hate to say it again: The Germans' propaganda machine was well developed, and they thought the Jews would go peacefully if they were told they were being deported to a 'better place' than the ghetto."

"And."

"And for the most part, they believed."

Peter recited the date of each event in the series, just as one would call off the birthdays of relatives. He sensed my reaction to his description by the horror on my face as I held my hand to my mouth. "I don't know what to say," I gasped. My mouth was dry.

"George, they consolidated small ghettos that were in nearby towns into the larger collecting points. Warsaw was one of the assembling or holding areas, growing from about 100,000 Jews before the war to a peak of over 450,000 crammed into a small section of the city. Radom held 30,000 or more. Krakow was another consolidation point with another 30,000. At first there were several hundred ghettos created throughout Poland and later Russia. It was from these that the process I described emerged. First the Jews were driven into a town, and some days or weeks later, they were again herded to larger ghettos, killed in a nearby forest, or placed onto the death transport trains and shipped to Auschwitz, Treblinka, and the other killing centers. The process was simple. It was a reverse of a distribution system, a plan to gather in masses of people and then distribute them to the killing points. It was a tribute to the German mind and ability to organize."

Peter held my attention. I hadn't thought about the process of the ghettoization, and I guess most people just focused on the shipping of the Jews to the camps. I didn't think about an organized system feeding the camps with the human material for the gas chambers.

I pondered how detailed the planning had to be as we walked back to the car. Peter drove the short distance to the railroad station, which was on the road we would be taking leaving Radom.

He stopped at the station and took me to the old ramp that was used for the deportations. It was on the far side of the busy new commuter station. As we walked through the station, trains were announced and commuters scurried to make their way onto departures for the local suburbs. At the far end of the station, the old platform was still in place, but it was in ruins along the tracks beside the new station that had been built after the war. The cement was crumbling, and here and there the old steel reinforcements were visible and rusting, as were the set of tracks next to this platform. The immediate area was dilapidated. The platform was about one hundred meters long and about ten meters wide.

"This is the platform where the Jews of Radom were pushed onto the death trains. Today, as then, a train could leave here and in hours be at Auschwitz or Treblinka. Then, these trains had a low transport priority and some of them would take four and five days to get to the death camp. With no food, water, or sanitary facilities, deaths in the boxcars could run as high as twenty percent of the human cargo. The Nazis didn't care."

As Peter spoke, I could visualize as many as 2,000 Jews with their baggage standing on the narrow platform with Wehrmacht soldiers, machine pistols at the ready forcing them into the old cattle cars and locking the sliding doors. With Peter's vivid description, I could imagine frightened people being herded and stuffed into the cars for their last transport.

I was subdued and depressed as we walked back to the car; we paused for a bit and looked back at the platform. Then as we drove on, Peter continued.

"The Germans were cynical about just everything. They even operated tour buses in Warsaw for visiting Germans. Civilians and soldiers on leave would ride these buses to see the ghetto as a tourist attraction. The buses would ride through the ghetto, and guides would point out how miserable these people, defined by the Nazis as 'subhuman,' lived. They would point out bodies of people who had died from starvation lying in the street, where the teams that were assigned to bring them to the cemetery had not collected the dead."

The more Peter spoke, the more uncomfortable I became. The abstraction of "the Holocaust" was becoming a personal story. I began to think of these people as relatives, kinfolk, and friends. They were Jews. I started to think about the United States. How comfortable we were. How safe we feel. How safe did these people feel? How could this happen?

Peter, in an apparent effort to ease my feelings, told me of the few survivors who escaped into the forest and became active in underground resistance groups and even participated in the Warsaw Uprising in late summer of 1944. He also cited that there were a few, very few, Christian families who took in Jewish families or their children. Some of these Christians were discovered by the Germans and were summarily executed as a lesson to anyone who would harbor a Jew. It was a miracle, but he said there were a few Jews who survived the entire war in hiding. "There is some shame among Poles that little was done to shelter Jews."

I told Peter of my short walk two days ago, seeing the Warsaw Uprising memorial, and my conversation with Anna the student. "I saw the monument two days ago, and I was amazed at the size and scope of the memorial park. It was a sorrowful but inspiring story. I felt honored to be there."

Although I told him that Anna had told me the history of the two revolts, Peter felt obligated to tell me his version. "You must appreciate that there were two uprisings. The first was a Jewish revolt. When the news came to the Warsaw Ghetto in 1942, brought by a young man who escaped from Treblinka, that the Jews who were deported during the summer were all killed, the Jews formed an organization called the Zydowska Organizacja Bojowa, the Jewish Fighting Organization. This force was led by a young man named Mordecai Anielwicz, and he organized the resistance when the Germans started to round up Jews, forcing them into railroad cars."

"When was this?"

"This was January 1943, and the Jewish fighters, with little more than handguns and homemade Molotov cocktails, attacked the German troops rounding up the Jews. At first the Germans were shocked by the resistance and retreated, pulling their troops back from the ghetto. It was a small victory, because the Germans came back in force, and on April 19th the Germans entered the Ghetto to deport the remaining Jews. Seven hundred and fifty Jewish fighters fought back and held out for nearly a month. You know the story of the defense and obliteration of Mila 18, the headquarters of the revolt, which fell to the Germans on May 8th. By May 16, 1943, the Germans had crushed the revolt. More than 56,000 Jews were captured, 7,000 were shot on the spot, and the others were deported to the camps. Most went to Treblinka, where they were gassed and the bodies were cremated in massive pyres."

"What was the second uprising?"

"The second, which is the revolt that we Poles call 'the Uprising,' occurred as the Russians approached Warsaw in August 1944. Knowing that the Russians were near, about thirty kilometers away just across the Vistula, the Polish resistance came out of hiding and fought the Germans. They wanted to capture the city and turn it over to the Russians with a minimum of damage. They called for help from the British and Americans, but the Russians wouldn't give their allies permission to fly missions from the west and land their planes on Russian occupied airfields just to the east. The resistance fighters hoped to free Warsaw and greet the Russians, who were just a few miles away. They called themselves 'the Warsaw Army Corps,' 25,000 men and women, but they only had weapons for 2,500 fighters. In one day, this group freed the city. They called for the Russians to cross the river and take over. The Russians didn't lift a finger to help. The Germans could not let the Poles hold the city and counterattacked, setting up a siege. They bombed, strafed, and set fire to Warsaw, annihilating it block by block. The Poles lost over 200,000 between August and October. Many of the Jewish resistance fighters who had survived the first uprising and had lived in hiding or had been active as partisans harassing the Germans joined in this battle."

"It gives me a sense of pride that the Jews fought," I said. "Many people have the impression that the Jews went quietly."

"The only time the Jews went quietly was when they were being deceived, told that they were being relocated to a promised land and told that there was work. Once the reality of the inevitable murder machine was realized, many Jews struggled, but it was individuals against machine guns. The fact is, the Germans conducted a very successful suppression of the facts of their killing machine. Those who were sent to the camps didn't live to tell of the slaughter. The few who escaped found that their stories were met with skepticism. The murders were an inconceivable thought to civilized people."

As we drove through several of the small towns beyond Radom, Skaryszew, Modrzjowice, and Itza, we would stop and review our information about the Jewish history that Peter had in the guidebooks and seek the local Jewish cemetery. On several occasions Peter pulled the car into one of the towns and pointed to a cemetery. He had been here as a guide. One cemetery was well preserved, and Peter showed me the little monument indicating that restoration of this cemetery had been undertaken by an American organization. In another he showed me an uncared for, unrestored Jewish cemetery that had been vandalized, first by the Nazis, then by local people seeking building materials.

"Building materials?"

"Yes, the granite gravestones made excellent road pavers, front steps, and foundation blocks for homes."

"Wasn't there any respect for these sacred sites?"

"The Germans started the process by using the gravestones for roadblocks and barriers. It wasn't soon after that the Wehrmacht needed pavers, foundations, and generally building items. The graveyards were easier than quarrying new stone. Sad to say, the local Poles joined in, and many of the homes began to have stone foundations."

I just shook my head, finding no words to respond to Peter's explanation. All I could do was grunt.

In some cases we were able to find the building that was the old synagogue in a town. Some of these old structures were empty but were identifiable by the Jewish symbolism still visible marking windows and facades. We looked for the shape of a window or the carving above a lintel, anything that would give a clue about the former use. It wasn't hard to find. Most were decrepit and in uses that ranged from warehouses to, in one case, a house with three well-appointed apartments. Peter spoke to local people and was often able to find remains of cemeteries and areas of former Jewish life.

In a few instances, the cemeteries were in good condition and were maintained by a charitable trust. We found small markers that indicated that families or organizations had donated to mark a home, business, or synagogue. Several cemeteries had been desecrated and left to decay. We were surprised these were the exception.

We wandered around a cemetery and looked at the gravestones. The grave markings were remarkable. It was an art form I hadn't seen in the cemeteries back home. There were elaborate bas-reliefs, designations of the tribes, and carvings showing occupations: lawyers, doctors, and students. There were family names that were familiar—Goldstein, Cohen, Levi, Schwartz, Zamen, Fleischman—and so many other Jewish family names. The headstone dates all ended before 1939. After that, the Germans took care of the need to record dates of the deceased and provide for orderly burial. They kept records but didn't bother about the burial details or the niceties of orderly grave markings. Mass graves didn't have headstones.

Chapter Twelve

The Road East: The First Evidence—Willie's Story

Early in the morning of June 22, 1941, the German army moved swiftly into Russia. One hundred and forty-eight divisions moved forward against a disoriented and surprised Russian army, advancing at a rate of twenty miles a day. It was an early spring morning over sixty years later that Willie drove out of Warsaw. He quickly picked up the Polish superhighway E 30 heading east and cruised the 185 km to the border of Byelorussia.

As he drove, he couldn't shake the uneasy feeling that had been with him since he'd left Treblinka. He realized that he was depressed, having walked through a site where the Nazi murders and atrocities had occurred. He realized this would not be the last time he would experience seeing a location or an incident that would disturb him. Willie started humming several old tunes to change his mood. The words and tune of "Lilli Marlene" streamed through his mind:

> Vor der Kaserne vor dem grossen Tor
> Stand eine Laterne, und stebt noch davor,
> So wolln wir uns da wiedersehn

Bei der Laterne wolln wir stehn,
Wie einst Lili Marleen, wie einst Lili Marleen.
Unsre beide Schatten sahn wie einer aus.
Dass wir so lieb uns hatten, das sah man gleich daraus
Un alle Leute solln es sehn,
Wenn wir bei der Laterne stehn,
Wie einst Lili Marleen, wie einst Lili Marleen.
[Underneath the lantern by the barrack gate,
Darling I remember the way you used to wait;
'Twas there that you whispered tenderly,
That you lov'd me, you'd always be,
My Lilli of the lamplight,
My own Lilli Marlene.
Time would come for roll call time for us to part
Darling I'd carress you and press you to my heart.
And there 'neath that far off lantern light
I'd hold you tight we'd kiss goodnight,
My Lilli of the lamplight,
My own Lilli Marlene.]

The song, although filled with nostalgia, lifted Willie's spirits, and he focused on the road ahead, crossing the Byelorussian border and entering what was Russia all those years ago.

Willie reflected on the political changes since the German invasion. In the postwar years, Soviet Russia had been monolithic, and the local states solidly subservient to their Moscow masters. The Soviet breakup in 1991 saw the reestablishment of an independent Byelorussia. Willie slowed the car and stopped to obtain a visa at the Polish border checkpoint. Crossing into Belarus, there was a perfunctory passport inspection and a mere glance into his car. The immigration officer waved him through.

Willie drove through the city of Brest and continued east. Wasn't this was the place of the Brest-Litovsk treaty? He had to research it. He knew it was significant, but what were the details? He couldn't remember; something about the end of the war in 1918 and Russia's boundaries. He was aiming to pass southeast and south of the Pripet Marshes, which were so formidable that the German generals had divided their army, one salient headed toward the north toward Moscow, and the other into Byelorussia, Ukraine, and toward the Caucasus oil fields.

The Second Panzer Division in the southern thrust, with Hans Kirchenmann, a baker, rolled with all its might into the lush, newly planted grain fields of Byelorussia. At first the resistance was light as the Russians withdrew in shock in the face of the surprise German attack. The Soviets started the process of trading land for time to equip and then fight. The Wehrmacht turned to the southeast and Ukraine, under the command of one of Hitler's favorite generals, Heinz Guderian. He was known for writing the book on the use of tanks in battle and the tactics of blitzkrieg. The army's aim was to drive to Pinsk, then on to Smolensk, eventually reaching Rostov. Papa mentioned these cities in his letters. These were the locations of the German triumphs during the first months of the sweep into Russia. From June to mid-November 1941 it had been a second blitzkrieg, just like Poland. The German army appeared unstoppable. The Russian army was crumbling.

Letter of June 25, 1941

Our unit moved into Russia in the second wave of the invasion. One of the men said that this was a day of great pride for us all. One of the officers proclaimed that we would have these Russians on their knees within sixty days. He may be right. We seem to be advancing with little effort. As support services for the fighting men, we set up quickly, prepare our meals, and serve them. We serve all the men of one division and some of the SS troops. They are assigned to clear the countryside of politically dangerous Russians. When the troops move forward, we pack our kitchens and move with them. I have seen long lines of prisoners being taken back to somewhere in our rear area.

Don't worry about me, I will return. Now we must move on. I send my love to you. Kiss my dear son Willie for me.

A letter written just four days later:

The Russians are very destructive and they try to leave nothing behind. I don't understand their barbarism. All about they live in filth, and their towns are more mud huts than real solid construction. They seem willing to torch their towns rather than let us capture them. The fields have all been burned away. It is obvious they will not let us have this year's crops. This is different from Poland. When there is fighting, we see much destruction, and our Army has many casualties. We are beating the Communist scum. Several times we have come upon villages that are totally destroyed and all that is left standing are burned-out chimneys. The fields are often littered with discarded uniforms, canteens, rifles, and other material. I will collect some souvenirs for Willie. There are shell holes that we use for the beginning of shelters where we must dig in. I do not see how the Russians can continue to fight. This all should end soon because we are taking thousands of prisoners and just continue moving deeper into Russia. I hope this is over quickly and I can come home and be with you and Willie.

Willie's first stop on this side of the border would be the city of Pinsk. His guidebook was at his side as he drove. He would stop and read that these first miles into Belarus were lands where during the last two hundred years, the ruling parties had changed many times. Russian Czars, Polish princes, and then again Russian governments had controlled these fertile fields so rich with grains of wheat, rye, and corn. Indeed, Pinsk had been Polish from 1929 to 1939, and then had been annexed into Russia from 1939 until the German invasion. Papa had mentioned this countryside. Willie read a letter from mid-August:

We are riding in open country and there are very blue skies and puffy white clouds. The good weather makes me homesick. The rolling open countryside is very beautiful. Since it is summer, it is very warm, and some of the camp discipline has been relaxed. We do not have to wear our jackets and we can open our shirt collars. There are some blessings of war. I can't tell you where we are, but we are near a city that is connected to a canal and two large rivers, south of the major marshes.

I was told we would set up camp here for several days to assist in the consolidation of this area. There is work to be done supporting the troops that stay behind the front to make sure the local population is under control. Now we are passing many small villages. Some have not been completely destroyed but are severely damaged.

There are special groups of troops that are dispatched to organize the local population. I am told there have been many deaths among the locals. This is very dirty work, and I am pleased not to have been designated to assist with these tasks. The men who are part of these units come to us to be fed. They have a different mentality from the regular troops. They are very similar in talk and swagger to the men who wanted the war, like the Brown Shirts of years ago. I try to keep my distance. They preach that our enemies are subhuman and must be totally destroyed. They take pride in being the instruments of destruction, following the instructions that come from Berlin. When they come to the camp, they are full of themselves and their extra rations of schnapps.

Along the road we saw many Russian tanks that had been put out of action by our Stuka bombers. The Stukas fly low heading to the front looking for targets. They look like eagles as they swoop down to attack. It is a contrast: the blue skies and white clouds in front of us and the black smoke from the fires left by the dive-bombers' attacks. Around us it seems peaceful, but we know that just a few miles forward of us, our men are beating the Russians back.

As Willie drove deep into Belarus, he was on straight, well-paved roads. Sixty years before, these had been narrow dirt roads poorly marked, dusty in the summer of the invasion and jammed with equipment, troop movements, and civilians fleeing the horror of war.

The spring planting was about six inches high in the fields. The wheat gave the land a golden glow as the sun reflected off the young stalks. He saw the peaceful fields but imagined the long lines of tanks moving forward, like great mechanical monsters, pushing the Russian army back, trapping and annihilating large numbers of the poorly trained and inadequately equipped Russians. Now Willie breathed the clean air as light, warm breezes wafted the aroma of the fertile land. He could almost smell the rich earth being ripped open as the treads of the large German tanks dug into the soil. He visualized their diesel engines belching black smoke into the air, their mounted guns spitting flame and destruction as they lurched forward.

As he absorbed the sights of the countryside, he realized the German army advance had slowed in 1941, as Russian resistance stiffened and the German supply lines were overextended. Willie stopped at the side of the road to eat an apple and relax from his driving. He took a letter from the pack, dated October 3, 1941.

> I haven't had mail from you for several days. I know you have written, but we have been moving and sometimes the mail doesn't arrive for days. Then I get several letters all at once. The letters lift my spirits.
>
> We are advancing following the main body of troops. The Russian retreat left the whole area desolate. The Ruskies are scum. They kill our prisoners and we have come to hate them. Hitler is right, they are subhuman beasts. What can be burned is in flames, and what can be destroyed is left in ruins. They burn the crops in the fields and in the silos, blow up the bridges, and destroy their own homes, leaving us nothing but barren ground.

For our supply battalions there is nothing to forage. The other day we came upon a farm and there was a flock of chickens left behind. That night we had a good chicken dinner for the men of our little group. I roasted the birds.

As our trucks and wagons move forward we see the fields are lined with the track ruts of our tanks. The tracks resemble the furrows of a plowed field. It is deceptive because we know war machines, not plows, left them.

The more I see of the destruction, the more I want to be home with you. Tell Willie that I am a good soldier and I follow orders. He should understand that it is our duty to serve.

Heil Hitler!!

Keep writing!

The vastness of Russia was defeating the German army. The distance between supply bases and the front lines stretched hundreds of kilometers. German fighting units ranged across the steppes, and coordination of the advance became a challenge for the generals. Supplies were delayed by poor roads and the lack of rail cars. Russian partisan activity made the rear areas dangerous, and Wehrmacht troops were diverted from the front to protect the supply lines.

Stalin had ordered a scorched-earth policy, and his army fell back, leaving the countryside barren so the Germans could not feed off the land. Now, all these years later Willie saw large fertile farms being operated as part of the new Belarus. The ground was carpeted with emerging crops of wheat and rapeseed. Scattered fields of yellow sunflowers added their splashes of vivid color to the landscape. Sixty years before, there had been a decimated peasant population. Now, there were well-organized, prosperous post-Soviet farm communities.

There were squat, one-story, one-room, brown, timber-framed houses with dirt floors that Willie associated with the "old country," pictures Papa had sent back. In envelopes in the car next to him there were pictures of these homes. Then they'd had thatched roofs. Now they had corrugated metal peaked roofs painted a dark olive brown. Willie thought these homes quaint. The vast distances in Russia were apparent to Willie as he seemed to drive and then drive farther between the small towns and villages. The driving was far more tiring than he had anticipated. How could Hitler possibly have believed he would conquer a land so vast?

Along the road, he looked up and saw that there were storks nesting on electric poles, a somnambulant pace of rural life. They were a change from the ever-present chickens scurrying about the homes. As he saw the storks, Willie smiled and mused, "There's plenty of babies to be delivered."

In Belarus there were still peasants wearing coarse cloth breeches and women in the fields in cotton print dresses and aprons. Willie looked closely for clues, but the villages Papa described were gone. In a few cases there were markers at some of the crossroads where towns formerly existed. The cast white cement markers had an uncanny uniformity; a base topped by a small obelisk or a cast metal plaque. The years had taken their toll, and some markers had started to crumble. Sixty years is a long time, especially for mass-produced commemorative stones. The base often had the name of the former town, and on some there were mounds of earth with dedication plaques. Many of the monuments had the names of the Russian army units, the battalions and the companies of men who had fought and died on this battlefield. The townspeople were gone and there was no community at the site, just a marker as an indication of a village that had been destroyed. These monuments bore no comment; they were tributes to a world long gone. At many of the markers there was litter. Empty beer bottles, scraps of food wrappers, candy packages, and cigarette butts were everywhere. He thought, "In Germany we have more respect for our memorials."

There was only one hotel in Pinsk where Willie decided to stop for a night, the Hotel Pripyat along the Bug River, a cement building about six stories high with very little allure. As he walked into the functional lobby, he noted that the hotel had seen better days. After checking in, he went to his sparse room to freshen up. Being restless, he had no desire to stay in the room and decided to walk along the river promenade in front of the hotel to get some air.

As he walked, he noticed the dilapidated walkway. The street here was littered. Empty beer bottles were scattered about; crumpled cement and cracked paint gave the impression that no one cared. Along the river wall there was the distinct odor of urine. At the end of the walkway was a small amusement park with a carousel and several children's rides. The stroll wasn't satisfying and he turned and walked back to his car.

There were several hours of daylight left in the afternoon, so he decided to take a drive along the canal and the river. The canal also was in poor shape. The bulkheads along the side of the water showed a deterioration, and Willie recognized signs of severe decay and neglect.

He again mused, "This isn't the way we would maintain our public facilities. Our cultures seem to be very different. The mindset of the last sixty years seems to build things and let them crumble. Why don't they put people to work painting, cleaning, and picking up the litter? We Germans wouldn't let things go this way."

His guidebook mentioned "the Great Pinsk Canal" had been in construction from 1775 to 1848, connecting the Bug to the Vistula River. Barge traffic and crops, as well as commercial goods, could reach the Baltic, making Pinsk a center of commerce for many years. Along the river, about five kilometers from the hotel, amid a beautiful and peaceful landscape, Willie entered a nature preserve that bordered the marshes. He stopped to read a stone monument. It was about four feet high, with a black plaque written in Russian on the front plate and a second white marble inscription just below. The writing on the second plaque was in several languages. Willie needed someone to translate.

A family consisting of a father, mother, and two young children were picnicking nearby at the river. Willie strode over and asked if anyone spoke German. The father said he did, and Willie asked, "Can you translate the inscription on the monument for me?"

The man left his family under the tree and walked with Willie. The engraving seemed to be in three languages: Russian, Hebrew, and Polish. The man started to explain: "This is a war memorial. It is a marker that notes where one of the massacres of Jews took place. It says: 'It was here on the nights of August 6–8, 1942, that 3,468 Jewish women and children were forced into the river to drown by troops of the German army.' "

Willie was shocked at hearing about the massacre and the subhuman execution method used by the Nazis.

"Did you know this was the area where the Einsatzgruppen of the SS were active in 1941?" the man asked.

"No!" Willie quickly shook his head in denial.

"The Einsatzgruppen were select killers. There were only a few battalions of them, but they swept through these areas behind the advancing army and systematically—with the help of the SS, the regular army, and local thugs—slaughtered Jewish communities. In addition, they killed a few of the Russian party faithful, but their mission was to make these areas Judenfrei."

Willie winced and stepped back, only to find the top half of his body leaning forward to hear more.

The man continued, looking directly at Willie: "When the Germans first captured Pinsk, there had been a mass shooting of the local Jewish men. A month later the Einsatzgruppen and Himmler wanted the women and children disposed of."

Willie felt uncomfortable and his heart seemed to skip a beat.

The man continued. "The German commandant had been ordered by Himmler to kill the women and children that hadn't been slaughtered but not to waste ammunition on them. They were to be taken to the marsh area to drown. This little area was set aside as a memorial to those people."

Willie was shocked. He felt bile rise in his throat, and his first reaction was silence, but he had to say something. "Oh, my God. I had no idea," Willie replied.

The man stepped back from the marker. "It was an SS operation assisted by the Wehrmacht."

"My father was Wehrmacht."

"It could have been him assisting the SS."

"But he was a baker!" Willie recoiled from the thought. He didn't want to contemplate his father being part of this action.

The man shrugged his shoulders. "I am a local engineer. My name is Egon, and I'm a native Russian." He extended his hand to Willie and smiled. "You must be German."

Willie felt the strong grip and warm, vigorous handshake. Egon was a stocky man about a head shorter than Willie. He seemed eager to have Willie come and meet his wife and children. The family was seated on a yellow-and-rose-colored picnic blanket. The grass field around them was filled with yellow and red poppies, with the sweet aroma of honey hanging in the spring air. There was an underlying smell of marsh marigolds, and the sound of crickets resounded from the river bank. Around the field there was a variety of maple, oak, and poplar trees that gave the area a pleasant amount of shade and yet created an open site. It was perfect for the picnic that Egon and his family were enjoying.

"This is my wife," Egon said. "Her name is Rakel."

She was a petite brunette who must have weighed half of Egon's 200-plus pounds. She sat with her legs tucked under her at the side of the picnic blanket. Her dark hair and blue eyes highlighted her slim face. As Egon introduced her, she smiled and nodded. Rakel wore a light print cotton dress, her feet were bare, and the sandals she had worn were off to the side of the picnic basket, between the blanket and a large willow tree. Egon offered to share some of their picnic, and Willie accepted a glass of white wine poured into a clear white glass. He was quite content to sit with the family. They reminded him of his son and his grandchildren. This was a pleasant change from driving.

The engineer leaned back against the tree, relaxed with his feet extended. His wine was cradled in both hands in his lap. Speaking almost into the air, he reflected: "I was trained in what was East Germany, before the unification. I was able to get a good engineering education. I now work for the Belarus state, as a specialist in water purification. I was living here in 1991 when Belarus became independent and I stayed on."

"Tell me about this area." Willie asked.

"As you may know, this was part of Poland, then part of Russia and independent during the two hundred years before that. We were in the middle of the civil war of the twenties. It was a battlefield that was fought over, changed hands, and changed hands again. Just about none of us living here can trace our origins to the people living here before the war. My family was originally from Moscow, and Rakel came from what is now Germany. She thinks her family roots are near Dresden. But who knows, it all got scrambled during the war. Her family was one of the ethnic Germans, *volksdeutsche,* who were resettled by the Nazis when they conquered the country, ceded eastern areas to the Russians, and settled Germans in the west. They were part of the Germanization of western Poland. I met her while I was at school, and we fell in love. She was studying nursing, and we lived in East Germany for the first years of our marriage. Then it all came apart when your country was reunited in 1990 and the USSR broke up a year later. We moved here because there was work for both of us. Now she is employed at one of the Pinsk hospitals. And as I said, I work in water purification."

Willie enjoyed watching the children play, skimming stones across the clear water and into the marsh. The scene reminded him of the picnics he and Hanna used to have when the children were young. He reminisced about how precious these moments were.

He was haunted by the image of Jewish women and children being forced into the marsh. He wondered how they were dressed, if the children were quiet, if there was hysteria—what was it like? What a nightmare. Were they praying, screaming? Willie's mind went back to the monument, and he asked: "Is there more to tell about the story of the memorial?"

Egon thought a moment: "It all depends upon how much you want to know. If you look about this area, you will find many monuments. This area was a mass execution ground."

Willie was interested in what Egon was saying but knew he was hearing something that polite Germans of the last sixty years didn't talk about. He wanted Egon to continue.

"Yes, I want to know what really happened."

Egon continued, "Well, before the war, out of the 130,000 citizens of Pinsk, there were 30,000 Jews. After the war there weren't more than a handful of the Jews alive. It was a community totally destroyed. As I said, at first the Germans killed all the men between the ages of sixteen and sixty. About 11,000 were killed in just ten days in 1941. The other Jews, about 20,000 of them, were concentrated into one section of town. This was done with just two companies of German troops. Then, about a year later, as the marker states, they tried to march all the women and children into the marsh. As fate would have it, the water level of the marsh was too low, and many survived, only to be rounded up and eventually killed in Dobrovolie, a nearby village. By then the Einsatzgruppen were more sophisticated and organized. Bullets were expensive for use on Jews, so they used portable trucks as carbon monoxide gas killing chambers. If you look, all through Pinsk you'll see markers like that one, and monuments."

Egon's explanation was more than Willie had expected. He was sorry he had asked the question. He was numb and couldn't speak or react. Egon went on. "I know you are German, so this must be difficult for you to hear, but you must realize that there were a few survivors, and they have kept the memory of the murdered Jews alive. The Russians built monuments for their soldiers and for civilians regardless of whether they were Jews or not. The Soviets were generous with their memorials, but they didn't distinguish between a Jew who was murdered and anyone else, although the Jews were the primary targets. After 1991 here in Belarus and in Ukraine, you will see specific memorials for murdered Jewish people.

"In Pinsk there is a large monument. Several of the few survivors reached Israel and were successful. They paid for the memorial to their past, and to those who died. In one of those tricks of fate, some of the Jews who survived had been deported to Siberia during the 1939–41 period, when Russia had control of the area. Stalin considered many of these people 'activists,' and he wanted them out of the way, so he sent them to the east as laborers. Their exile saved their lives. Some of the surviving men fought valiantly in the Russian army during the war."

Rakel, speaking in Russian, interrupted Egon and he smiled and looked at Willie: "She says I talk too much and shouldn't belabor the war to a German. She doesn't think you are interested, but if you have come, you should hear the stories. After the war, a few of the Jews who were alive returned and found nothing, and indeed some of the returning Jews were mistreated by the local people, so they left. Many went to Israel or the United States. You know they say, 'Europe is a ghetto, England is a haven, America is the Promised Land.' I guess that Promised Land applies to Israel too. They come back, always with their children, and see that cemeteries and memorials are maintained in good condition. In memory of their people, they erected many of the monuments you will see."

"Who were the German army killers—SS troops or Wehrmacht?"

"Some of the killers were local people. The SS encouraged them, and it didn't take much for them to take up the challenge of running their own pogrom. But after the first shots, the SS took over, and certainly the Wehrmacht helped by supporting the troops of killers."

"Do you know who the Germans were?"

"The German deputy commissioner in charge of the area was a fellow from Stuttgart named Abner Ebner, who with about seven other SS was tried about eight years after the war for the mass murder of between 20,000 and 30,000 Jews. He was never convicted because he claimed 'pseudo-dementia.' "

"And the others?"

"They all got a few years in jail. Their defense was that they were following orders."

Willie thought of his postwar days. As a struggling young man, he'd paid very little attention to any of the trials or comments reported in the newspapers. His stomach churned and he felt remorse for these victims. Could something have been done for the survivors to show humanitarian concern? Was he guilty of neglect as a concerned human? Could he have done something? He turned to Egon: "You have been most informative. I had no knowledge of these events."

"If you are interested, you should visit a small village near here named Rubel. A millstone serves as a marker for the mass grave of the men from that town. In this case the Belarus locals joined in that memorial because they were aware that Byelorussia suffered more than any other country under Nazi occupation. By the end of the war, 2.2 million—Jewish and gentile—civilians were dead. This was over twenty percent of the population, and thirty percent of the people were homeless."

The conversation with Egon was sobering, and Willie now felt ashamed. After finishing his wine, he thanked Egon and Rakel for their hospitality, commented on how well behaved their children were, and left.

As Willie started his car, he realized that this was the first time he'd associated any of what he knew was the destruction of the Jewish communities, the horrors of the Nazis, and his father's possible involvement. It hadn't occurred to him that Papa might have participated in the destruction or the murders. Treblinka and this were remote from his father. Weren't they? After all, Papa had been a baker. Now in Russia, what had been his father's role? What had Papa known? He couldn't get the mental picture of the women and children being forced into the marsh out of his mind.

More and more, Willie started to dwell on the thought that while his father wrote of what he saw, there was much that was not in the letters. Where was Papa during all of this horror?

Chapter Thirteen

A Turn of Fortune: Now It Is the Eastern Front—Willie's Story Continues

The time between letters from Papa increased, and by mid-1942 the tone of the mail to Mama had changed. The optimism of the early letters describing quick victories and coming home disappeared and there was no mention of progress or conquest. There was no mention of rolling forward. There were no pictures of smiling soldiers acting as tourists. There were a few pictures of a much thinner father, often unshaven and with the deep circles of fatigue under his eyes. The backgrounds for these pictures were destroyed Russian equipment, and in a few cases town squares with little identification. Papa offered little description of the events around him. He was holding back information. There was no mention of coming home, just reassurances of well-being and prayers. The German army was overextended and felt the might of the stiffened Russian defense. Papa's letters reflected the changes in the war:

> Please write often. The mail gets delayed and there are many days I do not hear from you. When I don't get mail I feel depressed. I understand there have been bombings of some

of the cities. Has Stuttgart been bombed? We hear that many German cities are coming under attack. They don't give us all the news. Please write often so I know you are safe. Things have changed. We are not advancing as we did in the past months. There have been some large battles and we no longer stay in one place for long. In some of the battles we did not do as well as our generals had expected and we are no longer advancing. I have been promoted to obergrenadier gefreiter [corporal] and transferred. No longer am I a cook and baker. I must do my duty in the front lines. I am a Landser [infantryman]. Do not worry; I will come home to you.

And so it had happened. Papa was no longer a support for the army; he was a fighting man. The innocent and gentle Hans Kirchenmann was now in the front lines. In the soldbuch Hans carried, there would be an entry with the promotion date and the increase in pay and benefits. There would be a second notation of the transfer of duties. Papa was now being exposed to maximum danger. He was one of the millions deployed along the long German/Russian front stretching from Leningrad to the Caucasus; from the freezing North to the semi-tropic Odessa area. His father must have been a replacement pulled from the rear echelons and thrown into the battle line to face the Russians. He was one more man knowing that he was to shoot or be shot, to kill or be killed. The German army had been running short of manpower, and Papa had been fed into the battle so the army could continue to fight. Hans was now an infantryman. Infantry was "the Queen of Battle." The army was manpower, men, men, men!

Willie remembered that when the news came over the radio in the spring of 1942 describing a battle with millions engaged in the fighting, Mama felt certain that Papa could have been committed to the front. A late September letter heralded the horrors of bad weather that would become a nightmare for the army:

> The weather suddenly changed and almost overnight we have winter. The temperature changed from pleasant autumn to minus thirty degrees of frost and then to a heavy snowfall. In the morning the wind came from the north, but the sky was cloudless and filled with brilliant sunlight. But the sun seemed to have lost its strength. I have never been so cold. We all long for the summer heat. This cold has slowed our progress. We wait for winter uniforms, which we are told will come. In order to stay warm, we wear many layers of clothing. Our boots aren't made for the cold and we must insulate them with items we pick up from the burned-out homes in the villages. Some of the soldiers take the boots of captured Russians. One fellow took a good pair from the body of a dead Russian officer. Some of the men have found ladies' fur wraps and wear them under their jackets. I found a long fur overcoat, and I wear it under my issued greatcoat and use it at night to keep warm. If you can, send me leather gloves with wool linings. The size should be extra large. Horst, my friend from Stuttgart, was killed in an action three days ago. He was buried in a new cemetery near where we fought. I was part of the burial party and I kept thinking of how much we love our homeland. I think of you every day and can't go to sleep without looking at the picture of you and Willie I carry at all times. Please tell Willie I love him so much.

Then, in the stack of letters was the note that had brought joy to Mama and Willie. Willie remembered the mid-November letter and how Mama had shouted her happiness when she'd opened the envelope:

> I will be home for Christmas. We have been in some heavy battles, and the officers told me that our unit will be relieved from the fighting area in early December and after some rest in a back area we will be able to get transport back to Germany. I should be with you by the 20th, in time for the holidays. I think I'll be home for three weeks. Our area now has Romanian troops relieving us and some other European troops serving around us in support of our activities. Also, there are many work battalions doing the cooking and maintenance, allowing us to man the front and show our determination to succeed. Some of these support troops are Ukrainians who have joined our army.
>
> The package with good cigarette paper and tobacco came in good shape and I shared it with my buddies. The sausages were appreciated and a great change from our army diet.
>
> I am writing this wearing the woolen gloves you sent. They are under my army issued pair. It gets very cold at night, and the snow is very deep. We whitewash our helmets and use white sheets that we have taken from some of the abandoned homes as camouflage cover for our uniforms, so we blend into the snow. One of my friends, Alex, went out without his woolen 'Kofschutzer' and suffered from frostbite of his ears. It took a great bit of careful massaging to thaw him out. We hope we saved the ears. There are times that because of the cold and the snow

we find ourselves looking for a hole to climb into and stay warm. It would be nice to be home and in our bed.

My hearty greetings and Sieg Heil.

Papa had his last leave home during Christmas 1942. It was after the defeat at Stalingrad, and Willie now understood from the letters that the mild-mannered baker who'd gone to war five years before had become a battle-hardened soldier. The battlefront was home to Papa. The German army had been decimated, and able-bodied younger men were transferred from support troops to be front-line soldiers. Troops from satellite allies, Hungary and Romania, had taken over large segments of the southern front, and the work battalions Papa mentioned were forced laborers from the captured Russian and Polish areas and men who had switched sides thinking the Germans would win the war.

When Papa arrived home on leave, he was much thinner than Willie remembered. His face was tanned and lined from being outdoors, and there was a cast of sadness in his eyes. Mama greeted him at the door and gave him an embrace that Willie remembered as being very long. He still recalled the two clutching each other, silhouetted by the light coming through the front door. Then Mama sent Papa upstairs to take a bath and shed the uniform, and she closed the bakery for the afternoon. Willie was sent to play at Aunt Hanna's. Mama went upstairs to join Papa. Father was home for three weeks, and he didn't talk about the war to Willie, but he would sit in the old overstuffed easy chair by the fireplace, hold his son for long precious moments, and sing lullabies. The smell and warmth of the fire log and the tuff of the deep brown mohair upholstery as it scratched Willie's leg remained in his memory.

Willie remembered squirming and saying that he was too old "to be held that way." He would get off Papa's lap, sit on the floor, and ask about the army. Papa would light a cigarette, look at Willie, and smile but never really answer the question. Papa and Mama were spending long hours of the afternoons with each other, often locked in their room. Papa would seem melancholy as they sat and had a drink before dinner; Mama would come to the dining area in good humor.

While on leave, Papa visited his uncles and his brothers. Willie and Mama would come along and watch as the men sat, drank beer, and spoke of war and peace, government, life, and then their families. It was his uncle, the veteran from the previous war, who took Papa aside. Willie overheard the older man ask, "What is it like? We hear things that aren't good. We hear about harsh army discipline, the panzers being a separate force and the SS doing things to civilians. We hear strange rumors about shootings, even of our own people. Is this true?" Papa didn't answer. Willie saw him shrug his shoulders, take a long pull on his cigarette, and lift his beer glass. Papa hugged his uncle and walked out of the room to eat. At the dinner table the men seemed to try to avoid talking about the war.

Then his leave was over. It was much too soon for Willie. Just as he'd started to get accustomed to Papa's warm hand on his shoulder as he was doing his schoolwork and the long hug Papa gave him when it was time for him to go to bed, his father was leaving.

Mama and Willie walked Papa to the train station. There was the embrace and the last kiss blown to Mama. Willie saw the train receding from the city as it left the Bahnhaus returning one soldier to his army.

There was a lapse of a month between the letter written by Papa on the train as he returned to his unit and the next note Willie had in the stack he carried on his trip. Papa must have arrived back and had been immediately sent into battle. From the ominous tone of the text, it was apparent that Hans knew the odds that faced him.

> It is with dread I arrived back in Russia. I can't see the end of this battle, and I know that I've been lucky so far. I must do my duty, but I also must try to preserve myself so I can return to you. My best friend Luther was killed two days ago, just before I arrived in camp. I will write a letter to his mother and father and tell them that he was a good soldier and followed orders to the end. It is a shame that loyalty has such a high price. This war has become vicious. We see men kill out of sheer desperation. I have learned the sad lesson that there is no mercy in battle, and the hate we generate continues after each fight. More and more I need your letters to give me something to be cheerful about.

The next letter in the pack of was dated four weeks later. Willie presumed that some of Papa's letters had gone astray or Mama had been disturbed by their contents and hadn't saved them. Papa had been in action:

> It would be nice to get into a clean uniform. You would not like how I smell after a few weeks without a bath and often days without a chance to wash up. We often go weeks before we get back to a base where we clean up, bathe, and get clean uniforms. Luckily the army has conscripted local people to do the work of washing our clothes. We do not have to do this work—we

just rest and recondition our equipment so we can get back to the front. It is amusing that I did not get a chance to shave for fifteen days and I came back to the rear with a beard. I have a lot of gray hair.

Then there was an almost embarrassing passage that showed Papa's depth of love and loneliness, and the impact of war was evident:

I am writing from a bunker. If my penmanship is poor, forgive me. It is night and I write using a small candle to see the paper. It is very cold and I often lie awake thinking of you and our love. I remember the moment of awakening before you when I was home, watching you sleep and seeing you in the first light of the dawn coming through the window. How beautiful you are. Your profile silhouetted against the dim light and the faint smile on your face. Were you dreaming of how we made love? How we started making love so gently after you came into the room from your bath, almost teasing while we both wanted to please each other, not worrying about our own satisfaction, then abandoning our inhibitions and letting our passion fill the night. How we kissed each other, never getting enough. How we held together for all that time, loving and not wanting to let go, and then letting each other become fulfilled and falling to sleep in each other's arms. Yes, I dream of those moments and hold them close in my memory. Sometimes I think they are all I have. They are moments that warm me despite the war and destruction that surround me. I want to come home to your arms, our bed, and our life.

With all that I am seeing, will I be the same man who left you five years ago? We are dug in across from a field of birch crosses, many with shattered helmets or the caps the tanker men wear resting on the cross top. Many of my friends and comrades are in that field. I must put these thoughts out of my mind and think of the good, sweet love we have.

Willie followed the path of the units where his father had been assigned. He crossed the border from Belarus into Ukraine and drove east toward Kharkov. It was difficult for Willie to match some of Papa's travels with events in the guidebooks. Because of losses and troop movements, the army unit designation would often change, and the commanders were often reassigned. Papa was often reassigned along with other Landsers when platoons or companies of men were depleted. The surviving members of the company would be joined with another remnant, and a new fighting unit would come into being. It was hard to match the guidebook, the history of the German army units that Willie was reading, and Papa's letters. The companies and battalions were shifted from Belarus to deep in Ukraine, and some even to the far north near Leningrad. The unit numbers changed as battle casualties decimated whole groups and the survivors were consolidated into other divisions. Replacements, both veterans and fresh young troops, were shifted along the long battle line. Papa's letters only told of staying in Ukraine. There was a letter from August 1943:

There has been a major battle near Kursk, and I was in it. I don't know if it has been fully reported at home. We were in the fourth line of defense, and the Russians penetrated right to our positions. We were not overrun, although the lines in front of us were. There were many casualties. I have never seen so many tanks, theirs and ours all in the field at once. The sounds were deafening, the smoke and mud unbearable. We killed many Russians, but they managed to push us back. They just seemed to throw men and tanks into the battle. There was no end to the number of men they sent to be killed. I was frightened, but I stayed at my post. The battle raged for about 20 days, and it was a rare day we were able to get a hot meal. At the end, a Hungarian army division relieved us and I'm safe in a rest area, cleaning up and getting fresh uniforms. I am proud to have been brave. There were two of your letters waiting for me when we came to the rest area. The picture of Willie was great. He is growing so fast. What a handsome boy we have!

With continued faith in Hitler and the love of the fatherland. I remain your loving husband.

Willie visited the Kursk battlefield and stopped at the Peter and Paul Cathedral and the bell-tower commemorating the Soviet victory on the Field of Prokhorovka. The hills upon which the church and the nearby tower were constructed gave him a commanding view of part of the huge battle area. He imagined the enormous battle scale as he wandered around the nearby countryside. The guidebook said: "In this battle, more tanks were engaged than in any previous battle. The Russians had over 1,300,000 men, 3,600 tanks, 20,000 artillery pieces, and 2,400 aircraft. The Germans had a slightly smaller force of 900,000 men, 2,700 tanks, and 2,000 aircraft. The battle started in July of 1943 and raged for six weeks. In those weeks the German Army lost over 100,000 killed and wounded."

As this battle ended, about four hundred kilometers to the south the last battle for Kharkov started. After these encounters and defeats, the German army would fight defensively all the way back to the Fatherland. The Kursk battle consumed much of the remains of the formerly crack German army. Whole groups, regiments, and battalions were annihilated as the German army started its withdrawal to the west. The book of World War II German army history and old guidebooks related that Kharkov changed hands three times. The Kursk salient and Kharkov were the farthest the German army penetrated into southern Russia. Kharkov, Stalingrad, and Kursk represented massive reverses for the Wehrmacht. The German army was operating beyond its supply capability and did not have the manpower to sustain the breadth of the war. There were battles where entire groups of divisions had been defeated, annihilated, and or captured. There were no replacements for these losses. Stalingrad had cost the entire Sixth Army; a total of over 400,000 Germans along with 450,000 Italians, Romanians, and Hungarians who were assigned to the German army.

From an army that had been well equipped and well trained at the beginning of the invasion and had been able to drive over one thousand miles into Russia to the Volga River, the remains of that war machine was in a battered state and started its inevitable retreat.

Willie looked around and felt the weight of history. As unsympathetic as he felt toward the Nazi cause, he could feel the sting of reading about the German losses and seeing these killing fields where hundreds of thousands of good men had died. The Germans who fought were his countrymen, just like his father. These were men who had left their homes as honest civilians, trained and committed to battle, and were now a beaten army. He could understand how a German soldier would not feel shame for fighting a brave fight. But, oh, the losses. Oh, the men who would not come home. Oh, the maimed. Oh, the futility. Willie felt exhausted by the weight of his thoughts as he trudged from his vantage point back to his car and drove on.

In the beginning, there had been no censorship. Now, after the reverses of Stalingrad and Kursk, Papa's letters were more guarded, and portions were blacked out. When the letters told of Papa being in the vicinity of Kharkov, it was late August 1943:

> I often stand at my post thinking of you and Willie. I have been in several major battles and I have seen events I cannot put into words. The sound of the artillery is terrifying. The sight of enemy tanks followed by hordes of their soldiers makes my heart stop, and I just pray to get it over with and to come out of the fight alive. When the shelling starts, we hide in our holes. There are times when we stay in our bunkers for many hours, cramped and cold. When there is action, the moments seem to last for hours and hours, and when it is over we realize that only twenty or thirty minutes have passed. The battle experience is exhilarating but frightening, and maddening. Life takes on a special dimension. The sounds and smells are beyond anything I have ever experienced or can describe. I get sick from the gunpowder odor, and the smoke of the battle blinds my eyes. The sight of dead and wounded makes me ill. Yesterday a man in my bunker was killed. He was standing beside me, and when I turned I saw he was shot. I often think, 'Why him, not me?' I have become a fatalist. If something happens to me, it will just

happen. I want to get through all of this and see you again. You are in my mind throughout each day and night.

As Willie drove through the Ukrainian forests, he saw women sitting by the side of the road on wooden stools or perched on a few logs piled on end. They seemed old, even older than Willie. In front of them there would be bottles or boxes of berries for sale. Several times Willie stopped and purchased some succulent and freshly picked blueberries or blackberries. The women's heads were always covered with babushkas; their wrinkled, aged skin made Willie sympathetic, and he didn't bargain, paying the few kopeks they wanted. Willie would prop the bottle of berries on the seat next to him and munch as he drove. It made for a pleasant feeling, and again he would start to hum one of the old songs he recalled his father singing. His mind turned to a letter he read before starting his daily drive:

We are entrenched in a cemetery on top of a hill. I have a rash, and the itch is making me very uncomfortable. Many of the other men have a similar condition. We think it is from the lice and the bad water we get to wash with. Fighting is in the valley below. We have been here for almost a week and I'm sure we will get the order to move from this protected location. I don't know if they will ask us to go forward or move to the rear. As I write, above me are about twelve German bombers diving to attack a Russian position about three miles to our north. The Russians have several fighters trying to shoot down the bombers. There is a lot of smoke, flame, and sound coming from that part of our front. The cemetery is a quiet zone, and there are chickens in the smoking village to our rear. We know there are eggs there, and one of our men will go over and get some for us this evening. I have become very good at mixing our rations with the items we are able to find, like the eggs, the chickens, or the horsemeat. It all helps.

At several vantage points along the road, Willie would stop to observe the landscape. Using his field glasses, he would observe the battlefields and imagine where Papa might have been. He trembled, thinking of the fears his father must have faced sixty-five years ago. Willie surveyed the scene and heaved a huge sigh. He'd read about the battles around Kharkov and tried to envision each encounter. The city had been captured by the Germans in October 1941 and had changed hands two times, until August 1943, when the Soviets finally liberated the city. It was the location of the last successful German offensive. The final German loss of the city was credited to the defeats at Stalingrad to the south, the Kursk battle to the north, and the resulting lack of German reserves to commit to the battles. Willie found the landmarks and telltale monuments marking the battle areas. He would compare these with his guidebook's battle description. This was as far as the German army had penetrated into Russia. He had come as far to the east as the letters indicated Papa had traveled. He knew his father was there. Willie then turned his Audi to the west and tried to follow the long road back to the area where the last letter, of January 1945, was written:

Many horrible things happen in war. The Russian prisoners all seem so thin. The Soviets send us pamphlets saying how "blessed" it is to be in Soviet Russia. We don't think this is so. The prisoners all look like imbeciles, and the few cities we see are poor and hardly near any standard we would live in. This is no paradise. The SS are very rough on the prisoners. I'm seeing things I will never forget. We have Waffen SS companies attached to our battalion. These are selected men, and they are very tough. In both battle and when we are at rest, they are stiff and formal doing their duty and making us stay loyal to the fatherland and our mission. Some of these men were in the Deutsches Jungvolk and then Hitler Youth and the labor service before joining the SS. They are dedicated party members. We are afraid of them and their attitudes. General von Manstein has urged that we "have understanding of the necessity of a severe but just revenge on subhuman Jews." The Waffen SS take this as an order to be extreme when we meet Partisans or peasants they believe to be Jews. I cannot turn my head and say I do not want to be a part of this. When they point to me, I must participate in some of their vicious acts. My duty to this Army is to be a soldier and follow orders. Someday I will make a personal peace, and perhaps admit to myself that I was a participant. I am no longer the man who left home in 1938. I long to come back home and have you restore me to those days of love and peace.

Heil Hitler. May we bring pride and prosperity to our great fatherland.

In his drive along the formerly battle-scarred roads, Willie imagined the massive army movements. He would seek a vantage point, stop, take his binoculars from the car, and survey the landscape. The generally flat areas would have a hillock that would provide some vantage, and Willie would look around and visualize the sights of tanks, men, and machines of battle and think of Papa. He would stop at a crossroad town, go into the local store or tavern, and have a drink. Some of the small towns had well-stocked modern food stores, so he would purchase lunch and take it to the car, drive, stop, and eat along the road. His little picnic would be in the shade of one of the tall cypress trees that marked the verge between the road and the beginning of the fields. His companionship for the lunch would be the butterflies, bees, and birds doing their job of pollinating and nurturing the black fertile earth. In some towns there would often be a market of farmers' booths selling local produce. In these he would ask where he was, although he knew, just to try to have the people engage in conversation. Several times he would find someone who spoke a little German and they would try to manage a conversation. Too many times he tried to find a town mentioned in his father's letters that was on his map, only to be told that the town no longer existed.

Willie would get in his car and drive some more. The roads in Ukraine varied from rutted country lanes to modern multi-lane superhighways. The secondary roads that he traveled were often long and straight. The forests were thick on the sides of the road, and visibility into the woods seemed to be limited to ten meters or less. The forests were dark, with the pine trees standing in tight proximity to each other and reaching thirty meters into the air, obliterating light from the needle- and cone-covered ground. Again and again Willie would think of the haven these woods gave the partisans harassing the Wehrmacht behind the German lines. He thought of Papa contending with the realization that even in the rear areas the German army couldn't feel secure. Where the forest ended, there often would be large tracts of wheat fields and grass sown for cattle. It was this difference between the dark woodland and the open tank country that intrigued Willie. This was a land of contrasts, the dark forest and open fields, the summers of extreme heat and winters of nasty cold, the hard road of summer, the deep snow of winter, and the mud of spring and autumn. Willie recognized the challenge the army had faced.

The German army hadn't had a training manual that described how to manage a withdrawal. The officers and men in the front lines became self-taught. Hitler proclaimed "no retreat." Berlin commanded the men to fight and hold their ground. To those in the front line this often meant a death sentence or at best a series of narrow escapes as holding actions became the order of the day. The life of a Landser became a firefight, falling back, regrouping, a little rest, a shower, a fresh uniform, and back into battle. There were just a few pauses to bury the men who had become brothers bonding together since Poland. There was a silent discipline grounded in the knowledge of your fellow soldier's capabilities, trusting those men who had been together since the beginning of the war. There was a quiet unspoken suspicion of those fanatics who still had hope.

> We pause to bury some of our comrades. Even when the ground is frozen, we dig a proper grave. In the burial service they said, "These men live immortally in that spirit which shapes a common spirit of our nation." That is a very high minded thought I cannot share. I feel all this is very futile. I have been designated as the one to write to the families of the men we lose. I always say something nice and tell how brave the man was. I hope you never receive a letter like the ones I have written. Of the 30 men who were with me when we left Poland, we are only nine remaining. Others have joined us; I hardly know some of their

names. Some are very young. Some of these new men come to us with thoughts that this war can still be a great victory. We older veterans just hope for a peace with the Americans and English and their joining us to fight these communists.

Willie felt a sadness following the steps of the defeated army as he headed west. He thought of the moral corruption of the Hitler years as he drove, thinking about the Nazi rise and fall and the lies told the German people. He tried to distance his mature mind from the hate that was preached in the schools he'd attended as a child. He thought of his life with Mama during the war and contrasted it to what he now realized was the desperate existence of the battle-hardened soldiers.

For Hans Kirchenmann at the front, it would be two years of falling back from the farthest advance to someplace on the Vistula, the scene of the last letter. For Willie, sixty years later, there was the growing feeling that this road was leading him to an unknown place. He also started to realize the possible frustration of not finding anything of the last days or hours of Papa's life. Perhaps he would come home with only the letters and the memories of this long drive. He would never be able to close the book on Papa's life.

There are times I am shaken by what I have seen. Blood rushes from my head and I know that experiences I have had and what I have witnessed will haunt me and lie heavily on my soul all my life. I have had to kill men. This is resting on my soul, but this is war. Sometimes we do not like the orders we receive, but we must obey. It is strange to write to you in a letter about this, but they say confession is good for the soul. I don't write these experiences to you because I do not want you to worry. However, you must realize that I must talk to someone about this war, and as time goes on, there are fewer and fewer of the men who started with me in Poland. I can't trust everyone here; there are too many who still unquestionably accept the brutal idea that might makes right. I have learned the hard way that this isn't true. I hope you can bring Willie to these moral beliefs. You have my love and every waking thought while I am in this great fight to survive.

Chapter Fourteen

Second Day on the Road: An Old Man's Story—George's Journey Continues

Our touring was at a reasonable pace, and Peter made no effort to hurry along. I wanted to spend more time and delve into the history at each site we were visiting and find witnesses or someone who could tell the story of the area's Jews. During our first day we found no one. It was just the two of us; Peter's narratives and the guidebooks. I was fully absorbed in the lessons of Jewish Poland. The cemeteries were the textbooks; the road markers and monuments were the chapter headings. As the afternoon wore on, I began to wonder where we would spend the night. Peter seemed to be in full command and found a bed-and-breakfast in Antonio, a little town about fifteen miles from Radom. It was about seven in the evening and Peter stopped the car in front of a home that looked as if it was an old manor house. At first I thought we had stopped for a necessary break to have a coffee and to refresh ourselves. "I know the owners," he said. "I'll see if we can spend the night here."

He was back in a minute with a smile and said, "OK, we'll stop here. They have two good rooms and the price is very reasonable."

Indeed, we had comfortable accommodations and a light dinner hosted by the proprietor, who turned out to be Peter's distant cousin. I laughed at the "coincidence" of his choice, but the hospitality relaxed me. At dinner there was no discussion of the reasons for my trip. The host seemed to accept that I was in Peter's care, and if we wanted to say something about my travels we would. The conversations between Peter and the host were in Polish, and Peter would turn to me from time to time and update me on what was being said. I relaxed with a bottle of beer.

In the morning we dressed and were on the road before breakfast. We looked around for a café near the center of the village and found a suitable place at a crossroad where we would be turning toward Ozarow.

We entered and ordered breakfast, to be served outside at a pleasant round table that had an enormous umbrella for shade inscribed "Browar Kormoran," which I took for the name of a local beer. Peter confirmed my assumption, and with a laugh said, "It's a little early for that beer, let's stick to coffee."

There was an old man sitting outside the café about ten feet from our table. He wore a yarmulke skullcap, an unusual sight in Poland. I reckoned that he was about eighty-five years old and not in great health. Although the spring weather was quite pleasant, he was bundled in two worn coats and at least one old knitted sweater. You could see the fringes of a tallis escaping from above his belt line and draped outside his oversized pants. He was bald under the yarmulke, and the hair on his head formed a halo of wispy gray that was shaped like a horseshoe framing his scruffily bearded face.

I decided I wanted to try to speak to him, and got up from our table and walked over.

In Yiddish, I asked, "Are you a Jew?"

"Ya, ich been a yid." [Yes, I'm a Jew.]

"Redden English?"

"A little."

I told him why we were there, seeking the stories of Jewish life and heading to Ozarow. He shook his head as he spoke: "You will not find many Jews here or any in Ozarow."

I asked, "What are you doing here?"

He heaved a deep sigh and spread his hands outward, palms up. "I had no place to go after the war and I lived here as a young man. My sister had married a Christian Pole, so I came back to find her. She was alive, but her husband had been killed, so I stayed with her. She died two years ago and I'm too old to move on."

"Tell me about life before the war."

"We had a great life. We lived in peace in a small village. My mother had inherited a home on the river's edge, the Vistula. The river divided our town, with the Jews living on one side and the *goyim* [non-Jews] living on the other. We were told as children not to cross the river, but to stay on our side. Our parents were strict about keeping us in sight. They were afraid we would be kidnapped and taken into the army. That was just one of their worries. Our house had a straw roof and mud walls. The floor was dirt, but it had been trampled flat and hard by many years of living. We had enough money to afford a woven mat that covered much of the floor. The house had only two rooms separated by a curtain, with one window. One room was used for eating by day and sleeping quarters for Grandma at night. The other room was where my father, mother, sister, brother, and I slept. I shared a bed with my brother and sister until she was about twelve and my mother then started to make a new cot for her. It was the room where I was born. The stove consisted of a makeshift fireplace where a large part of our daily activity was to keep the fire going all day. The stove was our heat and source for cooking. Because of a poor flue we were always black with soot, and the chimney often caught fire. When the fire happened, the neighbors, by the dozen, always volunteered with mouthfuls of water to help put out the fire. Sometimes it took a half an hour of 'mouth spraying' by the most experienced of our neighbors to put out the blaze. 'Mendel the Malamed' [teacher] from the *kheyder* [school] was the best of the firemen. Lucky the river was near and more water wasn't a problem."

It was evident that the old man enjoyed telling the story of his youth, but I interrupted. "What happened to the town and the Jews?"

"What happened? You know what happened! The Germans came. They knew who we were and where we lived. They took the records from the synagogue and then came at night and got us all out into the street and lined us up. They counted heads and called the names of the families. They shot two of the boys who started to run away—one was my cousin Schmuel. The rest of us were herded onto the trucks and taken away. First we went into the ghetto at Opole. Then we were transferred to the camps. I was sent to Buchenwald, where I was forced into work at the Gustloff Werke II munitions plant. We slave laborers were forced to do all the toxic and dangerous work. I spent two years there until I escaped and hid in the woods for about six months and then was found by a group of partisans, given a rifle and survived the war."

"And then you came back?"

"Since my sister and her husband had a farm near here and I didn't know anyone who had survived, I thought this would be a safe place."

"What did you find?"

"Nothing."

"There must have been something."

"Yes, Russians who looked for people they thought didn't belong. They would arrest people and ship them east. I don't know where, but they didn't come back. My sister and I kept our mouths shut and farmed. It was just the two of us. I didn't want to see anyone; I just wanted to be left alone."

"And that's how you lived?"

"Yes, I survived."

"Did you marry?"

"I had my sister to care for and there were no Jewish women around."

"And now?"

"Now I'm waiting my time. It will come soon. There has been so much death in my life that I look forward to joining my family and neighbors. I've seen too much." He looked at me, grabbed hold of my shirt, and pulled me toward himself. "Don't go to Ozarow!! There is nothing there. You must go to Auschwitz! Go and be a witness! See what it was like. Tell your children. How you say it? 'Never Again!' Jews must fight, not walk into gas chambers." His deep blue eyes burned with a heat I had never seen before. "For yourself, for us, go!"

"Yes, I'll go," I blurted out. I don't know if I said this because I meant it or just to have the old man release me.

"Go before you find the place you are looking for. *Farshtay* [understand] what you are going to see. Understand the size of all of the destruction. See that an entire nation, culture, people, your people, died." He then shouted: "They were your people!!" There were tears flowing from his eyes as he finished talking. Drool had started down his chin and he kept nodding his head from side to side. "Gay, Gay, Gay!!" ["Go! Go! Go!!" in Yiddish.]

I wanted to stay and talk, but he was haunting. He stood in front of me trembling as he held my jacket. I took him in my arms and held him for a moment as he sobbed. There was nothing I could say. I'm sure he had much more to tell, and I felt a sense of guilt as I released him. Peter and I sat and finished our coffee in silence, the old fellow crying, sitting on his chair just a few steps away. I paid the bill as Peter made a few inquiries in the café about memorials and the fate of some of the local communities.

As we left, the old man stood up from his seat and shouted, "Jews must fight."

When we were in the car I was silent for about ten minutes. "Do you mind if I want to change our travel plans?"

"Of course not, George, this is your trip."

I had been deep in thought, "The old man may be right. Perhaps I've been avoiding seeing something I know I will dread. But, I've come this far and learned more than I bargained for in just three days, some of which I really never absorbed from the books and papers I've read. It would be a shame if I didn't see at least one of the major concentration camps." After some discussion, we decided to head west from Antonio and follow the route to Oswiecim, the town that will always be know by its German name, Auschwitz.

The road we followed was parallel to the old railroad tracks upon which the death trains had traveled. Tracing our drive on the map, I saw that we were driving parallel to the Vistula River and toward its headwaters in the Carpathian Mountains. The railroad was on our right, and the river on the left. It was a pleasant countryside—the farms and quaint villages enchanted me. However, my thoughts kept returning to the old man. The image I carried away was that fierce determination in his eyes, clear blue but with clouds from age and tears; tears as he beseeched me to go to see Auschwitz.

Why have I had a mental block about going to Auschwitz? I am comfortable making the trip to Ozarow and investigating how the family died, but the trip to a death camp wasn't in my plans. The old man was so emphatic. What am I avoiding?

Peter didn't break any speed limits, and for the first two hours we traveled he was silent except for several polite inquiries about my family in the United States and how and where I had grown up. I could sense that he did not relish the thought of visiting Auschwitz. As we saw one of the first road signs with the destination "Auschwitz," he started to explain.

"You know, the concentration camps started long before there was an Auschwitz. As soon as Hitler assumed full power as both president and Reich chancellor, he established concentration camps for political prisoners. There was Dachau near Munich, Buchenwald near Weimar, Sachsenhausen near Berlin, and Ravensbruck near Mecklenberg, all within Germany proper. These camps formed the nucleus of the concentration camp system. In 1934 Hitler gave control of the camps to Himmler and the SS. They were given the full power to kill and to work people to death. Imprisonment in most of the camps meant a death sentence by either being worked to death on skimpy rations or by some method of extermination. Unimagined cruelty became a part of instilling fear and controlling the prison population. The administration of the camps was totally corrupt. It was slave labor. For as little as a few pfennigs a day, bodies were hired out to German businesses, with the money going to the SS. Men and women were used to break rock, build roads, and work in factories. Of course the prisoners received none of the money for their labor. People were beaten to death, or shot for no reason. These camps were the forerunners of the death camps, but also they were killing sites. They contained political prisoners, and 'asocial' prisoners who were basically criminals and sex offenders, and a third group made up of the 'inferior races,' mainly the Jews and the Gypsies."

"How many people went through these camps?"

"No one will know the exact number, but by late 1944 there were over nine and a half million people in confinement, most of whom were being worked to death. Only two million of these were captured prisoners of war, mostly Russian."

"I understand some of the prisoners worked for the big German companies."

"Yes, Krupp, I. G. Farben, and Siemens all used slave labor. There were laborers from the occupied countries and concentration camp prisoners. Small industrialists also were pleased to get cheap workers. There was a shortage of labor, and the SS was only too happy to supply these starving bodies. The people worked in the factories but were housed in the camps, or subcamps. The industrialists didn't feed the prisoners, but paid for the rations. Most of the money was siphoned off into the Gestapo pockets and never spent on prisoner food. The SS forced the prisoners to live on meager and inadequate diets, sometimes as low as four hundred calories a day while the prisoners were working at calorie-burn rates in excess of three thousand calories. The Kapos assigned to herd the laborers to the job sites mercilessly beat them, and the SS guards shot any who resisted, fell by the wayside, or got out of line. Rations were not enough to sustain the working prisoners, and within months starving workers began to die."

"Didn't the industrialists protest that their labor pool was being abused?"

Peter reflected for a moment and said: "Of course there were a few factory owners or managers who had a conscience. Oskar Schindler not only got his Jews fed, but also saved his workers' lives. You know the story; they did a film about him. There were others. Indeed, I know of one situation where former Russian slave laborers appeared as witnesses after the war to testify on behalf of the German factory owner during a denazification hearing. But this was rare."

"I find it hard to believe that a factory manager or owner would abuse his labor pool."

"To our knowledge, there was not a peep of protest. Just think, we are approaching Auschwitz, which supplied the labor and built the I. G. Farben Buna plant. Of the 35,000 Jews who worked building and operating this plant, at least 25,000 died. There was an entire subcamp of the Auschwitz complex across the road from the factory. Elie Wiesel was one of the slave workers at this plant when it was in operation."

"How can anyone say that the German people were unaware of the camps and the treatment of prisoners? They also worked in and around these slaves, and most of the camps were close to large towns. What crap! What lies! How can any German from that era say, 'I didn't know?' "

Peter interrupted. "In the system of organized killing, 'the Final Solution,' there were six major killing centers: Treblinka, Chelmno, Sobibor, Belzec, Maidanek, and of course Auschwitz-Birkenau. Each of the camps processed Jews and prisoners from a specific area. However, Auschwitz and Treblinka were the largest, and both were death-processing centers. Industrial killing machines."

"What about the other prisoners. Who were they?"

"The first prisoners at Auschwitz were Poles, prisoners of war, and political people who didn't fit into the Nazis' plans for running occupied Poland. Of course, there were also the unfortunate Russian prisoners, who were eliminated. Also, the refuse of the German civil and criminal prisons were dumped into Auschwitz and other camps. These criminals became the murderous Kapos in charge of working sections within the death camps. The Kapos became notorious for their inhuman treatment of the Jews."

"Do people visit the sites of the other camps?"

"Yes, but in some cases there isn't much to see. Auschwitz is a national memorial and it is preserved for the most part. It is run by the Polish government to preserve the memory of the Holocaust. There is hardly anything left to see of Sobibor and Treblinka, although there are memorials and significant markings at the sites. As the Russians were bearing down on several of the death camps, the Nazis tried to destroy the evidence. The places were cleaned up, first by the SS trying to hide their crimes, and then after the war by Poland to make these locations proper memorials. They are sacred grounds."

"And here at Auschwitz?"

"There is more than one camp here. Auschwitz is the main camp, but three kilometers away there is Birkenau, and there are several smaller satellite camps around the town, like the Buna Works and the munitions factory the old man described."

"What was the difference?"

"Auschwitz was originally a Polish army barracks that was used by the Nazis to house Polish prisoners after the 1939 victory. The camp was enlarged when the Nazis invaded Russia, and it became a concentration camp for political prisoners, POWs, and Jews. It was the original site, before Birkenau was built, and there were killing areas, gas chambers, and crematoria. But there were also areas where prisoners were housed for work in the factories, the forests, and the farms. Auschwitz was an industrial city where the working population had one destiny: death!"

"And Birkenau?"

"Birkenau was the expansion site. It was a death camp, pure and simple. It was built when the Nazi demand for murder outgrew the capacity of Auschwitz. It was designed and built as a killing factory. In addition, it was here that Dr. Mengele did his medical experiments on twins and women prisoners."

"How large is the camp?"

"Make no mistake, the camp was big business. Auschwitz was about 40 square kilometers in area. But it wasn't enough. They had to expand to be able to 'process' the massive numbers that were to be killed. So a sister camp, to accommodate their killing machinery, was built. And Birkenau was huge, a full 425 acres, with over 300 buildings that could hold as many as 200,000 prisoners at one time. The boundaries were a mile by a mile and one half. The two camps employed over 7,000 people in one way or another. In all, 47,000 people staffed the extermination industry. Realize that these employees had families and friends outside the business of killing. The camps couldn't have really been a secret, regardless of the German postwar claims."

We had been on the road since morning and it was getting late. I heaved a sigh as we approached the town of Oswiecim and Peter looked around for a hotel. He had selected the Hotel Globe from the guidebook and, after a few turns along the streets of the town center, found the hotel. It was a small white oblong building that had a lower area made from cement. On top of this "blockhouse" first floor, there was a four-story aluminum and glass structure that housed the hotel rooms. The upper area was almost all windows, and the building appeared to be "economy modern." It looked like a decent hotel, and if they had room for us, it would do. We didn't have a reservation, and Peter apologized for the fact that the rooms we were assigned weren't as luxurious as the room I'd had in Warsaw.

"That isn't a problem. But I am hungry. It's late, but is the dining room open?"

The clerk behind the desk heard me. "Our restaurant is still open and we'll take your bags to your rooms so you can go directly in and have a meal."

I had mixed feelings about sitting down and eating the night before we were going to Auschwitz. I was hungry, but I sensed from Peter that the Auschwitz experience would be unsettling. There seemed to be a sensation that I was going to experience emotions for which I had not prepared myself. I was uneasy.

To be accommodating to Peter, I agreed to have a light meal. We ate and then headed to bed. I anticipated that tomorrow would be memorable, and I wanted some sleep.

Chapter Fifteen

Auschwitz: The Education of an American Jew—George's Journey

Peter knocked on my door at 6:30 a.m. and whispered, "The dining room opens at seven. If we want the early start, we should be there when they begin to serve."

I growled, "I could use a cup of coffee."

There was a laugh from his side of the door: "George, you'll get it in half an hour."

Shaved, showered, and dressed, I was waiting for Peter as they let the first guests into the breakfast room. Breakfast was a buffet with hard-boiled eggs, ham, and cereals. There was a good variety of fruit. The coffee was the heavy black European blend I had come to expect and enjoy.

Peter came to the table with his mug of coffee and sat down. "A little heavier and the spoon would stand on its own." Peter seemed to have his mind on other things, but eventually said: "I won't be going into Auschwitz with you. I've been to the camp several times but I don't have the necessary license to do tour work inside the camp. What I would prefer is that I take you there and we agree to meet you when you are finished. When you go in, look for a licensed guide, they are all good. Ask his fee first, and if reasonable, hire him. You can do a tour alone with a pamphlet they have in reception, but I recommend having the guide."

I was disappointed and for some unexplained reason quite apprehensive about not having Peter with me. Even though we had only been together for three full days, I had come to trust what he said and was comfortable with his presence. His grasp of history made him a great companion. The thought of entering Auschwitz with a stranger was unnerving. I gritted my teeth, "I understand." It might have been over sixty years since the end of the war, but a familiar face would be welcome when entering what I knew would be a horrific site. I agreed and said that we should keep our hotel rooms, as it would be a full day. When we finish at Auschwitz, we'd decide out next steps.

He made sure that my cell phone worked so I would be able to call him. By 7:30 we were finished with breakfast, and by 8 a.m., opening time at the camp, we were parked at the Auschwitz visitor's entrance after passing the sign MUZEUM AUSCHWITZ.

Peter stopped the car and let me out. He nodded and drove off as I waved, took a deep breath, and looked around. Just like a child watching his mother drop him off at the first day of school, I would have preferred that he stay. Knowing something about Auschwitz from my readings did not make me feel comfortable standing there alone. It was reassuring that in a few hours Peter would take me away.

The air was crisp and clean. It was a nice early summer day as I walked on the flagstone-paved path across the little park in front of the tourist entrance. The walkway was framed with newly planted annual flowers. The scene seemed too pretty for the events that had occurred sixty years before. A neatly trimmed square of miniature pine trees formed the plaza centerpiece. I walked past the full tour buses and taxi parking lot, joining the throng being disgorged for their tours, and headed toward the camp entrance.

My mind dwelled on the number of Jews and other victims who had entered this camp but had not come out. At first it was a momentary thought, but it seemed to reoccur during my entire visit. I realized I was walking on ground that had become sacred with the blood and deaths of over a million and a half souls. Theirs had been a one-way journey.

The entrance fee was ten zlotys, and leaving the entrance hall I stopped one of the guards and inquired about a guide. He pointed toward a corner where there were several men and one woman standing about smoking. I approached and asked, "Guides?"

A short, barrel-chested man of about fifty years old came forward. He had a round face and a small moustache with a wide mouth and seemed to smile while still clasping a cigarette in his lips. A slightly oversized crumpled corduroy suit that wasn't blue and wasn't gray but was a nondescript somber color hung on his chubby body. It appeared that the suit hadn't been pressed in years. His very full head of hair was a mottled black and gray and swept straight back, slightly disheveled covering the rear of his frayed shirt collar. His voice reflected the raw effect of the harsh tobacco he was using.

"American?"

I replied, "Yes."

"My name is Florjan, and I'm an official guide. You should call me Florian, that's the anglicized version of the name." As he spoke he held up his identification badge.

"What is your fee?"

"It's $50 American for the morning and another $30 if I stay with you for the afternoon."

"Does this include Birkenau?" I asked.

"It does if you wish." After a smoker's cough, he continued, "However, you might want to do this camp today and then save a half day tomorrow for Birkenau, or we can do Birkenau this afternoon and you might want to come back tomorrow to finish a tour here."

"Can we make that decision later?"

"Yes."

Florian led me out of the administration building and onto the cinder path. I immediately saw the all too familiar entrance with the parallel railroad tracks leading into the camp. I remembered this from pictures and came face to face with the infamously cynical sign ARBEIT MACHT FREI [Work Makes You Free].

We were in Auschwitz! My heart was thumping as I turned around to observe each view. To my right was a board with a picture of the prison orchestra and a description in three languages (Polish, English, and Hebrew) of how the band had played as prisoners marched five abreast to work and back. Florian related how the prisoners had been required to sing as they came and went and he briefly hummed a marching song often played by the band. How cynical! A chill ran up my spine.

Florian stepped in front of me and gestured at the creosote-treated buildings that were just inside the gate and then at the rust red brick buildings that were along the path. "This is Auschwitz I, the original Polish army barrack area that became the death camp core. This camp is the beginning of the Auschwitz-Birkenau complex. Birkenau, three kilometers from here, was built as a second camp, an expansion facility. Also there were about forty work-area satellite camps. The original capacity to kill here in Auschwitz I wasn't up to the level that the Germans demanded. They built Birkenau so they could fulfill their fiendish plans for 'the Final Solution' with the capacity to liquidate whole masses of people."

I didn't want to interrupt Florian's narrative. He pointed here and then there. "These were workshops and the SS garage. There was a great deal of equipment to maintain, and the SS had vehicles to transport their personnel. The camp administration was here. These were reception, prison blocks, and laundry areas. Today, as you see, several are still in use for administration and the museum where we will stop later. These were the original barracks taken over by the Germans and converted to a concentration camp to hold Polish prisoners of war, mostly officers and then intelligentsia. In 1941 Russian prisoners were brought in along with the Jews, Gypsies, and other victims."

We stopped for a moment at the crosspaths between the barracks. "One of the camp *schutzhaftlagerFuehrers* [commandants] often greeted arriving prisoners with the statement: 'You have arrived here not at a sanatorium, but at a German concentration camp, from which the only exit is through the chimney of its crematorium."

I caught my breath at the bluntness of the comment. We strolled the 100 yards to the end of the pathway and I saw the double rows of pale white concrete fence posts with question-mark curled tops that had housed electrified barbed wire. There was no power on the wire now, but the fence and wires seemed as confining as they'd been all those years ago. Much of the barbed wire was gone. The posts were sentinels, exclamation marks, guarding the land of terror they once confined. In many spots there were openings torn in the fence. The posts and wire, along with the white insulators that held the electrification on every other strand, gave me the feeling of confinement, although I knew I could turn and leave. I kept reminding myself that I would walk out of this place in about two hours.

Florian took his time explaining the camp workings, which areas were barracks and where the women's quarters were, and then he paused. We were standing on the railroad siding. Florian looked in both directions and pointed to the grassed area next to the rusted railroad tracks that led through the center of the camp. "It was here that the trains stopped and disgorged their passengers. To the Germans it was subhuman cargo. Cattle would be precious and treated better. People had been herded into these cars in Warsaw, Radom, Krakow, and other Polish cities. They were scheduled here for arrival on a precise timetable coordinated to the capacity of this camp and later at Birkenau. Human beings were packed in without food or water. There were anywhere from 100 to 150 people in each railcar. Their baggage was stuffed in with them. There were no sanitary facilities, so you can imagine what they smelled like when they fell out of the car after from one to four days of confinement. Many died during transit. The human cargo was greeted by SS men shouting, 'Raus! Raus! Raus!' [Out! Out! Out!]. Those who did not move fast enough would feel the shock of a truncheon beating them along. Those who fell would be dispatched with a pistol shot in the head."

Florian took a deep breath and a long drag on his cigarette. In contrast to the deep breath of clean air I had taken when I stepped out of the car leaving Peter, I felt a tightening in my chest. The weather hadn't changed but I was perspiring. It was as if I were breathing a different atmosphere. "Those poor stinking people would fall out of the car climbing over those who had died in transit and struggle to their feet, wanting water or some food. They would be confused and disoriented. Families would be clinging together. Instead of being given food or water, they were told to leave their baggage on the siding, and their luggage would be brought to them. Then the men were separated from the women and sorted out on the spot. Those who could work were herded to the left, and all the others to the right. The same procedure was followed with the women. The children were sent to the right, often torn from a mother's hand. Sorted to the left and right. Families were separated, sometimes beaten as they clung together or tried to wave to each other to say goodbye. Those who went in the right column went directly to the gas chambers; those to the left were prodded to the barracks. They were shorn of their hair, tattooed with an identification number on their left forearm, issued striped pajamas and wooden clods for shoes, and crammed into the work barracks. In the few hours it took to process those who had been selected to live, their loved ones would have been gassed and their bodies would be on the way to the crematorium. For a while those in the barracks would live, then starve on an inadequate diet. Doing heavy forced slave labor, they too faced death. The turn to the left, for life as short as it might be, or to the right and into the gas chambers was called 'the selection.' The process was quick and organized. The trains had to be emptied, cleaned, and returned for the next cargo of victims. The siding had to be made ready for the next shipment of human cargo."

Florian let me dwell on my thoughts as we stood quietly at the siding. The more he spoke, the larger the hollow feeling grew within me. Feelings of insecurity entered my mind. How could this happen? Could it happen to me?

He went on. "The ramp where 'the selection' took place was here. It is gone now, but the vision of the selection process still haunts most of us who come here."

I reflected on his comments. I was looking at a peaceful scene, but my mind's eye imagined the trains arriving, the disembarking of the masses of Jews, and the cries of mothers being separated from their husbands, children torn from their parents, and all prodded the five hundred meters along the road to what was supposed to be a shower room, the gas chamber. The many thoughts that ran through my brain were difficult to put into words. I fell silent, unable to ask questions of Florian.

"And then Birkenau was the largest mass murder factory in the history of man." Florian quietly recited the statistics. Huge numbers: 2,000 persons per train, three to six trainloads a day, the capacity of the gas chambers, the matching of the capacity of the gas chambers with the capability of the crematoria. He again repeated that the demand for killing facilities had been so great that the Germans had extended the rail line three kilometers and built Birkenau. The combined facilities here and at Birkenau could slaughter as many as 8,000 to 12,000 souls—fathers, mothers, and children—a day and then cremate them.

"It was a depraved modern integrated production process. It was a business of receiving people, stripping them of their baggage and clothes, shearing them of their hair, killing them in the gas chambers, mining the bodies for the silver and gold in their mouths, and then disposing of the bodies in the crematoria. To the Germans there was little difference in this industrialization of murder and the construction of a modern slaughterhouse for cattle. Oh yes, there was a difference—these were human beings."

Florian grunted a harrumph, clearing his throat, and went on. "You see, the gas chamber at Auschwitz could only destroy 750 people a day, and the crematorium could only dispose of about 350 bodies a day, so the Nazis felt they had to build a bigger facility. Hence they built Birkenau. You know, matching capacity to their business—their 'business' being the supply of death to those they considered subhuman. This was a demonstration of industrial efficiency in the degenerate Nazi mind. It created a system designed for an unimagined hell, organized for efficiency of slaughter and killing in great numbers. The Nazis reality put the English author Milton's fictional description of Dante's Hell to shame."

We walked about thirty more steps along the dusty path. "For those selected to live and work, it was a living Hell. These poor souls were shorn of their hair and issued lightweight cotton uniforms called 'stripes.' They were crammed into barracks two or three to a bunk. The bunks were three high, with as many as a thousand men in a barrack with minimum sanitary facilities. In the wooden barracks there was a concrete open trough down the center of the building for excrement. The men couldn't relieve themselves other than at specific times of the day. They were fed a diet of watery soup and a crust of stale bread. The prison administration was 'authorized' to feed 1,500 calories a day to the prisoners. In reality it was less than 500 calories a day. The workload forced on the prisoners would require a diet in excess of 3,000 calories to sustain weight. The prisoners worked hard and starved. They quickly lost weight, suffered from dysentery, malaria, diphtheria, and typhus. Infested with lice, disease was rampant. They were beaten and faced the terror that any infraction would allow the guard to shoot them on the spot, no questions asked. Some guards would shoot and kill without any provocation. One demented guard shot a prisoner at random first thing every morning, before his breakfast. The average life span of a prisoner who escaped the first selection was about four months. Then they were fed into the crematorium, joining their relatives in death."

Thoughts raced through my mind. How did a prisoner stay sane? Did they go mad? How did the guards take it day after day? How did the townspeople not smell the smoke from the crematoria? How did they not see the flames from the crematoria and pyres? Was this a scene out of Dante? Did guards lose their feeling of humanity under these conditions? Were these murderers sane? My God, these prisoners must have smelled beyond belief.

Florian pointed to what appeared to be a mound, or a bunker. He identified this as the first sizable gas chamber. "Several hundred Russian prisoners of war were the first to be gassed. They arrived in mid-1941 and many died because of poor conditions in the camp. In early September of 1941 the remaining prisoners were used in one of the first experiments of the Zyklon-B gas. The gas came from the Buna chemical plant of I. G. Farben, which was just on the other side of the town. This plant was built by Auschwitz slave labor and then operated by prisoners selected from the camp. The Russian-prisoner gassing was a test of the chambers. You see, gassing was more efficient than shooting or hanging. The process was needed to accommodate the volume of Jews and others that were coming into the camp."

"Did they have a crematorium at first?"

"No. They used a nearby field to bury the first 200,000 killed." We walked toward an area that I took to have been the barracks. I found that Florian's descriptions were too devastating. I asked him to stop so I could catch my breath, and as we halted, I looked around.

Just outside the barbed wire were fields of grass now being used as forage by local farmers.

"How peaceful," I mentioned to Florian.

"Don't go over there. There are many bees, and they are aggressive and sting. They now are a natural barbed wire for the camp. But how ironic, now honey is being made where blood flowed. That was the field that was first used to bury the dead from the gas chambers. The Germans didn't realize that the decomposition of the bodies would create a morass and the field turned into a swamp that stank and was a festering bog. The SS then used *sonderkommandos,* special work details of Jews, to dig up the field and exhume the bodies, burning them in a huge funeral pyre."

He took me over to the area of the gas chambers and the crematoria. A hundred steps and we stood directly in front of the gas chamber and crematorium. It was at one end of the Auschwitz complex. I wasn't prepared for what I saw. The gas chambers were clean and smelled of disinfectant. The holes in the roof where the gas had been dropped were sealed, and the phony showerheads removed. The way it appeared, it could have been a very clean garage. The walls were painted off-white with a gray border, and the floor was scrubbed to a slight gloss. It was a clean, aseptic building almost appearing hospital like.

"This was originally an ammunition bunker," Florian said as we stepped into the gas chamber. He told how the gas had been developed, tested on Russian prisoners, and then used so efficiently on thousands of others. It was hard to imagine that this site, now looking so innocent, had been a place of horror. As Florian spoke, I started to feel queasy thinking of children dying first because they were closer to the floor and the gas spreading to snuff out the entire chamber of humans. I could envision the several hundred Jews packed into the room and the gasping death that took only a few minutes. I was obsessed with the image of couples and families clasped together in one final hug, an embrace as they died as others clawed at the entrance door trying to escape.

Florian described how the chamber was cleared, scrubbed, and prepared for the next victims. This was more work for the sonderkommandos, the prisoners kept alive even as they starved and were beaten, working to clear the bodies from the gas chambers and feed them into the crematorium.

"In some cases they had to pry people apart because they held each other so tightly in death." Standing there in the gas chamber, I didn't want to take a breath, although I knew it was clean and safe. The rough stone walls of the original bunker were immaculate and had been painted a pleasant light shade of green. Industrial lighting fixtures with bare bulbs cast a ghostly light throughout. The floor actually shined with an eerie gloss. Indeed, the odor of disinfectant offended me. The chamber was too clean!!

Out in the light, tears came to my eyes. Florian pointed out that to the right, about 100 yards away, was the pleasant house and marvelous flower garden where the commandant Rudolf Höss and his wife and children had lived, entertained, played, and enjoyed the use of servants who were prisoners. "After the war Höss's wife said that her four years living in that house were the most pleasant years of her life. Her husband was executed in 1945 for his atrocities."

The intensity of Florian's commentary was overpowering. I needed to break the tension building within me. For relief I wanted to change the subject for just a short moment and I asked where he came from.

"I was born in Krakow and went to university there."

"How old are you?"

"I'm an old forty-seven years old."

"Why do you say old?"

"When you get a job of being a guide at Auschwitz, you age very rapidly."

"Tell me more."

"It is one thing to walk through here and point out the fence, the barracks, and the gas chambers and crematorium. It is another to step on ground that has become revered. Every day I visualize the people who passed through and were murdered. Their ashes are part of this soil. I breathe the air that holds the dust and spirit of these souls."

"It has affected you."

"There are days I cry."

His voice choked as he pointed across the yard at what had been a prisoner barracks. To me it looked like a wooden stable. "Look at that building," he said. "There is a dirt floor, racks three and four bunks high. As I mentioned, each bunk was packed with three to five men. Think of the poor prisoners, beaten to work at horrible tasks, sleeping in their own excrement and knowing that they were dying from abuse. And those were the 'lucky ones' who hadn't been immediately consigned to the gas chambers. Think of the stench. Think of the meager food and the constant hunger. Think of the misery day in and day out."

"What jobs did they do?"

"Some of the better jobs were sorting the booty from the luggage that was left behind by the victims as they got off the trains. There were huge amounts of money, jewels, food, and assorted valuables that people had carried with them. The victims left their luggage at the rail siding, and a group called 'Canada' collected the luggage for looting and sorting for the Germans. The name derived from the prisoners' slang describing the enormous amount of the loot, which they associated with the far-off place they'd only heard about, 'Canada.' The Canada prisoners went to work as each transport of Jews went to the gas chambers. Just like scavenger ants, they cleaned the platform before the next train was to arrive. Then there were the sonderkommandos who manned the ovens and cleaned the gas chambers. Men who were 'dentists' stripped the gold teeth from the corpses before they were cremated, and a few more 'fortunate ones' actually had the run of the grounds keeping track of prisoners, food, and the camp administration. The Germans did none of this manual labor. All the dirty work was done by the prisoners."

I grunted, but Florian went on, "Yes there were some better jobs, but in reality for the most part the better job just delayed death. For those who survived the selection it was probably only four to six months before they would die from being worked to death, shot for some real or imagined rule infraction, or selected to go to the chamber because they were too weak to work and therefore useless. Of course a few, very few, survived for longer periods." Florian heaved a huge sigh and continued as he turned me in another direction. "See the crematorium over there. Look at the small mounds of what you see as dirt. Those are ashes. Sixty years later they are still resting in the corner. Think of the individual lives this dust represents. Between here and Birkenau, over one and a half million died. Big numbers. But each number is one person, just like you or me. There are no graves, just areas where dust and ash are buried outside the camp, dumped into the ground. In some cases where the ash spilled, it is still here. The traces are still with us."

Florian stopped to clear his throat and coughed again. "You Jews say the most important blessing is to bury someone. Why? Because the dead person can't thank you. I guess I'm blessed because every day I pay homage to these people: Jews, Catholics, Gypsies, Russians, Czechs and Slovaks. I do this every day, and every day I grieve. Yes, I feel very old."

Florian paused. He lit another cigarette and seemed to want to change the pace of his narrative. "You are well aware that the whole murderous process is called the Holocaust. Do you know where the word Holocaust comes from?"

I was surprised by Florian's question. "No, I don't, I never thought about it."

"The word comes from the word in the old testament 'olah,' which meant a burnt sacrifice. In the Greek translation of the Old Testament the word became 'holokauston' and the English definition made it 'an offering wholly consumed by fire.' So you see it was an easy transition to label this killing and cremation as the Holocaust. In Israel they use the word 'Shoa,' and the definition is directly applied to this type of massive destruction of human beings."

I wanted to know more about Florian. "Florian, are you married?"

"Yes."

"Children?"

"Yes, a boy of thirteen and a girl of nine."

"How long have you been a guide here?"

"I've been working here for fourteen years."

"How did you come to this work?"

"As I said before, I was born in Krakow and educated there. I went to university in Krakow and studied law. When I graduated, I looked for work in the legal field, but in the last days of the Soviet rule, before our breakaway and the new democratic government came into being, there were very few interesting positions. Also, I was known to be a thinker and too sensitive to our Polish complicity in some of the atrocities that occurred during and after the war. Some of my friends were anti-Semitic. They called me a 'Jew lover.' "

I nodded my head as he talked. "One day one of my friends said that if I had such sympathies I should go to Auschwitz and join my Jewish friends."

"And?"

"I came and applied for the post of guide. Had to study the history and pass several exams, mastered the history, and received a guide's license. I've been here ever since."

"How does it feel to be a guide here?"

"At first, it was a job. Now it's a dedication. I've seen people of every nationality and every religious persuasion. The Jews come in reverence. Some say they feel vengeance and hate when they see the scale of the atrocities, the efficient organization, detailed planning, and engineering. Others come and fall silent with horror. The Germans are the most remarkable. They seem to walk, how do you say, on eggshells as they look through the areas. They fall silent and become reverent. Germans are afraid to ask questions. They are afraid of the answers. I almost want to ask: What did your father do during the war? And they seem to dread that I might ask the question. Some of the Germans spend their entire time here shaking their heads in disbelief."

He guided me between buildings, ignoring the signs that set out the normal tour paths. He was interested in taking me through the camp rather than just along the paths where the large tours were guided. As we walked, he identified what had been housed in each of these buildings sixty years ago—the numbers, the conditions, and the horrors of starvation, beatings, and deaths. He showed the place of interrogation, the killing wall, the gallows, the building where medical experiments were conducted on women and twins, the assembly area, and the laundry. Each step had a story, a statistic, and a new dimension of cruelty and horror.

I asked him where he lived. It was the first time I saw him smile when we were in the camp. "I live here in the camp with my wife and children."

"Here in the town?"

"No, here in the camp."

I was shocked, but he quickly explained. "On the other side of the camp, the authorities have cleaned up some of the better buildings, and many of our staff live in the area. The area used to be where the SS were housed. It was almost a rest camp, with marvelous facilities. The accommodations are quite comfortable, and once you get used to where you are living, it is a very acceptable and economical home."

"Does the place haunt you?"

"Yes and no."

"Please explain."

"A man named George Steiner—I believe he is now a professor of literature at Cambridge in England—said, 'We know that a man can read Goethe or Rilke in the evening, that he can play Bach or Schubert and go to his day's work at Auschwitz in the morning.' That was his description of the butchers who heartlessly ran this place during the war. My wife and I enjoy a comfortable home in a tree-shaded pleasant surrounding. We brought up our children here. The murderers don't live here anymore; it is civilized now."

The gas chamber and crematorium stood just as they had sixty years ago. Seeing them was a traumatic experience. Forty steps later, Florian walked me into the crematorium. Haltingly, I placed my hand first on the door and then inside the oven. With Florian's description I could visualize the ghastly feeding of the bodies into the ovens' maw. The manufacturer's name, Topf und Sohn (Topf and Son) was on the doors. It was all so clean now. I could imagine the sonderkommandos at work, dreading their job and each knowing that it was just a matter of time before they also would be in the chamber and in these ovens. I looked at the ovens, the doors, the room, and the chimneys. How many souls had gone up in smoke? What had it smelled like? How had the wind been blowing? What had the townsfolk known?

Florian looked at the crematorium and said: "These are the actual chamber and ovens of Auschwitz. In Birkenau the chambers and ovens were six times larger. There were fifteen ovens in Birkenau. They were better organized there, a true killing machine. Birkenau operated for thirty-three months and in 1944 the SS tried to eradicate the evidence and destroy the facility as the Russians approached. When you are there, you will see the scale of the killing facility, but it lies in ruins.

"There are many stories of ghastly individual deaths. Most stories just personalize the mass murders. There is the story of the famous French actress who attacked one of the SS guards and was thrown alive into the furnace along with her child. Also, there was a sonderkommando who struck a guard; he too was just thrown into the flames alive."

I had heard enough and seen too much. It had grown quite warm and I had grown weary of hearing about death. It was nearly noon and I turned to Florian. "I think I'd like to move on and see Birkenau."

"Good, but on the way out to the gate, let's detour through the museum buildings. It's cool in there and you will see some of the exhibits that will illustrate what you have just heard."

We walked down the row of brick buildings, and Florian turned into one courtyard. "This is Block 11. It is a prison within a prison. To your right, they held a Gestapo court where prisoners were heard in 'trials' that often were less than three minutes, and death was the only sentence. And this is the wall where prisoners were shot. A bullet to the head or neck was administered. It is still pockmarked with the many bullet holes of the executions. The SS didn't want too much noise, so there wasn't a firing squad as you might imagine. It was just one officer firing a small-caliber pistol so there would be less noise, one prisoner at a time, day after day. They used the smaller pistol because they did not want to disturb the other prisoners."

He had me stand at the execution spot at the "killing wall," where the prisoner would be positioned as the German officer applied the economical one small-caliber shot to the base of the brain. Florian was extremely graphic in his description of the process—as he pointed his finger to the back of my head, a chill ran through my body. He laughed as he said, "Click."

"The prisoners," he continued, "women as well as men, were always shot naked and barefoot. A trail of blood reached across the courtyard where the bodies were stacked and then placed in a cart for the crematorium. Another inmate would load a cart and drag the bodies to the crematorium. We are told that the blood trail continued all the way to the oven."

Florian also pointed out the gallows where prisoners were hanged and in some cases left dangling for a day to instill fear in the men, who for the most part had lost all fear. "They used these mass gallows to show off their punishment."

All I could manage was a grunt, acknowledging that I understood what Florian said. He would not go on to Birkenau until we finished the museum tour in the two adjacent buildings. He showed me the enormous display of human hair, behind sealed glass. Again, a wave of revulsion swept through me. "There were seven tons of hair awaiting shipment when the camp was liberated."

"What would the Germans use it for?"

"It was woven into clothing, used as sealant for torpedoes; it was a substitute for cotton and wool, which was scarce because of the Allied blockade. It was used to weave slippers for use in submarines because the men needed quiet as well as warmth."

We then stood before another glass-enclosed case where thousands of suitcases were stacked. Names were stenciled on some, and there were baggage tags on others, all identifying individuals or families who had been delivered into the gas chambers and would not need the contents. I read the names: Kostek, Zamen, Marcol, Gradowski, Friedman; so many never to be claimed. Then I saw the cities and towns of origin: Leipzig, Breslau, Radom, Plawy, on and on from places all over Europe. Each suitcase represented a family. The pile of cases represented hope, future, and life that would never be realized. I wanted to cry.

"Florian, please let's move on."

"Very well, it's only three kilometers away to Birkenau. We can take my car, but first let's stop for a little something to eat at a café across from the entrance. The Art Deco Restaurant. It's a strange name for a place across the road from Auschwitz, but that's the name."

"Fine, but I really don't feel like eating. I've lost my appetite."

"A natural reaction to this morning, but a cup of tea will do you good."

Florian and I stopped for "a little something," as he phrased it. We were sitting at a very comfortable table with a white tablecloth in an air-conditioned café just across from the Auschwitz main gate. He ate a sandwich while I had a cup of tea and several very sweet biscuits. He offered to pay for his portion, but I waved him away and settled the bill. The restaurant was an unbelievable contrast to the scene I had observed across the road.

Florian paused between bites, "I don't know if you realize it, but the free-world Allies knew of this horror. Two Jewish men actually escaped Birkenau. They hid under a woodpile that the slave laborers had cut, and although the search dogs came right up to the pile where they were hiding, they weren't found. They made their way cross-country to the Czech border and crossed to Zilina, in northern Slovakia. There they wrote a 32-page report telling of the gas chambers and the crematorium construction, as well as the rail extension to Birkenau. This report was smuggled out to the Allies. The existence was verified by spy plane aerial photos which were taken when the Allies photographed the synthetic fuel plant on the other side of the camp, which appeared to be a possible bombing target. One of the guys, I think his name was Walter Rosenberg, who later went under the name Rudolf Vrba, went on to a career as a distinguished medical research doctor in Israel, the UK, US, and Canada. I don't know the name of the other escapee."

"I think I heard that Roosevelt knew. It didn't make an impression on me that it mattered when he knew. I think he was advised not to bomb the camps. I think the generals told him they were out of bombing range or that the effort to save the Jews was best served by winning the war."

"Yes, he as well as Churchill knew. Vrba even told the world that the rail extension was meant to be used in the transport of the Hungarian Jews. Auschwitz didn't have the capacity to do the killing in the time that Himmler knew was available. It is believed that Himmler knew the war would be lost by mid-1944, but he wanted the hateful Nazi mission completed. To accomplish this, the Nazis needed greater killing capacity and they wanted their demonic job done before the war ended. Birkenau and the larger gas chambers and crematoria were the needed capacity. Vrba heard the guards saying that 'Hungarian sausage' was coming. These details were in his report that was circulated among the Allied governments. The report was smuggled into Switzerland and then to England, where it made its way to the United States. It was secret, but widely circulated. It was even referred to in the *New York Times* in a small article buried in the back of the paper."

"And nothing was done?"

"There were some negotiations, but they came to little or nothing. There was some pressure on the government of Hungary, and some of the Jewish transport was halted. Maybe there were 100,000 Jews saved because the word was out."

I nodded my head in some disbelief that the world was so powerless or perhaps unwilling to stop the slaughter. "Could they have stopped the killing?"

"Probably not."

I muttered, "Think of how many people, as talented as this guy Vrba, went into those chambers, were starved, shot, or hanged. What horror. What a waste of humanity!"

"What do you think Roosevelt could have done? Could the Allies have bombed? Could they have done anything diplomatically?"

"Does it matter? Bombing the rail line into Auschwitz certainly would have sent a signal and probably would have slowed the process. It wasn't done. It didn't happen!"

Florian breathed a sigh. "We must move on."

We got into Florian's Audi coupe and he drove the three kilometers through the town, past a new motorway, to the rail siding at Birkenau. As he parked the car, he pointed: "There are the old warehouses that held the thousands of pieces of plunder that were being shipped back to Germany. Hundreds of trains left here with clothes, jewelry, extracted gold, hair, and even shoes. The valuables had been taken from prisoner baggage, sorted and classified, and then placed in those buildings awaiting transport. In May of 1944, in anticipation of the loot that would arrive when the Hungarian Jews would disembark, the staff was forced to sign an affidavit that they would not steal the property that would be part of the 'shipments,' and keep the annihilation of the Jews a secret. The booty taken from these poor souls then belonged to the SS and the Third Reich in no uncertain terms."

As we walked through the Birkenau main gate, Florian repeated that this was an expansion camp, built to handle the specific job of killing Nazi victims on a larger scale than ever before. Florian guided me to the rail platform that entered and ran through the site like a central spine ending at the gas chambers. This site was more massive than the Auschwicz camp. Midway along the rail line was a selection point; and within a short 300-meter walk, the efficient placement of gas chambers and the crematoria. The scale was massive. The grounds were four times the size of Auschwitz. There were two matched facilities of undressing rooms, gas chamber, and crematorium adjacent to each other. As Florian had said, they had been destroyed, dynamited. The roofs were askew, but in the ruins you could see an integrated step-by-step killing machine. This was an industrial design. There was little pretense. The camp was a factory, built for efficiency, built to kill. It did its job. The only concession to civilization were the willow trees standing as silent witnesses outlining the border of the complex.

Florian explained that these trees had been planted to shield this part of the complex from the prisoners. "Ha. The Nazis thought a row of trees and some flower beds would beautify the site of their murders. The scale of this system, the flowers, and the callousness still amaze me. I think the SS acted as if all this killing was as natural to human conduct as growing cauliflower or potatoes.

"Between Auschwitz and Birkenau, over a million and a half people were killed. We'll never know the exact number—the masses of men, women, and children, Jews, Gypsies, Catholics, Slavs, Poles, and Russians—that they sent through here, although the Nazis were diabolical in their record keeping. They overwhelmed any system they had for accounting for individuals. We have many names, many records, but trains with two to three thousand people were arriving four to six times a day, and the gas chambers were murdering as many as eight to twelve thousand a day. It was a big job, and the work of killing the masses shipped was paramount in the managers' minds. Keeping track of them wasn't on the agenda."

Florian walked me through the immense area of Birkenau. He had me stand at the selection point, and then we walked the 300-meter path to the undressing room, gas chamber, and crematorium. The landscape between the selection point and the crematoria was barren. I didn't hear or see birds. There were no flowers. The ground was an ochre dust that was baked dry and hard from the heat of the day. The grass was a thin stubble that crunched under our footsteps between the silent, empty remains of the barracks.

Florian took a bottle of water out of his small backpack and offered it to me. I thanked him, as I suddenly found myself parched. I took a long drink, and the cool water soothed my disturbed throat and body.

Florian stopped, and for the first time he chuckled. "Look at that pool of clear water," he said. I saw what looked like a swimming pool. "The Germans were a very strange lot. The Gestapo wanted to insure the camp against fire. The German insurance company said the water supply was inadequate, so the camp officers had the inmates build that holding pond for a water supply to be used in case of fire. The SS got their insurance."

"That story is hard to believe."

"It's true!"

The vastness of the camp amazed me. The remains of the empty barracks stretched to the horizon. I imagined the thousands of prisoners that occupied barrack after barrack, walking the dirt paths and staggering along the dusty road where we were walking. The scene created despair, as each individual knew what was at the end of this road: the gas chamber and crematorium.

I wasn't prepared for the size of the ruins of the dynamited gas chambers and crematoria. Florian pointed out the remains of the two facilities—twin L-shaped death factories with the foot of the L as a subterranean changing room that exited into the gas chamber, and the gas chamber sitting below the crematorium that formed the stem of the L. I looked down the stairs of the destroyed undressing room and visualized people standing awaiting their turn for the "shower." My impulse was to descend the stairs and stand in the place of those waiting prisoners. Florian restrained me, and the rope barrier barred my way into the destroyed area.

"During November and December 1944, as the Russians approached, Himmler gave the order to prepare the gas chambers for destruction. Dynamite was placed in the walls and supports of the buildings, and some of the ovens and equipment were shipped to Germany. Then in late January 1945, the facilities were blown up; as you see them now. Himmler wanted the 'evidence' destroyed."

The dynamited crematorium was resting with the roof split by the explosion, one half canted at a 45-degree angle, seemingly defying gravity and mocking the effort to destroy the ghastly evidence of what had happened here.

We walked a bit farther to a small pond with brackish green water. There was the stubble of swamp grass along one edge and three granite monuments, each inscribed in a different language. I read the inscription out loud: "To the memory of the men, women, and children who fell victim to the Nazi genocide. Here lies their ashes. May they rest in peace."

Florian said, "In contrast to what you saw at the fire water pool, this pond is the remains of a pit dug for the crematorium ashes. As you can see from the monuments, this is a sacred place. That pond holds the ashes of untold numbers. When it was full and there was no room, the SS hauled ashes over to the nearby Vistula River and dumped the remains there. Local people fishing on the river protested the sludge and odor of the residue in the water."

After two hours at Birkenau, I had reached the limit of what I could absorb. I felt emotionally drained and queasy. I asked Florian: "Can we head back so I can meet my guide by four o'clock?"

"We'll leave in twenty minutes, but let me show you one more thing before we go."

The Birkenau prisoner barracks we walked past were originally prefabricated stables. At Auschwitz most of the buildings were designed to be more permanent. There were many brick buildings that were substantially constructed. Any of the wooden facilities were well-built army barracks. At Birkenau the buildings were hastily constructed shacks that were originally designed as stables to hold forty-eight horses but housed a thousand to twelve hundred prisoners at a time. Florian once again described the squalor as the undernourished, starved prisoners lived in these buildings and did hard labor in local factories and in the camp.

"And these were the lucky ones who had survived the selection."

I walked into one of the barracks. The floor was dirt. Under the three-tier-high wood bunks there was a channel for the flow of excrement. It reminded me of a chicken farm where I had seen thousands of birds confined to a close space as they were farmed for their eggs. On the bunks were the numbers assigned to each location and carvings made by the men who'd occupied them layer above layer, where they were to sleep. There were initials, names, messages, and dates. This was the work of men who were doomed, except for those few who survived to be living witnesses. Carved on one was the "Sh'meh," "Sh'meh yis-ro-el Adnoi elehanou, Adnoi echod." (Hear oh Israel our lord our God, Our Lord is One!) (The most important prayer in the Jewish religion avowing monotheism.)

Florian pointed out, "Three and four men, maybe even five, were forced to sleep in each compartment. The only semblance of a mattress would be straw picked from the fields. The stench had to be unimaginable. Body lice were a major problem, and the diseases that accompanied the filth added to the death toll. Several times the plant had to be quarantined because of outbreaks of typhus. Men would become depressed and just give up and die or run to the barbed wire and be shot. Others would lose so much weight that they couldn't work. They would wander about as 'Muselmen,' a state of complete physical and mental exhaustion, waiting to be shot or dragged to the gas chamber."

"Florian, I've really seen enough!"

We slowly started to walk back to the gate. "As the war ended," he said, "the remaining prisoners, about 67,000 men and 35,000 women, were part of a forced march, a 'death march' from here to other camps. Many died during these marches. Anyone who dropped out from fatigue was shot. There was no provision for food, and the SS herded and beat the prisoners along what was a 250 kilometer journey to other death camps: Mauthausen and Buchenwald. The bodies of thousands of prisoners littered the evacuation routes."

"How did you master all this detail?"

"In order to be a guide I had to study seventeen volumes of detail about the camps. A copy of a summary volume is for sale in the administration building. You should purchase a copy." I said I would. "It's a summary of what I have told you, and it goes into detail we haven't had time to cover. Someday you will want to tell this story to others and they will question the numbers, horror, and the sheer magnitude of these two camps. The book will help you."

At the Birkenau administration building, I purchased the official guidebook. I used my cell phone to call Peter. Florian bid me farewell, and I paid him for the day and included a little extra. He asked if I would be coming back the next day.

"No, I've seen what I wanted to see. I want to get on to find out what happened in Ozarow. I really want to thank you for the tour. You have been a great guide and I believe you have become a friend."

Peter arrived within five minutes. He asked: "How was it?"

"I've seen too much. Let's go to the hotel. I need a drink."

I was silent all the way there.

Chapter Sixteen

On to Ozarow: The Killing Fields—George's Journey

By 7:30 a.m. we'd checked out of the hotel, gotten into the car, and headed east. I kept staring out the car window at the rivers and streams, and the multiple shades of green vegetation in the fields. Signs of life were everywhere. There were white and red poppies growing in the road verge and beautiful gardens in front of the homes that lined the roadside. The countryside was stunning. The extreme blue sky had contrasting puffy clouds scudding along. I kept looking at the towns we were passing and wondering on which side of the village the Jews lived. How many Jews lived here? Where were the Talmud schools? Where were the little boys with curls (payis) dangling down the sides of their heads? Where was the kosher butcher, the synagogue, the mikvahs (ritual baths)? How did the Jews live in this village? Where were the Jews? How did they die? There were none.

Peter quietly asked, "How do you feel after the visit to Auschwitz?"

I didn't believe my own voice, starting out very calmly, and then realized I was raging, speaking louder than I should have in the confines of the car. “The sons of bitches! How the hell could they call themselves civilized and create a killing factory like that? I can’t believe a society could create organized murder! They called us subhuman! They were the inhuman species—no human would do that to another being!”

Realizing that my rant wasn’t logical, but just pure emotion spilling out, I fell silent.

“I’m trying to think of what it was like for us, the American Jews during the war. What did we know? My family and neighbors remember Newark’s Rabbi Printz sermonizing that there were death camps. He was labeled an alarmist by other rabbis and the press. I remember finding out after the war that our hero, Roosevelt, had been informed but did nothing. There were no protests, no marches, no public outrage, not during the war or after. For most Jews the attitude was ‘don’t rock the boat,’ it isn’t happening here. Sure there was a ‘rally’ in Madison Square Garden, but no real outrage. It wasn’t like the ‘60s. There was no mobilization, no organized protest. Most American Jews just shut up. They closed their minds.”

Filled with emotion, I could not talk. A new anger was seething within me; my feelings were erupting. My stomach was rumbling with rage, and my mind was filled with fury. If Peter asked a question, I would respond politely, but I kept falling silent for long moments. Then, almost talking to myself, I started speaking. “As a kid during the war I did the patriotic things, collected tin foil from cigarette wrappers, old pots and pans and other metal in scrap drives and even collected the bacon grease from local restaurants. It was all for the war effort. I sold bonds and participated in the war stamp drives. I wrote to the war department and received posters to hang on the school walls, and we talked about the ‘Four Freedoms’ and how great it was to be free. There was nothing Jewish about all this, but in the Jewish community we participated as good citizens. We were in the war effort. Our fathers and brothers gladly joined the army. We knew that this was our war, as Jews and as Americans. Why didn't we become protestors? Did we do anything? If we had, would it have saved anyone?"

Again I fell silent. How could I tell anyone how I felt? I was a secular assimilated Jew. Had I been so concerned with my being an American that I'd missed some of the obligations I should have had as a Jew, as a concerned human being? Yesterday I'd seen the horror of the Nazi way of death, their "Final Solution." Now I was going to see and hear more that would anger me. I felt guilty for some reason. I didn't know why. What had the Jews of the United States been doing during that time? When Morgenthau and other prominent Jews went to Roosevelt, why didn't Roosevelt react? Roosevelt was a good man, wasn't he? Wasn't he? Did he feel powerless? If there had been a larger Jewish lobby, an active lobby, would it have helped? Hitler made it impossible for any group—Jews or other races and political activists anywhere on earth—to ever feel completely safe. Any minority could fall victim to a corrupt government.

Peter jogged me out of my reverie. "We're about fifteen kilometers from Ozarow. By the way, what was your guide's name?"

"Florian."

"That's amusing. Florian is the name of the patron saint of firemen and prison guards. What a coincidence!"

As we continued toward Ozarow, my silence filled the car. Peter concentrated on driving, as the road had many gentle curves. We passed through farming country with row upon row of great varieties of crops planted side by side in herringbone patterns of vegetables and grains. The many shades of green astounded me as spring growth carpeted the land. The scene represented a renewal of life.

Peter broke the silence. "I didn't mention it, but my uncle was killed in Auschwitz."

I was shocked. "I don't understand."

"Yes, he was imprisoned because he was a Polish army officer. He came home after the '39 war was over but was arrested within a month by the Gestapo because of his rank. They put him in Auschwitz with other Polish officers, and on October eleventh, 1943, he was shot along with about 750 other officers and intelligentsia."

"I'm sorry."

"During those early days of Auschwitz, Poles as well as Jews were the meat for the grinder. We Poles are very sensitive to the meaning of Auschwitz and are committed to it being a national memorial."

"I think I understand the significance of the camp to you. I'm sorry about your uncle; I don't think the outside world relates to the Polish losses in Auschwitz."

"George, it was a long time ago. Many others died during that time. Too many. My generation just thinks about moving on." Peter adroitly changed the subject and seemed intent to prove that as a guide he had command of the historical background. "George, you must realize that the war in the East in Poland and Russia was entirely different from the western front. The war in France and the occupation of Denmark, Belgium, and the Netherlands was harsh, but not like the regime imposed in the East. The western battles were comparatively civilized warfare. Because of Hitler's beliefs in a super race, he considered the Poles, Jews, Gypsies, and Slavs as *untermenschentum,* subhuman. Hitler wanted to eliminate entire populations for the concept of *lebensraum.* He wanted the area 'cleaned' of these so-called inferior races so he could place his ethnic Germans in these lands. 'Subhuman' beings were not worthy of life compared to the German 'super race' who were to become the owners and occupiers of these lands."

"I didn't realize the extent of the annihilations."

"Yes, our modern term for this is 'ethnic cleansing.' Hitler perfected the process in this countryside. This portion of Poland became known as the General Government. It was to be prepared for proper Germans to live here without Poles or Jews around to contaminate the population or the countryside."

The first road sign OZAROW came into sight, and a surge of excitement ran through my body. My anticipation built, and I became uneasy with a fear that this trip might be a waste. What would we find? What if there was no trace of my grandmother's family? I could just be chasing a phantom created in my mind. As we came down the road into the town, I had the feeling that it was all happening too fast. My heart was pounding. I was almost breathless.

"Peter, maybe we should stop and go to a hotel and take the trip into the town tomorrow."

"I don't think so. We are here and we might as well take our first look this afternoon."

Peter drove through the town center and circled the center square. I was impressed by the cleanliness and almost austere image of the town. The contrast with the walk through Auschwitz-Birkenau yesterday flashed through my mind. This wasn't the poor "old country" village I anticipated. I couldn't help but imagine a miniature papier-mâché snow-covered village with a model train set. That would be quaint. These homes and buildings were modern and well kept. The greengrocer's, butcher, and clothing stores were lined up along the main street. The white Catholic church, a squat structure with a pyramid roof and lofty spire and belfry, dominated the top of the hill at the town center. One main road led to the town, and three minor roads went off into the countryside. Opposite the church there was a large, wide square with several cafés awaiting customers to sit under the table umbrellas colorfully emblazoned with the names of the prominent beer brands.

We slowly drove around a traffic circle where several roads split the town into neat sections. The circle was filled with bowers of flowers in fragrant blooms of red, yellow, and green forming a center mound. There was greenery lining the road. It wasn't a "shtetl" image. Indeed, the ravages of battle a long time ago had eliminated the settlement my grandparents knew. The town was at a secondary crossroad not far from the Vistula River and just north of a new major east-west highway that ran from Lublin to Kielce. As we drove, we saw that where our older maps showed the Jewish neighborhoods, there now were three- and four-story Soviet-style apartment blocks. From a pre-war village of perhaps 7,500 predominantly Jewish people, there now was a small town of 25,000. Not only was it now "Judenfrei," but almost any relationship with its past had been obliterated.

We searched for the old Jewish section using several old maps that Peter had brought and from copies of several of Grandma's old letters, from her brother and from Grandpa's family. We had addresses for our search. Starting near the river, we traced the local roads to the side of town we were sure was the old Jewish area.

Peter asked for directions from a man sitting at one of the cafés. There was an extended conversation that was not translated for me. Peter looked at me and said, "We were invited to sit and have a drink." When we declined, the man stood up, taking a last sip from his cup of coffee. Peter introduced me and said, "His name is Thommée and he has agreed to show us the way."

Thommée was a well-conditioned man of about sixty-five who had been in the construction business for many years and was now retired. His pace approached a trot and he gave a commentary about Ozarow as we walked. Peter breathlessly translated. His first stop was a nondescript building housing a small electrical appliance shop. "This was the kosher butcher shop." He turned and smiled, "You know that would be the gossip center in the community." We walked together and I asked where "3 Mai Street" would be. In minutes we were in front of a vacant lot, a space between two creosote-coated old homes. This was the address of one of Grandmother's brothers who'd had a leather shop. We looked for another address of another relative, a lumber merchant. In its place was a one-story concrete warehouse that was obviously a postwar building.

Thommée was curious about our interest in the area. He led us to the east side of the small town square, past several modern buildings, and into an area that was rebuilt from partially destroyed buildings. One building, with old and new brick forming a two-tone mosaic, was about two and a half stories high and was a warehousing and plumbing supplies business. Most of the windows were conventionally rectangular. However, looking closely, you could see in the brickwork the shadow outline arches of the old religious windows. Above several were shadows of the Ten Commandment tablets and a seven-branched candelabra, the symbols of Jewish architecture. It was the old synagogue, once a proud centerpiece of a thriving community. Peter translated as Thommée told the story.

"It was in mid-August, three years after the outbreak of the war, I guess it was 1942. All the Jews had been forced to live in the old town. Wealthier Jews living on farms and in large homes on the west side of the village were forced out of their comfortable homes and into the Jewish area that had been established. Even Jews from some of the nearby towns were brought into Ozarow and forced into the tight quarters of that Jewish section. The conditions in that area were inhuman, with whole families confined to a single room. The Nazis would not allow the other townspeople to help the Jews with food or work, although many of our families were working for Jewish businesses and liked our employers and wanted to help."

He was talking very rapidly and Peter had difficulty keeping the translation even with the story. "The Jews gave their jewelry and valuables to the Germans as a bribe not to be deported. They were told that they could be safe here. But the Germans had lied and started their roundup of the Jews just days later. The police went through the town banging a drum and forced the Jews out of their homes and then herded them into the two-hundred-year-old synagogue. It was an old building then, but as you can see, it was sturdily built. It was what was known as a 'fortress synagogue,' built to house the congregation in case of a pogrom strong enough for defense of the worshippers in the old days. The Germans had lists of all the Jews. They corralled them out of their homes like cattle. Wearing their long green field combat coats, they would force their way in, breaking the doors. The soldiers were terrifying. Well armed with rifles and submachine guns, they used the butts of the guns to beat anyone who got in their way. They raged from house to house. As they ran they yelled, 'Raus, Raus! Schnell!' If they found old people or children or sick people, they shot them. After they 'cleaned a house,' they would post a six-pointed star on the door."

Peter interrupted and asked, "Where did they get these lists?"

"The Germans were well prepared. They had worked since the beginning of the occupation getting the names of the Jews. They even knew of intermarriages; no Jew was safe. They had the name of the synagogue members, the ration book allotment list, and of course they had enlisted Judenrat members, Jews who they forced to be their own police. The Judenrat also had to compile lists of known Jews."

Thommée took a breath and then went on. "When they thought they had them all assembled, they marched them into their synagogue and later into the town square and then down the road, past the church and the old Jewish cemetery. Somewhere down that road they shot them all. That night the old synagogue was burned, but later in the war the shell of a building was used as a stable. After the war, one of the new families brought into the area by the Russians as part of their repopulation program was given the property and they made it into the plumbing warehouse you see."

I asked, "Did any of the Jews survive?"

Peter translated, "Some of the younger boys tried to run away into the woods. The Germans hunted them like deer. They would be laughing as they found one and would shoot. If the Jew was wounded, an SS officer would shoot the victim in the head. They would leave the body where it fell, not even dragging the body to the ditch they had dug for the other dead. After all, that would dirty their uniforms. We know that a few Jews survived and went east and joined the Russian partisans, if they were lucky enough to find a partisan group that would take them. Young men seemed to make it; some of the young girls also got away. But of those who escaped that night, most didn't survive the war."

I asked, and Peter translated: "Who were these killers, the SS or the regular German army?"

"The Germans used Byelorussian and Ukrainian troops recruited as they marched into Russia. In these early days of the war, the Germans were looked upon as liberators in some parts of Russia, and there was no shortage of recruits for the Wehrmacht. The local Polish police helped searching for Jews. These were brutal killers; they did the dirty work for the SS. Some were former convicts let out of German jails to serve as paid murderers and do the Germans' dirty work. The SS gave the orders, the Byelorussians, Ukrainians, and their henchmen carried out the executions."

I was bold enough to ask: "What did the local people do?"

"For the most part, nothing," Thommée replied, and he quickly added: "Many of the locals wanted to take over the Jews' businesses and homes. They were pleased to see the Jews out of town. Of course, many Poles were afraid. There was a German order issued: 'Whoever hides a Jew, the whole family will be slaughtered.' Poland was the only German-occupied country where the penalty for harboring a Jew was death. Still, there were some who gave shelter, but they were very few."

Peter seemed pale as Thommée told of the Polish reaction. "Ha!" He exclaimed. "Many of these people who jumped into the Jewish property were killed as the Russians came through a couple of years later. The Soviets were ruthless, eliminating what they called collaborators and small business owners; they destroyed this entire area and settled it with their own people. Germans who had been placed in businesses were arrested by the Russians and either shipped to prisons or killed. Then the Russians changed the world of the local people; the town was 'Sovietized.' Individual businesses were shut down and all the agriculture was collectivized. There is little left of the Ozarow of the Jews, or the Ozarow of the pre-war Poles. There are a few like me, but very few."

I asked, and Peter translated: "Of those few Jews who survived, did any come back to this town?"

"No. None came back to Ozarow. In some of the neighboring towns, there were Jews who returned, but they were not made welcome."

Peter became quite pale as the narration continued. "In 1946, in the town of Kielce, not far to the west of here, there was a pogrom. Thirty-nine Jews were killed and 82 wounded from about 200 Jews who were Holocaust survivors. After that, most of the surviving Polish Jews emigrated to Israel."

I wanted to hear more about Thommée, so I asked, "And you, how did you survive?"

He went on to explain himself: "I was young and I was drafted into a labor battalion by the Germans and shipped to a factory near Dresden to make tank parts, I survived only because I had the skills of a mechanic, and I returned because this was my home."

Peter was becoming uncomfortable. Some of the Polish history we were hearing was not about Poles and Jews living in peace, an image he had wanted me to see. He shifted from foot to foot and interrupted the man's comments several times. Listening to a story of the postwar history of his country had an emotional effect on Peter. It was different from studying at school. When he was conducting a tour, he was able to control the content. Now, someone else was doing the talking.

Thommée accompanied us to the south side of town to a Catholic church, where he told us we might get some information about the Jews from the pastor, who had also been in the town many years ago.

For both Peter and me, the thought of what the next minutes and hours might tell us was exciting. I was breathless as we walked down the short road following Thommée.

We squinted as we moved from the sunlight to the dark confines of the church's main hall. A priest stood near the altar wearing a black cassock. Thommée said the priest would understand me and he introduced us and said goodbye. The priest appeared to be well over eighty years old and was holding a long walking stick for balance. His stooped shoulders appeared to carry the weight of the world, and the crevices of his deeply lined face showed each day of his long life. We told the monsignor what we were looking for and he pointed to two nearby old cemeteries.

He spoke in halting English. "I think I can help you a little. It will be good for me to practice my English. I was here when the Germans came. I was young then. Later the Russians came." He appeared to be well over eighty years old and his speech was halting. He would stop, think of his next words, wheeze, and speak. "I was ordained in 1940, and this parish was my first assignment. It was a good assignment for someone just out of the seminary, and I celebrated my first Masses after my ordination in this very church."

At a slow pace we left the church and walked into the adjacent Catholic burial ground. Weaving our way through the well-tended graveyard, we followed the old priest down the path between graves neatly decorated with cut flowers left by families and friends. We would stop, turn, and assist the older man so he wouldn't stumble as the ground sloped toward the road.

He had been here ever since the war. Indeed, we were in the presence of an eyewitness. He explained that this was a secondary lane leading to the river. At the bottom of the hill we looked across the narrow road. It divided the neat cemetery we'd just come through and a burial ground marked by a battered gate and a short stone wall on the other side. He heaved a great sigh and went on. "We just came through our Catholic cemetery. That is the Jewish burial ground and beyond is the field."

I looked at Peter. We didn't understand what he meant by "the field." Across the road was obviously a Jewish cemetery that looked badly overgrown with weeds and brush. Next to it was an orchard and a forest. It was just beyond the outer fringe of the old city. The priest showed us the approximate town boundary as we walked across the lane. About every ten yards, there was an elm tree, almost as a mileage marker. The trees were young in their early summer bloom, all less than fifty years old. Their leafy boughs hadn't yet reached across the road to form a canopy meeting the branches of those planted on the other side. The road was like a church aisle, with each tree marking a pew, where the roadside shade would have sheltered a praying supplicant.

We were getting a guided tour from the old priest. He stopped at the Jewish cemetery entrance. The wrought iron waist-high swinging gate was twisted from the hinges and swung askew with a Star of David welded within its center. We saw knee-high grass and tombstones in disarray, many knocked down and many more obviously missing. The few markers that were there were tilted in every direction. The old cleric stepped into the sacred ground and gingerly walked among the gravesites using his walking stick to point here and there at destruction and vandalism that seemed to tear at his heart.

"We keep our cemetery in immaculate condition. There is no one to care for this."

He stopped in the middle of the cemetery, turned to face us, and pointed to the decapitated gravesites where headstones were missing.

"The Germans had taken tombstones and used them for roadblocks to form battlements and tank diversions to stop the Russian advance. This is all that is left of the original Jewish burial ground."

Someone had taken several of the recovered bullet-scarred tombstones and laid them onto old gravesites, probably without regard to family or relationship of the marker to the grave. Some of the gravestones had weather-worn texts made faint and illegible by the erosion of time and others by the effects of war. You could see where bullets had scarred the granite and cement slabs and where fire had blackened others. Some were beautifully carved, and on more than one, there was the sign of the two hands, with mid fingers separated, of the Cohanim's priestly blessing. In the center of the old graveyard, were the remains of an *ohel,* the structure erected by a congregation over the resting place of a *tzaddik,* a most revered rabbi. In the corner of the graveyard was a destroyed mausoleum where the granite walls had been stripped off the supporting beams, probably to be used as part of a nearby roadblock defensive position which was hastily constructed by the Germans. The mausoleum front lintel piece lay on the ground with the family name "Kotell," Hebrew for "wall." My grandfather's name was Kotell.

Nearby was another, less damaged mausoleum with the Eisenstadt name: Grandma's family. I had never realized that the Kotell and Eisenstadt families had had enough wealth to construct mausoleums. Grandma's stories about her family's comfort and position were apparently true.

Peter was on one side of me, and the priest was on the other when I saw the names. I gasped, and with a sudden shortness of breath my knees buckled. Peter reached out to steady me, and the priest turned toward me in support. I was stunned and suddenly numb. Suddenly tears flowed as I stood at the graves. I was surprised at my emotions but felt cleansed by the tears. I recalled the image of my grandmother blessing the Yahrtzeit candles and the flickering flames glowing onto her tear-streaked face. I was unprepared for this moment. Seldom had I prayed, but now I wanted to pray. My lifelong profession of not being an observant person deserted me.

After a few moments Peter put his arm on my shoulder and turned me toward the priest, who seemed to want to show us more. I just wanted to stand before the family mausoleums, but the priest took me by the arm and guided us away to the edge of the cemetery.

Gingerly we walked between the graves, trying to avoid stepping on the burial sites. The priest took us beyond the cemetery wall. There was a large field dominated by two mounds, marked only by a small tablet. The tablet was written in three languages, and I was able to read: "Here lie the remains of two thousand three hundred and twenty Jews massacred on the night of August 4, 1942."

The priest explained. "Ozarow was just far enough off the beaten path that the commandant of the Einsatzgruppen, the special death squads that fanned out into the countryside to do this type of killing, didn't take the Jews to the railhead for shipment to a death camp. They didn't want to waste petrol, so he did his job here by machine gun. The mass grave was their legacy."

In a quiet, measured voice, the priest described what he had been told by local police and other eyewitnesses. He had repeated this story to others, many times. He described the forced digging of the large trenches by the young Jewish men brought to the site during the afternoon and their supervision by Byelorussian troops commanded by a small SS contingent.

"The SS Einsatzgruppen major ordered the Jews to be herded from the synagogue, where they had been taken after being rousted from their homes and held in the open town square for most of a day. First the men were forced along from the town to this field in what was then a forest. In their sense of order, the Germans had the Jewish men dig several oblong trenches with straight and orderly lines, the dirt piled along the tops of the trenches, one embankment higher than the other. There were three trenches, each about seventy meters long and twenty meters wide, dug to a depth of about ten meters. The instructions were precise: Make the trenches long, wide, and deep. The killers then forced the Jews to strip and leave their clothing in neat piles. Ultra-religious men with beards were pulled aside to suffer the indignity of a cold razor cutting off their beards. The men were lined up so that all would fall into the grave in place, like cordwood being positioned on a pile. Then the machine gun would bark and they would fall. Next the women, some carrying their children in their arms, were lined up at the pit edge and forced to stand so they would fall neatly over the men in their mass grave. We are told by some of the townspeople that there were horrible screams of some of the women and children sobbing as they witnessed the murder of those in line in front of them. Then there are stories of the incredible dignity of others as they stood naked knowing the shots would also be for them. Several of the men had bolted away from the trench and tried to run. The German SS commander shouted the orders, and soldiers dashed after them firing their rifles as if they were hunting game. One or two of the Jews got away. Most were killed as they ran. It was a busy night."

The pastor continued after taking a deep breath. "Then the Byelorussian accomplices took their shovels and filled the grave. At gunpoint they were helped by some townspeople who had witnessed the shooting. Some of those wounded in the trenches were still alive. It didn't matter; the earth covered them and the dead."

Bile arose in my throat. Sixty years later I imagined the sound of the machine gun. The whole scene resounded in my mind. The priest's description was all too vivid. I looked around; the forest was now an orchard with new fruit on the trees, but the gun's staccato seemed to echo through the woods. I heard the machine gun and my heart imagined the impact of the bullets. We could speak only in whispers. The priest held my hand as I started to say what I could of the Kaddish prayer.

The priest's description and Thommée's story merged in my mind with what I had learned at Auschwitz the day before. All I could do was think: "They're all dead! They're all dead! It didn't matter if it was by gas at Auschwitz or by machine gun in a forest—the Jews were dead. They are my family and they are dead."

I slowly walked back to the car and opened a little leather case. In it, neatly wrapped in a plastic packet, were the envelopes from several of the letters my grandmother had written years ago. There was one envelope addressed to each of the relatives. Each had been returned "Addressee unknown." There was a letter to Grandmother's brother Zwi and his wife Bracha Ajzensztain, a second letter to her sister Zaava, and a third to Lajzer and Rivka Wall, Grandfather's brother, the timber merchant and his wife. I walked to the center of the orchard, where there was a slight mound, and opened the plastic packet. I took each letter out, and the fragile envelopes crumbled as the slight wind lifted them from the protection of the cover, and fragments of paper wafted over the orchard. A small fragment caught a leaf of an apple tree just above me. I heaved a sigh and walked back to where Peter was standing. I had tears in my eyes as I said, "A bit late, but the mail has been delivered."

I had found the answer about my family. I now knew how they died and was standing at the family gravesite. I had found an answer to the question, "How did they die?" It didn't matter; they were gone, murdered.

The remains of the Wall and Eisenstadt families and their neighbors were in that field. There was an empty feeling in my heart. I no longer questioned why I had made the trip, and I realized that there was nothing I could do for the people in that mass grave. I had a new understanding that this wasn't something distant that had happened to unrelated people far away. This was my family. This was why Grandma had cried. I crossed into the field and stood at the edge of the mound. There were apple trees all around me, including several large ones on the mound. They were fitting tributes to renewal. I walked back to the broken mausoleum silently reflecting on what I had absorbed in the last hour and yesterday's trip to Auschwitz. The old man had been right. I'd had to see both Auschwitz and Ozarow to understand.

Peter placed his hand on my shoulder in comfort. I nodded to him. And as I turned to go, I placed the traditional symbolic small stones representing a visit from a relative or friend on the ruined mausoleums and the nearby graves. The occupants were no more, except in the memories of those who survived. My grandmother, mother, and I were among the survivors.

At the edge of the cemetery I went to the car and found the small prayer book I'd brought from home. I opened the Sider and I again said the Kaddish prayer. The priest chanted a prayer in Latin along with my prayer, then turned toward me at the conclusion and placed his hands on my shoulders. "Bless you for coming."

The graves and the orchard proved to be an epiphany. I thought that seeing the graves would "close the book." For some reason I could not just turn and go. There was a feeling that there was something more. I didn't want to leave, having come so far. Peter stood nearby, comforting me.

"There is nothing I can say to console you. All this is disturbing. I know! I feel ashamed as a Pole that this has happened within my country."

The elderly priest looked at me and again slowly chanted a blessing as I hung my head and wept. The priest then turned and started walking slowly on the road and up the hillside, through the Catholic graveyard back toward the old church.

We stood in silence for a long time. Peter's complexion was pale. When he started to talk it was halting and slow: "Seeing the site of the massacre has affected me. It is one thing to know of these events and atrocities from books and secondhand stories, but being here makes this personal. Standing at the site and hearing the story is another experience. I can identify with this being your family, and it has touched me. When the historians speak of thousands of deaths, it is a matter of history. When we relate to specific family members and how they were slaughtered, we begin to understand tragedy. It is a sense of reality I didn't have before."

He paused, took a deep breath and continued: "There was no monument in the center of the town and there was only a small marker in that field. What Pole will know what happened here when the old priest dies? Soon no one will know about Hitler's 'Final Solution' and how it was implemented in this town and villages throughout the country. Will they care? Five hundred years of Jewish presence in this area was wiped out. My country lost part of its heart and culture in this field, at Auschwitz and the other camps and fields. I feel angry at a world that made Poland a battleground for all of these centuries, but as a Pole I can only mourn for those who have died. These were innocent people who paid with their lives just because a fanatic took control of a country and declared them subhuman. They lived and prayed here in peace."

After a moment to catch his breath, Peter continued. "I have to wonder what the local Poles were doing during all of this. Did they just stand by? Who were the Poles who helped? Were they forced into silence? Were they standing at the side of the road as the Jews were herded out of town or were they hiding behind their white lace curtains? What did they think? What did they feel? What did they do? What did they do?"

Peter looked out into space, and then turned to face me. "You can voice your anger about Mr. Roosevelt and Mr. Churchill. I can feel the shame of knowing that Poles were also complicit in some of these crimes. Could they have done something? The answer lies in the souls of the older people who remember the war and were there. Their children's suspicion is that the real answer might be yes! I'm embarrassed that Jews weren't protected. I'm ashamed that more Poles didn't help."

Some of his youthful innocence was falling away as he mouthed these words. As profoundly as I was affected, I realized that my trip also affected this young man. In a more reflective tone Peter went on. "I know our Polish history and the war stories. We Poles were subject to arrest, confinement, hard labor, and, in some cases, death. As I mentioned in the car, many Poles were kidnapped and forced into slave labor. Thommée was an example. Many died in the camps. Poland was the only country where, during the occupation, harboring a Jew carried a mandatory death penalty. But, we can't just say we too suffered under the Germans. The Jews were our neighbors, they were Poles. The Nazis ranked Poles as the second lowest racial group in Europe. As a result six million Poles, both Christian and Jewish, were killed during the war. The Jews were singled out for specific slaughter, a 'final solution.' The Poles were destined for extermination through labor, because that suited the German cause. Although there was a resistance movement, most of my countrymen just stood by."

We had walked into the center of the cemetery. My mission was over, my curiosity satisfied, my mind saturated with images of the past. I took a deep breath, turned to Peter, and started to walk toward the car. I put my hand on Peter to slow him down before leaving the cemetery. I could go home, but something made me stop. I wanted to pause and remember it all. My mind was storing images that I would put into words telling of this experience to my family and friends. Having traveled this far, I wanted time standing here, in this space. I wanted to breathe this air and take in the sights. I walked to the edge of the cemetery and picked up several fallen pinecones from between the graves. I wanted to try to germinate these cones in my children's gardens back home. Perhaps their growth would symbolize a renewal of these lost lives. I put the cones in my pocket. Not wanting to leave, I started to tell Peter what I knew of Jewish cemetery headstone markings.

"Do you see that grave stone? It has the two hands of the Cohanim. Those are one of the three classifications of Jews within the temple. The Cohanim are the priestly class, a distinction passed from father to son through all these generations."

Peter pointed to another gravestone and then ran his hand over the carved relief of the marker. "George, what does this signify?"

The stone depicted water poured from a pitcher, the symbol of the Leviim. "A Levie is buried here." I explained, "The Levies, or Leviium, were the workers within the temple, the people who drew water, sanctified it with prayer, and carried it to the temple for ritual purpose."

"What is the third group? You mentioned there were three."

"The third of the classifications were Israelites. This consisted of all other Jews, not Cohanim or Leviium. The Cohans would be buried in the outer series of graves in the cemetery—priests were not supposed to step onto a graveyard. They would be buried near the fence so their children could visit but not walk on sacred ground."

I turned and slowly walked toward the road and sighed. "Peter, I found what I came for. I have learned how the Jews of Ozarow died. I know more than I had bargained for. The trip to Auschwitz and the killings in this field satisfied my curiosity about the destination of those letters. I have had a more memorable experience than I believed could be possible. It has been a remarkable trip."

My heart was heavy. I now knew the story of how the Jews of a town died. I would recite Kaddish at my grandmother's grave when I came home and tell the story of Ozarow and how her letters were finally delivered. "Peter, let's head home."

Chapter Seventeen

The Road Back—Willie's Story: Retreat—Kiev Coming and Going

Letter of January 1943:

We have become dedicated fighters in this struggle against the Bolsheviks. Even the new men coming to the front lines have this devotion to our cause. We are fighting for the great Germany the Führer created. All the progress of the last ten years is at risk. We must win this war to preserve our Fatherland and heritage. If we lose, we are sure the Russians will turn our country into a farmland and destroy our culture. No matter how hard it gets, we are brave. We are not the happy men that served in Poland just three years ago. Many of us do not believe we will be able to win, but we must fight to get a peace that honors our country. Very few of the friends we talked about when I was home are still here. What is left of my original group is now in the front lines as Landsers. We now know what it is to fight and fall back. We sit and talk about the old days, just three years ago. In Poland we were able to get very cheap schnapps and could spend hours sitting and drinking. Now there is no schnapps and no time to sit and talk. Sometimes we find vodka, but it isn't that good.

Most of the time our meals are rations, although the Army tries to serve us hot meals. The rations are nourishing, but boring. We were lucky the other day—a stray chicken was found by Fritz near a destroyed farm. Since the men think I'm a cook, I was asked to do the meal. Six of us were able to eat from this wonderful bird.

In hopes of a better tomorrow for the Fatherland!!

It was evident that the German penetration into Russia had reached its zenith. The letters showed a new tone. Papa had become hardened to the attitude of German righteousness in "the cause" and the changes from a victorious army to the Wehrmacht defending itself, often outnumbered, being beaten back toward the Polish border and the "Fatherland." The tide of the war was changing, and Papa's letters started to reflect the events occurring around him.

Letter of March 1943:

It is dark at only 4 p.m. here in the Russian winter. It is terribly cold and I'm wearing the gloves you sent me. They are one of the three layers of gloves I'm wearing to stay warm. I'm also wearing the wool cap Aunt Martha sent me for Christmas. We seem to be stalled here in the heights above Kiev awaiting either our general's orders to attack or to defend against the Russians. We hold the high ground and are confident that we are safe. Let them come. Many of the very political soldiers have been killed or wounded. We who carry on are doing our duty. All of us know the war has changed since the last few big battles. Now it is a test of our loyalty to our country.

The city of Kiev once must have been very beautiful. Much of it has been damaged by the battles. All I know is I want to be home. We sing a song to keep our spirits up. It is called "Unshaven and far, far from home, far far from home and unshaven." We are. The song is too true. We await the battle. I send you my love. If you can send cigarettes, it would be nice. We don't get good cigarettes here. The good cigarettes don't seem to get past the supply battalions to the front. Please save my letters. I want to read them when I come home. It will help me remember the horrible winter. This is a wretched land. I don't know why our Führer wants it."

The propaganda was explicit. There was to be no retreat, but bit by bit they gave ground back to the Russians. The surrender at Stalingrad in February and the battles of late 1943 in the lower Dnieper River area marked the end of the German tide flowing into Russia. After the battles of Kursk and Stalingrad, the Wehrmacht no longer had the strength to move deeper into the Russian heartland. In August 1943, Hitler ordered "no retreat." By September the orders were to pillage the areas where they were retreating. Now there was the torturous road back.

October, 1943:

I have been in the rear as part of a reserve group. We are no longer moving forward and have orders how we are to conduct ourselves as we fall back. We are commanded that nothing is to be left behind for the Ruskies, and we are to see that the land will be unusable for crops. It seems a waste. We fought so hard to gain all this ground and now we are slowly giving it back. We

> are being attacked by hoards of the enemy. They never seem to stop coming at us. On the steppes the clear fields make the tanks the king of the battles. I have been in a battle near Poltava, and we are proud to have slowed the Russians. We stayed in the city until the Russians swept around behind us. Then we moved back to our main forces. It was a job very well done. As a reward, our unit was pulled back and we were allowed to rest in the area near Kiev.

Willie turned his blue Audi to the west and started to trace the return journey the German army had faced after September 1943, some twenty-five months after they'd first crossed the Polish border. He stopped at a Russian equivalent of a small bed-and-breakfast, in a town named Fastiv, near the city of Kiev. This location gave him access to the modern north-south highway, M05, and allowed him to travel within the area of the German army's furthest advance. Before turning back, Willie re-read the relevant sections in his guidebooks, about the army history he had purchased before leaving home and several of his father's letters.

Just as the early letters had described the flush of German victories racing across Byelorussia and Ukraine, the later correspondence told of the army grinding to a halt and the start of the long retreat back to the borders of the Fatherland. The history of the war was spelled out in Papa's letters. While the Northern Army besieged Leningrad, the Central Army drove to the gates of Moscow, and the Southern army conquered the Crimea peninsula. Then the Wehrmacht's advances were blunted at the gates of Moscow, stalled in the siege of Leningrad, and devastated in the disaster at Stalingrad in autumn 1942. In June the following year there had been a massive battle north of Rostov in the area of Kursk. This was the site of the largest and most vicious tank battle ever fought, with over 2 million men engaged in the fighting. Willie realized that his father must have been there. After Kursk it was apparent to the German army staff that they could not win this Russian war. The massive German losses and the aggressiveness of the Russian army in the south started the German retreat that continued nearly two years, until the end in May 1945.

Letter of November 1943:

The mail came the other day. I received six letters from you all at once. This happened because we were at the front and mail delivery was delayed, as we are constantly moving. We crossed back across the Dnieper River several days ago. There were trees along the river and old clay-walled cottages with thatched roofs. The walls were white washed. There was a large sand bar with trees and bushes in the middle of the river. The birds were nested in the trees. They looked so peaceful, a sharp contrast to the fighting. Sometimes we can look across the fields and see the Russians cooking fires as they have their meals or try to keep warm. Our officers will not let us light fires, as they do not want to give our positions away. The fighting is very brutal. I hate the sound of the artillery shelling that seems to reverberate all around me. When it is our own, the explosions seem to surround us as we watch to see where the shells are detonating in front of us. When the Russians are firing, we tremble in our protective holes and dread the thump, thump of the shells as they land. Sometimes there are many casualties. The cries of the wounded are frightening. Several days ago in retaliation for a partisan attack, we were ordered to go into a town and shoot everything and everyone and leave nothing standing. Most of the Landsers did not agree with this action. I feel sick about it, but as long as the partisans attack us, we must do these horrible things. When it was over, I felt very guilty, but I know we followed orders. I know that if the tables were reversed and these uncivilized monsters were in the Fatherland, they would be much worse.

The severe change of tone in his father's letters was apparent. The conscript had become battlefield hardened and was writing home the message of the "Fatherland" that the propaganda officers were inculcating into the front-line troops. The promise of an early return home was now replaced by stories of battles and mention of duties performed and comrades lost. In some of the letters, there were longing, homesick, and loving passages punctuated by news of the war. Willie was brought to tears as he read the letter written from Belaya Tserkov, a town south of Kiev.

Letter of January 20, 1944:

My dearest darling and my Willie,

It is bitter cold, the night temperature drops to –30, and the days are seldom above –10. The sun sits very low in the sky and seems to have forgotten how to spread its warmth. Our equipment freezes and we spend more time battling the cold than the enemy. I long to come home to you and be in your arms. I miss the scent of your skin and the passion we enjoy when we are together. I miss your hair in my face as we sleep, and I miss holding you as you tremble with love in the night. I pray to be with you again. I just want to be your husband, Hans the baker, loving you and bringing up our Willie. When will all of this horror end? Yesterday, once again, they called my platoon together for a firing party supervised by the SS; this is something I do not like to do. I was lucky this time and didn't have to join the assignment. When the men came back from the task, they received a ration of schnapps and got very drunk. We are now slowly retreating toward the west. I am coming closer to you, but am I coming home? Are we going to get to grow old together?

The letter came from near Kiev as the German army was falling back. The battle chronicle that Willie carried in the car dated the second battle of Kiev in the months of November and December 1943. The German army lost the city and fell back to the steppe to the west. Willie read the letter about the firing party and realized that the Wehrmacht had been involved in some of the horrible incidents he had read about. He thought, Papa?

Willie wanted relief from the constant driving and tracing of Papa's movements. He wanted to see more than battlefields, so he headed toward a good hotel in Kiev. As he approached the city, he was surprised how quickly it appeared from the steppe flatlands, into a tall outer rim of apartment houses that formed the verge of urban development. Ten- and twelve-story buildings seemed to jump out of the flat plains planted with wheat, which defined the change from farm to town. Willie was surprised. These buildings had character. They weren't the uniformly dull Russian architecture that he had seen. They had to have been built in recent years, since the breakup of the Soviet Union. Tall white buildings with attractive balconies, the facades had startling modern mosaic artworks in beautiful colorful patterns, in contrast to the flat farmland.

Willie drove along the superhighway tracing the flow of the Dnieper River and exited when he saw the Slavutich Hotel sign. He had called ahead, selecting a hotel with a three-star rating where he thought he would be comfortable. The modern fourteen-story building was described in the guidebook as a "place for a discerning traveler." Willie parked the car and checked in. His room was on the eleventh floor, with an awesome balcony view of the huge statue rising above the heights of the National War Museum across the river. The accommodations were more than adequate for his purposes. He wanted to forget his father's war, have a hot shower, and enjoy the city as a tourist. Sasha changed that.

Sasha was a fifty-two-year-old guide suggested by the hotel concierge. He was six feet two inches tall, thin, with an assertive manner, and strode into the hotel lobby twenty minutes after the concierge called. He was a commanding presence, wearing brown slacks and a light green silk shirt with two buttons open at the neck and a gold medallion showing beneath the open shirt. His shoulders were partially covered by a fashionably cut light tan leather jacket. Willie looked across the lobby as he appeared and immediately knew that this well-dressed man was the guide. In four steps he crossed the marble floor and held his hand out in greeting with two crystalline blue eyes focused directly at Willie.

"I'm Sasha!"

"I'm Willie Kirchenmann. I believe you are the guide I'm supposed to meet."

"Yes. You sent for me—I believe you want to tour the city."

Willie fell into step with Sasha as they walked into the warm sunny afternoon. Sasha towered over Willie by about four inches, and his long legs and rapid pace made it hard for Willie to follow.

Sasha's car was a light tan Yugo that was a remnant from the pre-independence days, but appeared to be in excellent shape. The two tall men crammed themselves into the small car.

Willie asked: "Tell me about yourself."

"I was brought up just ten kilometers from the center of Kiev. Both my mother and father were Ukrainians and had been in the army. They settled here because this is where they were when the war ended. It's that simple. I grew up, went to school and became a guide because the government said I was smart enough to learn languages. In the old days I reported on whatever a visitor told me. Yes, we guides were assigned to visitors and were part of the 'keeping track' business. Visitors may have thought they were free to visit sites, but we directed their trips."

"How can I be sure you are not part of the old system, only working for the new government?"

"This is the free Ukraine," Sasha said, smiling. "No one cares where you go or what you say."

Willie chuckled. Sasha went on with a nationalistic fervor. "We were subjects of the Russians from the end of our revolution and Civil War until 1991 when the Soviet Union broke up. Now we can show the world who we are and what we stand for. We are a free nation."

His attitude and enthusiasm were contagious. Willie felt relaxed and pleased. Sasha was obviously proud to be a Ukrainian. His car even had the flag mounted on the rear window.

"Now we go sightseeing."

Exiting from the hotel parking lot, they crossed the three-lane Paton Bridge. With great pride, Sasha explained, "This bridge is not named after that legendary American general. It is named for our famous Ukrainian bridge engineer Evgeny Paton. It is over 1,500 meters long and was the first fully welded steel bridge when it was built. As a matter of fact, when it was built it was the longest bridge in Europe."

As they crossed the river, Willie looked to both sides and commented: "You seem to have many bridges."

Sasha again puffed out his chest and explained, "Since Kiev is located on both sides of the river, and the river is over several hundred meters wide in many places, Kiev has always been known as a city of bridges. In early history we had floating bridges, but from the mid-nineteenth century, the town fathers started building stationary bridges. There are fourteen in service for automobiles, trams, and pedestrians, as well as two under construction."

As Willie smiled at the explanation, Sasha went on: "Of course, we seem to be victims of armies blowing up our bridges and having to reconstruct them. All the bridges were destroyed during the 1920 war and of course again during the 1941 to 1945 war. But don't feel guilty. The Russian army destroyed the bridges first to slow the Germans, and then later the Germans dynamited the reconstructed bridges to slow the Russian advance."

Waving his hand and looking around at Willie, he laughed: "You blow them up, we blow them up, it doesn't matter. In Kiev we then just build them again. We keep the plans so we don't forget."

Willie and Sasha traveled the wide boulevards, dodging the buses tied to their pantographs hugging the overhead wires like giraffes nibbling on high tree branches. They visited the Cathedral of the Assumption, which dated back to the seventeenth century, and wandered through the National Museum of Fine Arts. The guided walk through Independence Square, with its huge Soviet-style buildings and beautiful fountains, was surrounded by wide sidewalks filled with widowed old ladies sitting on packing cases vending a large variety of everyday items. Sasha said that these ladies were, for the most part, war widows. Willie's spirits, which had been worn down by the daily driving through battlefields, were restored. Sasha's wry sense of humor forced Willie to smile again and again, and he would laugh as the huge Ukrainian told his stories about new freedoms and old Russian misadventures and his pride in the Ukraine.

"Kiev now has nearly three million people, and the restaurants are world class." They drove along the clean boulevards and the many small parks. Sasha told Willie their names and gave him descriptions of the persons or events honored in the dedication plaques and memorial statues they passed. "In Ukraine we have many parks to hold the statues of our many heroes. In Soviet days when we needed houses, they gave us monuments. Now Russians are gone and we like the parks."

The tour was a joy. Willie felt tired but hungry after three hours. Sasha said he knew of a great restaurant and detoured to the river to the Khutorok, a boat restaurant. They started their meal with several obligatory drinks of vodka, then had a relaxed dinner sharing a bottle of Ukrainian champagne. Willie was amused at the restaurant's nautical theme so far from the ocean, and Sasha tried to apologize for the meal's expense, but Willie felt that the cost was quite reasonable, about half of what he would pay in Stuttgart.

About halfway through their dinner, Sasha said, "You realize the German army was predominantly horse drawn. Although we talk about the tank battles and the massive amount of transport, in a typical Wehrmacht infantry division there were about 12,000 officers and men and over 4,600 horses. The vast amount of German artillery and supplies were horse drawn. At the beginning of the invasion there were 750,000 German horses and they needed over 16,000 tons of feed a day. The Germans thought that they would confiscate this feed from the Russians as they drove forward; but the Russians torched their fields and granaries. The Germans murdered townspeople and stole their horses and whatever remaining feed they could find. They needed replacement horses for their movements. The German army losses of horses from 1941 until 1945 exceeded 6,700,000 horses. Of these, we are told, 26,000 were eaten by the troops in the besieged Stalingrad. In contrast, the Soviets had a buildup of trucks and jeeps from the supply program from the United States and from their own factories beyond the Urals. For several years after the war there was mass starvation of the Russian peasants as a result of the destroyed grain."

"That's amazing," Willie replied. "I always thought that with the blitzkrieg concept, the German army had gone over to mechanization by the end of the Polish campaign. They even trained my father to operate a vehicle. I wonder if he ever got to drive?"

"Willie, in the beginning many Ukrainians were sympathetic to the German invaders. Some of the men even joined the German army, where they were assigned to all-Ukrainian units. They saw the German army as liberators from 'Uncle Joe' and the oppressive Soviet regime. Remember, our civil war had ended only about twenty years before, and we had become unwilling Soviet subjects. As the German murderers confiscated property and suppressed the local population, this sympathy changed. The Ukrainian peasant's attitude swiftly went from welcoming a new liberator to hate and resistance. The reaction created the Partisans, an army of irregulars who were mostly displaced people who took to the forests to fight behind the lines, harassing the Germans. In the rear of the German army, the

Partisans robbed supply trains and attacked any German unit they could ambush."

Willie was uncomfortable about Sasha's descriptions. The stories dovetailed into the fabric of Papa's letters, but in many ways didn't match what his father had written. He was hearing what Papa wouldn't or couldn't write.

Willie called for the check and paid the bill. Sasha drove him back to the hotel, said goodnight, and arranged to pick him up at about 8:30 the next morning. Willie walked into the hotel and looked forward to a good night's sleep in the plush bed and comfortable surroundings of his room.

It was just about an hour after Willie put his head down that he heard the "BOOM" followed by another "BOOM." He went to the balcony and looked out at a spectacular fireworks display, with rockets rising over the bluffs on the other side of the river. With each burst of the rockets and cascade of sparks, the great statue that dominated the other side of the river was fully illuminated, and the river water would shimmer romantically. The bombardment of joyous pyrotechnics echoed from the river to the balcony and seemed to reverberate back across to the city on the far shore. Willie stood at his open window and watched for about twenty minutes. He thought: "I'm seeing rockets in a land at peace where there had been so much war." He turned, went back to bed, and slept well.

Early in the morning, Willie sorted through Papa's letters and found what he was looking for, a letter dated September 1941. It was in the ribbon-bound pile of early war letters.

> It has been glorious. Our group has won Kiev, the city on the Dnieper. We were part of a great pincer that cut the Commie

troops off from their main army. I understand we captured over 650,000 prisoners. This war must be over soon. I cannot see how the Ruskies can continue to lose so many men. How proud we all are for these victories. The German might is superior to all that we face. We must be proud. I look forward to being back with you in our victorious Germany.

Willie searched for a second letter that he knew also mentioned Kiev. This one was dated October 1943:

Our group has been brought back to Kiev and we are guarding the city. We know the Russians will try very hard to take the city from us. I know we will fight very hard, and from our positions on the heights above the river we should be able to hold on for a long while. I know Stuttgart has been bombed. I hope it isn't in ruins like I see here. Write and tell me how you are making out. When you tell me that all is good, I am able to be comforted for the time between your letters. Please send a new picture of yourself and Willie. War is very bad. Please survive. I want to have our life together renewed when this is all over.

Willie took the several letters that described the taking of Kiev in 1941 and the retreat in 1944 and read them again over his breakfast. He sensed that his father had become a different person during the intervening two years.

After breakfast, Sasha was in the lobby to greet him. "We'll spend today looking at The Great Patriotic War Museum and then take a trip out of the city."

It was a short ten-minute ride from the hotel, crossing the Dnieper once more on the Paton Bridge and turning to the museum at the first turn at the end of the bridge. The huge statue dominated the escarpment that lined the Kiev palisade rising sharply from the river. The statue, a fully robed female figure, was about 200 feet tall, with a base of at least another 100 feet, holding a sword in one hand and a shield in the other, arms raised in a victory embrace to the sky. "We call the statue 'Rodina-mat.' The closest translation is 'Motherland.' There is another similar statue, but in a slightly different posture in Volgograd—you know, the former Stalingrad."

Willie stared upward from the base of the monument. "That statue is enormous. You really do everything on a grand scale! Sasha, I was awakened by a fireworks display last night. It seemed to be coming from this area. What was the occasion?"

"They had a reception at the War Museum for a NATO general who was in Kiev, and they made the fireworks to celebrate his visit."

Sasha parked the car at the base of the museum at the rear of the bluff. The entrance was at the top of the hill along a long promenade. Sasha smiled and walked about a pace ahead of Willie, leading him on. Willie was nearly out of breath by the time Sasha reached the raised area overlooking the river. On the massive flat platform were Russian WWII souvenir tanks and artillery pieces mounted on display. They were the largest Willie had ever seen. There were five huge monuments, each much larger than life, depicting men in battle, peasants tending the fields, and women building war material in factories. Sasha explained that these were dedicated to all the people who defended their Soviet homeland. Willie turned away and looked across the river. The view was commanding.

"Willie, this area was the battleground during the Great War. From here you can see the powerful position an army would have when it held these heights. When the People's Army struck back after the city had been captured, the Germans took these positions and defended their hold on the city. The city changed hands three times during the war. The Germans took control in 1941 and then lost and regained it during the next two years. In 1943 the Soviet army finally recaptured the city. There were many Russian casualties in each of these battles. We don't show the names of the dead heroes on the plaques; we show the designations of the battalions, companies, and groups that fought here. In many cases the losses within an army group were so huge that the unit ceased to exist and the Soviet Army just assigned survivors to another division or battle group being formed."

Willie was awed by these massive statues. The sheer size of each monument was a statement of the Russian attitude. Inside the museum he was impressed by the collection's scope. The documentation was set out in great detail, starting with an exhibit showing the rise of the Nazi party, complete with film clips of Goebbels and Hitler, to the start of the war and the German invasion of Russia in June 1941. A full wall was covered with a painting of the horror of the Kursk battle. The exhibit continued to a painting drenched in red and black paint depicting the fires, smoke, and hell of the fall of Berlin. Each phase of the war was portrayed.

It was all there in pictures and artifacts: the invasion, the retreat, the consolidation of the Russian defense, and finally the tide turning and the massive battles pushing the German army back to the German homeland and the final combat in Berlin. The last huge exhibition hall was about 50 meters long and 10 meters high from the marble floor to the immense ceiling. The room was lined with thousands of pictures of men, most in their uniforms, along with letters written from the front. Sasha said, "All of these are men who died, and some of the letters they had sent to their families." Willie thought of his father's letters back at the hotel.

After three hours of touring the museum and the battlements, Sasha turned to Willie and said, "I think you have seen enough of this part of the war, but I have something more to show you."

Sasha drove Willie back to Independence Square, the central square of Kiev, parked the car and took Willie to a buffet lunch at what Sasha described as a "typical Ukrainian bistro."

Willie was amused. The waitresses were in native costumes with colorful skirts and peaked capped hats. "Sasha, I know a tourist trap when I'm in one." The meal only came to only about 3.75 euros (US$5), and Willie thought it was a good bargain to be amused for an hour.

During the lunch Willie asked Sasha, "How do you feel about taking a German around a Russian war museum?"

Sasha thought a moment and replied, "I have no problem with you or any other German today. We are one generation away from that hate. However, there are memories of the past that still anger me. The killings, of course, are on our mind. The Nazis considered us to be subhuman and wantonly murdered and plundered the Ukrainians. The senselessness and futility of the war reminds us of acts that are beyond belief. When the Germans captured Kiev, they plundered our museums, taking trophies from the library of the Ukrainian Academy of Science that had singular manuscripts of Persian, Abyssinian, and Chinese writings. There were also priceless incunabula by the first printer, Ivan Fedorov, and rare editions of

Shevchenko, Mickewicz, and Ivan Franko. They took these items and unfortunately they were destroyed later in the war. Any artifact that could be shipped out to the SS plunder warehouses or Goering's collections was stolen from the homes and museums. They had no respect for our people or heritage."

Willie sat quietly during Sasha's answer. He wondered what the guide really thought.

After the lunch, Sasha took Willie out of central Kiev for a short fifteen-minute drive. He parked the Yugo along the side of the major highway heading west and locked the car. Sasha said, "Let's walk along this path."

The path was made of cast concrete pavers about two meters by two meters in size, four pavers across with a five-meter divide of growth and another four paver path running parallel to the walkway. The center greenery was overgrown and appeared not to have been trimmed or cared for in years.

"Willie, this is the path to the ravine at Babi Yar. Where I parked the car, the German army had emptied the wagons they used to transport the Jews of Kiev from the ghetto. They had concentrated over 50,000 Jews into a confined area of the city, and in this major action they started to clear the ghetto. One by one they filled trucks with Jews, telling them they were being transported to a 'promised land,' and each family was allotted 70 kilos of luggage. At the base of the road they were forced off the trucks. The Jews were then herded along this trail—mothers and fathers, children, and the elderly. They carried their baggage with them. The path is approximately one kilometer long. At the top is a monument to those killed here. You will notice that there is a deep ravine to our left as we walk."

Willie had a hard time keeping up with Sasha's pace walking up the slight hill. At one point he reached out and tugged at the leather jacket to get Sasha to slow a bit. It took about five minutes to get to the clearing at the top of the rise. There was a large Jewish candelabrum in a paved cleared square about fifty by fifty meters. "The Jews call this seven branched candelabrum a menorah. This a tribute to those killed in the ravine."

After stepping back from the candelabrum, they stood on the lip of the huge deep natural amphitheatre between the two hills. Within the ravine was a large gray granite statue depicting people struggling upward, pushing children to the heavens. Sasha turned to Willie and said: "This is Babi Yar."

Willie stood there in silence.

"This ravine is about six miles out of the city. On the day of the Jewish holiday Yom Kippur in 1941, the most religious day of the Jewish year, the Nazis assembled the Jews of Kiev and systematically murdered them. There were several large trenches at the bottom of this ravine. The Jews were taken to the lip of the trench and machine gunned or shot in the base of the skull. Within the first two days they killed over 33,000. By the time they were through, it was estimated that over 100,000 were murdered here. At one point the Germans were running out of ammunition and, according to one historian, they would put two people head to head; so one bullet would do a double job of killing. They shot people from morning to night. It took over five days. Trucks came with people from the ghetto and left with piles of clothes and valuables."

Looking over the ravine, the scene was so peaceful; Willie felt the bile rising in his throat over the revulsion of what occurred here. He couldn't think of anything to say. The two men stood still as Willie cast his glances into the area where the pit must have been, where the thick undergrowth covered all evidence of the massacre so long ago. It had started to rain, but Willie and Sasha stayed at their vantage point. Willie turned up the collar of his jacket but felt the dampness seeping through.

Willie wanted Sasha to stop talking, but Sasha continued: "The hundred thousand Jews that were killed here are the story that everyone knows. But there are two other stories that tell of the depravity of the Germans. As we were told, there was a group of SS assigned to killing Jews by gassing them in portable vans out in the countryside. For recreation they had a night visiting the bordellos in Kiev. After satisfying their pleasure, they rounded up the girls from the nightclubs and told them to enter the vans to bathe. The girls were gassed and their bodies were added to the pyre of Babi Yar."

Willie said, "I never heard of that story. Are you sure?"

"Yes," Sasha replied. "And there was also the story of the local football team that was brought together to play a select team from the German army. When they won their match, they were told that there would be a replay. The Ukrainians won the second time, although the German commander advised them to lose the match. Most of the members of the team wound up at Babi Yar. The German army didn't like losing."

Willie could only utter, "That's horrible."

As they stood in silence in the light rainy mist, a group of children, obviously Jewish by the skullcaps the boys were wearing, came up the walk from the parking area. They were quiet and respectful. A woman, their teacher or guide, assembled them at the base of the menorah and they began to sing. It was a pleasant melody, and Willie listened to their beautiful voices as the sound of their music floated across the clearing to him. It was a comforting song, made mellower by the rain that continued to fall.

"What is that song?" Willie asked.

"The song is called 'Hatikvah.' It translates as 'hope' and is the Israeli national anthem, although Jews sang it for many years before there was an Israel."

Sasha continued. "If the original murders weren't enough to desecrate this place, in 1943 as the Germans started their retreat, the SS was ordered by Himmler to eliminate the evidence. They assembled a work force of slave prisoners, exhumed the corpses that were in the mass graves and hadn't been burned in the original pyre, and created an enormous second pyre. Every prisoner assigned to this task was shackled. The job took six weeks of digging, sorting, carting, and feeding the flames. They destroyed the evidence. All that was left was a mound of ash. At the end, the prisoners knew they would be murdered as part of the SS cover-up, and they revolted and tried to escape. All but fifteen were killed. Those few who escaped told their story."

"Years later in 1961 our great poet Yevtushenko published his poem *Babi Yar,* and the memorial you see was sponsored by the writer Victor Nekrasov. There were many protests because the Russians wanted to make this ravine into a sports stadium. The poem caused an upwelling of opinion, and the site was preserved as you see it." Sasha quietly recited the poem:

"The wild grasses rustle over Babi Yar.

The trees look ominous, like judges.

Here all things scream silently,

And, baring my head, slowly I feel myself turning gray.

And I myself am one massive, soundless scream

About the thousand buried here.

I am each old man here shot dead.

I am every child here shot dead.

Nothing in me shall ever forget!"

Willie and Sasha said nothing and slowly turned away from the ravine and walked down the path. The rain was soaking them. Willie held his head down as he walked, the rain dripping from his head mixing with the tears that streamed down his cheeks. He imagined the lines of Jews carrying their meager belongings walking the other way along this path. He saw whole families shuffling along. They were almost real as he visualized them parading to the death that awaited them. Willie looked around the forest. He didn't see birds or flowers. There were just the pine trees, deep undergrowth, and a dank odor coming from the surrounding forest. Dampness seemed to rise from the heart of the woods, and just as tears would fall, drops of rain came off the pine needles along the path. He could feel the spirits that saturated the air. They were around him, surrounding him. He shuddered as a chill ran up his back. He kept swallowing, wanting to express thoughts that were racing through his mind. Opening his mouth, no sound came out. Willie wanted the walk to end, wanted to be in the confines of Sasha's car. He was afraid of what Sasha would reveal next.

"Willie, it was as if there were two wars. One was a war we understood. The Germans wanted to conquer land for their 'Lebensraum,' room to expand and feed their people. They wanted a large sphere of influence and power. The other war was ideological. They thought they were a superior race. The Nazis had the concept that there was a hierarchy of human beings and they were at the top of the pyramid. Ukrainians, Jews, and others were subhumans, to be considered as vermin and exterminated. At places like Babi Yar, they fought that second war. Thank God that we won the first war on the true battlefield."

Willie was silent for most of the ride back. Nearing the hotel, he turned to Sasha and very quietly said, "Thank you." Then, almost whispering, Willie said: "I know it may be hard for you to believe, but I never heard of Babi Yar. I come from a generation in which many things were not discussed. We just did not talk about the things I have seen on this trip. I am almost in disbelief at what you have told me."

In the driveway, Willie shook Sasha's hand to say goodbye, then pulled Sasha toward him into a hug. The embrace lasted for a moment. With a deep sigh and his eyes still red from the emotion of the afternoon, Willie stepped back and hurried through the lobby and to his room.

Willie ate alone that night and went to bed before 10 p.m. He felt emotionally drained and wanted a good night's sleep. He kept thinking about the awesome number of 100,000 dead and the image of that parade of people walking to the killing point. Resounding in his head were the harmonious voices of the Jewish children singing the song "Hope" at the Babi Yar menorah. It was difficult to sleep peacefully.

Chapter Eighteen

Encountering Krista: Return to Poland—Willie's Story

The next morning traveling west, Willie left Kiev crisscrossing roads and battlefields. He was thinking how the victorious German army had moved into Russia and then suffered the defeats at Stalingrad and Kursk which had turned the tide. At each rest stop, he pored over tour books, letters, and atlases tracing the movements and engagements of the two armies. Now he had reoccurring images of the retreat and the massacres. He could not dismiss the sight of the ravine at Babi Yar. To his amazement, he was looking at more than battle areas. He considered the other people who had been war victims. He had heard the stories of Pinsk and Babi Yar and they were haunting. He could not put these massacres out of his mind. The question of his father's role was reoccurring. Had he taken part? Willie now suspected that there were no innocents in the Wehrmacht.

The great slogans of the war surround us. I may have thought they were silly just two years ago, but I have come to believe. We must do what we have to do to make us victorious. I must survive, and our Adolph Hitler must be victorious to bring about the great future we are fighting for. If we lose this war, the Bolsheviks will destroy all we have lived for and wanted for Germany. We have been told by the officers that if we lose, our Fatherland will be torn apart and turned into farms and pastures. Our cities will be leveled and our people scattered around the globe. Our great recovery from the last war will have been for nothing.

My love for you and Willie and for the Fatherland grows every day.

Willie recalled the letter about the firing party. Papa said he hadn't been part of this assignment. Was this true? Were there other assignments that Papa had taken part in? Had Papa been at Babi Yar? How many other Babi Yar murders had there been?

Willie found himself humming as he drove these back roads. Now he wasn't singing the Germany army battle songs or the lullabies of his youth. That song, that melody, "Hope," the Jewish tune he'd heard the children sing at Babi Yar, entered his mind again and again.

Each night he would re-read several of the letters and seek the passages in the guidebooks that described the activities in the area. In one of the books, *The Good Soldier,* written by a war survivor, there was a passage that described how the Nazi army had marched into Russia in 1941 with the belief that they were on a grand crusade and that it was their mission to rid the world of Bolshevism. The book detailed how the German troops were told that the Russians, the Ukrainians, and the Jews were "subhumans" and could only be the object of destruction by the superior Aryan Germans. It documented how the army commanded that the killing of these subhumans was justified and was to be commended. Now as Willie was heading west following the path of the retreat, he wondered how the spirit of that glorious German army had been as they'd fought holding action after holding action, without having the resources to match the strength of the Russians and now knowing that the end of this road was an inevitable defeat.

The retreat had been marked by short, intense battles, with German tanks and infantry mounting attack after counterattack, only to be stopped by the Russians and thrown farther back. As the Russians went on the offensive, the German army did not have adequate manpower or materiel to stop the inevitable progress of the huge Russian force that had been assembled, and had been thrown into defense of their homeland. The German army, once invincible, was being forced farther and farther to the west.

> We often face wave after wave of these fanatical Russians. They seem to have no regard for their lives when they attack. We fight very hard and then at night withdraw to prepared positions. The commanders are working hard to minimize our losses, but I have to admit we have suffered. My friends from training days are gone. This has been a costly war. Pray for me to come home.

Entire German armies were being trapped by Russian pincer attacks engulfing large areas of the steppe at a time. Some German units fought their way out of the Russian encirclement and retreated. Other army groups were decimated and surrendered. There were counterattacks and withdrawals. The army fell back behind the Dnieper River, and Willie was sure from one letter that his Papa had fought at Dnepropetrovsk. The postmarks on the letters seemed to move all over the map of the German army's southern front. Papa's unit was being moved from point to point. There was a letter with a postmark dated November, from a town far to the west, Kirovograd. Papa been wounded.

> I have been taken out of the fighting for a short time. I am all right. I had a slight leg wound, high on the thigh, and I have been brought to a rest area to recover before I go back to my unit. The good part is that when I came to the hospital, I was able to receive some letters from you, and I'm so happy that Willie is doing well at school. How tall is he? I'd like to see him and see what a good man he is growing to be. Please send pictures. We are all discouraged. More of my friends have disappeared or fallen in battle. I promise you that I will try to return to your arms. I love you. Take care of Willie. Bring him up to understand our values and to be a good man. I will write as soon as we are back in rear camp.
>
> Heil Hitler, we must live for the glory of Germany.

Willie wove his way west using the new postwar highways, traveling on wide cement roadways designed for modern high-speed travel. These highways didn't exist in 1944. On some of the long straight roads, he could see for miles ahead across the flat plain. There were tall pine forests and wheat fields lining the roads. The occasional oak tree among the ubiquitous pines reminded him of the parks in Stuttgart. His pace was one to two hundred miles a day looking at battlefields, traveling where sixty years before, a day's progress by either army was measured in meters. Some of the towns Papa wrote about were hard to find. Towns such as Bender, mentioned in one letter, now had a new Russian name: Tighina. There were so many other changes. These highways didn't resemble the war-torn rutted mud roads of spring and the iced roads of winter described in the letters. There was remarkable beauty in the flat fertile land covered by the high blue sky filled with scudding spring clouds.

Willie experienced the June heat. Thermal rivulets rose as the heat beat down on the tarmac. A sudden cloudburst soaked the landscape and the road. It was an eerie sensation as the cool rain reacting to the hot asphalt created a cloud of steam filling the air. Willie approached and sped through the mist as the rain evaporated around him.

After his time in Kiev, he traveled following the route of the withdrawing German army. He envisioned the tanks and men, the mud that had mired the army during the spring campaigns and destroyed timetables for attack. He pictured loaded vehicles stuck, wheels spinning, men and mules straining to get trucks and wagons back on the road. He pictured horse-drawn columns halted because the roads were impassible; the countryside hazardous with partisans raiding rear supply units. He pictured his father, once proudly telling of his well-tailored shirts, now just wishing for a bath and a clean uniform.

In many small towns, such as Skvira, Smela, and Talnoya, there were commemorative monuments. Sometimes it was an old T-34 tank preserved and memorialized with a plaque; in other larger cities, like Ternopil and Bedichev, the statue depicted a soldier cast in concrete in a heroic pose, right arm raised with rifle or tommy gun in hand moving forward to attack. Again and again there were only lists of local "Heroes of the Soviet Union" who had fought and sacrificed in this catastrophic war. Just as at the museum in Kiev, some of the memorials had only the names of battalions and regiments carved into their stone bases. Several times along the road, far between towns, there were huge monuments and tall obelisks marking battle sites, engraved with the names of local heroes. Several had eternal flames as centerpieces.

> We have come to appreciate dust. Dust means that there is no snow on the ground and there is no mud. The weather is a factor in everything. The summers have been unusually warm and we are told that we have just been through the worst winter in the history of local records. We are ordered not to mention casualties, but I think you are getting some news back home that all is not good. My group is no longer at full strength. There is a shortage of new replacements. We must do with what we have. The landscape, which must be beautiful in peacetime, is bleak and desolate in war. We passed through villages that are now nothing more than rows of chimneys standing like sentinels silhouetted against the sky where homes once stood. We have had horsemeat steaks to eat because animals have been killed in the bombardments. I wish I could say more. I love you and hope all is well at home.

There were enormous Russian cemeteries. They were orderly places, not elaborate but massive fields with orderly white markers beautifully maintained. There were very few cemeteries for German soldiers. When Willie came upon one, he would stop and walk among the graves. He didn't know what he was looking for, but would wonder if this Landser was from Stuttgart, or was this Papa's buddy? These were the fallen, left behind during the retreat. The burials were orderly but not well kept. The haste when they were dug and abandoned was evident. On a side road he occasionally would come upon gravesites with minimalist markings showing where one, two, or three German soldiers were buried. In some cases an inscription of no more than a name and rank on a small wooden board served as the marker. The markers were weathered and the inscriptions faded. Willie would stop, try to read the meager inscriptions, and place a flower plucked from the nearby field on the grave, and then move on.

One letter haunted Willie; the date was late in July 1944, and the war had turned disastrous for the German army. Willie believed he was in the approximate area of Ukraine where his father had written the letter. He was amazed that this letter had passed through the censors:

> My dear loving wife! Yesterday under the unceasing blast of artillery and the constant roar of incoming Katyusha rockets we celebrated the survival of Hitler from a bomb attempt to kill him. We are all pleased that our Führer is alive. I thought the squall of the bombardment would never end. We thought the Russians would attack, but they seemed to hold back. My friend Schultz believes they are gathering strength for a big push. We are resting and hoping for the best. I am saddened by the lack of additional men and supplies. Our unit is less than a quarter of the authorized strength, but we must hold our positions. That is the command of the day. I'm not happy that your letters rarely reach me. I know you are writing almost every day. Please continue writing. For now I embrace you and the glory of our country.

Some towns were missing. Names that were on the old maps were no longer there. Some villages had just disappeared. The closer he got to the Polish border, the more pronounced was this phenomenon. In many cases there were places that Papa mentioned that no longer existed. Willie thought it was strange.

About two nights before he planned to cross over into Poland, he stopped at a small, clean, quaint hotel in the center of Buz'ka, which was between two of the secondary roads marked as "P" roads on Willie's map. He sat in the bar drinking an Obolon lager beer, a local Ukrainian brew. He was surprised that the Ukrainian beer, called *pyvo,* tasted as good as some of his German favorites. He thought it was remarkable that Russians and Ukrainians could brew something besides vodka. He was hungry and asked the barman for a waitress.

The waitress's name was Krista, and she escorted him to a table near a window. As Willie followed her, he couldn't help but notice that she was strikingly good looking. She was a tall blond, about 5 feet 10 inches, with crystalline blue eyes and shoulder-length hair. He judged her to be about thirty years old. Her hair was pulled back from her face and held at the nape of her neck with a plastic clip. She was shapely, and her looks, posture, and poise caught Willie's eye. She strode ahead of him in her black leather clogs, as they walked through the dining room to the table. Her appearance would easily attract most men.

She seated him at a table near the lone window and gave him a menu. It was too dark to see outside, but the faux white lace curtains lent a pleasant touch to the otherwise rustic dining area that was lighted by a simple brass chandelier. The room was dominated by a huge fireplace with a large log emitting a bright warm flame. There were six other tables, all the same size. The table could comfortably accommodate four diners, with the expected oil-cloth table cover, a glass sugar bowl, and square clear glass salt and pepper shakers with bright stainless steel tops centered on the table with a standing menu wedged between them.

By now Willie had enough understanding of the Ukrainian language that reading the menu presented no problem. In the dining area only one other table was occupied. Four men neared the end of their meal. As there were very few people in the bar or the dining room, Willie started to chat with the waitress. Traveling alone, he'd had no one to talk to during the day and felt a real need to just speak. She seemed to welcome the opportunity for a conversation in German. She was wearing a white half apron over a peasant skirt. Her name, Krista, was on the badge of her blue blouse engraved in white on the blue background. Willie joked, "It's a nice name," and she quickly replied: "A nice name for a nice girl, but only to nice men." As she finished saying it, she tossed her head back and flashed a bright wide smile.

Willie complimented her on her German pronunciation.

"All of us in Russia and now in Ukraine must take several languages in school. I took German and English. I don't get to use either language often. It's a pleasure to talk to you and practice the language."

Krista was well groomed and had the bearing of a well-disciplined thoroughbred, not the image of other waitresses Willie had encountered at other inns. Willie smiled and said, "I wish I were twenty years younger."

"You wouldn't be here if you were twenty years younger," she quickly snapped back with a smile on her face.

Again, he chuckled at her response. This was a relief from the dull meals he'd had at most of the other stops along his travels.

Krista was all business, recommending several menu items, particularly the *holubtsi,* the Ukrainian version of cabbage rolls stuffed with rice and hamburger meat that she said were a specialty of the chef.

Willie was more attracted to the tone and meter of her voice than the decision of selecting a meal. He quickly agreed to the holubtsi preceded by a small bowl of borscht. Krista took his order, returning to his table to talk to him while the food was being prepared. While he was eating, she first asked if everything was all right and then paused to chat. It was obvious Krista didn't feel pressured by the other occupied table, and she found the presence of the German interesting.

"Krista, I have a question for you. Are you from this area?"

"Yes, I was born within twenty miles of here. I'm thirty-eight years old, and I was married for six years. My husband was in the army and was killed in Chechnya. I don't have children, and this is a way of earning money and getting out of the house. There, you know my entire life story."

The quick, short answer and forthrightness impressed Willie. "I have another question, but before I ask, let me tell you why I'm here." He then told of his journey, and how he wanted to know about the war from the point of view of traveling where the German armies had fought and where he believed his father had been.

Willie asked if she would sit down and join him.

"I'm a bit tired," Krista said, sitting down opposite him, positioning herself where she could look across the room and observe the other occupied table.

After Willie finished his explanation, she looked up to see that all was well in the dining room and began to speak in a very low voice. "First of all, let me give you my background: I was a student at the university when I met my husband. I was studying history and languages. I wanted to be a translator. I fell in love; we married, had a glorious time while I finished my studies. Then he was conscripted into the army, remember we were Russian then. After graduation I didn't take the job offered by the government as a tourist bureau guide so I could move to be near his army camp. Then he was sent to Chechnya. A year later I received the message that he was killed. His name was Mikhael, and I really loved him. He was a very handsome man, tall, gentle, and loving and took very good care of me. We were two idealistic students. When I got the news of his death it took the life out of me. My ambition was drained and I moved back to this area so I could be near his family. This is a job, nothing more."

Soberly he said: "I guess we are all damaged by war."

"Some more than others. Very few of the people in this area are from here. The native population was decimated, first by the Germans coming through and then by the Russians during their recapture. The Soviets had a scorched earth policy as they retreated in 1941 and then the Germans destroyed the towns as they retreated in 1943–44. The Germans razed and burned over 28,000 villages and over 700 towns as they fell back. Many of these places no longer exist. In 1943 Himmler said the Germans would leave not a single person, no cattle, not a ton of grain, and not a railroad track standing or usable. Everyone has a story of their family and the way they survived or were relocated here. Ten million Ukrainians died in the war. It was murder, murder, and murder with destruction, destruction. If it wasn't Hitler murdering Jews, it was the Russians being indiscriminate in how they slaughtered to recapture the land and then eliminated anyone who they thought collaborated with the Germans or might be dissatisfied with the Communist way of life. Of the twenty million Russians who died, we Ukrainians were half the total.

Willie was moved by Krista's conversation. As she spoke she still surveyed the room and then returned to her story. "Willie, these were the lands of the death squads. Troops from the army, yes, the regular German army as well as the notorious SS, were dispatched to each village. As the army went East in their conquest, these squads followed. Some were 'special units,' others were drawn from the ranks. They were well organized and they didn't miss any village, some as small as three families living at a crossroads or at a farm. Villages that had been in existence for three or four hundred years became targets for Nazi searches and killings. The Jews lived peacefully, except for some harassment years ago by the Cossacks who would come through and occasionally wreak havoc. But the Germans weren't the Cossacks—they came to annihilate, and they did."

Willie interjected, "Were they sent to the concentration camps?"

"Not here. The concentration camps were in Poland and the west. Most of these Jews were killed on the spot. They weren't sent to death camps. The Germans didn't want to waste time and spend the effort of bringing them into the killing system they'd established in the Polish camps. For many, their fate was sealed in their own villages. The Germans came, killed the innocents, destroyed the village, and moved on. In some villages they herded the Jews into their synagogue and set the building on fire, shooting those few who escaped the burning building. Other times they just lined up the villagers and shot them all. They were very efficient. They used the village records or lists given to them by the synagogues to find each home, each family, and to account for each member of the household. The damn Germans kept excellent records of how many they murdered. They awarded medals and commendations for the officers and men doing the killings."

"I know of the numbers, but were there survivors?"

She continued. "Some of the Jews escaped and joined the Russian partisans. For the most part they weren't welcome there either. A few survived, and after the war some even made it to Palestine."

Krista took a deep breath, and Willie sipped his beer and then asked, "What happened when the Germans retreated?"

"When the Russians recaptured the area, they saw no need to keep the Jewish place names. There was nothing left of these settlements. In a few places you will find a marker naming the old village. If there is a monument it has generally been erected by either an American Jewish family who wanted to commemorate their origins, or one of those lucky survivors who reached Israel and became prosperous. You are traveling through an area that was once a vibrant home to over a million Jews. It was the cultural center of an entire ethnic nation. I am often haunted by these thoughts. I can hear them praying. A culture died here."

When she had ended her comments, Willie had little to say. He had finished his meal. She got up, cleared the table, left him with a fresh beer, and agreed to join him for an after-dinner drink. Krista had finished serving the others in the dining room and gave the bill to the guests at the far table. The dining room was now empty except for Willie and Krista.

Krista served coffee and busied herself straightening out the tables. As Willie finished his coffee, Krista returned with a cognac bottle and two glasses, not the fancy stemware Willie was used to seeing, but solid functional glasses. She poured a drink into the glass tumblers. Both inhaled the aroma and paused as Krista toasted, "To world peace." They clinked glasses and she continued: "It's a trite toast, but very appropriate sitting with you."

They sat and talked. Krista asked about Willie's past. He spoke about his work at the bank during the German reconstruction, his love of his wife Hanna, and her passing. He told of finding the letters from his father and his feeling that he had to make the trip.

Krista was blunt, "Why are you searching for your father's grave?"

He heaved a sigh: "I guess I'm trying to preserve the thought that he might have been just a loyal soldier, fighting for a country that commanded him to fight. He was brought up to believe that loyalty to a country was the obligation of all citizens. That was my father. He was my hero. I believe that most children think of their father as a noble person and have their father on a pedestal, looking up to them all their lives and are obedient. I have mixed feelings that I want to resolve. I want to find the father I didn't know."

Her answer was simple: "Give it up! You can't find your answer. Anything your father did was buried with him."

"I know, but as a son, I believe I must honor the memory of my father."

"Do you know where your father was during this time? Was he in this area?"

"He was in this area; I'm using letters sent to my mother to trace his wartime locations."

"The German people must feel the guilt, but then again the horrors are not something to be denied. Your country must recognize its heritage, good or bad. I know it is long past the end of the war and you can't pay for the sins of your country, any more than I can pay for the excesses of Mr. Stalin and his ideology. Stalin murdered as many or more people than Hitler. He did it differently. All that was yesterday. It's gone. I don't know what my husband did in Chechnya. Does it matter? We can't believe in collective guilt or we all would be emotionally immobilized."

Her deep blue eyes seemed to bore through Willie and penetrate into his subconscious. He thought her attractive and was mesmerized by her story. He heard her voice drop an octave as she poured two more drinks. She changed her seating position, moving closer, and her body language conveyed her intensity as she leaned her head across the table.

"Every man and woman wants to idolize their parent. It's human nature. You're looking for your father because you are curious to see where he died. That's your rationale for making this trip. You want a hero. Yes, in war there are many heroes, but in the front line they are all killers. In the Russian army we had good killers and we won—so, are they heroes? Your father gave his life for a morally corrupt government whose crimes against humanity are well documented. You would like to believe that your father was an innocent victim of the war. Willie, you won't find evidence for that. All you are going to find, if you are lucky, is a gravesite. As you travel, you will discover the enormity of the Nazi crimes. The remains of those immoral crimes are all around in missing people, cities, and cultures that no longer exist. You can only find graves: cemeteries filled with Poles, Ukrainians, Russians, Gypsies, Catholics, and Jews.

For many there are no marked graves, just mounds of earth where people were slaughtered like cattle and entire communities buried together. These were the true innocents; people who happened to be born to one ethnic group or another. They lived in these rich lands that grew enormous grain crops. These people were peaceful and did no harm. They just got in the way of history. What was Hitler's lebensraum was their graveyard." Krista added, "Those villages are out there. Some are just shadows and ghosts. You just have to look. And when you find them, think of how they died."

"You make it sound as if I'm going to hear voices and see ghosts of these people."

Krista smiled, "Who knows?—you might."

She poured another drink and Willie started to comment, but Krista put her finger to his lips and whispered: "Sometimes silence is the best answer to a woman's long speech. I'm sorry to have gone on, how you say, a soap box." She took a full sip from her drink and set the glass down, closer to his.

"I guess I have to thank you for being honest to an old German man. You have said a lot that I have to think about."

"I'm sorry. You seem nice, but you are a German and I am a Russian, or I guess a Ukrainian now."

At the end of the evening, Willie wished he could spend more time with her. She hugged him and kissed his seventy-four-year-old cheek and said: "Good night, I hope you find what you are looking for."

"If I were twenty years younger I would want to take you with me this evening." He said.

"If I weren't tired and needed to get up early in the morning, the twenty years wouldn't matter. You are an attractive man. Don't think about the past too much. There is nothing you can do about it. If you come by here again, give me some advance notice, I'll wear something nice."

Willie went to bed. The hotel was quaint and his room was simple, with walls painted an off-white yellow gloss. He slept in a massive feather bed in a simple wood frame that brought back memories of his childhood bed, many years before—before the war, before his father left. When he awakened and went for breakfast, there was a pleasant surprise. A small note was attached to the bill for his room. It read, "If you delay your leaving by about an hour I will join you for the day and show you some areas I spoke about. Let the man behind the desk know and he will call me. Krista."

Willie told the desk manager to call Krista and said he would wait for her. He then went into the restaurant where he'd had dinner the night before and ate breakfast from the ample hotel buffet. By the time he went to his room and finished packing, she'd arrived at the hotel.

Krista looked scrubbed, fresh, and well rested. It was a vibrant young woman who bounded into the lobby and smiled, pecked him on the cheek, and exclaimed, "I thought you would need a guide."

Willie blushed and said, "Yes, you are most welcome. I look forward to what you can show me. Why did you change your mind and decide to come with me?"

She didn't answer but leaned over and took his rolling suitcase and headed out to the yard where his car was parked. She also carried her large personal handbag slung over her shoulder. Her long strides punctuated their way across the parking lot and he willingly followed. "I really want to thank you for spending some time with me."

In the car Krista said, "When we talked last night I thought it sad that you had no one to share your thoughts with and certainly you had no one to show you around. So I said to myself, 'Krista, do this for Willie. The restaurant owes me a day off. So here I am!' "

Willie turned to this attractive younger woman sitting in his car and said, "All right, where do we go now?"

"We are going to a field near here. I'll direct you to the town of Izaslav, it's only about fifteen kilometers away."

Willie enjoyed the drive. It was so different from traveling alone. A light scent of rose wafted across the air as Krista's perfume filled the car and her smile cheered Willie. Her light banter made time fly. Then her voice dropped into a lower register as she became very serious. "This area is along the Horyn River and was occupied by the Germans within the first ten days of the invasion."

As they neared the town of Izaslav, Krista started telling a story. "The story starts in the summer of 1941. The time was glorious for a reserve officer in the Soviet army. One such officer was Savely Kordsey, a major, his wife Rita and their seven-year-old daughter Sveta, who was the joy of their lives. Savely was pleased to be able to spend the month of June on leave from service deep in the Ukraine with his mother-in-law, swimming in the local river, fishing in the early morning, and lying in bed listening to the early morning birds. His wife Rita was a beautiful twenty-eight-year-old blond Jewess who Savely had met during his first military tour in Ukraine during the days after receiving his army officer's commission. He was a 1930s officer, schooled in the post-revolutionary army buildup as the Kremlin assembled a force to balance the power of eastern Europe. He had seen brief active duty the year before when Stalin had joined the German war against Poland, and now he was very happy to be back in Moscow in the army administrative service. Rita had also joined the government as a nurse in the public health forces."

As they approached the town, Krista interrupted her story and instructed Willie: "Take the road to the left, the one with the market on the right as we pass the town square."

He slowed the car and followed the directions, although he was listening intently to Krista's story. She continued, "Late in June the couple and their daughter went camping in the deep woods and when they came back to Izaslav they were greeted with the news that the day before, without warning, Hitler had invaded Russia and was rapidly approaching central Ukraine. Savely was immediately summoned to active duty and he headed to the front. Rita reported to the nurse corps. Little Sveta was placed in care of Rita's mother."

The car was now on a long flat road with a forest on one side and fields filled with potatoes, turnips, and the unmistakable watermelon vines lying flatly on the ground on the other side of the road. It was good black earth farmland.

"About a week later, Izaslav was occupied by the Germans and shortly thereafter the Einsatzgruppen came to Izaslav. The Jews were rounded up, and little Sveta and her grandmother were among the 5,000 Jews who were assembled in the town square. They were told the transport place was just out of town, and they would be going to Palestine, the Promised Land. Holding her grandmother's hand, Sveta walked the one-kilometer dirt road. The road was lined with tall poplar trees that swayed in the breeze of the warm August evening. Here and there were nests of storks in the upper boughs of the trees. From time to time one would sweep out of its nest and scan the long row of Jews shuffling along the highway. The little girl carried her favorite stuffed, ragged, ever-smiling doll as she walked, reassured that the Ukrainian policemen lining the route were her friends. She was oblivious to their rifles cradled at the ready. Grandmother held the little girl tightly as the column of Jews walked into the field."

Krista had Willie stop the car, and they got out next to a field with a lane of grass that had been flattened by footsteps. The field was huge, stretching across to a clump of maple and poplar trees and a pine forest beyond. Krista helped him step down from the verge of the road and cross the drainage gully and onto the path. She continued to tell the story as they walked onto the field. "The sweet smell of the young crops filled Sveta's nostrils with a honey-like intoxicating aroma. There were butterflies dancing from bud to bud on the blossoming crops. From the woods at the other side of the field came the sound: 'pop-pop-pop-pop.' They passed the huge pile of baggage left by those who had walked before them. Grandmother held her hand more firmly. There was more of the staccato 'pop-pop-pop-pop' sound echoing from the forest in front of them. Grandma held more tightly as they entered the clearing: 'pop-pop-pop.' "

Willie knew, this was the place.

"There was no burial in the forest, just a pyre of stacked bodies ignited to destroy the evidence of yet another small Jewish community. There was no marker, no plaque. At the end of the war, Savely and Rita came back to Izaslav. They wanted to find out what had happened. There had been two series of mass murders. Savely wanted to find out where his daughter had been killed. He had advanced to become a general during the war, and Rita had become a medical major. They were able to use Savely's influence with the local police to determine which of the massacres had taken their daughter. Savely was distraught and again pleaded favor to have the area of these killings marked with a memorial to the Jews killed in this forest. At the site of the funeral pyre, the grove was planted and the memorial you see was built with a small obelisk and commemorative stones. Savely had a bronze bust cast of his daughter Sveta. You see it there. He then made it known that when he died he wanted to be buried near his daughter."

Willie was silent, holding Krista's hand tightly as he gasped breathing deeply from the walk across the field. He harbored deep rage that increased as she told the story. The sight of the bust of the little seven-year-old girl and a second life-size statue next to her was seared into his memory. A new feeling of shame engulfed him. The second bronze had the strong features of a man in a general's uniform.

Krista read the inscription on the second bust. The inscription was simple, "I have come to you my little daughter."

Willie started to cry. "Why did you bring me here?"

"I think you are a kind, well-meaning man, and you are seeking the truth and your father's story. This memorial in a forest grove is just one little truth you should see."

He sobbed, "Who did this?"

"Does it matter? Whether this was done by the Wehrmacht, the Einsatzgruppen, or the local Ukrainians, the German invaders were carrying out the depraved policy of mass murder. Now we call it ethnic cleansing."

Grief stricken, he sat on a stone monument for a moment. "What shame! What shame! What bastards!"

"I want to take you one more place, can we go?"

Krista took Willie's hand as they started back through the field. They walked very slowly. He was pale and his eyes were red where he had rubbed away the tears. His heart was pounding. He was feeling the impact of the memorial and the story he had just heard. He raised his head as they crossed the field and took a deep breath and sighed, as he noted the contrast of the peaceful surrounding planted field and the memorial.

When they reached the car, Krista gave Willie a drink from her water bottle. They sat still for several moments as Willie regained his composure. After fumbling with his keys, Willie started the car. Krista leaned across the front seat, kissed him gently on the cheek, and instructed him to head north along the country road.

When they reached the main road, Willie followed her directions. They were traveling along roads where there was an occasional house with unpainted weathered board sides. The houses seemed to have only one large room and white lace curtains on the one large window that faced the road. They all had tin slanted brown roofs and an ornate front metal fence with individually unique designs that defined the personality of the homeowner. Sunflowers, some five feet tall, decorated the area just behind the fence and there was at least one dog in each yard. The dogs barked at the car as they drove by; the sun beat down on the fields and shimmering heat waves blossomed up from the road.

"I am seeing a landscape that I have always imagined."

Krista asked, "Is it much different from your thoughts?"

"I never thought there were that many dogs," he chuckled. "My father didn't write to us about houses like these, or families and dogs. He wrote about the weather; how hot it was in the summer, cold in the winter, and muddy in between seasons when it rained."

As they drove, Willie realized that it was down these side roads, the paths into the woods within the unseen depths of the forest, that the stories Krista wanted to tell him were played out. He shuddered at what he had missed as he had driven by country lanes that he thought were of no interest. Again and again his memory went back to the trampled grass leading into the field at Izaslav.

Krista kept up a pleasant banter about the countryside and her own life. She was a good traveling companion and Willie enjoyed her company. As they drove through a village named Slavuta, Krista mentioned that there was a good small market in this town. They stopped and Krista purchased the few things she needed for a picnic. She bought some water, sausages, and peasant-baked bread. Willie thought the town was quaint, something out of the distant past with the farmers' stalls in the market, the bees buzzing about, and again the numerous dogs that seemed to be scurrying about under foot with no apparent owners. A faint odor of perspiration hung in the air, mixing with the earthly smells of the vegetables as they meandered through the market stalls.

With her arms full Krista said, "Good, now we can stop along the road and have our picnic." Leaving Slavuta they passed the bus station. It was an old and decrepit building and the buses appeared to be from the Soviet era.

"Krista, where do these people come from?"

"Slavuta is a small market town. There is a little cement industry about five kilometers from here and the housewives come here to the market. The local men like to come here for the bistros and little nightlife. The town can be quite lively on the weekend, when there is a lot of beer and vodka flowing."

Following her directions, Willie smiled as they drove out of the town on a gravel road.

It was very pleasant driving. Krista occasionally would hum a tune. Sometimes it was one of the popular ballads that Willie would instantly recognize and other times she hummed what sounded to be old Russian folk music. It was comforting. After about half an hour Krista said, "There is a turn off the highway on the left, in about two minutes and there is a table where we can have our picnic."

He saw the turn off and pulled the Audi into a large clearing next to the road in a pine grove. Krista quickly moved out of the car and from the bag of food items she had purchased, produced a brown butcher paper table cover, the sausages, the loaf of bread, and a plastic container of butter. There also was a cucumber some tomatoes and a knife that seemed to appear from nowhere. He was impressed at what she produced in seconds.

"Now relax and sit down."

Soon he was presented with a very appetizing and tasty lunch of a salad, sausage, and black bread. Krista bantered during the time they ate. She pointed out the bushes nearby laden with berries and was delighted when Willie complimented her, once again, on her German.

After eating, Krista spread her peasant skirt and stretched out on a bed of pine needles and said, "Come take a rest. The pine needles are clean."

She moved to a side of the clearing and sat down on the pine needles. Willie laid down beside the sitting Krista who adjusted her position so Willie's head rested on her thigh. Within seconds he had closed his eyes and was asleep.

About fifteen minutes later he was awakened by Krista's gentle stroking of his hair.

"It's time we moved on," she whispered. "You know I told you there was more to see today."

Back in the car Willie asked, "Where are we going?'

"You are going to see a site where there is a proper memorial that shows how cold blooded this war was."

"Why do I want to see this?"

"As we discussed, I think you should know what was done back then."

Krista directed Willie back onto a major road and after about a five-minute ride pointed to the right and said, "Turn down this gravel road."

About one hundred meters on the gravel road in another pine forest there was a dead end with an impressive monument. It was a startling sight. There was a larger than life-size white granite image of a man in "stagger" position as if he had just been shot and where the heart would be there was a symbolic bullet hole surrounded by a Star of David.

"Please come out of the car with me." She said.

He slowly got out of the car and walked toward the statue. Now he noticed that there were two other monument markers near the staggering man.

Krista took him over to the first monument; the inscription appeared to be in Russian. She read the inscription. "At this site thirty one thousand Soviet Heroes were murdered by Hitler's soldiers during the Great War of 1941–1945."

Krista took Willie to the third monument and read it, "On the night of August 4th 1941 Hitler's soldiers murdered seven thousand Jewish citizens in this forest. May they rest in peace."

"What is the difference between the thirty one thousand and the seven thousand?" he asked.

"Willie, the seven thousand were Jews. The other twenty-four thousand were prisoners of war, partisans, and just citizens the

Germans didn't want around. As far as the distinction between Jews and Soviet Heroes, prior to 1991 the Soviets didn't recognize the Jewish people. Jews killed were just fellow Soviets."

He said, "How strange."

"After 1991 some of the Jewish agencies found these killing sites and memorialized them. At this site a Canadian, who lost his family here, financed the statue."

"But Jews and Soviets were killed here."

"Yes, since this is an out of the way area the Germans thought was a good place to do their murderous work. Once they started with the Jews, they continued the killing and kept the funeral pyre going. Why start another fire in another forest? This one was working so well."

"You make it sound so matter of fact."

"It was. If you were Jewish, you were murdered. If you were a captured soldier, you were murdered. If you were a partisan or suspected of helping the partisans, you were also murdered."

Willie turned away from the memorial and slowly walked back to the car. Krista took his hand and stopped him, turned and went to a raised area of the pine grove about 20 meters from the monument. "Willie this was the center of the pyre."

A chill ran down Willie's spine.

"We are standing on the ashes of those murdered innocents."

Back in the car with the door open, Willie sat in silence bent over with his feet on the ground and held his head in his hands.

"Krista, thank you. I would have never found these sites or heard these stories but for you. It's one thing to be told about these murders, but it is another to see where they happened. This doesn't make me an eyewitness, but it shows me what no one would talk about in my country for all these sixty years. I would have to have a heart of stone not to be affected."

"If it has come to mean something for you, then I have given you a gift; and I am pleased."

Turning to Krista he asked, "What do we do now?"

"Drive a little. We are about an hour from where I think you should spend the night."

Willie headed out onto the road.

She said, "I know this all means something to you. There is so much more. I don't think we have to see more sights to day."

"Are there more sites near here?"

"Too many, about fifteen minutes from here there is an old salt mine. The Germans herded a small village of about two hundred persons into the mine and blew up the entrance, sealing them in alive."

"That's horrible. Insane."

"Yes, but they were told that Ukrainians and Jews were a subhuman species and should be eliminated. They were following orders, orders from the top. The army was only too happy to oblige."

It was still light about seven in the long spring twilight evening when they arrived in Slavuta, the small town they had passed through earlier in the day.

Krista said, "There is a good hotel in this town and it isn't too expensive. You can stay the night here and be comfortable."

Willie walked into the Slavuta Hotel, a nondescript four-story cement building. Krista acted as translator requesting an available room. The desk clerk, who appeared to be the hotel manager, was a hefty large-bosomed woman well past middle age. She cast her eye over Willie, inspecting him from head to toe, and he was offered a small suite of rooms on the top floor. There was a well-appointed bedroom with an eclectic mix of modern bed and side tables with an eighteenth-century classic tsar period chifferobe. The sitting room had what appeared to be an Ikea modern couch, coffee table, and flat-screen television. In the bathroom was a nice stall shower just large enough for one person. Krista helped Willie bring all his bags up into the room. She had advised him that it wasn't wise to leave good items in the car over night.

Krista then said, "Can we go to dinner?"

"Of course, where do you suggest?

"I live just in the next town and know all the good places. Unfortunately I can't afford them. Would you take me to a nice place?"

"Which is the best?"

"The Four Tsars. I have always wanted to go there, but I had no one to take me."

They walked across the town square and Willie chuckled at seeing the statue of Lenin. He also couldn't help but notice the sway of Krista's skirt as she walked. There was a rhythm that he hadn't noticed in women for a long time. Krista was a bit taller, but reminded him of Hanna. He hadn't walked with a woman since Hanna's death and he was surprised how welcome was the sensation of holding her hand and stepping with her stride for stride. He felt a slight arousal as she smiled at him during their brief walk.

"I think that's the one thousandth statue of Lenin I've seen."

"He is still a hero to many. Also, it takes too much money to tear these statues down."

Willie smiled at the answer.

Dinner was delightful. The restaurant was all that she said it would be. Willie asked, "You haven't been here, but you seem to know all about this restaurant."

"My customers at the tavern talk. They come and rave about this place and I envied them for being able to dine here."

Willie relaxed. First he had a beer and then at Krista's suggestion they tried a bottle of Ukrainian champagne. Willie didn't think much of the champagne, but Krista seemed to enjoy the bubbly sweet taste. She didn't wear lipstick, and when she licked her lips she had a pursing action that showed her naturally even white teeth which with her perfect complexion added a glow to the evening. He obviously felt attracted to this vibrant woman.

"You know you are a very beautiful woman."

"You have had too much to drink, but I'll accept the compliment," she said this with a little laugh to punctuate her comment.

About halfway through the meal, Krista reached across the table and held his hand. A surge went through Willie's body, a rush of warmth he hadn't felt for many years. Fleetingly he thought back to Hanna and his youth. He responded by returning the grasp. She continued to hold his hand.

They chatted about their respective childhood memories. Willie told Krista of the good part of being the son of the local baker, and Krista spoke of the wonders of being young and carefree when she was at school.

After dinner they walked back to the hotel. When they were just where Willie had parked the car he asked, "Shall I drive you home?"

"No, I shall walk home from here; it is only a short walk."

"I can't let you do that. You have been too good for me not to see you home."

"You are such a nice man. I know I have said things about the Germans that may have hurt you and I'm sure I've shown you places that you never would have found on your own. If I have helped you learn something about the past, I am happy."

"It will take some time to absorb the impact of today. What you have done is break down part of some walls of denial I have built and accepted about the war and how the German army conducted itself."

Krista stopped him from saying more by tenderly placing a finger over his lips.

"We have talked enough. If you come this way again perhaps you will remember and come and see me. Give me a warning; I will want to have a nice dress to wear when I see you."

Krista climbed into the Audi and within five minutes she guided Willie to a small one story house with an iron fence and a front yard garden."

"This is my in-laws' home. It's where I live."

With that, she pecked Willie on the cheek, hurriedly left the car and opened the fence gate. Willie slowly watched her go and feeling very lonely drove back to the hotel. The next morning Willie packed his car and left quickly. He felt Krista's absence from the moment he started the car. He missed her voice and her presence. As he drove out of Slavuta and turned toward the Polish border he started to think about the stories Krista had told him. Although she wasn't there and obviously not near, in his mind he spoke to her. He recalled how, just yesterday, she would point to places for him to observe and how he would see more through her eyes than he could on his own. Deep within his thoughts he would not forget how she opened his eyes to the horrors of the German presence in these lands.

The possible truth about his father depressed him. Hero or villain, his mind imagined his papa as a peaceful, innocent man who left him so long ago. With all he now knew he was confused and discouraged; he didn't think he would ever find the closure he was looking for. On the other hand he was exhuming a past that for the last sixty years his generation did not want to acknowledge. He felt uncomfortable about the entire Hitler era. This trip was forcing him to face those suppressed thoughts. He asked himself: "Do ordinary citizens share responsibility?" Then, almost trying to get to the bottom of his reflection he asked himself, "Responsible for what? Responsibility for an unjust war? Responsibility for the murders? What about the masses of the German population that were bombed. We were victims too!"

He spoke to himself trying to resolve these inner conflicts. These new doubts filled his thoughts as he wandered back and forth heading west on the Ukrainian motorways, northwest on the lesser "P" roads to see the small towns. Without Krista's guidance it was hard to find many memorials, those markers of the past.

Sixty years ago, his father's letters described muddy and icy roads, not well-marked highways.

> When we are not in the fighting line, we spend much of our time helping the transport people. In the spring our trucks are deep in mud, and it slows everything down. We have to pull trucks out of the ditches where they have slipped into what seems to be an endless sea of mud. It is difficult to keep our uniforms up to the standards our officers' demand when we are pushing

> and pulling cars out of the mud. The squalor we have to live in is very different from what the German army would call acceptable. We go for days with our uniforms caked in the mud, longing for a bath and a change of clothes. For the last week we have been lucky enough to be able to sleep in what was an old Jewish prayer place. There are no Jews around, and the army used this place as a stable. We forced some of the local people to clean out the manure and we moved our troops into the place. It's a roof over our heads and it is warm and dry.

Then there was the part of a letter that was written when winter had frozen the roads:

> We all wish for a thaw. It is very cold, and to keep warm, we work to help keep the trucks out of the snow and back on the road when they slide on the ice. This is the same work we did when we had the mud. One week we have snow, the next the mud. We remember the dust of just a few months ago. We have come to feel that dust is good, or at least better than the snow and mud. There is no good weather in war. It is a mad world. The horses have a difficult time, much of their feed is frozen, and we work them very hard pulling our cannon and wagons filled with ammunition. Our trucks freeze overnight and we have to work to start them in the morning. It is difficult to move our materiel on these roads, as everything is frozen—the trucks and the men. We don't get a hot meal every day, and must live on field rations most of the time. If we are lucky, we have time to heat some of the food. Since I was a baker, the men look to me to find ways of dressing up the rations. We were lucky last week and found a lot

of turnips in the cellar of a destroyed house. I have used these to make soup and add to some of the rations. One of the men found a chicken and I made some soup before we ate the boiled chicken. I'd like to be able to bake bread again. We long for the coming of summer, but we know that will bring more fighting, and we dread the inevitable battles. By the way, four of your letters were waiting for me when I got back to the base. I'm sorry that there has been more bombing of Stuttgart. I feel hopeless when I hear of the bombings. Hopefully you are not near the bombing. We all hope this will end soon.

Willie tried to imagine what these country roads were like sixty years ago. He now traveled to the north here, to the south there, but always heading toward Poland in the west. He had been sensitized by Krista and now, along the way he occasionally spotted the markers directing tourists to villages destroyed many years before. Often he would stop by the side of the road and look out at the fields that seemed to carpet the entire landscape. It was truly "the breadbasket" of Europe. In his mind he could picture the battles, the tanks marshalling for the attacks, and the encamped men awaiting the orders to move forward. He imagined he could hear the diesel engines as they belched their exhaust and moved forward. He would breathe the clean air of the countryside and envision the clouds of acrid smoke that blackened the sky during the battles.

As he passed fields of vegetables, he now sought the little paths like the field at Izaslav. He looked for trails into nearby woods and wondered what might be hidden. He constantly thought, "Where was Papa?" And then, into his consciousness was the second question,

"Why am I always confronted with and thinking of the massacre of these Jews?"

Several times Willie detoured down a dusty road to seek a village that was mentioned in his papa's letters. Krista was right each time. There was the marker, dedicated to a place that didn't exist. There was the date of annihilation. One marker even said, in English, Russian, and what appeared to be Hebrew, "Here were killed 1,265 Jews." A chill went up and down his spine as he stood at the base of the stone monument. It had the name of an American family that had paid to commemorate their past with the monument. In this case it was a small stone with a brass plate, but the event, probably repeated hundreds of times across this area of Ukraine and Byelorussia, weighed heavily on Willie's thoughts. How many killings were there? How many families came to find the crossroads that had once framed a village square? How many had left a marker? How many had just left? How many other places were liquidated with no trace? How many had no one to remember or write a commeration? Was his father part of all this? Was his father fighting facing one direction, while others wearing the same uniform were doing this killing? What had his father known? What had his father done? How had his father felt?

As Willie drove, in his mind he now heard the voices that seemed to be the ghosts of the millions killed on these fields. His visions of the dead were everywhere. Russians killed in battle. Germans killed in battle. Jews murdered by Germans, or Jews killed by fellow Ukrainians. The killers might have been from the other German armies like the hired mercenaries from Bulgaria, or the divisions from Hungary. Everyone killed. The partisans killed. The Germans killed. Slaughter. One flow of killers worked as they swept into Russia and then Russians slaughtered as the German army moved east. There were the civilian deaths. Angry armies of Russian and Germans killing day after day, night after night. Then as the tide changed and the fortunes of war reversed, there were German soldiers dying by the thousands as the Russians drove them back toward Poland and eventually German soil. In Willie's mind's ear he heard the roar of the guns and the creaking of the tank treads. He heard the screams of the wounded and the curses of the fighting men as they were surrounded by death and all too often consumed by the fires of the war. Gotterdammerung! Now, for some strange reason he heard in his deep subconscious, which he had suppressed for many years, the soft chants of Jewish congregations that were there, but never would be again.

Willie continued driving toward the Polish border. He passed through the city of Ternopil and came to the village of Drohobych. The guidebook referred to "a charming city in Western Ukraine." As he entered the town he was struck by the impressive wooden St. George Church towering over the downtown area. It seemed familiar; he stopped in the town center and retrieved a letter Papa had written in May 1943:

> We have been in the rear area for two weeks. Our group was called out to help the SS and local police as they rounded up several hundred Jews who had been used as laborers for the last few years. We were assigned the job of getting the Jews out of their homes and taking them to the cemetery. The SS commanded them to dig pits and then we watched the Ukrainian police shoot each of the Jews. A Jewish musician played the violin as the Jews were marched to their graves; he was one of the last to

be shot. The Jews did not try to escape. One of the old Jews said, "This is fate, this is God's will, but our blood will be on you and your children for seven generations." After the action, we all went back to the camp and drank vodka that had been taken from the Jews' home to go to sleep. I am a little cog in the whole wheel of the army. I must remember that.

In the envelope, along with the letter was a picture of Papa and two of his buddies smiling with the church in the background. The church spires had been slightly damaged and repaired, but Willie was able to walk across the square and stand in the approximate spot where the picture had been taken. He shuddered, turned around, and returned to his car.

Then, driving along the road, it dawned upon Willie that the Germans were the aggressors. The German nation wasn't a victim of the nations who won the war. This was a reversal of fortune and the truth. These peasants were living in peace when the German people looked for a leader and "fell in love" with a false savior. Soldiers swore an oath to the man-god and killed in the name of Hitler. Justices violated their pledge of law and their knowledge of ethical practice to please Hitler's executive orders. The German people were responsible for the actions they allowed to be committed in their name. The guilt of the nation's actions weren't talked about. In the postwar silence there was the denial of the responsibility for the actions and deeds of their own nation. Even this silence contributed to the nation's guilt.

Willie reached the new Ukrainian/Polish border. He was in the region of Koval and wanted to cross over into Poland so he could head toward Lublin. He crossed the border at the Bug River from the

Ukrainian town of Brezci to the Polish town Dorohusk. It was just past Chelm, on the Polish side where he stopped the car, stretched his legs, and went into a café before deciding where he would drive to spend the night. The café was clean. There were five tables with four wooden chairs. The tables were covered with white oil cloth. The manager, an elderly man, came to the table and wiped the already clean surface with a damp cloth almost as a gesture to reassure that the restaurant was a sanitary place to eat. The name of the restaurant was "New Little Poland."

The manager presented the menu and stood next to the table as Willie reviewed his choices. Willie was hungry and ordered familiar food. It was a Polish meal that any German would understand, an order of loin pork schnitzel topped with egg and a small order of boiled spinach pierogi, and a kompot to drink.

The restaurant was quiet except for an old plastic radio behind the counter playing Chopin. As the meal was being prepared, the elderly manager approached Willie's table and asked if everything was acceptable.

Willie replied, "Yes, what is your name?"

"My name is Lucca."

His German was good and he stayed next to Willie's table. Business was slow and his German visitor intrigued him. "We don't get many German visitors here."

Willie looked at the wall above Lucca and commented on the restaurant motto that was on the menu, "The food we serve is as good, as music of Chopin," and they seem to have arranged for the radio to be playing his music.

Lucca chuckled, smiled, and said, "Yes, the music selection was just for you. Polskie Radio cooperates with us to entertain visitors."

Willie asked, "Tell me about this area and something about yourself."

Lucca was more than willing. "I was a young boy during the war. Since I was a kid, no one noticed me, and I smuggled ammunition from the Russians to the partisans hidden in the woods." His chest seemed to puff out with pride as he spoke of these activities, so long ago.

"Were you afraid?"

"Of course. The penalty for being caught was instant death. But a kid doesn't consider this, and it was exciting." Lucca sighed and went on. "Now I have an old bald head where once I had beautiful red hair, and with a lame leg and potbelly all I can do is work several hours a day in a roadside tavernera just to occupy time, and earn some zlotys."

Willie told him about his travels of the last several weeks and how he hoped to find his father's grave. He described how he had traced the action and retreat of the German army, and he told Lucca that the last letter from Papa had come in January 1945. He believed his father had been captured or had died somewhere in the area.

Lucca responded, "The Russian offensive had crossed the Bug River in July of 1944 and then stopped to gather its forces for the final push to Berlin. They used the area between the Bug and Vistula Rivers, the ground around here, as the staging area to gather their troops and supplies. This whole area was a parking lot filled with cannon, tanks, ammunition, and men. They were just across the river," Lucca pointed to the east. "Then our people in Warsaw, north of here, thinking they would be helping the Russians, rose up and started to fight. They freed most of the city."

Hate oozed from Lucca's face as he told his story. "The Russians didn't push their army on to Warsaw and they did not assist the Warsaw Uprising. They held their army on that side of the river and let the Germans annihilate our men and women. They let our best men and boys die just so they could run the country after the war without the cream of our young Polish patriots. The Russians didn't want any of us who would fight for a free and independent Poland."

He shifted from foot to foot and used his hands to emphasize his anger. "The Warsaw Uprising was brutally put down by the German army, costing the lives of thousands of Poles who rose up to fight. Even as they heard the pleas for ammunition and food from the entrapped fighters in Warsaw, the bastard Russians sat still. It was here, between the two rivers, that the Russians sat and watched the Germans destroy the partisan army that had taken control of Warsaw. The Poles called for help. They called for Churchill to send fighters, for Roosevelt to send bombers. None came. The offensive started on 16 January. Of course, by then the Uprising had been put down, the Poles had surrendered, and the men who had fought were on the way to prisoner camps to die, if they hadn't perished in the siege."

Lucca spit out the words, " 'Uncle Joe' said, 'Let the Poles die.' Then, when the Germans put down the Uprising and Warsaw was destroyed, the Russians struck. Their first actions were massive bombardments; bombardments that drove men mad and leveled the countryside. Then on January 15, 1945, the Russian horde crossed the river, led by their massive numbers of new T-34 tanks and followed by the huge waves of infantry. They moved, as lava would flow from a volcano, across the plain moving through the small towns between them and final victory. They suffered huge losses of men, but there always seemed to be more men to replace the wounded and dead."

He took a breath as he was speaking fast and was totally caught up in telling his story.

"They took just four months to fight from here to Berlin. The Russians knew they had won the war. This last campaign was the coup de grace. On the other side of the river, there were only the remnants of the German army; beat up and dispirited men who once had been proud when they marched east. Now the remnants of the Wehrmacht stood with the fanatical SS troops who vowed to fight to the end and would shoot any of the soldiers who would not stand with them. Fourteen- and fifteen-year-old German boys were alongside old men pulled from their homes and handed guns to defend their homeland. That last campaign started here in January and ended in Berlin in April. One of the first objectives for the Russian onslaught along this southern part of the front was to capture the crossroads not far from here at Ozarow."

Willie mentally compared the dates, the last letter dated 15 January. The letter came from near here. He knew that his father must have died in that Russian offensive:

> We have a river between us and the Russian army. We feel safe, but we know they will come across any day soon. It will be our duty to stop them. We all know the end of this war is near. I must survive to come back to you. Throughout the war I have been loyal to you, my dear. I have seen many things I will want to forget, and you; you of all people will make me forget them. Night after night I think of our meeting long ago. From the first night I saw you, I saw your ankles and my eye traced your legs

upward and I saw your face and fell in love. I haven't seen a more beautiful face or met a more marvelous person. You have been my soul, my love. This war has taken me away from you and from the person I was, the man who appreciated our peaceful and productive life. The image of you is burned into my brain and I want to be back with you to share our future, no matter what the future brings. You were my love then, now and forever. I do not know what the next days, weeks or months will bring. If I am to die I know it is for a noble cause and to protect you from these uncivilized Russian hordes. I have faith in our country and its cause. Yes, I am afraid. You can be assured that if anything happens to me you will be in my dying thoughts. There is only you. I love you very much. Take care of yourself and Willie.

For our heritage and the glory of our land. Heil Hitler.

Willie left the café and found a small bed and breakfast. The next morning he was eager to scout the area to see where this explosive breakthrough took place years ago. He realized he was near his father's last battle. He doubted he would ever find a trace of Papa, but he had learned so much. He realized that his personal quest had shed light on German actions that he and his generation did not want to contemplate, admit, or analyze. His trip had forced a personal confrontation, not only with his father's fate, but also of his generation's denial of the truth about the war and the responsibility for the war crimes. He was part of sixty years of denial by the German people. It had left a scar on his soul he would long endure. He asked himself if he was feeling sorry for himself and Mama—or was he developing an empathy for those other families and people who had also lost loved ones in this war?

After a quick breakfast of black coffee and a hard roll, Willie reviewed the maps of the area and started his daily drive. He wandered the roads on the other side of the river, discouraged but hopeful of seeing some sign of the action. He rode on to Krasnik, then north to Poniatowa, then back over the Vistula River to Radom, crisscrossing the area and finally driving back south toward Sandomierz. He was traversing an area about 30 km wide (approximately 18 miles) and 30 km from north to south. At each crossroads, he stopped and tried to compare what he had been told of the Russian offensive. Was his father here?

He was tired of traveling and was losing hope of ever finding where Papa was when he wrote that last letter. He despaired that there was nothing to find, and now accepted that he never would find his fathers grave. He went on although his sense of reason told him he should just go home and admit that he had seen enough.

It was about 30 km (18 miles) from Sandomierz, where he wanted to spend the night when he came to the village of Ozarow. He realized that this was the crossroad that Lucca had described. It was midafternoon, he was tired, and it looked a good place to rest.

Chapter Nineteen

The Meeting: Confrontation or Accommodation

Willie slowly approached Ozarow, winding his way through the lush farmland enjoying the pleasant drive. The temperature was well over 32 degrees Celsius, and there was a high blue sky with puffy clouds that resembled large floating cotton balls. The Audi's windows were down to capture a little more air as his back was sticking to the seat, his shirt starting to show wet stains spreading from beneath the armpits as he perspired. It was just after midday and Willie was exhausted and emotionally drained from his travels.

The few hours he'd had with Krista had given him a burst of energy. However, the viewing of former killing sites now preyed on his mind. The thoughts of tracing the path of a noble but misguided army had been replaced by the knowledge that the massive denial of the wartime atrocities was the postwar shame of the German people. Papa may have fought well, but the cause was immoral and the leaders were criminal, as were the executioners who'd pulled the triggers and the troops who'd stood by and assisted. He longed for his travels to end. At the town of Annopol, where Lucca said there had been an old Russian camp, he approached the Vistula River. This was a jump-off point for the last offensive against the entrenched and waiting, debilitated but still dangerous German army. Lucca had told him where the Russians encamped, and Willie found the area. It was now a farm. He stopped and walked through the field, his head lowered, seeking some sign of the encampment. The scent of the growing wheat permeated the air. Butterflies emerged from between the wheat buds, now about a foot high. Sixty years of plowing, sowing, and gathering had obliterated any sign of the tents, redoubts, and supply dumps that once had covered these now peaceful fields.

Unhurriedly he drove across the narrow, high, two-lane bridge looking down at the peaceful river. Sandbars and verdant growth covered the several midstream islands. The bridge spanned the two riverbanks, with 30-meter cliffs (about 100 feet) on either side. In crossing, he traveled from the former Russian staging area to the German defenses, the Russian lines to the German lines. It was only about 500 yards, but this short distance from one riverbank to the other was a journey from the positions of a vigorous, well-equipped army about to go on the offensive, to the defensive area awaiting the inevitable attack they knew would come.

Standing on an abutment above the river Willie thought where his father might have been entrenched, part of a worn and beaten army still determined to fulfill their oath of loyalty and service. The Russians were facing west ready to fight the remaining distance to Berlin. The defending Germans stood looking east into the sun, their backs to the Fatherland. Willie observed the area, as would a defending Wehrmacht soldier. He visualized his worried father knowing that the Russians had time to prepare, reequip, and stage masses of fresh men for the attack. It was certain as the sun would rise one day, the Russians would come across that river. For the

Germans, it had become a defensive war to try to block or slow the expected Russian onslaught.

> *December, 1945:*
>
> We know an attack will come soon. The Russians have been quietly building their strength for two months. We have had replacements come to partially fill our ranks. They seem to be very young men, almost as young as Willie, and a few are older than my father. Maybe we will not have to fight before Christmas. That would be good. The few old veterans who are still left all hope we can delay the Russians long enough for peace to come before the Russians reach Germany. That is our job. We stand between the Russians and home. I will be steadfast in holding the ground. I love you and Willie and will fight to keep you safe.

The insane "orders of the day" had been not to give an inch. But, these had been the orders for months, as the German army fell back farther and farther toward the Fatherland.

The men of the Wehrmacht knew that one morning there would be a huge barrage from a thousand or more artillery pieces; the Katuska Rockets with their "whoosh–whoosh–whoosh" signature sounds would be supported by "carpet bombing" from the Russian air force. Would the barrage be for an hour, two hours, or for the entire morning? They did not know, they only knew it was coming. Then the mass of Russian troops in small boats and pontoons would bridge the width of the rapidly moving river. The water was cold in January, but the river wasn't frozen. For the well-equipped Russians, it was more of an annoyance, not a real barrier. The entrenched Germans knew that their enemy was willing to pay the price, however many men or material they would lose. The Germans only hope was to bleed the Russian advance until it halted.

Willie stopped the car again and looked out at the river. He observed the width, depth, and the water. The scene seemed so innocent, with the river running clear blue with little ripples rushing toward the sea. Of course, there had been no bridge at this crossing sixty years ago.

Willie took the first turnoff, a small secondary road marked Highway 755 with a marker and arrow, "Ozarow." The farmland was flat and the road was straight, no different from the hundreds of small roads he had wandered along during the last weeks. Linden trees lined the road, like tall solders at attention, planted as markers every ten or so meters forming a wall, separated from the asphalt by a green well trimmed verge. Beyond was the beginning of the fields.

As he approached Ozarow he noticed a church dominating the hill near the town center. He could see that the old church had been badly damaged and then restored. The relatively new brickwork had cemented over pockmarks of old battle scars. Its white stucco steeple rose high above the town, and the body of the church was white-washed stone, with an uneven surface where the outer wall repairs were still visible. A cemetery next to the church extended down to a dirt side road that probably also led back to the river. The secondary road appeared to have fallen into an abandoned and overgrown state.

The village was small. He could see all the way to the crossroads that were at the town center and observed the homes and shops to the other side of the town. He stopped the car to inspect the area. The signs of action had not been completely erased. A closer view showed shells of buildings that were still abandoned and in one of the fields the crumbled remains of a brick wall and chimney. There had been wartime activity at this road juncture some sixty years ago.

An old priest was standing in the churchyard, and Willie stopped the car for assistance with directions. The priest was wearing a white cassock with black trim and seemed to be praying as he slowly walked through the graves. Willie approached and apologized for interrupting his prayers and asked in German, "Pardon me; I would appreciate directions to Tarnopol."

The priest replied in excellent German, in a soft voice and gave directions to the nearby town. As an afterthought Willie asked, "Do you know of the battle of January 1945 that occurred in this area?"

A wry smile came across the priest's face: "This seems to be the day for visitors inquiring about the past. Yes, I have heard the stories of the battle from the local survivors."

"Please, tell me what happened here."

"What is your interest?"

"My father was in the German army and I believe he fought near here and was probably killed in this area."

The priest heaved a huge sigh and for the second time that day told the story of the battle in the area. "There had been a huge Russian bombardment and then the Russians came pouring across the river. The Russians seemed to be a human wave, first the men in their pontoon boats and then the tanks on their barges. Then soldiers surrounding their tanks that rumbled forward. It was a wall of men and tanks that came down the road and across the fields. The Russians didn't seem to care about casualties they took or inflicted. The town was almost obliterated in the first minutes of the rolling barrage. There had been a roadblock mounted just the other side of the church, over there, to seal the approach to the crossroad. The Russians easily surrounded the roadblock, and after overcoming the resistance of the German rear guard, in a short but devastating firefight, they quickly moved on, leaving the defenders' bodies. After the battle, the local people came out of their cellars and tried to clean up the destruction. The Russians left the German dead where they had fallen, and the townspeople dug graves along the roadside and buried the German soldiers. You can see some of the graves along the road over there. The grave capstones had been used by the Germans as part of the roadblock and came from the cemetery across the way."

Willie thanked the priest and walked slowly through the church's cemetery down the embankment and to the gravesites laid out in single file along the roadside. He felt compelled to pay his respect to these fallen German soldiers. As the priest said, each grave was covered by a granite slab had been blasted away by the direct fire of the Russian tanks. The slabs bore the marks of bullets and shellfire. Willie looked down the road toward the river; he could envision the Russian T-34 tanks coming down the short straight road and across the nearby fields. Their 75 mm cannons would be firing directly at the area in front of them, and their machine guns would be spewing fire. The cannon shells would have splintered the roadblock, but the mass of Russian infantry following the tanks would always be moving forward.

There were eleven German graves along the road. They were probably quite shallow and appeared to have been hastily dug without the precision of a military cemetery. They were aligned head to foot, and the granite gravestones were used to seal the contents. Each grave had a name painted on the marker. Inscriptions were simple, "German soldier," and a name. The paint was faded and some of the letters were chipped and peeling. Willie could make out the inscriptions. The fourth grave had the name "Hans Kirchenmann," and his rank, "Obergrenadier Getfreiter." It was Papa's!

His father's grave!

Willie's knees buckled, but he caught himself before he could fall. Willie was overcome with a hollow feeling of fatigue, and sadness filled his mind. He felt he should cry, but his breath only came in short gasps. His lungs seemed to empty, and he was starved for air. His legs lost strength, and he sat down on a low-lying stone fence at the side of the road and tried to compose himself. He sat for about ten minutes. He started to cry. "Mama, Mama," he gasped and sobbed again, "Papa, oh Papa!"

Fatigue overcame him and a cold sweat chilled him from the base of his spine to his shoulders. He shuddered. He reached into his rear pocket and took out his handkerchief. Willie tried to blow his nose, but was only able to muffle his sobs.

He now knew where and how his father died. Willie wished that his mother were still alive and that he could tell her that he found Papa's grave. He now knew the place, and could envision the roadblock, the bombardment, the Russian hoard, and the brief firefight. He imagined his father's fear, when the certainty of being killed became a reality.

He sat for about twenty minutes, then slowly stood and walked toward his car. The car wasn't near. Willie was trying to get his bearings, looking for his car, which was parked on the other side of the church at the top of the rise. He couldn't focus on where he had left it. His mind was numb and he felt crushed; he wanted to go home now. Willie's quest was over.

I was standing with Peter about sixty feet away from the edge of the road. I saw a man walking toward us breathing heavily, slowly shuffling, and trying to stay on his feet. He seemed to be staggering as if he were drunk. Once across the road he used gravestones as supports, seemingly looking for someplace to sit down. He was obviously disoriented.

We were in the old cemetery looking at the graves, trying to decipher the symbolic meanings of distinguishable markings. As I finished my description of the classifications of the Jewish grave markers, I looked up and saw a tall man staggering toward us.

He appeared to be in deep thought as he haltingly approaching us, grabbing the few upright grave markers to steady himself. Although casually dressed, he had the aura of a man of stature. He was flushed and perspiring profusely and appeared to be confused. He said in English: "I overheard you talking."

Both Peter and I nodded.

"May I sit down? Is there a place to sit?"

He was exceedingly polite and appeared to have tears in his eyes. "Are you all right?" I asked

The reply was a quiet, "No," as he sat heavily on one of the gravestones and seemed to try to take a deep breath. He blurted out, "I have just found my father's grave, after sixty years of wondering where he died."

My immediate response was the polite, "Oh, I'm sorry."

We let him sit in silence for a few moments, letting him catch his breath. Then to initiate a conversation, I said, "We are visiting this old cemetery, and I have family buried here."

"Is this a Jewish cemetery?"

"Yes."

He asked: "You are Jewish?"

"Yes."

"American?"

"Yes."

His voice was hoarse and gravely moist with phlegm. "Are you doing a Jewish tour and visiting the camps?"

"No, we are not on a tour. I came to find what happened to my family."

The stranger whispered, "I have come to find my father, and I found him. I found his grave. I found his grave. It has been a long search."

I asked, "You are German??"

"Yes, I'm German, my father was in the Wehrmacht," was the very quiet reply. "He's buried under that gravestone along the road, over there."

"Oh!"

"You, why are you here?"

"My family, my grandmother and grandfather's family are in a mass grave over there." I gestured toward the field behind me and told him of the massacre that occurred there.

The man looked at the cemetery and the field. There was a querulous expression on his face.

I explained, "The field is where the Jews of this town were killed."

Willie stood up and looked across the wall at the orchard and around the cemetery and then across toward his father's grave. He seemed to take inventory of the Jewish cemetery, placing it in relation to his father's gravesite. Then he sighed, took several deep breaths, removed a white linen handkerchief from a pocket, and blew his nose and wiped his eyes. He was continually shaking his head as he stood there. He said, "Oh I'm sorry."

Then he breathed another sigh and sobbed. "My father, your family, all those people. Oh! Oh!"

We were both silent for a few moments. Three people standing in a field. He was obviously affected at finding his father's grave. I also was devastated from the experience of the cemetery and the field beyond. I was confused. The anger from seeing Auschwitz yesterday was still with me. The field where my family members had been slaughtered amplified a rage that I had never experienced, a heat within that made me want to strike out at someone. The appearance of this stranger, a German, added to the confusion. I tried to decide how to react to him. I looked at his obvious disorientation and for some reason I wanted to reach out to ease his grief. He was in great discomfort. I felt sympathy for him even though he was a German. He needed someone to talk to and I needed to relate to someone other than Peter.

Again, he sighed and sobbed. "Do you have any water?"

"Yes, in our car."

Peter quickly crossed over the graves and to the road and came back with a water bottle. The man took a long sip from the bottle and seemed to catch his breath and revive.

I asked: "Do you want to sit and talk? I could use someone to talk with."

"That would be nice. I've had a rather upsetting experience. Just talking might be good."

"Do you want to stop and have a have a coffee?"

Nodding his head in agreement, he whispered, "Yes, and perhaps something stronger."

We walked together to the road to our car. He rode in the back seat and Peter circled around to the other side of the church to his car. He followed us to the town center, where we parked near a local café. Both of us needed the air. We selected an outside round metal café table, although it was midafternoon and the day had started to cool. There was a place for an umbrella for use on more balmy days, and the metal chairs weren't comfortable but would do and we ordered drinks. We both ordered a whiskey. The man also ordered a Zyweic beer. Peter ordered a Coca-Cola.

"I have never heard of Zyweic beer. What is it?"

"It's one of Poland's most famous beers. Most people don't associate Poland with beer, but this is beer with a refreshing taste. I've had it many times, and enjoy it. Do you want a sip?" He offered me his glass.

I was expecting a standard Euro lager taste. It turned out to have a bit more character than that, some definite body and vigorous freshness, without the aftertaste that sometimes comes with some crafted lagers.

"I'm not really a beer drinker, but if I see Zywiec on a menu in the US I'm ordering one. I think I'll enjoy telling the story of how I discovered it."

For the first time since we met, the stranger smiled. With a full swallow of whiskey and a few sips of the beer he seemed to perk up and color returned to his face. Once again, he took a deep breath, cleared his throat a few times, and then blew his nose into his handkerchief.

"I'm George Bluhm. I'm from New York, and I came to Poland to see what happened to my grandmother and grandfather's family. They were killed in the Holocaust, and the murders took place here. I wanted to see what happened to them and the other Jews of this town."

The man took a sip of his beer and nodded. "I'm Willie Kirchenmann, a retired banker from Stuttgart. I am the son of one of the German soldiers who was killed in the local action in January 1945 and was buried along the roadside."

We looked at each other, both sensing the irony of a Jew and German sitting near a cemetery in Poland. Peter sipped his Coca-Cola with a wry smile.

"How did you come to this road?" I asked.

Willie told how he was retired and wanted a project, had come upon the box of old letters, and had started his search, ending just an hour before at the gravesite where we met. His eyes filled with tears again and he sobbed, blew his nose, and smothered a sigh with a sip of beer. "It has been a long road, and I feel a sense of relief and peace, knowing where my father died. At least I have a grave to visit."

I told him of our finding the cemetery and how the priest related how the Jews of Ozarow were killed that night long ago.

Willie said: "That must be the old priest who directed me to the German soldier's graves."

I told him, "The cemetery where we met held the remains of the Jewish population of the town in 1941. The field next to the cemetery, which is now an orchard, is where the local Jewish men, women, and children were slaughtered in an extermination action. The orchard is directly across from your father's grave."

Willie looked away from me and stared off into the distance. He couldn't make eye contact. I related the story of the killings as the priest had told us. I retold the facts—the herding of the Jews from the town to the site, the stripping of the victims, the acts of humiliation before the killing, and the digging of the mass graves. I described how the Jews were shot, one bullet to the head, men first, and the killing of the children before their mothers. How they were buried all in one grave. Willie sat shaking his head; he turned ashen and was muttering: "No! No! No! On one side of the road a mass grave of murdered Jews, on the other my father! Unbelievable."

Once again Willie took a breath and swallowed some beer. With a great effort he started to talk slowly, almost as if he were speaking to himself, at first staring off into space and then focusing his eyes directly at me. "During the last two weeks as I traveled through Poland and Russia, I have learned a great deal. My generation rebuilt Germany. We didn't talk about the war, the deaths, or of our father's participation in the war. These things were just not discussed. When the subject might come up, we just moved the conversation on. You did not ask, 'What did your father do during the war?' It wasn't a polite subject. We were in denial, or better than denial, we thought that if we didn't acknowledge war crimes, they didn't exist. I'm sure I went to school with some of the children whose fathers committed these murders, fathers who supported the Nazi party and fathers who also died fighting. The crimes of the war were so enormous that we could not grasp them. We did not want to hear or think about them. Yes, we Germans were guilty of denial and trying to be too busy to care. We blamed 'that' generation."

Again he stopped to sip the beer. "We heard the stories. We avoided any topic that might examine who was involved. We didn't want to know who did what. Indeed, most of us denied what happened. Some said the 'stories' were propaganda. I guess we were afraid to ask questions about the past. We didn't want to know who was to blame or how it came about. The atrocities I have learned about while traveling did not come to our attention; the deaths, the murders, and the concentration camps were minimized or brushed over. Collectively our postwar attitude was to keep our head down and move forward. Among many there was a belief that we were the victims, first of Hitler and his cronies and then of the bombing and being conquered and occupied."

Willie took a swallow of his drink, cleared his throat, brushed his hair back and went on. "Now I must reflect on all that I know and have learned and place it into a personal perspective. I am one of those who considered himself a victim of the war, along with my mother. Papa wasn't part of the Brown Shirts, the SA, in the early '30s. He was anti–Brown Shirts and didn't approve of the 'Jewish business.' Maybe he was just one of the many who stood by and watched, afraid to protest or stand out, content to enjoy the return of some prosperity. My mother and father were standing behind their lace curtains as their neighbors were taken away. It wasn't 'their business,' so don't protest. They looked at the Nazis as something that was 'just politics,' and would pass. He was too busy to care. Business was good and his generation became proud again after the losses of World War I and the disaster of the postwar inflation. I loved Papa. He was a decent man, a simple baker. My mother lost the man she loved and I lost a father. Those were our personal losses. Others lost their fathers, their entire families. Now I see that an entire generation of Russians, Poles, and Jews were lost. So many Frenchmen, British, and Americans died, cultures were destroyed. The war was mad. It was mad! And for what? Germany went to war based on the demonic vision and the ambitions of an insane Hitler, who captivated the soul of a nation. The country wanted an easy solution to economic and social problems, a people who accepted hate as a medicine and a fable of ethnic superiority as a narcotic. The leadership grew from a band of thugs who became murderers. The nation, the country of my forefathers, followed blindly, and in too many cases, with enthusiasm."

There was a silence as he paused and I didn't want to interrupt. He seemed to be reciting a reverie, a confessional. Willie continued, "I cannot accept guilt for crimes I did not commit. I don't know if my father was one of these killers or guilty of these crimes. However, my nation must accept the responsibility that comes from our fathers blindly following an ideology that permitted men to kill as they did in that field. Hitler led these crazed men and they followed orders blindly to the destruction of your people, and indeed the greatness that was Europe. My father is in his grave about a mile from here. I don't know what my coming here has proven, but inside me, part of a book has been closed."

After a moment, I started to tell him why I came to Poland. I spoke of my grandmother and her family and how important this location was to my family. "This was the 'old country.' This was their ancestral home for the last five hundred years." I went into detail of how my grandmother had come to the United States and how she looked forward to the day she could bring relatives to America, her promised land. I spoke of the letters posted each week and how the letters were returned in 1939 and in 1945. I told about grandmother's brother who owned the local dry goods store in this town and Grandpa's twin who was the local timber merchant. Then there was the other brother who did nothing but study the Torah and was honored in the family as a religious scholar. "Each of these men and their families were buried somewhere in that trench in the orchard."

Willie reacted to my comment with a gasp.

"I realize now that the Holocaust really applied to my family. Before I came, I didn't feel any direct connection to the Holocaust." I continued: "I wanted to walk the streets where they walked. I wanted to sit in the synagogue where they prayed. I wanted to see their world. What I found was that the Holocaust wasn't something that happened to someone else. Seeing the cemetery and the mound of graves next to it made those letters that were returned to Grandma sixty years ago a confirmation that the slaughter was personal for me. It wasn't a distant news story that happened to someone else. It took over sixty years for me to imagine the sound of those guns."

We were silent as we gathered our thoughts and sipped our beer. If someone came by and observed us, they would think we were two old friends at a café having a drink. Willie ordered yet another beer, and I joined him. I don't know if it was the last beer, or Willie was feeling sorry for himself, but he seemed to talk into the air, almost ignoring Peter or me.

"Millions of Germans were members of the National Socialist Party during those years. Where did all the denial come from after the war? Can't a mature person just confess that it was stupid, wrong? Guilty!"

Almost in a whisper I heard, "I'm German, do you hate me?"

"No, you seem to be a very decent guy."

Peter, my guide, sat silently and observed the two men from diverse backgrounds who came from opposite sides of the world. He was silent during our conversation. I would look over at him and he would be shaking his head. For him, the student, this was a lesson in listening. He absorbed every word of our dialogue. Then Peter excused himself.

"I'm going to leave you two alone. I'll be back in an hour I want to purchase something in town."

We stayed and talked, neither of us wanted to break away. The late afternoon sun darted behind dark clouds and Willie said he was chilled and we moved our seats into the tavern. We both spoke of family, compared our backgrounds and stories of our youth. He told of growing up without a father and how his mother had been deprived of the love of her life, never remarrying. Pictures in his wallet showed his children and grandchildren, and he described where they lived and how they had prospered. He smiled as he said one of his sons was living in Westport, Connecticut, working for the American affiliate office of the bank where Willie had been an officer. He talked of his deceased wife and how his father had missed all of this; not seeing Willie mature and not meeting his grandchildren. We compared career notes and found we had a common acquaintance and mutual knowledge of certain business associates.

We talked about experiences of this trip, his and mine. Willie told of the travels in Ukraine, the battlegrounds visited and the towns where he'd stopped. He told me about towns he could not find; "missing towns," he said. He talked of his growing awareness of the effect the war had on individuals and how his comprehension of the Nazi murder policy against civilians grew.

"The Nazis fought more than a war. I see that now. War is one thing, you fight to destroy an enemy, gain territory, and win or lose. The Nazis had this hideous other agenda of not only fighting the war, but eliminating whole masses of people: Jews, Gypsies, Slovaks, and other innocents. For them there was a war within a war; their 'Final Solution.' Going to war was an excuse for political murder, at least in the war in the East. The atrocity was genocide. I understand the meaning of the monuments and memorials now. Two weeks ago I felt nothing when I saw them. I could walk or drive by them and they were just pieces of stone that someone put in a park. Now I think I comprehend why memorials are built. I will never be able to pass a memorial or gravesite without thinking of what I have learned on this journey. Each stone, each statue, is the personal heartache of individuals just like you or me; thousands of them; millions. Seeing my father's grave and the field across the road brought it all home."

I talked about the trip from Warsaw to Radom, Auschwitz, and then to Ozarow. We compared our reactions to the memorials in Warsaw. His analysis of what he saw in Warsaw was different from mine. I described the martyrdom of those in the ghetto uprising and the impact of the deportation walk to the railcars, the Umschlagplatz. I told him of the railhead at Radom and how it was used as a transshipment point to the gas chambers. Willie was solemn in saying that he saw the monuments in Warsaw and he didn't have any emotional reaction.

"If I went back, I would see Warsaw with different eyes. I now realize that my father was one of the soldiers who purchased clothes, a fur coat from one of those Jews held in the ghetto. So he knew. My mother wore that coat, proud that her husband sent it to her. What other possessions did the Jews have to sell to stay alive; for how long? I'd also want to see the deportation point where they loaded the Jews. I'd appreciate the monuments where the Jews resisted. And now I know about the Poles' uprising and how the Russians didn't come to their aid and let them die."

He quickly added, "I saw so many sites where horrible deaths took place, and heard of murders that are too hard to imagine. The killing of millions of Jews for no reason at all, except they were Jews, seems unconscionable. The word 'atrocity' now has a personal meaning for me. The shock of those sites and stories has affected me. Today, I can't view the monuments with indifference. These sites are sacred. It doesn't matter where they are Warsaw or Ukraine or here in Ozarow, they must remind future generations that vibrant people once were here. The memorials commemorate members of the human race who were classified as subhuman and then humiliated, discarded, and murdered. Every German must acknowledge the guilt. My country made the inconceivable, real. Monuments are inadequate, and men like me must make people remember."

I interrupted his comments. "I visited Auschwitz on the way to Oazrow. I was there just yesterday. I'm still digesting my reactions to what I've seen. My image of humanity is changed. How can human beings be capable of dong unimaginable acts of cruelty to one another? Auschwitz is a reminder not only to the brutality of man, but a symbol that we are not that far above the animal kingdoms in our behavior. I believe every German, Pole, Russian, American, or any person who considers himself civilized and moral should go to Auschwitz and bear witness. It is not only the killing of this mass of Jews, Gypsies, Russians, and other innocents, it is the way that the task was organized, industrialized, and executed with pride by the sick Nazi mind."

"Do you think that I, a German, should go there?"

"You should. You have come all this way. You should see the gas chambers and the crematorium. You should see the atrociousness of the crimes; the mechanics of mass murder. You should become knowledgeable. Complete your education."

Willie reflected on what I had said about my visit to Auschwitz. He took another taste of his drink and almost as if he were talking to a ghost, looked away and said, "As they were using railcars for transporting Jews to camps, my father and others were fighting short of supplies and ammunition. They endured three winters in inadequate clothing, clothing not fit for the Russian weather."

Then almost shouting, he raised his voice and pounded the table with his fist. "What fools! What damn fools! How could they? How could these men?"

Shaking his head, he reflected, "My father participated in the war. I have to believe he was a good man. I was brought up to love him and respect his memory. I lost him to an evil he couldn't control. He was a loving father and wonderful husband to my mother. I wonder if he was the same man to whom we said goodbye to in 1938. My last memories were of him kissing my mother, stroking my head and leaving the house to go back to the front. All German soldiers weren't criminals, but we, their children, will never know for sure who squeezed the trigger back in that field or the thousand other slaughter sites. We will never be sure. And if we were, what good would it do now?"

I said that there were some who desired vengeance and would stand by and cheer as all Germans were eliminated. Willie winced. "Isn't that just as bad an attitude as those who did all the killing?"

He told me how he had been traveling these past two weeks and had visited many of the battlefields. He talked about many Russian monuments and memorials. As he spoke, his voice was choking. "Of course there were no German memorials." He sighed. "The size of the fighting fields was so vast. As I drove my car, I was awed by the scope of this war. It was thousands of miles of battlefields, hundreds of miles of rear areas, millions of men on each side. Every encounter seemed to cover huge areas with hundreds of thousands of men and thousands of tanks. Reading about it and seeing where it all happened was an awesome education. It comes down to the actions of individuals; the men's heartbeats and feelings were the human components of the battles. Each soldier fought his own personal battle facing his fears and trying to survive."

I asked him if he had visited Dnepropetrovsk.

"Yes, it was a monumental battle, and I know my father fought there."

"In Dnepropetrovsk at the start of the war there were 80,000 Jews in a population of over 500,000. As the Germans approached, many Jewish families were evacuated to the east. There were over 20,000 Jews in the city when the German army took over in August 1941. Two years later the Red Army recaptured the city. Only 15 Jews were alive. The others had been taken to a large department store in the city as a collecting point, and then trucked to a ravine, shot, and pushed into a ditch. Over a period of three days they were murdered. These deaths were part of the work of the Einsatzgruppe C."

I took a breath and continued: "Willie, just think. There were approximately six million Jews killed in the Holocaust. There were only four battalions of the Einsatzgruppen and each battalion had at most 3,000 men. This small contingent killed 1.3 million Jews. Who were these killers? They were educated professional men, lawyers and even some physicians. There was even one clergyman in the gruppe.

What kind of man can get up morning, morning after morning, and go out and kill like these men did?"

I had Willie's attention as I went on, "And just think, they had to have support from the Wehrmacht. They had to have regular troops for their logistics, for their food, bread, clothing, and even their ammunition. They could not have acted without the knowledge and approval of the generals and the acquiescence of the other soldiers around them. Was there any outrage? Were there protests within the German army?"

I took another sip of beer. "Here in Ozarow there were 2,146 Jews murdered, men women and children. Ozarow was a small operation by comparison. But it was all bad. All ghastly."

Willie paused, and seemed to be speaking in self-defense: "I hired a guide when I visited Kiev. I was surprised when he took me to a place called Babi Yar. Believe it or not, I never had heard of the incident. It was one of those places we didn't hear about, even after the war. Not in Germany. Over 100,000 were murdered there in about three days. I cried. I still cry and choke every time I think about Babi Yar. What dirty bastards could do this? It was a horrific site to visit. I can't excuse German men for doing that. Today it is bucolic and peaceful. Now I think how many other incidents are there that I don't know about; that my fellow German doesn't know about."

He again sipped his drink, heaved a sigh and spoke slowly. "The ideology the Nazis preached was immoral and heartless. Since the war, German children have been brought up with a blind spot about the years from 1931 to 1945. The children of Germany should be making these trips and see the cemeteries, the battlefields and the remains of the camps. We are too old. I have learned too much late in life. When I return home I want to speak to children and young adults, not about the memory of my mother or father, but about what I have seen. It isn't only 'Never Again,' it must be 'Never Forget.' The Jews didn't believe that a country that believed it to be the height of civilization could slide from acceptance to overt discrimination and persecution to deportation and death. The people who did this killing, this labeling of 'subhumans' as targets for elimination violated more than human rights. Germany has desecrated man as a civilized being. They proved how thin the veneer of civilization is. The Nazis and indeed the sympathetic Germans committed that sin. How futile, how stupid."

There was little I could add to Willie's monologue. I wanted to stay there and continue our talk, but Peter returned and prompted me: "If we are to have you on an airplane in two days, we should start back on the road to Warsaw."

Willie pushed himself up from the table, threw his shoulders back, and took a deep breath. "I think I'll stay the night here in Ozarow. I want to visit my father's grave again in the morning. Having traveled this far, I want time alone with Papa. I have so many cherished memories of him." Willie then shocked me. "Could you stay, have dinner with me this evening, and make the trip to Warsaw tomorrow after breakfast?"

I looked at Peter. A wry smile crossed Peter's lips and he said, "You could still make your plane if you stayed the night."

I agreed and we asked Peter to find us accommodations. About thirty minutes later he returned with three sets of keys to rooms at a small hotel, the Hotel Zacisze about a three-minute walk from the bistro. We smiled and thanked him for his efforts.

Peter said: "Don't thank me until you check in and see the place. It definitely isn't Le Bristol in Warsaw. I don't think either of you will find it other than a place to get a night's sleep. It is a two-star hotel and it does come with private toilets and showers."

We went to the hotel and freshened up. As Peter advertised, the hotel was a small concrete building that showed a great deal of wear and tear. The rooms were decorated with green bedspreads that seemed not to have been washed or cleaned in the years since Polish freedom was declared in the early 1990s, but it was an acceptable bed for the night. We rendezvoused in the small lobby a half hour later, and the proprietor, a Mrs. Chabrowicz, recommended a local restaurant about a five-minute walk away.

As Peter, Willie, and I strolled to the restaurant, Willie talked of his family and how when he returned home he would tell them of his travels. He said, "There are some things they should acknowledge. As time blurs the history of WWII, someone has to reveal and retell the fact that these horrors have been committed."

"The Jews keep saying: Never Again," I uttered.

Willie replied, "It has to be more than the Jews saying that."

There were only five tables in the restaurant. Each table had a white homespun cloth covering, and candles fashioned from an old drinking glass with white wax drippings on the side. To me they looked like the Yahrzeit candles my grandmother used to light as memorials. The restaurant floor had a carpet that showed the traffic between the tables as worn paths, trails between the kitchen and customers. The waiter led us along one of those paths and sat the three of us at a rear corner. There were quaint faded pictures of old Polish landscapes on the white stonewalls.

Willie again ordered a Zywiec and I demurred and asked for one of the other beers I saw in the display case, a Stella Artois. It was a Belgium beer that I had liked for many years. When we were served, Willie pushed back his chair away from the table. He seemed to relax as he spoke. "I want to thank you for staying on and joining me this evening. Today was a significant day in my life. I have been on a long journey dreading what I might find, thinking that perhaps I would find nothing. But at the end, seeing my father's grave, the Jewish cemetery across the road, and then hearing of the killings in the field has put some feelings of the last sixty years in perspective."

"It has to be a closure for you, at least knowing where your father is buried."

"Yes, it's a strange set of bookmarks, the mass murder graves on one side, the German graves on the other side of the road, and the old Jewish cemetery between them."

"Perspective is important for both of us. I have spent much of my life not really thinking of the Holocaust. I was a red blooded Jewish American boy. Of course I went to Memorial Day parades, looked for the best fireworks on July fourth, and celebrated Israel Independence Day. At the right times I saluted and waved the American flag, and then carried the Israeli flag on other days. I didn't give much thought to the war sacrifices or to the human cost represented by the Holocaust. It all was peripheral to my mind, to my everyday existence."

"That's getting on with your life."

"Yes, but now I have to reflect on something I have never wanted to think about.

A surprised look was on Willie's face. "What is that?"

Just then the waiter came and asked us what we wished to eat. Willie and I were absorbed in our conversation at the moment and couldn't focus on ordering a meal, but the waiter was patient and Peter broke the silence by saying, "I'll have the steak please. Make it medium rare."

The waiter listed the available vegetables and Peter selected a baked potato and carrots for his side dishes. As a starter, after some deliberation he selected the asparagus when the waiter said that it had been freshly cut in the afternoon.

Willie and I spoke at the same time, "We'll have the same."

The meal was served but I found that eating gave me little satisfaction. I had no taste and I barely ate. I glanced at Willie and noticed that he also had hardly touched his food. Peter seemed to eat everything in sight. He seemed embarrassed when he looked across the table at our still full plates, nodded a few times, and seemed to apologize, "I can understand your lack of appetite this evening."

Willie then asked me: "And what is this you never wanted to think about?"

"You know I grew up during the war, just as you did. I collected tin foil and old pots and pans and other aluminum scrap and old steel for the war effort. We campaigned for war bonds; we did all we were asked to do, and volunteered, even as kids, to do what had to be done. We were loyal and understood the magnitude of the effort needed to defeat Germany and Japan. I listened to the radio and I read the *New York Times.* The *Times* didn't feature the genocide of the Jews on the front page. Some of the most sensational stories of the mass killings were in the back on page fifteen."

My anger was mounting as I spoke. A polite upbringing kept me from banging the table in emphasis as I went on. "Although the publisher of the *Times* was Jewish, a man named Sulzberger, he buried the news of the massacres deep in the paper, and always referred to the victims as part of larger groups like Poles, Belgians, or 'refugees,' never singling out the Jews. Sulzberger was an assimilationist and wanted to avoid the claim that America was engaged in a war for the Jews. He knew what was happening but didn't spread the word to the American people. The *Times* had the news but did not publish it. Their reporters attempted to get headline stories prominently placed in the paper, but the reports were suppressed or minimized. We will never know if the newspapers had printed the truth if the American public and world opinion would have reacted differently. If the news had been more prominent, had the editorials been more persistent and aggressive, would it have made a difference?"

This time I was the one to pause and take a breath. I was avoiding eye contact with Willie as I went on. "We Jews believed in Franklin Delano Roosevelt. Overwhelmingly we supported him. He was our leader; we listened to his every word. More than anything we trusted him. My father voted for him in each of his elections and in our home you couldn't say a bad word about that man. It is only now that we know that he had early knowledge of the magnitude of the tragedy. He chose a politically safe path of demurring to his anti-Semitic state department rather than helping to get some of the Jews out of harm's way."

Peter interjected: "But he was one of the great men of the twentieth century."

"I visited Auschwitz and have seen some of the areas of desecration and murder of the Jews of Poland and Europe. Before the knowledge of Auschwitz-Birkenau became public knowledge in 1944 Roosevelt, Churchill, and the leaders of the West knew of these killings; knew of the horrors of the concentration camps, the ghettos and the selective ethnic murders. Word was getting out through to the free Polish government in exile, and this news was being shared with the United States and the British governments. Nothing was done to really conceal the work of the murderers."

Peter continued, "That's all true. The Poles knew their neighbors were being rounded up, ghettoized, and then shipped out to some hell. The Polish underground sent the messages out to England asking for some assistance from the British or Americans. No answers came from either government. All Churchill and Roosevelt did was to make speeches warning that any people who committed war crimes would be punished after the war. That's not saying anything to influence a fanatic who expected to win the war."

I picked up on Peter's comments, "Did the German people really believe there was a pleasant work camp where all the Jews would live in bliss? The Ukrainians supplied some of the most vicious killers to the Einsatzgruppen. Surely the word was out that genocide was taking place. Where was the outcry? Why weren't there protests in the streets of New York, Brooklyn, Newark, and Los Angeles? Why wasn't there a march on Washington? Were we Jews too impotent as a group? Were we so insecure that we wouldn't march for our ideals? Why couldn't we bring the president out into the public to threaten, denounce and take action? Were we cowards? Were we too insecure of our position in the United States to raise our Jewish voices? Why weren't the camps bombed? Early on they knew of Dachau. Hell, Dachau was opened in 1933 and people were disappearing from the streets of Germany and later Austria. The diplomats knew. They were trying to get American visas for Jews. Roosevelt did not act."

Again Peter interjected: "As a student I was told that your state department was decidedly anti-Semitic at the time."

"There is sufficient evidence to prove that the state department was anti-Semitic, and Roosevelt was unwilling to challenge them. The entire Jewish question was not popular according to the polls conducted during the war. It wasn't until the word of the Holocaust became known that opinion changed. Think of Roosevelt's unwillingness to admit the passengers of the St. Louis, as it was turned away from Havana in 1939. He was aware of the plight of the refugees on board. Even his wife tried to get him to act and give haven. Nevertheless Roosevelt turned his back on them. Most of those passengers eventually died in concentration camps after they were returned to Amsterdam. When Holland fell, they were rounded up with the other Jews. Then, in a too-little-too-late reaction, it wasn't until 1942 that any act of Congress was passed to let an additional small quota of Jewish children into the US."

By now I was red in the face and obviously so aroused that Willie reached out and placed his hand on my arm, trying to calm me. Peter said, "I heard that some Jews were able to get out of Germany from 1933 until 1940."

"That's true, but while Roosevelt and the state department were holding back on letting Jews into the United States there were over 400,000 visas within the quota system that were not issued. That's 400,000 lives that could have been saved with very little effort."

Willie asked, "Didn't Roosevelt have some Jews in his cabinet?"

"Yes Willie, some of his closest advisors were Jewish. His secretary of the treasury, a fellow named Morganthau, was Jewish. Morgenthau told Roosevelt about the murders in early 1942. It took two years for the government to organize any effort to accommodate the flow of future Jewish refugees. In the most critical of times, Roosevelt did nothing."

"Was there a strong Jewish voice at the time?"

"Not really. A rabbi, Stephen S. Wise, met with FDR in September of 1942. As a matter of fact, he went with Morganthau to see Roosevelt. He was a well-known Reform rabbi and assimilationist who led several rallies to publicize the killings of men women and children. Wise was renowned as a leader but did not have that much political influence. The *Times* buried the story of the one Madison Square Garden rally, and there were no real results or public outcry."

Willie asked, "Were these rallies publicized?"

"Yes, in the Jewish press. But they weren't followed up. The Jews of the United States were meek and afraid. Also they were divided. Those who practiced as Orthodox did not want to work with the Conservative or the Reform sects. In some cases there were divisions between those of German origin, who were generally Reform Jews, and those who came from Eastern Europe. One prominent Reform rabbi thought that those who spoke of the rescue of Eastern European Jews were alarmists. Contrary to gentile thought, there was not a real 'one voice' among the American Jews. One rabbi who had come out of Germany pleaded with the government, and had said 'the most urgent, disgraceful, the most shameful, most tragic problem is silence.' Unfortunately those who spoke could not speak loud enough, and there was no television or Internet to mobilize vast numbers of sympathizers. The responsibility to spread the word fell to the printed press, and they failed."

Then as an after-thought I said, "We were silent. Why do I feel guilty that we didn't do anything?"

Both Willie and I took sips of our drinks and there was a moment of silence between us. Willie spoke first. "You were the victors, you were a just and righteous people who defeated Hitler and a morally corrupt and inhuman government and culture, and you should not feel guilt. One man, Adolf Hitler defined the mission of the extermination program. The obsessivness of the men who brutally implemented the program defined the extent of the insanity a nation was willing to self-righteously accept without examining the morality of the orders or acts. We Germans were the killers, we should never forget."

Willie paused in his commentary and seemed to cross a line that I was surprised to hear. "Hitler promised us that he would deliver a greater Germany. He promised 1,000 years of prosperity and glory. We know his vision was insane. We can also accept that his hatred of Jews, Poles, Slovaks was so crazed that he used the excuse of the war to mask a desire to eliminate these innocent people. His monstrous crimes against humanity stand as just one of the many horrible deeds of a man and regime that abandoned all moral basis for governing. The crime of the German people is they accepted this genocide, how do you say, lock, stock and barrel. Many even gloried in it."

"Willie, you make a strong argument, stronger than anything I have ever heard indicting the German people. And yet as I sit here I feel this disappointment in the American government and Roosevelt. They did nothing to get Jews out of Europe before the war, and did nothing to stop or slow the killings during the war."

"George, maybe the multiple factors that existed at one time, the politics, the war situation, the events and bureaucracy, may have tied the hands of your Mr. Roosevelt. Don't you think it is ironic that Roosevelt, the man that Hitler thought was a Bolshevik Jew, is the man who many Jews look at and say he had sympathies that precluded his helping Jews? The world may be more complex than the black and white, guilty and not guilty verdicts you may want."

I felt exhausted from the buildup of my rage and the experiences of the day. As we finished our meal, our conversation turned to the mundane table chatter of how good the steaks were and the comparative virtues of Russian, Polish, German, and American food.

Willie smiled: "And look, it's sixty years later and we can now buy a Big Mac in almost every city you and I have visited. Even your McDonald's is in Poland and Ukraine."

Peter laughed: "To the victors goes the hamburger."

The shared memories of the day had made friends of strangers.

We ordered coffee and after dinner drinks. Neither Willie nor I wanted to break the spell of this evening. We just wanted to sit and talk.

Again Willie surprised me. He asked if I was an observant Jew.

"Willie, that's a harder question than you might think. My grandmother and grandfather were observant, Orthodox, and regularly attended services. On the way to work, my grandfather would often stop and pray. I grew up in a generation that was attempting to prove ourselves by joining the American mainstream. I lived in a Jewish world on one hand and a predominantly non-Jewish on the other. I personally could not conjure up the faith, nor submit to the discipline of the Orthodox lifestyle. Between my time in the army during the Korean War, and university, I became a secular American, Reform Jew."

Willie furrowed his brows and asked, "What is the difference between Orthodox and Reform?"

"It's more complicated, Willie. You can be Orthodox, meaning that you observe the kosher food laws and attend a very traditional synagogue. In the United States we also have Jews practicing as 'Conservatives.' These people may or may not keep kosher, and their service contains some English, and they modify the service into a modern format. Then there are several groups of Reform and Reconstructionist Jews where much of the litany depends upon the congregation and the rabbis select a format that the congregation feels comfortable with. Eventually, I became a Reform Jew while my children were growing up. Willie, of those Jews who affiliate with a synagogue in the United States 46 percent belong to the Reform movement. I guess I call myself a Reform Jew. Yes, secular and assimilated. I only attend High Holy Day services."

"George, who are the fellows who dress in the black clothes and wear the wide brim black hats?"

"They are the ultra-Orthodox. Their dress reflects the costume of the seventeenth century, and the customs of the rabbis they venerate and follow. Obviously they aren't fully assimilated into the American mainstream. Indeed they represent the extreme interpretation of the religion even in Israel."

Willie nursed his coffee and his drink, and told of some of his encounters with the Ukrainians. "None of the people I met seemed to hate me because I was an old German. They all wanted me to understand what had happened in their lives during the war. How could they forgive us? Thank God there are decent people in this world. I was lucky to meet some of them."

I looked at Willie and thought a moment. "Elie Weisel, who was liberated from Buchenwald and had been in Auschwitz, wrote that when the war ended the inmates didn't pursue the SS, didn't seem to want revenge. They were free. They wanted food. They wanted life. They wanted to move on."

It was late and Willie looked at his watch. We signaled for the bill and prepared to leave the table. Peter, who had been silent during much of the meal, interjected a comment that brought us to attention. "When I made the reservation at the hotel, I spoke to the hotel manager. She told me that there was an older man in town, who was a youngster living here during the war, and eventually became the local bank manager. She said that it he might be an interesting person to meet."

Both Willie and I agreed that talking to this man would be a remarkable encounter.

Peter excused himself, "Let me walk back to the hotel first and tell her to arrange the meeting."

Willie said, "If we can see this man in the morning, I will then head home. But first I want to stop by my father's grave for a few moments. Then I will go to Auschwitz, it isn't that far from here. Probably I'll also go to that town Radom you mentioned, and go on to Warsaw. I'm in no hurry. I want to take a good look at what I missed when I was more interested in seeing where my father traveled. I saw the monuments, but I really didn't comprehend their significance. I realize now that the war was about people, the tragedy of those millions."

"You know, Willie, although we won the war, six million Jews were dead as well as twenty million or more additional men women and children. That's a Pyrrhic victory."

Willie added, "George, it keeps haunting me that the culture that gave birth to men like Albert Einstein and hundreds, thousands more worthy souls, were killed by people to whom I'm related."

I asked Willie, "Do you believe in collective guilt?"

"No, but I now know that the German people realized what was happening. They knew when they received recycled clothing from the government that it was coming from some victim. They knew when people disappeared from their midst, and they knew when the Jews were taken away, and businesses and Jewish property became theirs. Individuals were guilty, perhaps not of the murders, but of receiving the stolen goods from people who were their neighbors. They were guilty of complicity. The Nazis made human life cheap and many Germans experienced the schuldenfrei, it's better them than us! Yes, I now believe that ordinary citizens share the responsibility."

Willie paused in his comments and shook his head several times. "Innocent as I might wish my father to be, he probably became a killer. He must have participated or observed or even did some of the shooting. Once a man kills in battle he changes; something changes within the man. My father was an infantryman (Landser); he must have been one of the many who realized the war was lost the day Stalingrad fell. He loyally soldiered on. He followed orders and stayed at his post until the end. Was he the one who murdered innocents? We will never know. I will never know. But if his other comrades were pulling the triggers he lived and fought among them. My father was just as guilty as others."

I tried to put my hand on Willie's shoulder to comfort him, but he brushed it aside very gently. "Whatever you might say, I must accept this. Yes, I loved him as a father. I cherished my memories of him. I must also face that he wasn't the hero I might have wished him be. None of that generation was."

I tried to interject, but Willie continued on. "George, there were two wars being fought at the same time. The German people thought there was one war going on, but the government used that war to mask a second war, Hitler's Final Solution. One war was being fought by armies here on the Eastern front. The other war was an army of irregulars, the Einsatzgruppen, the SS Special Forces, the OPW police killers, and the details of Hungarians and Romanians all charged with killing innocent citizens. This was the second war, heavily armed troops against unarmed civilians. It was an unequal match. This wasn't fighting in the field, armed man against armed man. It was ideological and ethnic murder. There was an agenda of hate. Sadly the German people and the German army accepted this."

"Willie, I believe that activism has a place in society. We experienced the power of a country's conscience when my generation protested during the '60s. We saw our children demonstrate for causes they believed in. They took to the streets protesting Vietnam. Modern history has shown us that the man in the street has a voice. Not one murder in the name of an ideology is just. The lesson from knowing these events is we cannot remain silent. As long as there are decent people protests must be heard. Millions have died, but the message of their deaths must be to civilization that 'Never Again' must apply to all injustice and every innocent victim."

Willie was hushed to a whisper. "I have spent sixty years struggling to be successful, to rise out of the rubble and dust of my city and country. There is a moral responsibility that my nation must stand for. Our children and our people must accept that responsibility."

Willie and I settled the bill at the restaurant. I wanted to pay for Peter's portion, but Willie insisted on "splitting the bill up the middle." We then walked to the hotel in silence, each lost in our thoughts.

Peter was in the hotel lobby awaiting us. "We have an appointment to meet this fellow who was here during the war. The only time he can see us is 10 a.m. The mayor is going to send an official of the town to accompany us."

Both Willie and I thanked Peter for arranging the meeting.

Peter replied, "Don't thank me, thank our host Mrs. Chabrowicz when we see her tomorrow."

We agreed to meet in the lobby to go to breakfast at eight in the morning.

Chapter Twenty

The Old Man

The sun shone through my dusty window, and the hotel room looked more tattered than it did the night before. Sunlight didn't clean walls and furniture; it highlighted the grime. I showered in the small shower cubicle, ignoring rust spots on the wall and was pleased that at least there was a powerful water pressure to awaken me. My khaki travel trousers still held their crease and looked presentable. I took the last clean shirt from my bag and prepared to meet Willie and Peter.

Willie and I were in the breakfast room before eight, anxious to meet this man who could tell us what happened many years before. Peter joined us at about eight fifteen, apologizing that he was a little late.

The hotel breakfast room was a bright alcove with a slanted glass roof and clear glass- paneled sides for three of the walls. The entry wall from the lobby was painted a bright yellow and added to the cheerful atmosphere. The sun drenched the room and warmed us as we sat and enjoyed our coffee and croissants from the basket centered on the tables.

At nine o'clock a stocky man with broad shoulders and a barrel chest walked in, looked around and came to our table. He was wearing a white short sleeve shirt, gray twill trousers, and black work boots. About two inches of his belly hung over his beltline and a smile burst across his face as he spotted the three of us sitting in the far corner. He approached the table with his arm extended, grabbing Peter to shake hands first. In accented English he introduced himself, "Hello, I'm John Chernofski. I'm the mayor's assistant and the water commissioner of Ozarow. I understand you want to meet Mr. Twyouick. I'll take you there."

I asked, "Is Twyouick the man who was here during the war?"

"Yes, he is an interesting old man. He was a child here in Ozarow and then, after his university time, became a bank manager in the town."

I said, "Do you have time for a coffee?"

"Yes."

Willie jumped up and brought John a cup of coffee and several of the croissants.

John was affable. The smile we saw in the first moments remained as he talked. He spoke about the town and how it grew during the postwar years because of the two highways that intersected just to the north. He described how the Soviets had socialized local industry, and although those had been good times for most of the residents, the local people longed for an independent Poland with a free economy.

Both Willie and I were a little impatient to get going to see the old man. We were polite as we watched John enjoy inhaling the aroma of his coffee. He finished the coffee and two of the croissants, aggressively dunking the second roll. "It's time to go; we don't want to keep an old man waiting."

The four of us rode comfortably in the rental car, leaving Willie's Audi at the hotel. John sat in the front seat giving directions to Peter. Crossing through the town, we were guided into a residential section of low-lying one-story cement homes with courtyards and masses of flowers covering the fences. John told Peter to turn into a driveway in the middle of the square of homes. Peter followed the directions to a six-foot-high green steel gate. It had curlicue ornamentation rising across the top and a steel rod vertical bolt at the center of the two hinged gates. Roses were growing over the fence and onto the sides of the entryway. Peter stopped the car in front of the gate.

John got out of the car and rang a pull string bell at the side of the entrance. There was an immediate answer from within and in seconds the steel passageway opened and we went into a large front yard. There were several metal tables and many children's toys scattered about. Two middle-aged men in sleeveless shirts were playing baccarat at a table and a toddler was playing with a small orange ball at the far side of the yard. Standing in the doorway was an elderly man about five feet eight inches tall supported on two canes. Shifting onto one cane he motioned to Peter, Willie and me into his small dining and living area. He pivoted himself aside so we could pass into the room.

He was wearing a light tan silk short sleeve shirt with a tropical scene imprinted along one front panel of the shirt. A pair of spectacles were in the left breast pocket. His matching tan shorts were Bermuda length, but extended slightly below his knees revealing his swollen legs and the telltale sores of a diabetic. He was wearing sandals and short white socks. His angular face was clean-shaven, but the pronounced liver spots on his cheeks and forehead showed the age of a man who otherwise would have looked far younger than we knew him to be.

An old desk chair was in the center of the room and the dining table was beside it. I could see that the room had been arranged for this conversation. It normally was the dining and sitting area of the home. One wall had a glass-enclosed, dark wood bookcase with a sparse collection of hardcover volumes. The other walls were painted in a dark green. One of the walls closest to the kitchen had a picture of Jesus, while the wall nearest the entry door had a troika horserace print. Peter leaned over to me and pointed to the picture. "Did you know that the horses are each a symbol? The black one represents sorrow, the chestnut one love, the white one represents peace. The three horses must be in balance to move life forward. It's a traditional scene."

An old-world charm pervaded the small house. The worn furniture contrasted with a television in the corner of the room as well as a few toys that must have belonged to the child we saw outside. Several generations lived in this small but comfortable home.

He signaled Willie and me to sit opposite him on a couch compressed thin by use; we sat and nearly dropped to the floor, our knees awkwardly and uncomfortably near our chins, as we assumed a squat position sitting there. I surmised that Twyouick's chair came from the bank and was retired with him some years before. The old man shuffled over to this chair and sat down setting one of his canes on the floor between us. We sat facing him as instructed. A third seating position, off to the side, was where Peter sat so he could translate. John had come into the room with us, but remained, arms folded across his chest, standing at the door.

Once seated, our host reached across, extended his arm and shook hands with Willie and then gripped my hand with a firm and vigorous motion. "I'm Twyouick." Peter translated, "I want to welcome you to my home."

Peter translated as Twyouick finished each sentence.

"Can I offer you something to drink? I suggest some tea."

Willie and I agreed to the tea and Peter took a glass of water. An elderly woman, who we assumed was his wife, quickly produced the tea. She placed a cup of tea and two sugar cubes on the table next to Twyouick. Willie and I balanced the tea cups and saucers on our knees.

"I want to thank you for coming to see me. I don't get many visitors, and I was pleased when I was called yesterday that people from America and Germany were interested in meeting me."

As Peter conveyed the comments in English, Twyouick rested his right arm on the table and his other on the second cane. "I'm eighty-three years old now and was sixteen when the war started. I have lived in this town all my life except when I was at university. When I finished my schooling, I came back and worked at the local bank for forty years. It was just after the socialist years ended when I retired. I was a young boy during the entire Nazi occupation. I witnessed a great deal during those years."

Reaching over he cracked one of the sugar cubes in half in the side of his mouth and took a sip of the tea.

Peter caught up with the translation as Twyouick swallowed. "In 1944, there were many fierce battles around here from mid August until late September. Most were on the other side of the river. The Russians came onto this side about 45 kilometers south of here and controlled the city of Sandomierz. In this area they did not cross the river and we could see their campfires and hear the roar of their tank motors at night. With the buildup in place, there was a very quiet period from October until January. Everyone was nervous. Poles wanted them to come and liberate us, and the Germans were anxious awaiting the attack they knew would come. We knew that where the two roads from the river met the road leaving town there would be a clash. During that quiet period the Germans built their defenses hoping to make an effort to slow what they expected would be a major push."

Willie took a swallow of tea and said, "I guess my father was here digging in."

"When the Russians started their drive it was January fifteenth. We all remember this because it was our liberation day. The barrage was tremendous. None of us had ever heard anything like it. We all went into our cellars and prayed. The shells and rockets were very precise and leveled much of the east side of the town where the defenses were concentrated. Then, leaving only a few men for a rear guard holding action, the German general abandoned the town and the Russians moved in. There was a fierce skirmish near the Catholic church and the defenders, poor souls, were wiped out very quickly."

Willie sighed, "Yes, that's where my father died."

Twyouick understood Willie's comment and replied in a halting German. "I was told that you are the son of one of those Germans."

"Yes, I want to thank you for telling me what happened."

"I understand some of your language; after all we were occupied for nearly six years. Was your father in the army a long time?"

"He was conscripted when I was eight years old."

"Is this the first time you came to see his grave?"

"I just found the grave yesterday. I have been visiting the places where I knew he was stationed during those years. It was a shock to finally find out where he was killed."

Twyouick reverted back to Polish and Peter picked up on the translation. "I have three stories to tell you. The first happened in late August 1944. My father sent me out with our wagon into the fields about three kilometers from here to bring back straw for our horse. We were filling our barn with hay for the winter. As I said, there had been fierce battles around here and most of the German army had been pretty badly shot up. It was not unusual to see army stragglers wandering about looking for their unit or seeking their way to a supply station, or to see ambulances bringing wounded to the rear. After I filled the wagon and started back to town I was stopped by a German, I believe he was a sergeant. He was an older man, maybe about forty or forty five years old and his uniform was worn and in need of some tailoring and cleaning. He had several days' growth of beard and hollow circles for eyes. I'll never forget the deep dark eyes. He had four Jews with him. They had escaped from Majdenek, you know, one of those death camps."

Peter asked, "The concentration camp?"

"Yes, the death camp. It was to the northwest of here and they were probably trying to get across the Russian lines to someplace in Ukraine. The Jews had tattered clothing and their feet were bleeding. Their shoes were worn and they could hardly walk. They were in very bad shape. One had blood seeping out of a bandage on his leg. The sergeant stopped me and asked that I take them onto my wagon. He said they couldn't walk any further and needed help. We lifted them onto the back of the wagon, covered them in the straw so they would be comfortable and he joined me in the front of the wagon. The sergeant instructed me to go to the railhead about twelve kilometers from here. Along the way he told me to ride as carefully as possible because these people were in bad shape. Just before we reached the railhead we were stopped by a young boy, he couldn't have been more than seventeen years old, a Hitler Youth who was obviously newly drafted into the SS and wore a new, clean and finely tailored uniform. The SS boy wanted to inspect the wagon, and walked to the rear and uncovered the Jews. He pulled his pistol out of his holster and was about to shoot. He was shouting, 'Raus, raus,' demanding that the Jews get out of the wagon to be executed. The sergeant countered by leaping between the SS man and the Jews. He too drew his pistol and pointed it at the SS man. He shouted, 'Young Himmler, get the hell away from here! These are people who need medical help. Your war has been lost! We who have fought the battles know this. If anyone is going to be killed today, it will be you. I have had enough, but you might as well be one of those I've killed. Let us go on.' The youth holstered his pistol and shouted, 'I will report you and you will be shot.' The sergeant laughed and climbed back onto the wagon. When we arrived at the Red Cross hospital at the railroad station, the sergeant asked that I help him lift the Jews into the operating theater where other wounded were waiting. He then thanked me for my assistance, turned his back and walked into the hospital to be sure the Jews were treated well."

Willie spoke first. "That's quite a story. Did the Jews survive?"

The old man shrugged his shoulders. "I don't know. I hope they survived. I also hope the sergeant survived."

I could feel Willie relax slightly. The story gave him some satisfaction that there were some honorable soldiers. My throat felt constricted from hearing the story. Each of us took a breath and a sip of tea. The older woman returned and served more tea.

I said. "What is the second story?"

"The partisans were active in this area. They harassed the German rear supply lines and worked to keep the German rear unstable, pinning down many Wehrmacht who were guarding the rear. In one incident in June of 1944, just after we heard that there had been landings in Normandy, a German supply convoy was ambushed and partially destroyed. The Germans were understandably angry. A German general and a platoon of the Wehrmacht came into town and forced all the citizens into the town square.

Willie asked, "Were these regular army troops or were they SS?"

Twyouick thought a moment and went on, "They were regular army people. They forced all the people out of their homes, this included women and children, the sick and the infirm. They were surrounded and penned inside the square. I was one of the people in the square. The Germans kept us all there for three days. There was no water, food or toilets for us. The general came to the square and said, 'If you turn in the men who made the attack, you all can go home.' Of course, no one came forward. Then, after the first day he came and said, 'If no one comes forward, I will select eleven men and shoot them.' He then started to make this announcement every hour day and night."

Peter was spellbound by the story and said, "You said this went on for three days."

"Yes, and there was no food or water. As a result several sick and older people died from the stress. The place was filthy. People were crying, and the women were pleading with the German soldiers to let everyone go. The German troops kept their guns trained on us and several times fired shots over the heads of the women. There was a lot of crying and much praying."

Willie was totally absorbed in the story Twyouick was telling. He leaned forward looking directly the older man and listened to Peter's translation.

Again it was Peter who said, "And then what happened?"

"On the third day the general separated the men and women. He walked among the men and selected eleven men at random. The men were pushed against the wall of the school and shot. Each man was shot in the head by the general. He just walked down the line of men and put one bullet into the head of each man. He then turned, and ordered his men to mount their trucks and left town."

Willie looked at me and then at Twyouick. "Is that all?"

"No, on the way out of town about four kilometers from the square where the road passes through a small forest, the troop was ambushed by the partisans. Most of the Germans were killed in the first series of shots. The head of the partisans sought out the general, who tried to surrender. The partisan refused the general's surrender, turned him around, and shot him in the back of the head, just as he had shot the men in town. The area is just out of town. There is a memorial. You should see it before you leave Ozarow."

Willie grunted at the moment Peter translated the word "shot," and I sat in silence. It was a war story we didn't expect to hear.

Then Twyouick turned his head and looked in my direction. He stared into my eyes and spoke directly at me. "Let me tell you how our Jews died. We never had a problem living with Jews in Ozarow. We had good relations. Many of our better businesses were Jewish owned; our lumber business, the tannery, the local tailor, and many merchants. In business there were two groups: the craftsmen and the merchants. They were good and fair employers who always came into other areas of town to find employees. There was an economic dependence between the Jews and the gentiles. In some things they kept to themselves, but for the most part they were just citizens as we were. They lived throughout the town. Although there was a section called the Jewish quarter, many Jews lived in other areas and many had large homes on the higher ground far from the railroad. I can't remember a single incident between the Jews and their neighbors."

Twyouick paused and smiled. He seemed to reach deeply into his memory, "As a matter of fact, when I was young, before the war I was hired to ignite lights on their Sabbath and do some of the things they were prohibited from doing Friday night to sundown on Saturday. I enjoyed working for them."

I asked, "Was that unusual?"

"No. Of course, there were stories that in some towns there was friction. But for the most part we got along fine."

Again there was a refill of tea and Twyouick received another two sugar cubes, and immediately bit into one and sipped more tea. He reminded me of how my grandfather drank his tea.

"When the Germans came in 1939 they moved all the Jews into the section of town near the synagogue. My family saw neighbors on each side of our property forcibly taken from their homes and moved. One of my best friends, a nice Jewish guy was shot because he didn't move fast enough for one of the German bastards."

Willie shifted uneasily in his seat next to me.

"The area the Jews were in became very crowded. Some houses held entire families in one room Jews from nearby towns were brought and forced to live in this ghetto. There wasn't a wall, but there were troops surrounding the area and they would only let Jews come out for supplies when they received permission. Some of the local merchants tried to supply the Jews. The Germans stopped this kind of trade. It was horrible to walk by this area and see the people. We lived like that for a little over a year."

Twyouick shook his head and took another sip of his tea. "Just after Hitler invaded Russia in 1941, a group of the Wehrmacht came and camped just outside of town. After they were here about three days they started to force all the Jews out of the Jewish section and assembled them in the open area of the city square. An SS man was in charge of the counting. They counted the Jews and checked that all were accounted for. Included were about forty Jews that been brought here from Vienna and lived in one of the houses. These Jews refused to come out onto the street. The Germans went in and went room to room and shot them in the house. They even shot infirm old ladies as they lay in bed."

Peter was having a hard time translating Twyouick's story because the old man was breathing heavily and seemed to gasp from time to time as he told the story. "During this time I and another boy hid in a home on the other side of the town square and watched what was happening. We couldn't do anything. The other Jews were marched out of town to the area beyond the Catholic church to the other side of the Jewish cemetery. The first day they separated the men and marched them in a column of five across. There was a large field surrounded by tall pine trees. There they made the Jewish men dig several long trenches in the field. They then shot the men one by one forcing some of the Jews go into the grave pit and pile the corpses like logs. The trench was filled with the bodies. Before they were shot they made them strip and they had the religious men with beards stand still; they bound their hands behind them and shaved them. Then nude and shaved, totally humiliated, they prodded them to the side of the ditch and to be shot."

Twyouick wiped a tear from his eye as he finished this part of the story and as Peter was translating he took a handkerchief from his pocket and blew his nose.

Willie leaned forward, "And what did they do to the women?"

"The next day they paraded them to the gravesite. First they either shot or bayoneted the children right in front of the mothers. Then they made the women strip and shoved them to the lip of the ditch to be shot. In some cases they raped the younger girls before killing them. The Jewish women didn't go quietly. There was a lot of screaming and several tried to attack the killers with their bare hands. Those that resisted were shot on the spot and the Germans made the others drag the bleeding bodies into the ditch."

Peter asked, "And how did the townspeople react to all this?"

"Most of the people did as they were told. They stayed inside behind their white lace curtains, and watched. There were some who went out and tried to give the Jews water. But these few were hounded away by the soldiers with their rifles. Shots were fired at the townspeople who tried to help. None of our people were injured. Many of the women cried as they realized what was happening."

I felt enraged as I realized that some of these Jews he had described were my family. My breathing rate increase as the story was told and I was taking deep breaths as Twyouick finished. To calm myself I asked, "After the Jews were shot what happened?"

"The Germans took about twenty men from the town and made them cover the grave. The Germans stood guard and if they saw movement in the ditch they shot into the pile of bodies. When this was done, the Germans left, heading east. Of course there were a few who couldn't care less. In two cases that I know of, Jews escaped the shooting and were housed by neighbors until the Russians came years later. Many of the townspeople went to the field and planted trees to mark the area. After the war an orchard was planted and a memorial plaque was placed in the field. It wasn't much, but we wanted our children to remember. It was the right thing to do. To us the orchard is a symbol of the cycle of life."

Willie was twisting in the seat and appeared uncomfortable. He had become quite pale during the last few minutes. Twyouick looked at him and asked if he had any questions. Willie slowly shook his head and said, "No."

I asked Twyouick about his family and career and he smiled and told us about his son, son-in-law, and his grandchildren. He told us how he built his house and planted the courtyard garden. He seemed relieved to have told us his story and when he related this personal information Willie began to smile and catch his breath.

It was evident that the visit was over. John stepped into the room and looked at his watch. We helped Twyouick get to his feet and he ushered us to the door, standing at the door as we stepped down the two steps. As we passed by, each of us affectionately put our arms around him and said our farewells. The courtyard had the pleasant smell of the roses in the warm air. It was a peaceful family scene, with his son-in-law playing a game of chess with his son and the toddler wheeling around on the tricycle.

As Peter backed the car away, Twyouick balanced himself on a cane and waved to us and then raised his cane in a form of salute. We waved back.

"Where to now?" Willie asked.

I said, "I'd like to see the monument where the general was shot. We are so close; I'd like to see where the ambush happened."

Willie nodded and Peter took directions from John. In a few minutes we were at the monument. It was a large boulder with a cross about ten feet high imbedded into the rock. Peter translated the simple Polish, "Here General Karl Gruber was shot. He was responsible for the murdering of eleven innocent heroes of Ozarow."

There was silence as we drove back to Ozarow. We left John at the town hall and we then returned to the hotel; each packed and met at out cars after we checked out.

"Where will you go from here?" I asked Willie.

"I'm going to take your suggestion and see Auschwitz and then drive to Warsaw before I head home."

He shook my hand. "And you, George, where are you headed?"

"I'm going to Warsaw to catch a plane and head back to the US."

He extended his hand and reached out for an embrace. I could feel his body tremble as we held each other and then separated. We checked that we each had the other's address. When we parted, we agreed to "stay in touch."

I got in the car and watched Willie leave the parking lot and turn to the road that would take him past his father's grave and then onto the main highway toward Auschwitz.

Peter and I went to the little bistro where we had our drinks with Willie yesterday and had a light lunch knowing we had a four-hour drive ahead of us to Warsaw.

As we were getting into the car, I told Peter that I wanted to pass the cemetery one more time before we left. We drove back to the graveside and stopped. I left Peter in the car and slowly walked into the cemetery. The ground was familiar now. First I found my families' graves and said Kaddish. For some strange reason I felt the visit was incomplete. Gingerly I weaved my way through the burial areas, sidestepping toppled headstones and reached the wall between the cemetery and the orchard. Here, again I said Kaddish. Then I walked across the road and looked along the row of German gravesites and found Willie's father's grave. At first I stood silently not knowing why I came over to this German site. I felt remorse that a man supposedly so loving to his family as a husband and a father could be converted into a killer. Then I placed a small pebble on the marker just as I had placed the stone on my family's graves across the road. As I left, I said the brief last lines of the Kaddish, "Oh Say shalom bimrov hu yasay shalom." "He who creates peace, may He create peace for all of us."

Chapter Twenty-One

Epilogue

Take heed to thyself, and keep thy soul diligently, lest thou forget the things which thine eyes saw, and lest they depart from thy heart all the days of thy life; but make them known unto thy children and thy children's children.

—Deuteronomy 4:10

At Kennedy airport there was a commotion as I exited the baggage hall. Dragging my one piece of rolling luggage, I walked across the area to see what was happening. About twenty people were jumping up and down and cheering two elderly women in an embrace. Media people and television photographers surrounded the group. I asked a man standing nearby what was happening.

"It's a reunion. The two ladies are sisters." He smiled as he spoke.

"They were separated as children in Poland during the war. Both survived not knowing that the other was alive. I am the son of one of the ladies. I was doing genealogical research and discovered my aunt was alive and living in Israel. We brought her here for a visit."

I congratulated him on the happy event although inwardly, I was saddened. The Nazis destroyed a whole family and the only survivors; the two sisters had been separated for sixty years. Now they had a few precious moments late in their life to try to reconstruct a lifetime. It was a joyful moment, but I had a bittersweet taste in my mouth.

At home, the story was on the evening news, along with an interview about survival and the joy of reuniting the sisters. In the morning, the newspapers carried the story on page one. The *New York Times* had a picture of the embrace. Buried deep in the paper there was another little news article, only one column by an inch and a half, about a "former Nazi," who had been hunted by the Simon Weisenthal Center of Vienna, dying a natural death in Paraguay. I grimaced: "The Holocaust still doesn't make the front page."

The following day dawned; a hazy, hot, and humid July morning. Because of the time change, I was up early. After reading the newspapers and catching up with some of the local gossip that my wife seemed eager to tell, I drove the twenty-five miles to the cemetery where my grandmother, grandfather, mother, and father shared a gravesite. It was a cloudless sky but the car air conditioner kept me comfortable. Stepping out of the car I was met with a blast of hot air and inhaled the fragrant scent of cut grass and summer blooms that covered the well-trimmed graves. A cherry tree near the area I was seeking was blooming with small bunches of soon to be ripe fruit and the birds were starting their feast, darting into the branches to pluck fruit and then scurrying to perch on nearby gravestones. The leaves of ivy and ground covering yews blanketed each gravesite and reflected the sun with a green luster. The little blue marker on the side of many of the gravestones, "eternal care," showed families' commitments to maintain the graves in a pristine manner.

Looking around I found the family burial plot. Although I knew that I would come again before the High Holy Days, a traditional time of cemetery visitation, this visit was special. It was an appointment consciously made while in Poland.

Standing at the foot of the four family graves, with a small prayer book borrowed from one of my grandchildren, I recited the full Kaddish prayer. Then I silently recounted my story. Once again, the nine year old in corduroy knickers was taking the mail to the post box, only now he was returning with news. I was the postman. The events of the journey were recalled and how the wind took the tattered crisp letters written so long ago, and the fragments seemed to rise and then waft to the horizon. When finished, I placed a small visitation stone on each grave. A warm feeling infused my psyche during the entire trip to the cemetery and my return home. I thought I should cry, but the tears never came; I felt strangely at peace.

The lessons of history encountered during the trip to Poland and the town of Ozarow and Auschwitz will never leave me. The awareness that those Jews murdered that night were my family had been branded into my mind. There was more. I recognized that the Jews in that Ozarow orchard, and every one of those gassed and cremated at Auschwitz were my extended family. All of the six million were family. The trip had personalized the events of long ago. My family was murdered.

At home, much to my surprise, there was an email from Willie:

Dear George,

I want to thank you for the few hours we had together in Ozarow. Our meeting means a great deal to me. Encountering you at the moment I saw my father's grave was a shock at first.

Then the realization of why you were standing there at the cemetery and slaughter site placed much of my experience of the last several weeks into perspective. As much as I had seen I had to see more. There was more to my trip than finding a grave. I was in the process of ending sixty years of suppressing thoughts about responsibility and culpability about certain events of the Nazi era.

After we parted I went to Auschwitz and then back to Warsaw. I spent a half day at Auschwitz and hired a guide as you suggested. It was a profound experience. It is difficult to convey the deep pain and shame I feel for my generation of Germans who have avoided talking about the war. This avoidance must end. There must be some way of bringing this experience to the younger generation who are ignorant of the past, and deny the facts. If I can be a little part of that mission to expose and to teach, it will be a worthwhile legacy. I am convinced that the idea that the German people were victims of Hitler's madness rather than its sponsors had been a convenient mask in my nation's post war culture. I was part of that generation that accepted this idea of our being the victim of history. My journey has changed all that.

I hope you will respect my wish and correspond. My experience of the last month has shown me that the world is made up of diverse people who share a common history. We were on opposing sides of a horrible conflict. We grew up in two different cultures. When we met, one would think we had little to share, but I have learned differently. We were two people, who might never have met, save for that coincidence in Ozarow, Poland. That town will form a bond between us. I may be naïve but I hope you feel as I do, that you also found a friend when you stopped at that Polish crossroads.

Our families have both suffered in the last century from events that were out of our personal control. History is made up of the stories of individual people and families. As we were told in Ozarow: "the death of millions is a statistic, the death of one individual is a tragedy." We learned of Death, and heartbreak.

At the beginning of my journey I had no idea that the stories I would hear and the people I would encounter would change my perspective of life, my country and the war. A huge anger now wells up within me at the mere mention of the word Nazi. This is more than shame, it is disgust. My question, the question that haunts me, is what I can do now?

Attached to this email is another that I am sending to my son in Connecticut. You will remember that my son has moved to the US and is working for the same bank I worked for all those years. He is living just outside Westport. He is my "American boy."

Please write.

Sincerely,

Willie

There followed a copy of the email to his son:

Thomas,

I have had an experience that has changed my life and my thoughts about much that has happened in the past. The history of the war years was well known to me but I and most other Germans suppressed thoughts that our families had anything to do with the horrors of the Nazi regime. I choose to believe that our family was a victim. We lost my father, many of our relatives died in battle or bombings and we praised those who had died as heroes in a cause that was noble but unjust. I did not know where or how my father died during the war. We knew that he had participated in the Polish campaign and then spent the next years on the eastern front. My generation did not want to know what had transpired during the Nazi era. Hitler was a madman, he led Germany to disaster, and my generation had to do the cleaning up of the rubble and the rebuilding of the country. We were busy, and that was the extent of our interest. We wanted to rebuild and get on with life.

About two months ago I found the letters my father sent to my mother during the war and I undertook a journey to trace the path he took during his military travels. I tried to find where he may have been killed in his last battle. The trip took three weeks and at the end I found his grave at a roadside near a small town called, Ozarow in Poland. It was a stroke of luck that I came upon the grave and, I was intensely affected by the discovery. I cried and was overwhelmed by grief feeling the love I had for the man taken away from me when I was so young and for the years my mother was deprived of the love of her life. However, within minutes of finding his grave, I discovered something that shocked me and forced me to face a reality I had ignored for all these years. In a field across from my father's grave there was a site where several thousand Jews were murdered during a two-day massacre in 1941. The impact was profound. To see the juxtaposition of the grave and the atrocity site was an enormous shock. And even now, just the thought of the proximity of the two sites sets my heart pounding. I am choked just writing these words. My father didn't murder the Jews in the field across from his grave, but the organization he was part of certainly participated or enabled executions and slaughters similar to those in that field.

In my travels the two weeks before I saw many massacre sites in the Ukraine and in Poland. I even visited Auschwitz. However the connection between one grave, our grave and a massacre site where several thousand died drove home the lesson of the Holocaust. The Holocaust was our doing and in my generation and your generation and the generations of Germans to follow must keep the lesson of these unjust deaths alive.

When you were growing up I'm sure you realized that we didn't talk about certain aspects of the war. Most of my generation did not know whether our fathers were good soldiers, or were those who had perpetrated dreadful crimes. Some of our neighbors even claimed that because the victors of the war wrote the history, the stories of the Nazi murders were exaggerated. Many even denied the Holocaust happened at all.

Thomas, I now realize that these stories of atrocities are not only true, but also what we heard in post war Germany understates the monstrosity of those crimes. I went to Auschwitz and saw what remained of the crematoriums. I put my hand in the oven and I felt the Holocaust; in my mind that oven was still warm. I cannot forget what I saw; The German actions of the war and the long-term implications of these murders are unbelievable. The Nazis created a huge killing machine, and I only saw a small part of it. It would take a lifetime to see the remains of all the camps and chronicle the murders in Poland, the Ukraine, Austria and other areas of Europe. There is an idea among some members of my generation that the German people were victims of Hitler rather than sponsors. That is false. The German people nurtured the Hitler causes and underwrote his ideology. They supported him without protest until it was too late. In the end, there were even those who justified their actions by claiming that it was good for the Jews, because the Holocaust caused them to pull together and resulted in the establishment of Israel. This is nonsense.

My father will always be an unknowable person. I only remember him as an eight year old as a visitor back from the front. My adoring eyes could and would not want to see a killer. We do not know his participation in these murders. But Germany cannot remain naïve. We cannot be in denial; We are not innocents, many German civilians knew, but they didn't form an opposition to the Nazi practices, not before the war, during the first terror acts against the Jews, Gypsies and the infirm, or during the conflict. These acts were happening to our neighbors, taking place right in front of the eyes of the civilian population. We chose not to react; there was no protest. When Jewish neighbors were taken away there were opportunistic party members who moved into the abandoned apartments and took over Jewish businesses. During the war, when clothes were distributed in bombed out areas we knew where the clothing originated. Nazi policy succeeded because it was part of a deep weakness in the German people. Very few denounced anti-Semitism and fewer reacted when news or the rumors of exterminations circulated. People who considered themselves among the world's most intelligent and educated society accepted propaganda they knew was false and actually quite brainless. The German public knew there were atrocities; but they chose to look the other way.

Your grandmother and I lived in a bombed-out cellar. Party members who moved into homes formerly owned by Jews lived quite well. They knew where the former owners were. They understood that the Jews weren't going to return. These were rewards for loyalty, silence, and acquiescence.

The German people were guilty when the first Jew was murdered and when the first window was broken because a shop owner was Jewish. Justice was not pursued. The day the judiciary stood by and allowed these crimes to continue, Germany became corrupt. When the police and army became instruments of the Nazi political machine, the soul of Germany was lost. The defeat of the Nazi regime was lady justice arranging the scales of life.

During my father's last leave, Christmas 1942, he visited his uncle who was a First World War veteran. They must have discussed the atrocities that my father had seen. His uncle was aware of killings on a vast scale. My father confirmed this news and added to the story by telling what he had witnessed in Russia. I was a young boy, but I remember them with hushed voices and shaking their heads with words like "killing" and "Jews" whispered. But no German did anything to protest. Were we afraid or were we sympathetic? In either case, their acquiescent silence and our lack of public reaction made all Germans accessories to murder. My father was a killer.

After the war there was an expression, "Stunde Null." To us, our loss of the war wiped the slate clean. We were thoroughly defeated; some acted as though the loss absolved the people of any guilt. We approached the subject of the Holocaust with confusion. We didn't want to accept the guilt that we knew deep in our hearts was ours, so we tried to ignore it. Many Germans believed that with the payment of some claims to Israel or to some individual Jews the score was settled. We have never paid our moral debt. Mere payments cannot erase the guilt of crimes committed in our nation's name.

Six million Jews were murdered. If they had lived, had children and had normal lives they would probably be sixty million people today, sixty-five years later. They were a peaceful community before the war. Think how much better this world would be if they had lived.

I still can't reconcile how these men, these German men, just like my father, who we thought were the cream of modern civilization, could get up in the morning and kill innocent people the way they did. How did a nation that held itself to be the pillar of European civilization acquiesce to the Nazi ideology? I want to talk to my grandchildren about this. I want to impart to them the journey I have just completed. We Germans cannot circumvent, repress, or deny knowledge or responsibility for the Holocaust any more. It happened and we let it happen.

Your father has become a crusader. Although it is late in my life, I hope I can influence those around me. In my retirement, my mission is to speak to my children and grandchildren and tell them that Germans should and can feel remorse. We must see that no one forgets, so it never happens again.

I look forward to seeing you soon. I'll come to your home for Christmas.

Your loving father,

Willie

I closed my computer and sat at my desk deep in thought. Some time later my wife reminded me to change into my tuxedo for a B'nai-Mitzvah of two girls, the granddaughters of an old business associate, Irving Sakaloff. My wife and I drove into New York City. The affair was at an exclusive club. It had a huge dining room and other facilities for the four hundred and fifty invited guests, a magnificent place for a celebration. I commented to my wife that this was opulent as we entered and observed that a great amount of money had been spent on flowers to make the enormous entryway a fragrant garden in a marble hall. The brilliant flower colors contrasted the black formalwear of the men and the women's elaborate couturier gowns. The sweet aroma of the array of blossoms perfumed the large room. The women's jewels radiated in the bright lighting. An attendant approached with a sliver tray and we were given a choice of wine or champagne. The white-gloved waiters were circulating and making sure that each guest was pampered. As soon as a crystal flute was near empty a white glove emerged and replaced the drink. It was a gala event.

It was about the moment we anticipated being guided into the dining room we were brought to silent attention by a fanfare blown by six trumpeters, three on each side of the dual Regency stairway. There were about thirty rungs on the matched staircases descending from the second and third levels of the lobby. Violinists took their position on every other tread and started to play the Hatikvah. Everyone stood, faced the stairway, and joined in singing as this song of hope sounded. One by one members of the host family took their place on the stairway. There were about 60 family members, men in starched shirts and formalwear and ladies in couturier dresses ranging in age from young teens to several quite elderly, standing between the ground floor and third landing when the music ended.

Irving and his wife, Anne, stepped to a microphone. Irving was in his late seventies and Anne was a tall, slender, and still a very beautiful woman a few years younger. He started his comments. "My wife and I want to thank all of you for being our guests honoring our two granddaughters, Miriam and Hanna on their B'nai-Mitzvah. Many of you attended the ceremony this morning and I am proud how well they did."

There was a round of polite applause that interrupted his presentation. "What you see on the stairs behind me are all of the members of our family. They include our five children, their spouses, and our grandchildren. These family members represent a tale of our Jewish heritage that I want to share with you."

He cleared his throat. "Anne was born in Poland. When the war broke out she was eight years old and the Nazis quickly overran the town where her family lived. Her father was arrested by the Germans on the second night of the occupation, and has never been seen since. Her mother, realizing the danger, went to a Catholic neighbor and requested that they care for her daughter. The family raised her as their own, took her to church, taught her the rituals to protect her and passed her as a non-Jew. My wife lived with them for the entire war. She learned the catechism and practiced their religion. This family was at great risk for harboring a Jewess. They could have been executed for this act of kindness. When the war was over, my wife, on the first Sunday, asked if the family was going to church. The father of the family said, 'No, it's time for you to find your own family and become the person you were born to be, and practice the religion you were born into.' After an exhaustive search aided by the family that sheltered her, Anne found two living relatives. Eventually they came to the United States, where I met Anne about two years later, and we married and had our children. On the stairs are the result of our marriage, our children and their children, and those immediate members of the family who were the original survivors. There are sixty people standing before you."

There was a resounding applause for the assembled family. The host raised his hands for quiet. "But there is more. This righteous family who saved Anne asked for nothing in return. Although through the years we made many offers, but there was always one answer. 'We want nothing.' The head of that family is now ninety-three years old."

There was a dramatic pause while the host drew a breath. "I would like you to meet him."

A stooped, gray-haired man, aided by a cane and a younger man, stepped into the room from a door beneath the stairs. The band played the Hatikvah once again as Anne and the old man embraced. The microphone was placed in the hands of the old man, who said something in Polish. Anne translated. "He just said, 'I did nothing you would not have done. Thank you for remembering.' "

Again there was a thunderous applause. I caught my breath and blinked hard to keep back the tears. A uniformed waiter stepped into the room and announced. "Dinner is served."

Later that evening, I sat at my computer and wrote an email to Willie. We have corresponded almost every week, and he is coming to the US to see his grandchildren in Connecticut this Christmas. We will meet and share a drink once more.

I was in my den and turned on the radio. There was a program of Israeli popular music and suddenly the following song was being played. I was transfixed, listening to the words:

Muslim man and Christian man,
both get killed in the bombing.
Hindu man and Jewish man,
they all get killed in the bombing.
Poor rich man
or rich poor man,
both get killed in the bombing.
Father and mother,
sister and brother,
they all get killed in the bombing.

Enemy of yours,
Brother of mine,
happens again and again,
time after time.
Brother of yours,
enemy of mine,
are politics and greed keeping us blind.

Muslin boy or Christian girl,
both get killed in the bombing.
Hindu girl and Jewish boy,
they all get killed in the bombing.
In our schools or in our residence,
they all get killed in the bombing.
A heart filled with hate
or a heart full of innocence,
both get killed in the bombing.

We hear it on the radio,
see it on TV,
Read it in the papers,
it's all the same to me.
A world full of anger,
and mistaken hate,
Justified explosions,
smart bombs don't discriminate.

Soldier of the homeland,
or soldier on foreign soil,
both get killed in the bombing.

They all get killed in the bombing.

(Copyright "Haifa/In The Bombing" 2003 Taiowa/Timothy G. Sheridan/Thane Hake BMI Music, with permission of Russian River Records--www.riverrox.com)

I smiled at the irony of the song and then found the book I had been searching for. It was *The Righteous,* by a Holocaust scholar, Martin Gilbert. I was looking for a quote that had been running through my mind. It was near the back of the book and discussed the many that "turned against the tide of terror," and risked their lives to shelter and save Jews. It was a simple statement, "We did what we had to do," "Anyone would have done the same,"—the words of many rescuers.

I closed the book and I thought, who is anyone?

Author's Note

This book was started as a remembrance of my childhood. I then turned those first notes into a novella of about thirty-two pages. With encouragement of a friend and neighbor I wrote the full-length novel.

The reason for writing is my grandchildren. They, like many know about the Holocaust. However, the detail, the scope, and the personal nature of the murders and crimes are most often told in non-fiction text fashion. The details are many; the stories behind the details are the lives and history of millions of people, thousands of towns and encompass the tides of war, murder and death. There are also the stories of life. I wanted to personalize and paint the story of these awsome events on a canvas with a story that would be read. I guess the way to qualify this novel is, "the events are true, and the people lived, but are imagined."

I want to acknowledge the members of the Galaxy Writing Club and particularly Heather Cariou, Florence Friedman, and Len Litof for the inspiration, guidance, and encouragement they gave during the writing. My guide in Ukraine, Anna Royzner, was invaluable in educating me about the atrocities that occurred and having me meet survivors who could authenticate incidents I was fictionalizing in the book. In Poland Maria-Margret Skierniewska and Ewa Lucznska guided me through the Auschwitz and Treblinka horrors and Maria was able to find those Jewish cemeteries that would have eluded the casual visitor and worked to have me meet the eye witnesses I needed to validate my story. Here in the United Sates I had the pleasure of meeting Suzanne Brown-Fleming, Senior Program Officer, University Programs Division of the Center for Advanced Holocaust Studies of the United States Holocaust Memorial Museum. Suzanne was invaluable in briefing me on the innuendos of the German mindset during the postwar era and the psychology of denial that pervaded much of the German culture. And finally I must thank and express my appreciation to my wife, Arlene, who edited page after page and chapter after chapter. She discussed, corrected, and even argued some of the approaches to the story. Her input was appreciated and with great love I acknowledge her efforts.

Sandy Simon

September 2008

Printed in the United States
130484LV00003B/6/P

9 781434 393173